THE EDGE OF DISREPUTE

By Elithe Hamilton Kirkland

Love Is A Wild Assault
Divine Average

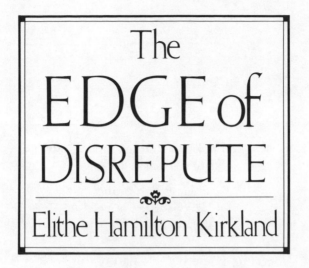

The
EDGE of
DISREPUTE

Elithe Hamilton Kirkland

SHEARER PUBLISHING

TEXAS

To My Son and Daughter
James Benjamin Beal
and
Beverly Jean Allen
*for the understanding heart
and accomplishments that
encourage and inspire*

FOREWORD

Sarah Belle's New Orleans

It began in New Orleans in the 1840's, this story of Sarah Belle and her House of Recovery established for patients of the opposite sex only, personally solicited when discovered in the agony of a traumatic betrayal, interned one at a time. She was a woman more inclined to conform to the voice of conscience than to dictates of social structures in this time and place.

And what was this *Queen City of the South* like when Sarah Belle was driven by the forces of love and loss, sympathies and remorse, into its vortex? The racial heterogeneity of this self-proclaimed supercity was beyond classification.

If you were of *African* descent, you might be slave or freeborn. If slave, you were bonded to the privileged bloodstock and baptized into the Catholic Church and might practice *voudou* in secret; or, if one of the unteachables, you wore a heavy iron collar and leg chains and were hustled out to dig drainage ditches, lift marble, generate the back-built levees and ramparts. If you had the measured good fortune to be born free as black, mulatto, quadroon, octoroon, or any other color designation, you might be in that special class, the *gens de couleur libres* (wealthy, educated, talented); or a work-a-day colored engaged in services and modest enterprises of your own selection; in either case, your freedom was strictly limited by law and custom.

If you were *French*, you could be of the *French Creole hierarchy*, native of New Orleans, descendant of French Colonial stock; or, second best, a French immigrant. . . . If of *Spanish* derivation, one of the same distinctions. However, if you were *American*, you didn't really exist in the consciousness of the city fathers until General Jackson in the War of 1812 rescued the whole amalgam from the pirating British. Even then, it was not "many thanks" but "bien des remerciements" and "à la bonne heure!"

The bounty of all middle America was heaped on the docks of this imperious French lady of a city, her opulent river commerce feeding into the trade channels of the world. She considered her Spanish lineage an accident, and her American marriage a forced contract. The Spanish were Latin enough to be tolerated. The Americans were imposters and unacceptable. Thus, from 1836 to 1852, the city was divided along ethnic lines into three municipalities; the first, at the city heart, the exclusive Latin Creoles; the second, mostly Americans, along with German and Irish immigrants; and the third, a mixture of Creoles (native-borns) and immigrants from many lands.

Innate differences, prejudices, and outright hostilities prevailed among the races drawn into the magic crescent. Yet, the civic-ego in its entirety, presided over by a mayor, was so inflated that the "royal compound" with its bulging slave-based economy was heralded by some of the *haute noblesse* as an incubator of "the strongest civilization on earth"!

Consider: The astonishing display of opulence in lavish application of Greek Revival classicism within the city's architectural wonderland . . . palatial hotels, awesome in size and appearance, the majestic structure on St. Charles Avenue with a dome rivaling St. Paul's in London.

Behold: Exchange buildings and banks—megalithic marble, Greek temple facades—and on the impressive entrance to the enormous

City Exchange Building, Tuscan and Doric orders reconciled to announce hotel, bank, private stores, sumptuous dining rooms, and ballrooms with motifs from Persian fantasy to Louis XIV splendor.

Applaud: The eminence of the performing arts, where gold-fringed curtains part on a stage that beckons the fame-crowned of the world to New Orleans theatre; and, after opera, drama, ballet—on to ballroom magnificence for the ultimate in terpsichorean delights. . . . *Hourra!*

By the mid-1840's, class strata ran through the second municipality. As an American, you might be a river flatboatman ("half-alligator-half-man"); an enterprising Yankee from the North; a puritanical New Englander, shocked by the plethora of pleasure marts and Sunday entertainment; or, a prototype of the energetic American making your division of the city an example of order and public improvements—ably assisted by your German and Irish neighbors, who cherish their own type of exclusiveness, eschewing slavery and turning a lofty countenance on the Latin climate of perpetual song and dance, drinking and dueling, riotous festivity and romance.

Nowhere in the world could the heroine of this book have carried out her peculiar self-assigned mission so effectively as in New Orleans. Where else could circumstances have brought her friendship with a voudou queen, a merchant prince, a humanitarian genius of disguise among the *gens de couleur libres*, and an antiquarian-adventurer who, in the misery of a bitter disillusionment, would change the course and purpose of her life?

References and Personal Notes

Background references informative and inspiring are listed; some subjects were fruitful with detail (New Orleans), some sparse and lean (the little known South American Guaharibo Indians of the upper Orinoco), and some exciting and challenging (the Mayan ruins of Palenque).

Benjamin Moore Norman's 1845 guidebook, *New Orleans and Environs*, replete with facts, alive with sketches, one of the Louisiana Bicentennial reprints published by the Louisiana State University Press, enriched with an introduction by Matthew J. Schott, professor of history at the University of Southwestern Louisiana. . . .

Another L.S.U. Press bicentennial reprint, Henry Castellanos' *New Orleans as It Was* (1895), supplements Norman's reference with historical episodes of Louisiana life.

Creole Voices (1845), musical poems in French by free men of color, Armand Lanusse, poet and editor; English translation in a centennial edition by the Louisiana State University Press.

Lyle Saxon's *Fabulous New Orleans* (1928, 1950): Part II, "French Town and Spanish City"; Part III, "Gaudy Days."

Diary of Hervey A. Adams (unpublished), sections on New Orleans and the Republic of Texas (1836–37), and the Somervell Expedition against Mexico (1841–43).

Assisting with leads into the meager information on the wary primitive Guaharibos were the Department of Anthropology at the Smithsonian Institution . . . the Tozzer Library at Harvard providing photoduplication from *The Geographical Review* (1925) of "Plans for Exploration at the Headwaters of the Branco and Orinoco" by A. Hamilton Rice . . . the Public Library of Abilene, Texas, with duplication of "In Humboldt's Wake" by Ernest G. Holt, *The National Geographic Magazine* (1931) . . . the J. A. B. Miller Library of Coleman, Texas, giving prompt service on interlibrary loans.

The John Lloyd Stephens books: *Incidents of Travel in Central America, Chiapas and Yucatán*, Vols. One and Two (1841, 1969); *Incidents of Travel in Yucatán*, Vols. One and Two (1843, 1963). The warmth and sympathy poured into the detailed narration fully realizes Stephens's "hope to snatch from oblivion these perishing, but still gigantic memorials of a mysterious people." The full illustrations provided by Frederick Catherwood from daguerreotype views and drawings taken on the spot are superbly executed.

A century after Stephens, my own travels in Central America, Yucatán, and Chiapas with my friend and world traveler, Dorothy Kurtz of New Jersey. From the excellent Kurtz photography of our observations at Palenque, I was able to make valuable comparisons with the Catherwood illustrations and the impressive Palenque section of the recent publication *Maya Ruins of Mexico in Color* (1977) by Ferguson and Royce.

Through all the seasons of structuring *The Edge of Disrepute*, personal assistance has been provided by my physician husband and business advisor, Dr. R. D. Kirkland, who has given thoughtful analysis to all I have written . . . by Glenda Cash, English teacher and literary enthusiast, with secretarial services extraordinary available on call . . . by Barbara Gates, scholar and research specialist, through the resources in her private library and her meticulous research assistance into other collections . . . by Carol Peabody, resident artist and naturalist, with labors of love in the interest of author and book.

Ever a part of this author's work and interest in history is the Texas State Historical Association, its director L. Tuffly Ellis, he and his staff always responsive to inquiries pertinent to a writer's progress.

The characters in this book, whether historical or emerging from invisible life forces, are a part of all that I am, have witnessed, read, been taught by friends, relatives, and educators, those who have sought me, loved me, disapproved of me, or passed me by. My gratitude to all of you for bowing me down or raising me up! You have made another book—*The Edge*. Read cautiously!

ELITHE HAMILTON KIRKLAND

Big Sky Ranch
Coleman, Texas
April, 1984

O Thou Desert of My Mind!
O Thou Guarded Hidden Glory!
Let me somehow somewhere find
Essence of the human story.

Sarah Belle's Song

CHAPTER ONE

S ARAH BELLE WAS A MOST UNUSUAL WOMAN of the streets. She was not a street-walker in the traditional sense, but in the eyes of the public, she violated the mores of her time and place enough that her color was scarlet.

She was more enlightened than the average woman in New Orleans in the year 1846. She subscribed to two city papers—the *Louisiana Courier*, published in French and English, and the *New Orleans Times* in English—also a London journal, and a Boston almanac. She read Balzac (in the French), the Bible (in spots), and adored the romances of Sir Walter Scott.

Sarah Belle had a strategy unique, no doubt, in New Orleans or any other place where a woman might meet a man. She was youthful and good-looking, and, in the pursuit of her chosen work, forthright and dedicated.

She lived alone in a modest house in the second municipality, located on the fringe of respectability and the edge of disrepute. In her own mind, she called her place the House of Recovery. You might say she was a kind of missionary.

It was mid-afternoon, an idyllic, softly cool day in early summer, when she discovered in Lafayette Square another candidate for her attentions. She had rented a carriage in her usual manner when on a recruiting mission, and set about surveying resort areas, public squares, loitering places and entertainment fronts, shipping docks, and riverside walks—even the slave mart, and especially the comings and goings at big supply stores where men were outfitted for wilderness exploits and treks to the West.

The driver, aware of her interest, brought the carriage to a halt so that she could pursue her observations. The man sat alone on an iron wrought bench, bareheaded, a tropical straw hat at his side. His arms were stretched across the back of the seat, his head thrown back, his eyes closed. She must get closer, study him unaware before he aroused.

She gave the coachman a wordless signal to dismount and help her from the carriage. He did so with a deference that implied high station, and they exchanged smiles that spoke of shared discovery. They were friends and co-conspirators. She stood for a moment, her hand upon the gate that complemented the handsome iron railing surrounding the square.

She made her way toward the man without any attempt at concealment. The path was bordered with ornamental shrubs, and overhead the shading branches of a Eurasian maple in full flower. She stopped for a moment as if listening to birdsong, and again to caress a flower; all the time her excitement was mounting, her intuition sharpening.

His leathery tanned face was sun-lighted in an effect that revealed taut features, deeply lined. Sarah Belle was fascinated. He would not be easy to approach, she surmised. His mind was roving in a domain far removed from his surround. He was unlike any man she had ever selected to bring to her house.

With expertise, she evaluated. Probably near her own age though he appeared older. His attire, though carelessly assembled, indicated he was no stranger to cultural environs. He was clean-shaven. Thick brown hair was trimmed without vanity of grooming. The loose coat was no doubt fine linen, his boots made for him alone but showing no recent shine-boy service. Pants were fitted and suggested a litheness and firmness of figure that could have been acquired under a fencing master. The shirt was full, loose-sleeved and tight-cuffed, open at the neck.

Now she could see the hands—such revealing maps of character and desire hands were! Their shape and movement often open pronouncements and revelations. These hands were large and as tanned as the face—their experience had been . . . she was baffled, bereft of her usual perceptions. Instead she seemed to be reading a caution of some kind. Do not touch. Do not disturb.

He aroused. There were occasional passersby. He did not observe them—nor the watchful Sarah Belle. He reached into a coat pocket and placed something to his lips, hands cupped and the object not visible. Sarah Belle listened for the sounds of a harmonica or Jew's harp, but what she heard were haunting tones, yearning, alien, peculiarly insistent, like a summons to an ancient temple beyond the curtain of time. No one but Sarah Belle was paying any attention to him or the strange soft sounds being emitted through his presence. That which was alien was commonplace in New Orleans.

Sarah Belle felt a tingle, a shiver of anticipation (or was it trepidation?). The tones opened her senses, told her plainly that in one way this man was like all the others she had brought to her house. He was wrestling with a loss, an inner force of man-woman involvement, and had not yet declared himself the winner. Devotion betrayed, passion thwarted. The valleys of sorrow on his face were deeper than those she had identified on other men, but nature's handwriting was plain if one studied well the hieroglyphics of the heart.

She was at the bench, her full pale yellow skirt of finest batiste almost brushing his knee before he noticed.

"Will I disturb your curious piping if I sit here? I've heard nothing like it before. I play a———"

He leaped to his feet, a quick hand to the pocket, concealing what had been at his lips. He gave her a look that seemed to question her reality, then to resent it, then to accept it.

"Certainly, madam, have this seat. These beautiful flowering shrubs all around do not disturb me, why should you?"

The statement was not an invitation. It was a dismissal. He did not intend to be seated beside her, nor to stay.

She remained standing. She smiled, but it was not her usual smile at this stage of acquaintance.

Her hands trembled a little and her mouth seemed dry. "You have sisters, no doubt."

"No doubt. Gone, but not forgotten." He did not ask her why she thought so, as she had expected.

His hat remained on the seat near her skirt; she moved imperceptibly, she thought, in order that he might have to reach behind her and not be able to make an abrupt departure.

Blue-gray eyes met hers in a level stare, cool and aware.

She blushed.

His eyebrows raised above the cool knowing.

She must not let him go! With an effort, she held his gaze and tried to bring about a responsive warmth.

"Please tell me—music is important to me—the tones you made were like nothing I have ever heard. There was an appeal, a summons inherent——"

"And so you came!" Pure satire!

Forsaken by her patterned approaches, she spoke in an impulsive rush.

"My name is Sarah Belle——"

He interrupted, "Sarah Belle what?"

"Just Sarah Belle——" She talked faster. "I live alone in a house of my own. I have no family of any kind—in the city. Two elderly servants share my life. I am in trouble of no kind——"

An inner voice warned: "You soon may be."

"I make no trouble. Please don't go away——"

There was a quirk of a smile at the corner of his mouth. "That was my initial impulse, as an animal has a flash of instinct in the presence of a well-baited trap. But the animal is curious. He moves a little closer—" (at this moment he moved a little closer to Sarah Belle) "—in order to examine the bait and why it is so attractive to his senses."

He folded his arms and looked at her like an attorney trying to get a hard-pressed witness to confess. And again he moved a little closer.

"I . . ." To her own surprise she was almost in tears, turned her head away, and wished she were not so close to him. But the

4

bench was to her back. "You can't believe me because . . . because I am so different . . ."

"New Orleans abounds in differences."

Now a tear slid down her cheek.

"And many of them weep very charmingly."

"You are different too!" she declared in a tone of desperation. "Different . . . and . . ." she tried for objectivity, looked up at him, demanding recognition, "and . . . and Mr. _____?"

Now he did smile, but it was not comforting. "Mr. Spench," he made it very distinct, and in answer to the doubt in her eyes, "It is an old New Orleans name devised when a Spanish ancestor of mine mixed with a French colonial—simplification for posterity. I have thought of adding an 'a' for the American infiltrations in the bloodline since 1803, but *Spencha* would sound Italian and the Romans have not yet laid seige to the city."

Sarah Belle turned to a major principle of her strategy: ignore cynicism. Override it with directness. She pretended acceptance of his invention.

"In your heart, Mr. Spench, you are very miserable."

There. She had said it, but must avert her eyes even as she spoke. She was angry with herself and trembling, for composure and the eye-lock were a part of her *modus operandi*.

"You *are* discerningly different," he conceded wryly, his tone changing to the tolerance of curiosity. "Although I have never considered the sharing of misery salutary, let me inquire: What is your burden that you seek out a complete stranger, and—I might add convincingly, I trust—a man of no potential means, in case you——"

This time Sarah Belle's blush was a fiery red from throat to hairline.

"Sir, I am well provided for. I have an income that cares amply for all my needs. You . . . you . . ." Very real tears ran down her cheeks. Accustomed to living alone and conversing with various aspects of herself, the inner comment behind her tears was free of subtleties: *Long time since you wept for yourself. Long time since you heard a heart-call. How will you work this one out? Your pattern won't fit Mr. Spench! Your net has come apart. Face it, you're in a jam—with yourself, that is.* "I do not desire money."

"What then?" Positions were reversed. Now he was the inquirer.

"To be a companion and servant to man—not just *a* man, but man-*kind*." Her throat tightened. "*Hu*-manity." The word had a hollow sound in her own ears.

"Perhaps you should have given yourself to missionary work."

"I have—I have! But the nature of it——" How could she possibly explain to such a man? "I can't help in the *way* I have set out to do except——"

"Do you seek out strange women, who, as you put it, are miserable?"

"No, no——" She turned her back crying, lost to words, bereft of stamina and the formula that had proved flawless in similar encounters.

Now credibility was achieved through the ageless and instinctive formula of tear ducts in authentic function, which to Sarah Belle was a form of self-defeat.

A handkerchief appeared over her shoulder. She accepted it.

When she turned, she met his gaze directly. "Will you come to my house for refreshment and let me explain, Mr. Spench, please?" She used his name in the tone of pretense with which he had presented it.

"Yes, madam, I will." His smile was more natural, but still disquieting.

"Why do you address me as 'madam' instead of 'miss'?"

"Because it is my impression that you have been wed."

She turned away quickly, her hand to her mouth.

He recovered his hat, touched her elbow and they moved toward the carriage.

CHAPTER TWO

S ARAH BELLE AND HER GUEST ate sparingly of the buttered pound cake, cold milk, apricots, and cheese set before them. He partook with equal deliberation of the conversational gambits she set before him as she delayed her testimonial. He glanced around at inviting book-shelves and a secretary crowded with printed matter, but made no comment. Fanaalis, the servant, came and cleared the table. Sarah Belle left her chair to assist with restless movements here and there. The stranger stood and made courteous comment on the excellence of the repast, and she nodded.

She turned to him impatiently. "I cannot continue to call you 'sir' or that ridiculous 'Mr. Spench' every time I address you. What is your real name?"

"It might sound even less appealing to you, and that would be a disappointment to both of us, wouldn't it? Remaining incognito seems to be a mutual choice. You have not given me your wedded name, and were I a man of ordinary caution, I would consider this information essential."

"I told you I live alone. I chose to lay aside my family name—and my wedded name. There was no—no blemish on either name. I elected to be just—just myself."

"Is your husband deceased?"

Sarah Belle paled. "I . . . I . . . do not know. I only know he will never . . . be . . . back."

"An assumption, at this point, but we'll rest on it. Sarah, you solicited my attention in the park, then my presence here. Why?"

"To help . . ."

"Me?—or yourself?"

"You . . . I thought . . . but you are like none other who has . . . come here."

"Been brought here, you mean."

"Ah . . . yes. You have the same symptoms, but somehow I realize now you carry your own cure."

"What symptoms do you refer to?"

Sarah Belle looked at her interrogator appealingly, but his steady gaze did not release her. She felt like a benevolent trapper securely snarled in her own soft rope devised for catching wounded animals. It mattered not that the intention was to give sanctuary and healing. Who would release the trapper herself? Certainly not the *trapped*, who understood the nature and intent of ordinary trappers.

Her choice of words would have to give extraordinary content to her explanation. The clear gray (or were they blue?) eyes reflected a quality of discernment that tragedy whets to a finer edge.

Oh, my Conscience, guide me! she pleaded inwardly and began, "A man who has lost a woman he loves," she spoke very slowly, her voice barely audible, "Whatever the cause—death, a rival, deceit, difference in station or race, or simply the divisive currents of time and events—no matter if he be a gentleman or a ruffian—reveals the nature of his loss through certain body movements and postures, expressions and marks on face or brow, and, most certainly, through the language of his hands."

She paused and took a deep breath. "I do not mean that all the gestures, postures, expressions are the same for different men; but through these, you read the story, not in detail, but in category, you might say."

Her listener looked thoughtful, interested. "A doctor friend of mine told me that he had trained under a medical authority who taught him to diagnose certain ailments in this manner."

Encouraged, Sarah Belle continued. "I was led to this study . . . and this . . . mission . . . by personal experience."

"I should think so," he commented in a level tone.

"I . . . I want to tell you about it."

"Do you think it would be wise? I am a stranger. Your discernment must have its limitations, you know."

She tried to pull back from the compulsion that had laid hold of her. Her reasoning self protested.

"Surely you're not going to tell him all that has happened to you in the arena of love?"

"I feel that I am. I want to."

"But you've never done this. It's dangerous."

"I'll tell it like a story and not feel it."

"In the square, you cried."

"I'm more composed now."

"The way you feel about this man, you could go to pieces and have him just feeling sorry for you."

"That would be a beginning."

"Weakling! You know quite well this man won't really love again for a long time—if ever."

"But every man eventually can forget—can find another love. That's what . . . what I teach."

"That's teaching. Now you're about to *learn*."

"Regardless of consequences, I must tell all—everything!"

"No woman should tell *all* to any man. That's basic!"

"I'm going to tell all to this one!"

"You're an emotional goose!"

"So be it!"

Sarah Belle took a deep breath. "You're not a stranger. You're—you're a deliverer. I can trust you."

"God of the Ages! I've never been called that before! What makes you so sure?"

She didn't reply. She rushed over to the secretary, and took from a drawer a casket of shining ebony. It was bordered and banded in gold with rich jeweled inlay on the lid. She placed it on the table and indicated a chair across from her. He sat down. A ray of afternoon sunlight embraced the glowing pearl in the center of the lid's design and gave added luster to the gold lettering beneath. *To My True Love, a Pearl of Great Price.*

She pulled her chair a bit to one side and closer to the table so that she could touch the casket for reassurance and fix her gaze upon it, and, if she looked up, she would not be face to face with her listener.

She told her narrative softly, rapidly, sometimes in a kind of silken monotone, at other times in cadences modulated with occasional notes of joy, but more often of loss, of self-analysis and atonement.

"His name was Orlando. We all called him Lando. He was the son of a gifted craftsman who made furniture for some of the most beautiful homes in the Southland and in this very city. Lando was motherless and worked with his father when not in school. He had a royal look about him, a princely bearing. He was popular with boy and girl companions alike, good-humored, yet serious; truthful, lovable, unmatchable—that's the way he looked to me at sixteen, and I think I would have felt the same at sixty. I was still sixteen and he was nineteen when we declared our love and for a while knew what it was like to be in tune with the wonders of the universe. At seventeen, I was having suitors and my parents were evaluating them carefully when I told them that Lando was the only one, and I would not be put forward as a prospect to anyone else. They lost no time in making it clear to both of us that he had no right even to pay serious court, when his means were so limited and his background without status or promise. His father was a man of talent but not careful of finances beyond the needs of himself and son.

"Orlando was not so easily turned away. He had a wealthy uncle in Boston, who was in lucrative shipping trade in the Orient and had offered Orlando a position of future partnership, if he would learn the business and work for a few years in the foreign ports as his representative. Orlando asked me if I would wait five years for him. I told him I would wait forever! That I would die before I would wed another. If he were successful and alive, he would be back in five years to claim me. I begged that we elope, that he take me with him. But he would not commit me to any hardship— would not blemish our love with family grief and hostility. We parted, and never had I known there was such bereavement. My mind was despair. My flesh and my bones ached, felt dried out as if mummified. I wept and lost weight and made all around me miserable until finally I had my first packet from dear Lando. He was happy with his prospect for good fortune and the generosity and affability of his uncle. He was soon to take ship for the Orient, and would be gone several years, but I would have word from him, never fear, and the little locket with the tiny perfect little pearl, I was to wear—and some day he would find a large and lustrous pearl more worthy of me. His words of love and endearment were manna and medicine. I became my natural active and gay self again, sustained by the magnificence of my dream and expectations."

Entranced with her fixation on the great glowing pearl before her, Sarah Belle paused and recaptured the fullness of her every dream of Lando and love. Her eyelids were almost closed, the long lashes quivering, and her breath shallow and hard to detect. From across the table, a comment, almost in a whisper, "A dream long held is a powerful thing."

He had aroused her to continue. "Yes, yes . . . powerful! . . . dreams clothed in gossamer, rainbow-hued, then shattered in a thunderclap of emotion—and there stands reality, stark and demanding! My dreams, fed on packets of love letters and exotic gifts from the Orient, held out against parental anger and eager suitors.

"Yet, there was one—what a name he had—Defender Locke. And what a will, and what patience! He had everything but my love—wealth, my parents' affection, a happy disposition, and a good mind. He towered in height, dark of beard and hair, in every way Mr. Eligible. I told him about Lando. He said he would wait out the allotted time and more if I desired. In the meantime, he would be my good friend. I accepted this arrangement and thus eliminated the annoyance of others. We rode and danced and dined together. We visited and talked together many hours, reading the same books, sharing interests. My devotion to Lando never wavered.

"Then there came the last year of the five. Months went by and I had no word from Lando. His father had died—so Lando had told me in earlier correspondence. I wrote to the uncle but had no reply. I began to wonder if Lando had another love. If he were dead, somehow I should have known. Then one day my father brought in a newspaper and showed me there in the ship news—lost at sea, the company ship that I knew Lando had planned to take passage on for his return to Boston Harbor. It had been lost to the sea lanes for several months and was believed destroyed in a storm known to have raged in its path. I wept in the arms of my friend and refused to accept it. The five-year promise had run out. But the 'forever' I had said I would wait had not—the vow of 'die before I would wed another' weakened in the comfort of Defender's arms. I accepted him, and he accepted me, knowing the depth of my attachment to Lando, but now confident that death would seal off the matter, and I would be his and his alone. I was not the wife to him that I would have been to Lando, but he was tender and protective, wooing me with the certainty that he could erase the Lando image in my heart—an image that had had so little of the physical realities of love to build upon."

Sarah Belle took a deep breath, sighed deeply, and for the first time looked directly at the man she was addressing. The anguish in her eyes moved him so that he said gently, "You do not have to go on."

"Yes—yes I do. I need to go on. Thank you for listening . . .

"One day I received this box, this jeweled messenger that threw my mind and body into an agony inexplicable. It contained a lengthy account by Lando of his experience: his ship in the storm, too crippled to control, a prey to the winds and finally run aground on a barren isle. He and the crew had maintained themselves in the wreckage until a freighter off course had spotted them. He was writing from Boston. The ordeal had temporarily impaired his health but he would be well again, would have his business well in hand. He now prospered in full partnership with his uncle. Though he had overstayed his five years, no woman had ever been in his mind or heart except the one love of his life. All had been accomplished and endured for me alone. He and all his were mine to claim. He begged me to advise him at once of my circumstances and of his place in my life.

"I told no one of my dilemma. Defender was not at home. I was tempted simply to disappear and go to Lando. We could get lost to the world except for each other. Then I thought of my husband and what such a betrayal would mean to him—and still married to him wherever I went, I could not be the woman and wife that Lando had cast in his dreams. I wrote in anguish that I was wed and must remain so. 'Thank God you live, as does our love,' I wrote. 'Now, dear Lando, we must make room for other love or we die.'"

CHAPTER THREE

"FOR WEEKS, DEFENDER WONDERED at my pallor and languor, and had the family physician prescribe a tonic, hoping, I realized in deeper misery, that the sickness was prelude to parenthood. Another year moved across the calendar of my life, and I found myself renewing energies and interests, though I still had a little secret room in my heart reserved for Lando, and in imagination would sometimes retreat there. If I lingered too long, however, in this dream preserve, I would find myself beset with jealousy in absentia, over the woman whom Lando might come to love or wed.

"What fools we can make of ourselves in our imaginings, in ways known only to ourselves but no less shameful! And so it was with me. Reality gave another loud knock on my door and delivered documents to me under an ornate and impressive legal seal. When I had read what was set forth there, I felt like a stunned player suddenly alone at center stage in the drama of life—no book to go by for playing my part, no prompter. Yet I must keep the play going or all the cast was doomed.

"The papers were legal and clear and irrevocable in their statements of fact. Lando was dead. He had left for my use or disposal a large trust fund, placed with a New Orleans banking firm. There was also, the trustees advised me, a collection of jewels of no small value, vaulted there for me as further inheritance from a 'distant relative'! All was done and finished properly. This was simply notification. The trustees would be at my service when I called upon them.

"I hid the papers, wondering how long before I should tell Defender and what would be his feelings. He still knew nothing of Lando's return. I had to try to move back into the state of mind and feeling I had achieved when I married Defender, assuming that Lando did not live. But it wasn't the same. There was a new permanence to his death now. Also the guilt building up.

"If only I had been more faithful to my love—more determined, more patient—held firmly to my avowal, and resisted my parents' will, refused the surcease found in Defender's loving arms and ample fortune. Then Lando would be alive and I would be in his arms again. Defender would have stepped aside, his heart bruised but pride intact, and not having known me as wife, would have been less bereft.

"So what about my feelings now before my new loss and self-judgment? Before I told Defender anything, I reasoned, I must convince him that I loved him exclusively and past romance was indeed past. I achieved this and a sort of relief through inner arrangement with my dream self. Now when I met Lando in that little secret room of my heart, I did not have to deal with jealousy—no other woman would have his love—he was all mine, for always. This was selfish and unhealthy.

"I didn't realize how strong the mind can build where the imagination flourishes. I allowed myself to dwell upon Lando's affections and closeness to the extent that I no longer felt any guilt and became even more tender and considerate of Defender. After a while, I realized that I was accepting Defender as a sort of stand-in for Lando.

"And then one fatal night, in a dreamlike trance, I fully accepted Defender with a release and a response never before given in our marriage—and then—O betrayal from the overfed and overgrown emotional self: I cried out, 'O, Lando, Lando, my love, my only love!!!' My husband left my bed and never again touched me in caress or even courtesy.

"Soon after that, he left me, and when I asked him where he was going, he answered only one word: 'West!' and added, 'I leave you well provided for,' before he turned his back on me. In due time, another set of legal papers came my way and another endowment from a man who found me weak in promise and loyalty. He, too, may be dead. At least he is dead to me, for I know that as long as I live he will not come to me again.

"What I destroyed in these two men, I must help other men to restore and rebuild. What I did to myself, I must more fully recognize and understand and somehow pass this along to women who fashion for themselves the disguises and self-deceptions that I created with such dexterity."

Sarah Belle looked up. She was dismayed. Her listener's face had turned a deadly gray—his eyes bulged, as if viewing a scene of incomprehensible devastation. "Guafana! Guafana!" he moaned, his countenance in a fixed stare.

Sarah Belle knew instantly that something she had said was a goad to the rooted pain that had drawn her to him. And the name *Guafana*, how unearthly it sounded through his lips.

"My name is Sarah," she reminded him softly. "Sarah Belle. And I was just——"

"Yes, Sarah Belle, you were telling me about your husband, Defender Locke." His eyes were cool gray again, and the key she had thought for a moment might open an exchange of confidence was snatched away and deep hidden.

But there was communication of a kind. Sarah Belle felt a stab of sympathetic pain just below the diaphragm as rough and thorny as any reality.

She drew in her breath sharply, spoke in broken phrases. "Your eyes turn dead, like slate, when you are moved in a certain way. Defender's eyes changed like that—darkened—when he was angry or upset in some way. Only his were different!" She tried for a deep breath, as though she had been struck in the chest, and pressed a small fist against the pain. "I mean his eyes were different . . . each eye . . . one blue . . . one brown. It wasn't so noticeable except . . . well, when he looked at me . . . the last time . . . they blazed, one a blue flame, the other a black thrust of malediction."

"Don't you think you have told me enough?"

"Oh, no, no! I have only begun. I want you to examine what I have kept here—a full account of every guest——" She started to raise the jeweled lid of the box that was Lando's love gift.

"Do *not* open it!"

It was a staccato command, and she froze in astonishment, her fingers at its latch.

His grim expression held her transfixed for a moment, and then it relaxed, and in a gesture almost of tenderness he touched her hand and spoke softly.

"Beware! Surely you have heard of the jinnee of Oriental mythology. How will you deal with it when it appears? Have you the supernatural power to control it?"

"I don't know——"

"You don't know? Then that would leave it up to me. And I am no Solomon with a magic ring to control whatever might appear with the raising of that lid."

"I mean—I do not know what you are talking about."

He gestured toward her library shelves crowded with books.

"All this hunger for enlightenment and you do not know about *Arabian Nights*? No awareness of the powerful nature demons of Arabian lore?"

"Fairy tales—references in literary fantasies——" Inwardly she was dazed and asking herself: What is happening to me and this man in this room? What is he saying or trying to say to me? Her hand was still resting on the box, the pearl pressing against her palm. It was heating, and with it came apprehension. She gave the box a little shove as if to disengage it from her sensations, and clasped her hands in her lap.

"Any knowledgeable Arab would prepare a secret chamber for such a casket—place it on a shelf as ornate as a pagan altar—bow to Mecca five times a day in its presence, and open it only when he felt Allah favored him with the power to control the contents for good or evil."

Bewildered by the unreality of the conversation, Sarah Belle gazed at the little box, in silence, feeling a pulse throb in her throat, making an effort to still it.

"You see," he continued, "the carvings are in the ancient symbols of enchantment. Your Lando paid as much for workmanship as he paid for the matchless pearl. No doubt he was enchanted himself with the mythology of the Orient, and its subtleties of meaning."

"I *know* what is *in* the box. It has nothing to do with enchantments and subtleties of meaning. I——" she hesitated.

"Are you sure? How long since you have opened it?"

"Several months."

"When you opened it, did you review all you had placed there before that time? Did you study the contents?"

"Why, I—no. There was no reason to."

"Did you close it quickly—as though something might—might escape?"

She looked at him wide-eyed and did not answer.

Fanaalis had lighted the candles in brackets that gave a golden illumination to the room. A small blaze was flickering and whispering behind the ornate brass andirons in the fireplace so the evening dampness was transmuted into a soothing envelopment of the man and woman sitting before it.

The casket had been removed from the table.

"John (I must call you something)—it somehow seems to fit."

"That will do."

"You have not walked out the door, and I thank you. You know what I do, see how I live, but have prevented me from telling you of—of my work—of the ones who have been here before—before you—and——"

"And the recoveries you have wrought?"

"Yes. When I said to you that you were a deliverer, I did not mean that the weight of confession was on me and that in you a victim for this passion had appeared. Father Confessors abound in every square of New Orleans. You were scornful when I said I did not seek out women who are in despair because of shattered romances. What I have done——"

"I presume you mean what you *are doing*——"

She did not answer at once. She did glance at him appealingly, but his focus remained on a dancing blue flame, and his profile, partially shadowed, affected Sarah Belle so deeply that her hands moved as if she would like to sculpt and preserve it for her heart's sustenance.

"What I have done——" she repeated softly, "I would like for women to know about and thus achieve their own salvation in these matters. It would be a *man's* work to help such women after the damage is done—to—to work as I have done."

"Are doing," he repeated, and chuckled at the idea of a masculine mission in the same realm of romantic chaos.

Sarah Belle felt that she was functioning on two levels of mind and emotion: In one she could still hear a lover's agonized call to *Guafana! Guafana!*, see the stress lines deepen on his face, feel the surge of panic that struck and was cast off by a thrust of will. On the other she was conversing with a man of needle-sharp insight and satiric evaluation.

"Perhaps—I have—I mean, do I have enough of your confidence that you would tell me what you do—what is your mission——?"

"Mission? I have none. A drive, yes. I am an antiquarian. I search for answers among the ruins, not in museums mind you, but on the site of manifestation."

"Ah! Then unwittingly I have guided you to one of the most ancient sites of all, the ruins of the human spirit."

He was quiet before her acumen, then responded. "Touché! And now I find my mummified essence in this glorified tomb, awaiting the pulse that signifies resurrection."

Did he mean that he was accepting residence and awaiting her response to the sparring that was taking place between them? Since she had abandoned her role as his rescuer and he had rejected her designation of him as her deliverer, how could the impasse between them be resolved? Instinctively, she knew he would sit silently by, for hours, if need be, waiting for her to untangle the net he had woven around her.

After a while, she inquired, "Is there any place where your presence is expected this evening?"

"None."

"Is there——" she hesitated, and then ventured, "Is there— any place—where you'd rather be?"

"Yes indeed. At a camp of my own contrivance, in the main tower of the Mayan ruins, near the village of Palenque, in the state of Chiapas, Mexico." He paused, waiting for Sarah Belle's response, and when there was none, he added, "Listening to the screaming monkeys in the jungle round-about."

The additional remark prodded Sarah Belle to answer abruptly, "Are you assuming that such a diversity from reality would drown out the thought-sound of *Guafana?*"

It was her turn to follow up a delayed response. "Have you ever been to Palenque?" He still did not answer, but Sarah Belle sensed he had not been there. And she regretted the sharpness of her thrust for he had stiffened at the name of Guafana and his head had jerked as though he had been struck. "You have violated your own principle of nonretaliation," she accused herself bitterly. "You are teetering on the precipice of jealousy."

"You must have read John L. Stephens's *Incidents of Travel in Central America, Chiapas, and Yucatán,*" she commented quietly.

He turned and looked at her sharply. Her heart began to beat violently and she blushed again and was thankful for shadows diffusing the candlelight.

"You have read that book?" Surprise and an edge of incredulity in his voice.

"It is there on the shelf at the end of the mantel, almost within your reach."

He glanced that way in verification. When he spoke it was in a tone subdued and at a level of acceptance Sarah Belle had been reaching for. "An antiquarian named Dupaix visited the ruins some ten years before Stephens, and the government of Guatemala sent a Captain Antonio Del Río there in 1787, the first to make an extensive exploration and provide a description of the area."

"I had not heard of those."

"Del Río's report was not published until 1822 and created quite a stir in Europe."

"A stir perhaps, and even awe, but how many readers or even discoverers, ever feel the importance of learning *why* lost civilizations became 'lost'? Such knowledge might better equip us to preserve our own."

Again he turned on her a keen glance of appraisal. "We do not think it important because we consider ourselves the most important and knowledgeable civilization that has ever existed, and no such obliteration could possibly be our fate. There are always surmises and some evidence for conquest, destructive drouths, floods, but no attention to discovering the effects of what the people might have been thinking, believing—what were their hungers or denials beyond the commonplace? And, was the accumulated wisdom of the times being abused and perverted?"

"Do you plan to go to Palenque and search for clues to these intangibles?"

"Yes."

"Soon?"

"Yes."

Sarah Belle felt chilled, denied. She rang for Fanaalis, asked for the fire to be rebuilt, while she fed her desire to keep him near with contrivances of delay.

She gave the appearance of utter composure as she inquired gently, "I assume you have explored in other areas, visited the ruins of other fabled kingdoms?"

"Yes." He was silent a space, then added, as though speaking to a newborn flame in the wood just placed on the fire. "In South America, along the upper Orinoco Valley among the Guaharibo tribes——"

He's about to tell me . . . he's about to tell me . . . Sarah Belle was thinking, holding her breath, motionless.

But he did not continue. Sarah Belle sighed, and after a while rang the small silver bell that brought Fanaalis into their presence again.

"If our abode pleases you, and you would like to rest with us a while, sir, Fanaalis will show you to a comfortable room and attend your needs there," she invited formally, as inwardly she addressed a force beyond herself: *Don't let him go! Don't let him leave me now!*

"One does not turn aside from so charming a private hostel when notified in advance that reservations have been made," he countered. "Compliments of the day, madam. Yes, thank you, Fanaalis."

Sarah Belle reached for the Stephens book and began a more

thorough appraisal of its contents in an effort to lay aside her deep disquietude. Two, three hours passed. Shealia interrupted gently, "Are you not a-hunger, ma'm?"

"Nothing now, Shealia. What is our guest about?"

"He supped in his room, ma'm. Fanaalis brought him chocolate and a muffin. He would have nothing more. Black tea later, he said."

"Has he retired?"

"No, ma'm. He is writing—writing very fast."

"Light the music room for me, Shealia."

Sarah Belle followed her servant and was soon seated at a tall golden harp of classic proportions, the centerpiece of the room. It was a high-ceilinged room, not large but complemented with arched windows, the arcs at the top of stained glass and the lower sections clear and framing the blossoms of tropical plants just outside.

She sat and fingered the strings and then began to sing softly the tuneful imagery of her thoughts.

"O Thou Desert of My Mind,
   O Thou Guarded Hidden Glory,
   Let me somehow somewhere find
   Essence of the human story.

Let me find within my desert
   Secret pools so pure and sweet—
   Let me find within my desert
   Fellow nomads I can greet.

Let me share the fronded shade,
   Offer fruits that satisfy,
   Gaze in wonder at the dune shapes
   Bonded to a blazing sky.

O Thou Desert of My Mind,
   Bathing me in searing sun,
   Chilling me through bone and marrow
   When the burning day is done.

What the light that plays so grandly
   On the harpstrings of my brain?
   Where the Source that rives the darkness,
   Brings dissolve to crystal pain?

In the desert of my mind,
Now I stand constrained and mute
Without a song of love to sing,
While conscience and desire dispute."

The music of the harp continued without the voice, almost fading into shadows and then came back to accompany

"O Thou Desert of My Mind,
O Thou Guarded Hidden Glory,
Let me somehow somewhere find
Essence of the human story."

When the harpstrings were silent, from another part of the
house came the tones that Sarah Belle had heard in the park. The
quality of resonance was so singular, its appeal so pervasive, that
her senses seemed bonded to it as though it were a signature to her
own song.

He is with me. I am in his thoughts and he in mine. He is writing, writing what he could not tell me. He is in my house. I will
rest now—and tomorrow——

CHAPTER FOUR

S ARAH BELLE USUALLY AWAKENED at dawn and
waited for early morning light to caress the pic-
torial stained glass of a large window to the east.
The scene represented was of a fertile verdant place in the desert.
The oasis was not peopled but there were small birds and animals
and one camel at the waterside to animate the landscape. The
morning light was ever changeable, from the dimmest illumination when fog blanketed the city in thick folds or clouds hung low
and heavy, to the brightest of sunshine when every detail of artistry shown out and the pool of life was clear and light blue.
There were other times when morning haze was thin, and pink
and gold played over the window like a dream in motion.

On this morning the fog was master and allowed only a shaft of
light on the camel in a surround of dark blue, shadowed greens,
and recessive browns.

Shealia entered the bedroom with fragrant coffee and small banana patties, a specialty of her native island in the West Indies,
and Sarah Belle's delight.

The house was very quiet. Sarah Belle sipped her coffee and tasted a pattie as Shealia awaited the usual compliments. *What shall I wear this morning that I'm sure will please him? What shall I order Shealia to prepare for breakfast that will be sure to appeal? And there should be several courses so that we may have time to get used to each other.*

She noticed her servant looking at her anxiously and realized she had not given the praise expected.

"Perfect!" she said. "Absolutely perfect, Shealia. I shall eat only one now. Make these the first course, and have butter and a small bowl of honey available. After that——"

Shealia stammered an interruption, "Ma'm. Ma'm, I . . . we . . ."

"What's wrong, Shealia? You appear distressed. Are you ill?"

"No. No, ma'm. No sickness in me, but I . . . I supposed to tell you——"

"What are you supposed to tell me? I sense it's not good news. Tell me at once."

"The gentleman . . . the gentleman . . . is . . . gone . . . not here . . . not here."

Sarah Belle began to chill. She was shaking and her voice came out harsh and demanding. "Why was I not told?"

Shealia picked up a large shawl and wrapped it around her mistress. She reflected Sarah Belle's distress and her hands trembled as she secured the shawl.

"I knew no thing about what happen. Fana told me and told me tell you when you wake up. When he took tea last time, man asked him to stay in room for a while. When he finish writing, deep in night, before cock time in morning, he asked Fana to go to door with him . . . he not want to leave your house without the lock back in latch."

"Bring Fanaalis to me at once—at once! Do you hear?"

Shealia scurried to the door and when she opened it, there was Fanaalis.

Sarah Belle glared at him. She wanted to say: You fool! Why did you let him go! You should have had sense enough to come to me, I could have persuaded——. But she stopped there. She clutched her shawl tightly around her and asked, "What did he say to you before he left?" And before he could answer she repeated harshly, *"What did he say?"*

Fanaalis stooped even more than his natural disability required, as though Sarah Belle's displeasure were a physical reprimand.

"He say, 'Tell your mistress what she'" (he recalled the exact wording but found it difficult to enunciate), "'what she desired of me has been given—that it will fit well in her Pan—Pan—' I do not know the word, ma'm—Pan—box."

"Pandora's box?"

"Yes, ma'm, yes, ma'm, that was it! Pan—dor's box."

What else?"

"That was all, ma'm."

"Are you sure—very sure?"

"Yes, yes, vera, vera sure."

Sarah Belle went directly to the guest room. The bed had not been slept in. On a desk nearby where she kept writing materials, a calendar, a clock, and a small bowl of fresh flowers, was a rectangular shape of folded white paper. She knew instantly that it was folded to fit easily in the Lando box he had not allowed her to open. She picked it up and released the first fold. Lettered small and lucid was

For Pandora's Box
Guafana's Web of Passion

There were several pages, and one more movement of her fingers would lay the story of Guafana open for her reading. She felt like an intruder who could pull the curtain aside and see that which was meant for other eyes alone. At the same time she felt rooted to the spot, as though she couldn't move away—the curtain was in her hand.

She called out, almost screaming, "Shealia! Shealia!" and when the frightened woman appeared, "Bring me the box! Bring me the box! You know where I keep it. The jeweled box!"

When Shealia returned, her eyes wide in apprehension, Sarah Belle directed, "Place it on the desk. No, no, do not run away. Stay right here."

She pressed the paper in her hands back into the original fold, tightening the edges with her fingernails. She fumbled with the latch on the casket as if she had never seen it, and when it sprang open, she thrust the antiquarian's account inside in one quick gesture and slammed the lid shut.

"Take it back, Shealia. Take it away at once."

Then she sat down and wept, wept until she felt loose in body and drained of emotion.

Still in disarray and barefooted she went to her bookshelves and took down a popular book on Greek mythology. She sat in the chair that she had occupied the night before. A small fire was freshening and drying the air. Wordlessly she accepted the strong hot tea Shealia brought. She looked at the empty chair beside her as if imagining a presence, then consulted the index for "Pandora" and turned to refresh her acquaintance with this legendary character and consider the significance of her mythical creation.

She read:

Pandora: A beautiful woman (the all-gifted) whom Zeus caused Hephaestus to make as punishment for the human race because Prometheus had stolen fire from heaven. She became the wife of Epimetheus, brother of Prometheus. Zeus gave her a box enclosing all human ills, which escaped over the earth when the box was opened by her out of curiosity. *Hope*, which was in the box, was all she prevented from escaping.

"Hope was all she prevented from escaping," Sarah Belle repeated to herself. She returned to the room where the man she called John had been writing through the night and sat for a while in the chair where he had been seated at the desk. Did she dare to hope that he would return?

She walked restlessly about the room touching the objects he might have touched. At the marble-topped washstand, she rearranged the soap dish and water pitcher and saw a green object near the bowl. She recognized it as a piece of jade. It was flat and shaped to an arc that would fit easily between the lips and could be held between the teeth—it was perforated in a manner that must have produced the sounds she heard in the park and in the house when she had ceased her music on the harp. To what ancient ceremonial pattern had it been attuned originally, she wondered.

Surely, he had not left it behind accidentally. Could she hope that he would return to claim it? And, if so, when? After he had conducted his search through the ruins of Palenque? Months, years away, if ever. What should she do with it—treat it as a talisman or amulet? Cherish it as a symbol of the hope left in Pandora's box after the mischief was done?

She returned to her bedroom and placed it on her dressing table where it was reflected in the mirror. She studied it for a while but did not place it to her lips. Deliberately she began the morning ritual of her toilet, with Shealia assisting, trying various arrangements of her abundant brown hair, selecting with care her attire for the day.

"It is a dreary day, Shealia, and rain likely. Let's make a bright spot with my rich blue ensemble for sky and my gold poplin cape for sun."

She studied herself in the full-length mirror. "Hmm—Pandora: a beautiful woman and all-gifted. Do I qualify for the part, Shea?"

Busy with hooks and buttons, understanding only the essence of the question, Shealia replied, "Deedy, deedy, ma'm. You make Mardi Gras Queen, or real queen for sure!"

"It's cheering to have an attendant who talks like someone right out of a fairy tale." She saw her smile at Shealia reflected in the mirror and liked what she saw.

"A smile is good for the face, Shealia, and in the presence of others it is a gift and a communication."

She continued to study herself in the mirror and rehearse a repertoire of smiles until Shealia laughed aloud.

"But when a smile carries mockery or disdain, it is no longer a smile, it is a grimace. See!"

"Oh, yes, don't do! You spoil beauty."

"Shealia," she was serious now. "Tell Fanaalis I will go out this afternoon for a long drive. He must get in touch with my hackman right away and have the carriage ready for me at two o'clock promptly."

Shealia was disturbed, disapproving. "This day, ma'm?"

"This day, regardless of weather. And make the usual preparations while I am gone. There will be another guest tonight. I shall see to it."

CHAPTER FIVE

AT A TABLE RESERVED FOR TWO at the Isle of the
Blest on Elysian Fields Street, a man and
woman are seated for leisurely dining and visit-
ing through late afternoon and evening hours. It is a setting where
romance flourishes—soft lights, perfume of fresh flowers, choice
food and wines, soft music of strings at intervals from behind a
screen of garden wall. For these two it is a lovers' delight—he so
fair, eyes of deepest blue, so ardent, she French-dark with small
and restless hands.

The meal has only begun, the dark red wine in the glasses, small
tasty crackers and tidbits of delicate meats before them. He raises
his glass: "To the love of my life—the one and only Ange! The
eternal song of my heart!"

Her eyes moisten. "It is so good to be the one and only, above
all else in a man's life, *mon amour*. So good—so important! So
exciting!" She lifts her glass, saluting him, and her eyes hold his in

a look of such intense passion that he feels bound to her, riveted to her in a bonding that more resembles being possessed than possessing.

"My all is yours!" Her burning gaze holds until she looks down and sips from her glass, releasing him.

She begins nibbling at the savory morsels before her. Her partner begins drumming on the table, his fingers in action as though striking piano keys. He begins to hum in time with his fingers.

"Da-da-*da*—Dum-de-dee-dee-da."

She flings her shoulders and head of dark curls about like a highstrung mare on too short a tether.

He becomes more animated with his concentration on fingers and da-das and de-dees. He pauses and reaches into a side pocket, then frantically reaches in other pockets, using only one hand for the search—the other for the compulsive composition hammering at him.

She, too, is becoming more animated—with anger.

"Darling, darling," he pleads. "You couldn't possibly have a bit of paper I could scribble on. I've found a nub of pencil."

"You are absolutely right! I couldn't possibly have a bit of paper about. I wear only cloth and have yet to offer up a piece of my skin for parchment."

He misses the irony.

"Go. Go quickly to the maître d'hotel and ask him to procure some paper for me. I'll stay here and hold it in my fingers lest the dance music start again and distract me. You know how I always get inspired at meals—this is my best ever! Help me, dearest. Help keep this precious time and tune. Hurry! Hurry!"

She rises, enraged, pushes her chair over, "I cannot live with this . . . I will not . . . I am lost to you . . . I could be Aphrodite herself and you would ignore me when a cursed tune takes hold. You had rather caress a piano any time than me! I am nothing . . . nothing! I hate music! I hate you!"

She grabs her wineglass and throws it at his drumming fingers. His hand flares and opens as the glass strikes the table and there is a red splash of wine. Then utter stillness between them. The string music starts behind the screen. He picks up his napkin and wipes his hand. The red stain doesn't rub off. It continues to ooze and flow.

"Oh, Mon Dieu! Mon Dieu! Your hand, your fingers, it's blood! What have I done? Oh, darling, darling, darling . . . ," she gasps in a deep sob.

He looks at her with hate-filled eyes that do not make the switch back to love as hers have done. In his rage, before rushing out, he screams at her: "You've killed me, you Jezebel! I'll never play again!"

"Oh, no, no, my precious! I love you! I love you!"

"A harlot would have loved me more. You pig of a woman! You belong in a slaughterhouse!" He flings his blood- and wine-stained napkin at her as he grabs up her napkin to bind his hand tightly and rush out in search of a hackman. She follows him calling out piteously.

At the steps of the restaurant, he turns on her, "If you come any further, I'll kill you!"

He spots a carriage near the entrance, its driver apparently waiting to serve customers at the Isle of the Blest.

Frantic, he stumbles and almost falls against the vehicle. He raises the bandaged hand like a red flag and shouts to the solemn man seated above him, "Can't you see I'm bleeding to death? Get me to the Franklin Infirmary! It's nearest." Then he retracts, "Oh, no, no, that hussy will follow me there."

He jerks open the door without inquiring if the carriage is in service. He catapults onto the seat, then shrieks, "Madre de Dios!" He's sitting by a woman. A very calm woman. He twists about and fumbles wildly for the doorlatch. She takes a firm grip on his arm.

"We'll take you to your residence, sir."

He groans. "God, no! She'll find me there for sure. I'll take the nearest steamer before that."

"Then to my house." She calls to the driver. "Quickly, Hudson! Home as fast as you can make it."

The hackman lifts his whip and the carriage hurtles forward.

The wounded musician is panting. "How can you explain me to your family?" And then back to his dilemma, "I should have killed her and myself. We could have gone to hell together!" His arm jerks. "The center of my hand! The ligament, for sure. I'm ruined. It's paining me now. I'm all pain. Oh heaven! Oh hell!"

"We'll soon be able to examine the damage and learn better the nature of your injury. Have hope and don't worry. I live alone, except for two aged servants, not slaves, with many remedies from the West Indies. Together we'll help you."

"You live alone? In the Ramparts?!" he groans, his agony compounded that she might be a quadroon concubine taking him to her cottage.

"Do not distress yourself as to my place of residence. I have no protector to challenge your presence. My living arrangements are my own choice."

He groans again, but notices her closely for the first time. "Men come to your house?"

"Occasionally there's a guest. They know naught of me. I discover them. Let me tighten your bandage and secure it and we must keep pressure on the critical point. Where's the cut?"

"The deepest in the center of the hand. I caught a cursed fragment of the wine goblet—there's the blood-letting."

"I'll hold your hand and apply pressure there until we arrive."

"Are you a nurse?"

"Sometimes. When we get to my place, come in quickly and Hudson will hurry on. If you should be followed, the carriage will not be at hand."

"I place myself in your hands. Nothing worse could happen to me now."

She speaks quietly, "My house is not an open house. It is a House of Recovery."

He looks at her again, searching for what he cannot identify. "For males only, I suppose?"

"Why, yes."

There is a silence—the driver sets a faster pace—the passengers sway against each other.

"Do I qualify?"

"We shall see. I usually select my guests with care. You were delivered up to me."

"You are not voudou?"

"You must find out for yourself."

"Curses!" The white napkin is now soaked with blood.

"I feel like a cadaver—nothing but a beating heart and a mess of blood. That monster of a woman has castrated the musician in me!" He jerks his hand from her, holds it before his face, and gasps in self-pity, "Why should I be maimed and she have a good hand of no more use on the keys then a hoof!"

CHAPTER SIX

HREE DAYS LATER, the distraught pianist and
composer had changed little. He had the constant attentions of Sarah Belle's servants under
her supervision. The wound had been cleansed, tightly bound,
and poultices applied. Hand and arm were swollen, but not in-
flamed. Sleeping draughts had been administered. Nevertheless,
he punctuated the nights with sobs and fevered deliriums of recall
until his caretakers knew every detail of the incident at the restaurant and of the love affair in which, with jealous tenacity, Ange
had competed with his devotion to the goddess Pianoforte.

In nightmares of confusion, he was at times the lover who had
lost the emotional shelter provided by the beloved and was calling
for her presence; at other times he was in the concert hall and
unable to reach the chords, or found the keys soundless. He ate
and drank little but was conscious enough of those who attended
him that he revealed nothing of his identity—the swollen eyes
were dry and responses abbreviated.

When Sarah Belle entered on this morning, he gave no recognition of her presence. She carried a newspaper in her hand. She stood by his bedside and addressed him. "Good morning, Mr. Lahart. Mr. Sutton Lahart, I believe."

He blinked and she knew she had his attention. "Your brother Justin is offering a ten-thousand-dollar reward for information leading to the solution of the mystery surrounding your disappearance."

"Very generous of Mr. Marbleheart. Leading to my dead body, he hopes."

"I've been thinking you should be in the care of your family physician."

"And my captor, the so-white witch, gets ten thousand dollars?" He glared at her.

Sarah Belle recognized the implied insult; that he was searching for a color mark. Her brown eyes met the challenge in his but she smiled as if in response to a compliment. "It is possible that the value of my estate might not suffer in comparison with that of the Laharts. . . . Now, as to the main topic: your recovery. Shall I call your physician?"

"If you do——" his voice threatened.

Sarah Belle smiled again. "It would not disturb you if your dead body were left on my hands and I must account for your condition?"

"Not in the least. You brought me here."

"I have a certain sympathy for your brother Justin."

"If he were in my place, it would be love at first sight. You were both chipped from stone."

Sarah Belle laughed. "You're improving. That's the longest statement you have made since you accepted my bed. I'll send Fanaalis with a brew of Java's strongest. He has freshened your fashionable attire, but if you'd like something more comfortable, you'll find a selection of garments in the wardrobe. And if you make it that far, he can show you to my music room for I have missed my regular hours of practice on my——"

"Oh God, preserve me!" He sat up wild-eyed and moved as if to leap from the bed. "Nothing could compound my misery more than seeing and hearing you at the piano!"

"Nothing could compound your misery more than to leap off in the custody of the nearby gendarme, and on into the presence of dear Justin and your high-spirited Ange Déchu. There is no piano in this house."

"I hate those dainty lady harpsichords with their gold-crusted cupids, all glitter and squeaks!"

"Your comments indicate you're still feverish, or a rude fellow that Ange is well rid of."

"How do you know her name?" he growled in accusation.

"Easily. You have alternately screamed at her and begged for her caresses in your nightmares. And that is not all. A gris-gris has been placed on my doorstep."

His eyes opened wide in alarm. He stared at her in disbelief. "Oh, no! Ange wouldn't!"

"Ange did. She's desperate. She's asked Marie Laveau, the young voudou queen, for assistance. As you must know, Marie has widespread popularity with lovers in troubled waters."

"How does she know I'm here?"

"We would have to inquire of her."

"If she knows, why hasn't she betrayed me?"

"You evidently have little acquaintance with the god of the voudous and his adepts here on earth, particularly in New Orleans."

"Heaven forbid!" Sutton crossed himself, moved his lips in silent prayer, and fixed his gaze on Sarah Belle as if she were another apparition from his frightful dreams.

"In one respect he resembles the God of the Old Testament: he is all-powerful, the source of all that was or ever will be created. When offended, his anger is terrible and his vengeance certain. His symbol is the serpent, and you will recall that Moses raised a brazen serpent upon the cross in the wilderness that all might be——"

"Blasphemy! I will not listen to such heretical satanic——"

"Yes, you will, Mr. Sutton Lahart. I did not force you over my threshold. I offered sanctuary and you accepted it. You've enclosed yourself in a cocoon of self-pity. The circumstances of your crippling condition have caused a gris-gris to be placed at my door, and, until we have an understanding of what it's all about, and the actions I must take, I'll keep talking, and you'll not pull the covers over your head like a pouting simpleton. Not unless you want Fanaalis to dress you and escort you into the street."

Sutton fixed his eyes on Sarah Belle's with a look that expressed his own kind of maledictions and then turned on his side, his back to her while she continued.

"I was about to point out that the serpent has been through the ages a symbol of the all-powerful, whether the power is for good or evil. To the followers of voudouism, their god is monster-size and utterly—" she paused and raised her voice and slapped her hand on the marble-topped table—"*utterly terrifying!*"

Sutton jerked to a sitting position, his eyes wide in fright.

"That's better. The god of the voudous will countenance brutality, but not rudeness. You'd be better served to hear me through. He can control and outwit evil and is wise and crafty in his use of supernatural powers. His workers of black magic are adept in the powers, and the more learned are knowledgeable in the use of herbs and potions, including subtle poisons. They are accomplished also in the manipulations of mental states and emotions." She paused again. "Look at you!" She held him in a steady stare. "You are a good example."

Sutton gave her resentful attention.

"You are fearful as though a demon were in your presence and you had no control over it. That is the tool of power they have exerted here since colonial days!"

"How do you know these things? Have I landed in an ungodly nest of witchcraft?"

"Let's put it this way: you've brought witchcraft to my doorstep. If you have slaves in your household, it is likely you have been reared, protected, waited upon day and night by the practitioners of this particular religion."

"Ridiculous! All influences over both slaves and family members in the Lahart household have been in the true Catholic tradition, and all, including slaves, baptized into the faith."

"True of many households in this area for generations. The slaves have found the Catholic rituals and saints' days a satisfying adjunct to voudouism—their open festivities on St. John's Day and other observances useful as a covering for their secret ceremonies."

"I've heard of these—who in New Orleans has not? They engage in savage, maniacal orgies——"

"Some are frenetic, savage, true—others offer an outlet, a hope that in playing the game with the evil force that hangs over all, there can be winners, though their god is often frivolous and malicious and sounds no moral tone. To ease your mind about this small household: my servants not only are informed but also at times are my valuable informants. Their faith in a benevolent god is based on a different experience than slavery espouses. In irons and under the lash it is more profitable to be crafty than to be good."

"Then perhaps you'll include in your discourse what is the nature of the gris-gris placed at this house because of my presence." Sutton's voice was a mix of sarcasm and fear.

"It's the traditional little red bag containing cayenne pepper, powdered brick, and yellow ochre. From your initial reaction, I judge you know this is expected to bring about some dreadful injury to the recipient. In addition, your, or we might call it *our*, gris-gris has a chicken gizzard and buzzard feather attached."

Sutton paled and looked so revolted and fearful, she thought he might vomit.

"You must know, Mr. Lahart, that these spells lose their potency unless you accept their intended authenticity with a possessive fear."

He did not answer.

"She is telling us quite plainly that we must meet and parlay if we want the spell of the gris-gris removed, invalidated."

Sutton paled, moistened his lips but could not speak.

Sarah Belle raised her eyebrows. "So Marie with her little red bag of dust, a feather from one of nature's essential garbage collectors, and a vital organ from an inoffensive chicken, has damaged you as certainly as the shattered crystal of Ange's wineglass. Don't worry. I'll do the parlaying. How I parlay depends on you. If you want to reappear as mysteriously as you disappeared, then Marie will rank high in Ange's favor, and many more women of high station will seek the services of the high priestess of voudou. I will add a few compliments to her powers and a gold coin to give weight to any statements I may make. If, however, you insist that she keep your whereabouts secret, it will be a bit more complicated."

"If she knows, others know."

"No doubt. But the voudou line of communication is a very

tight web over the entire city and none would violate her orders. Ange no doubt told all, and Marie conducted her own investigation. She's a free mulatto, born of free mulattoes, and operates independently when and where she pleases. Is your brother your closest relative?"

"Yes. Other members of my family perished in the plague of '32." His voice was flat, toned with a burdened memory.

Sarah Belle was still. She had heard countless horror stories of ravaged families, some where all had perished and homes had been set ablaze for cremation. She inquired softly, "And yet you hate your brother?"

"Despise would be a better word."

"And Ange, your amour?"

"I would mate with a fiend from purgatory before returning to her." He made a sweeping gesture with his bandaged hand and gasped in pain.

"Don't fret about the gris-gris. Marie will not be hasty. She's too cunning for that. She'll let heartbreak simmer and passion smolder. Giving fear time to develop into something grotesque and destructive is the wisdom of her station. She's gaining in favor among the social set as a hair-dresser. Her customers admit her into their homes unaware that one so young and personable could be proclaimed a pythoness by a sect so ancient and currently populous in our midst. I shall summon her here as a hair-dresser."

CHAPTER SEVEN

S ARAH BELLE, GOWNED in a long flowing morning
robe of pale blue silk and a matching cap that
covered her hair done in multiple curlers, rose to
greet Marie Laveau as Shealia admitted her into the boudoir.

"Je vous souhaite le bonjour, Marie."

"Bonjour, madame."

"My name is Sarah Belle."

"Ah! La Belle, the bee-ou-tee! Madame La Belle!"

"Marie, we are freeborn persons in private converse; just call
me by my name, no 'mesdames'."

Marie smiled broadly. Her compelling eyes, pools of glowing
darkness in which the black pupil was hardly discernible, met
Sarah Belle's in a perceptive flash of empathy. "La Belle," she answered simply.

The two women stood quite still for a moment studying each
other with undisguised interest. Marie, bronze and statuesque, was
an imposing figure. She was not garbed in the expected vivid col-

ors; her gathered skirt and her blouse with low-cut bodice and winglike sleeves were of creamy hand-loomed cotton. Around her waist she wore a bright blue sash that hung to the bottom of the skirt, and wound on her head turbanlike was the same blue cloth. Her ornamentations were ear loops with a cluster of tiny shells attached, a wide copper bracelet, and on a cord around her neck a black cross carved from ebony held in place just at the bosom line.

Sarah Belle moved to her mirrored dressing table, sat, and put aside her cap. With nimble fingers that did not pull a hair, Marie began removing the kid curlers—strands of wire covered with the softest kid leather—until swirls and coils of shining brown hair covered Sarah Belle's head and shoulders.

Marie began talking rapidly, now in French, now in English, as she gathered the hair this way and that showing possible coiffures, some in high styles, some original. No mention was made of their underlying purpose in meeting, each seemingly intent only on achieving the most complimentary hairdo possible.

"We do all this for one purpose alone, do we not, Marie?"

"Oui, La Belle, to please un homme comme il faut."

"There is a gentleman in this house I would like to have turn his sour words to sweet in my presence. Could we help this along with an entirely different coiffure?"

"Mais certainement. La Belle is wise to know this."

"Not wise enough to do it. That's up to you."

"We will not do the straight part in the middle that is so fashionable with or without the curl. We will make something that softens your presence, La Belle, and brings a kind of mystery around the face—so—a frame of curl along the forehead and over the ears, trailing over the bare shoulder—but the bodice will be high in front, you understand, only showing a dainty locket chain around the throat. There will be a scattering, maybe no more than five, very small rosebuds in the hair, none centered, one just peeking at the shoulder. No other adornment, your gown only a hint of color."

"Where did you learn such tricks?"

"My mother dressed the hair of many a fair quadroon for the ballroom where the white young gentlemen were waiting for romantic connections."

40

"Ah, yes—a fate of bittersweet romance, a virgin's rapturous taste of passion, then naught but dregs."

"At least the beauteous one can choose her own protector, if her charms are sufficient to beguile him. As a child I assisted my mother."

"Do you do hair-dressing for the quadroons now?"

"Non. I go here and I go there for high ladies and for the jeune fille caught in the net of Cupidon."

"I see." Sarah Belle studied her reflection. Indeed Marie had wrought a transformation—replaced independence of expression with dependence. Shyness and innocence could be assumed if one brought the eyes and lashes into proper compliance. It was astonishing.

"It makes me feel silly, Marie, and rather brainless."

Marie laughed. "Very useful, La Belle, if you care to change sour to sweet as you say. We will try another way, at your pleasure."

"No, leave it like this. I will add the rosebuds later, before curtain time." Sarah Belle smiled at her other self in the mirror and at Marie. Now must come the delicate interplay of comment and inquiry leading to unspoken compromise and agreement.

"Seat yourself comfortably, Marie, and liven my morning with a tête-à-tête. Do you come prepared with love potions when you attend these women grooming for competition in the game of hearts?"

"I brought none today, La Belle."

"Why not?"

"You brew your own."

"Not to any advantage so far, Marie. I thought you might have brought some for me to administer to the guest in my house, not for myself, of course, but for the distraught Ange."

There was no inclination of either woman to engage in side glances. They looked directly at each other as they spoke. The mention of Ange brought no change in Marie's expression. It did seem, however, that the natural brightness in the dark eyes took on a higher sheen.

"Lovers must behold each other for the potion to excite passion."

"Ange's irrational amour would accept a poison with more grace than he would agree to see Ange again. The passion that consumes him is to create music and to execute it, and the music of the great masters, through the piano. Ange inflicted the hand wound that separates him from the piano as surely as an amputation would do. Though some day he might forgive her the act, there is no way through the mind or body that this mode of expression can be restored to him. And the love passion for Ange is just as permanently severed from his existence."

This was additional evidence to Marie. She absorbed it in silence.

"No fear that could be devised would change this, though it could move him toward self-destruction."

Both knew that this had reference to the gris-gris. Marie remained silent, relaxed as though the occasion were merely a social one.

"It is a most strange quality in human nature, is it not, Marie, that what we accept into our minds as valid, no matter what the intrinsics, governs our day-to-day performance."

"Vrai, La Belle."

"And one who can affect or control, by whatever means, the thoughts of another, is exercising a power more potent than is ever inherent in a pill or measured from a bottle—or injected through symbolism."

Marie's eyes squinted ever so little, and her mood seemed to switch into something very remote from the boudoir and its occupants.

Sarah Belle felt a tingle high on the back of her neck. She smiled ever so slightly.

"Marie, I do not care to invade the secrets of your art, nor intend to be governed by them except for that which we can accomplish together in restoring Sutton Lahart and relieving Ange. I know that you have been called before the magistrates for certain acts that they label 'black magic'—this of course enhances your reputation."

Marie's expression betrayed her amused agreement.

"I also know that you sometimes exercise your talents in directions that assist those in dire distress—this you keep as secret as possible. It would dull the weapon wherein your power resides. In a society such as ours here, based on human bondage, a regular Babylon of prejudices, race mixtures, and class distinctions, the emotions of love and fear——"

"And *sexe*, La Belle, the hunger, the passion, the dragonhead that cannot be severed——"

"Oui. Common to all. And it is along these avenues that you move and exert your influence for evil or good, which is, after all, a variable classification, depending upon our viewpoint. You are reputed to have a gift of divination along with other supernatural proclivities. I envision your influence widening, your wisdom increasing——"

"And my success as a procuress, an increase?" Her smile this time was light mockery and implying more than her own status in certain facets of public opinion.

"You are much more under public scrutiny than I, Marie, but I must say there are certain aspects of our activities that would place an onus upon us should we seek admittance into circles of the circumspect. But tainted nomenclature can often be worn like a mask, concealing a mission that would be even less understood, more reviled, than the apparent activity."

"You are wise and generous, La Belle. You encourage and give hope——"

Sarah Belle laughed at the superfluity. "The mask of flattery draws followers in countless numbers. Fear and flattery—what a partnership! It would be hard to find a person in New Orleans who feels more secure than Marie Laveau. So—I have a suggestion for a little drama in which you and I, Ange and Sutton, and brother Justin will be the main characters."

Marie shifted into a position even more relaxed and attentive, though the eyes were never shielded, always alert, penetrating, sifting the relationship of fact and thought.

"You know that Justin is offering ten thousand dollars for establishing Sutton's whereabouts. I know that Sutton can recuperate only if he is kept separate from Justin and Ange, and continues to believe that he has foiled them. Would it not be within your province to forecast for Ange a lover more satisfying, more attentive, more replete with masculine charms than Sutton? Doubtless you know a rejected suitor who could be cast in this role, and how a meeting could be arranged?"

Sarah Belle waited for a response. Marie left her chair, wandered over to a vase of freshly cut flowers, removed one, kissed it and then threw it at Sarah Belle's feet. She did not smile. Her expression was fathomless.

So we talk in symbols, Sarah Belle said to herself.

She picked up the flower, smoothed it a bit, placed it in her lap, and continued.

"Then perhaps you could arrange for a meeting between me and Justin Lahart. I could meet him in a closed carriage at a designated spot, and we could talk. You would see to it that he comes to me without talking to anyone else. I would see to it that the reward would be placed in your hands—for—your good works."

Marie simply placed her right hand over the black cross on her chest.

"When this is arranged, Hudson, my hackman, can bring me your message."

"Oui, La Belle." Sarah Belle stood carefully holding the flower. Marie walked back to the dressing table. "Will madame be so kind," she used the word carefully, changing the status between them, "to let me examine, hold in my hand, the piece of ancient jade that attracts my attention."

"Of course." Sarah Belle felt the strange tingle again. "It has a peculiar tone value, and (why was she saying this? she asked herself) you may try it, if you like. When placed in the mouth, it can invoke a quality quite different from the standard scale."

Marie studied the object, looked at Sarah Belle with the piercing insight she had evidenced earlier, then placed the object between her lips and brought forth the same sounds Sarah Belle had heard from the stranger who had aroused her to such an emotional tide of yearning.

"The owner at this moment yearns for your presence, madame. He will return."

Sarah Belle felt her heartbeat quicken, and a peculiar sensation race from shoulders to fingertips, but quickly resumed objectivity. "Thank you, Marie. And now what are your charges for the remarkable change you have wrought in me through a coiffure, and for the bit of pleasant divination just spoken?"

"For you, madame, there is no charge. For me there is waiting ten thousand dollars—in gold."

Sarah Belle rang the china bell on her table in signal to Shealia who appeared so soon that the two women smiled at each other, knowing but not caring about the servant's proximity. There was a certain kind of bondage in which each was held and all understood.

From the provident collection in the guest room wardrobe, Fanaalis had selected a discreet dressing gown and slippers and persuaded his ward to sit in a chair while he pulled out a small dropleaf table and spread a teasing repast—small servings of Shealia's most tempting meats and sauces and bits of colorful garden vegetables lightly sautéed in fresh-churned butter, emitting the most enticing of odors. Then Fanaalis withdrew, leaving the diner to his own maneuvers. He also left a newspaper within reach.

Later when Shealia came to clear the table and picked up the scattered newspaper, Sarah Belle entered not far behind. Sutton looked up startled and came to his feet in automatic gallantry.

Score one for Marie, Sarah Belle thought. *When he kisses my hand, we will have accomplished the turnabout.*

He stared at Sarah Belle like one who has just recovered his eyesight. His instinct and training signaled "a lady to the manner born." He even bowed slightly.

Sarah looked the part and spoke the part, her voice low and gentle, her smile and dewy glance a caress of sympathy.

"Dear Mr. Lahart, you cannot know how relieved and happy we are to see you so improved. Do be seated or perhaps you had rather recline."

"Oh, no, no," he demurred, as if this would not be quite proper in her presence, and remained standing until she was seated.

"Fanaalis reports that the swelling is reduced and you have been able to sleep with more comfort."

"True. I am indebted——"

"Not for a bit of it."

He kept looking at her in bewildered wonderment, thoughts and emotions whirling and hardly relating to what had passed before this moment. This beautiful creature was like a storybook heroine, all kindness and grace and reserve. And the hair—the glory of it—could it be rosebuds held there? Fresh tiny rosebuds, he mused; as though they had fallen from an arbor upon her head, unable to cling to the vine above with such beauty shining below. What an idea for a festival feast of music, a serenade to loveliness. (The lame hand forgotten, the mind was composing.) And she was holding a flower in her hand.

He seemed entranced. Sarah Belle wondered if he had forgotten where he was, and the circumstances. She augmented his mood by coming to his chair and laying the flower in his lap. It was the blossom Marie had thrown at her feet. He looked at it and back to her and could not speak. She felt it was time to rationalize somewhat and yet not lose the impact of the part she was playing. She would not even mention the gris-gris or the queen of voudous.

"Mr. Lahart, sir. You are not to worry one bit—all has been arranged. There will be no need for you to see *anyone*—from the outside—until you choose to do so, not anyone. This house, you might say, is protected—or blessed—nothing to fear."

"Thank you." He spoke absent-mindedly, his eyes glazed, though he was watching her. He began to move the right hand now bandaged around the palm, with the thumb in a stall. The free fingers fumbled with the flower in his lap, and laid it on the table. Then he began to drum his fingers on the table. "Paper!" he whispered hoarsely, "Pencil!" With his left hand he began to search the pockets of the dressing gown and started to get up from the table.

"Stay right there, sir, please, I'll be back with paper and pencil at once." She was thinking, is it the same piece that came to him at the restaurant? Has he slipped back into—oh my! In a swift moment she was back and placing music score paper before him. He grabbed the pencil but the stiff fingers would not respond. He tried frantically, then grabbed the offending hand with the other and his eyes filled with the anguish of pain and frustration.

Sarah Belle hastily pulled a chair to the table and sat close to him. "Look at me."

"Circe . . . ," he murmured.

"No. Sarah Belle."

"La Belle."

"If you like." She was taking the paper and pencil from him. "I know music, not just parlor jangle. Now say the notes to me as you hear them and I will write them down. I will be hearing them too."

The long tresses that had lain to the back of her shoulders fell forward around the paper as she began to write for him. She raised her head and flung the hair back in place. A rosebud fell out.

"Don't do that!" he said pettishly.

Startled, she looked up.

"There is the melody. Do not throw it behind you." He reached over and touched her hair, fingering a small strand, and the notes he spoke were like winged phrases in her ears, and she could hear her harpstrings singing the rhapsody of it.

He finished and sat back in his chair, his eyes closed, his posture utter relaxation. "It will be heard at the festival for St. Valentine and the balls next season. . . . My sweet," he whispered, his eyes still closed, "my very sweet, the title is 'Serenade to St. Valentine.'"

"A la bonne heure!" She raced to the music room and her harp, and soon the notes on the script were actual tones that embraced him, enfolded him in an ecstasy where dreams and reality merged. Then he spoke softly to his music (or was it to the woman?): "You came to me like a whisper from the dewy lips of morning . . . tender . . . wistful . . . loving."

CHAPTER EIGHT

SARAH BELLE'S HACKMAN, HUDSON, was one of the *gens de couleur libres*, a handsome man, lively in expression and movement. He was of the community of free persons of African descent in New Orleans, noted in the mid-nineteenth century for their learning and wealth. There were some nine thousand of this caste in the city's population of over one hundred thousand. They worked mostly as craftsmen and domestics but were thrifty and shrewd in types of highly remunerative business investment, and not infrequently served as trusted public servants. In proportion to their numbers, they were more distinguished in literature than any other class.

Hudson not only was available as hackman to selected clients, but also was part owner of a thriving personal transport service operating many sizes and styles of carriage from stately coach to the small elegant French fiacres sometimes festooned for public appearances of ladies in high station.

The friendship between Hudson and Sarah Belle was important

to each. There was trust and mutual understanding for both the realities and the masquerades in their life styles. Their conversations were free of restraint, and matters of confidence need not be wrapped in vows to secrecy.

Sarah Belle had been notified by Hudson of the arrangements for her meeting with Justin Lahart. They had discussed it on their weekly drive to St. Mary's Market. Hudson explained that Justin was a shipping magnate of no small dimension. He maintained elaborate headquarters within an elegant suite located in the architectural gem of New Orleans, the magnificent St. Charles Exchange Hotel. He had neither wife nor offspring, was seemingly wed to his far-flung merchandising enterprise. Nothing could be of less interest and validity to him than the voudou "exercises." Not one to bend easily to any scheme that smacked of hoodwinking, still he was resolute in examining any clue that might clear the mystery of his brother's disappearance.

Hudson described him as robust, fearless, and not to be stopped in the pursuit of whatever he sought. He had forthrightly promised Marie the ten thousand in gold when he should become certain of the information which she shielded. First, let him meet and talk with the woman who claimed to have Sutton in her house. Then he would have the payment delivered. He was not pleased that he was given no name or status of the woman he was to meet, but agreed on time and place and that he would appear without escort, conducting the whole matter personally and in utter privacy.

On the day of the appointment, curtains of fog lay over the city, thinning here, thickening there, moving in phantomlike wisps as breezes tossed small cloudlike patches into restless treetops. The meeting was set for high noon at the Royal Street entrance of the St. Charles Hotel in order that it might seem circumspect and not unusual. Sarah Belle would arrive in a closed carriage. Hudson would dismount from his seat and wait at the door of the vehicle as though having been summoned for private service. He would recognize Justin Lahart and nod to him an invitation.

When Hudson arrived for Sarah Belle and opened the yard gate as she came out, they eyed each other as performers checking out costume and lines.

"Hudson, what a surprise! A really elegant coach. I like your choice of a two-seater. I'd rather face Justin Lahart than have him at my side. And your livery is handsome indeed. Man, horses, vehicle, in high style."

The coach was a cool rich green in color with lines of accent in silver. Hudson's attire was a modish shade of gray with waistcoat, hat, and gloves in Robin Hood green. When he opened the door for Sarah Belle to step inside, the upholstery revealed was a display of luxury cushioning in soft leather and satin, cool and inviting.

"What of my outfitting?" she inquired of Hudson as she stepped in. "Is it appropriate for an appointment with a Merchant Prince?"

"Madame, I'm not engaging in flattery when I say you are Master Shakespeare's perfect Portia. Though Monsieur Lahart would be miscast as the lovable and generous Antonio in the *Merchant of Venice*, still the pair of you are destined for high drama. It's regrettable that I will be the only audience for the play."

"I think it's extremely fortunate. Do listen carefully."

"Do I not always? This coach, as all that I reserve for personal use, is equipped with a sounding pipe."

Sarah Belle stepped inside, carefully selected her place in the back seat, thus facing forward in advantageous position. She was wearing an outfit completely of her own designing, the skirt not as full as fashion dictated, and the long open coat all of misty blue voile over an underdress straight and fitted with mandarin collar, and cut from imported Oriental cloth of daintiest multi-coloring and faint intriguing design. Instead of the usual open bonnetlike headpiece, she wore a hat shaped like a small round box, silver banded and framed with white veiling to be lowered or pulled back as she desired. Her hair was netted in a wide cluster at the back of her neck and escaped in wispy tendrils at the brow and ears. She wore white gloves, no jewelry, eschewed perfume, and cosmetics accented only eyes and lips.

The drama began as Justin Lahart arrived and, without hesitation, stepped inside the coach. Hudson closed the door, leaped to the seat, and signaled the team into an easy walk, then a smooth trot.

The protagonists faced each other in silence, without greeting. Sarah Belle waited for Justin to speak first. He was dressed in the latest attire for the affluent merchant, including a modish dress-coat of cerulean blue complementing an ensemble of soft gray. His posture was stiff and correct, his eyes at first cool and guarded, with swift appraisal which warmed to curiosity for the unexpected. Sarah Belle's steady gaze never wavered while she carried on her habitual inner monologue: *He favors Sutton but is taller and more muscular, strength built into his body and mind. Where Sutton's eyes are a dark flashing blue, Justin's are the steady blue of sapphire ready to command, appease, reject, or, when he chooses, almost to hypnotize.* (Justin removed his bell-crowned hat and carefully placed it on the seat beside him, turning his head as he did so as if to relieve the shock of her presence.) *His hair a darker brown than Sutton's and the glints in gray, not gold. His features bear lines that tell of the intense effort he applies to all he does, whereas Sutton's brow and face are smooth. Has music made this difference? I wonder.*

Justin cleared his throat. "My dear—uh—mademoiselle——"

She did not supply the name he waited for, but she did smile slightly. "Anonymity is my shield, sir. I will relate as briefly and accurately as I am able, the event and the aftermath that brought your brother Sutton into my household, which is composed only of myself and two freeborn elderly servants, competent and loyal. What I recite is not as a supplement to Ange and Marie—it is for you to make comparisons and come to your own conclusions through our independent accounts."

Holding his cane as a prop between his legs, he leaned forward in eager anticipation. "Dear lady, you are, I must say, the most unusual—the most different—and I have seen women from every clime and class in guises and disguises——"

Sarah Belle interrupted abruptly, "Mr. Lahart, tell me truly, are you fond of your brother? Do you carry in your heart a real affection for him? Or is your concern more a loyalty for family connection?"

She had the reaction she hoped for: surprise, an emotional jolt, an inner thrust of genuine anxiety and affection revealed. "How could you doubt my feelings?" his voice was hoarse, accusing. "He is my family, all my family, the only one left."

"He considers himself despised by you."

"I do not believe it! You are trying to hoax me!"

"When I have finished my account, you may tell me plainly whether you believe me or not and, if so, we'll return to this subject."

Hudson had stopped the coach at Lafayette Square, as if waiting for a passenger, in order that the dialogue inside could proceed in the stillness and the seclusion that the location and fog provided. He would move on from time to time at other inconspicuous locations until they were done.

Sarah Belle's soft flow of speech was seldom interrupted by the other passenger. At times, he leaned back with his head bowed, cane and gloves laid aside; at other times, his hands on his knees, he watched Sarah Belle in unguarded fascination. Once he took out a large handkerchief and wiped his brow and face, then loosened his vest and tugged at his cravat, as though breathing were difficult.

When she had finished, he turned aside, craved her pardon, and blew his nose as quietly as possible. Then he faced her again. "I believe your every word, and I'm not easily bamboozled. Tell me why Sutton has such a low opinion of my motives. I thought he might have some pride in my attainment of—of means and position."

"Did you give audience to his musical talents—support his ambitions in this work?"

"Support? He had an open account for studies in New York, tours in Europe, and all that, while I waited for him to show enough interest in shipping to become my full partner, wed properly, and hopefully extend the family line."

"Perhaps he expected you to do that."

He was startled, but replied sharply, "I never found a woman like you, or perhaps I would have." Then he stared at her in fixed astonishment that she could have provoked such a statement from him, could have caused the sudden burning thought to burst forth in such a barren framework.

For the first time, it was Sarah Belle who averted her eyes, looked out the window, found no answer. Inwardly, she was telling Hudson to hurry along back to the hotel. However, her silence after Justin's flat but convincing declaration had resounded through the pipe to the driver's seat, was cue enough. The coach moved with the team in a more animated pace then previously.

"My dear, may I beg of you, and I assure you I'm one who seldom begs a woman's favor, tell me your name that I may address you with more assurance—that I may hope to see you again; and since you have revealed that you are a woman alone except for worthy servants, perhaps I could . . . could enjoy your presence again, could attain to your more . . . more personal attentions." He was perspiring and mopped his brow in an endeavor to get her to look at him with some response to his plea. And plea it was—Sarah Belle had no doubt, and had not anticipated nor desired such a heady victory.

He continued, "Not only for Sutton's sake but for the noble nature that you have revealed in caring for him and perceiving the sensitivities that I was blind to, must I crave your indulgence for further acquaintance."

The horses seemed to be trotting faster and Justin hurried on. "I pledge to you I shall not invade his privacy until you give the word or he comes to me of his own accord. And I must insist that you allow me to provide you and him unlimited means for whatever you or he may need for complete recovery and every comfort——"

"Sir, I must refuse." Her throat tightened, for she sensed the deep loneliness in Justin, his grief at his brother's plight, and his frustration at her aloofness. His dejection was abysmal. She longed to reach out and touch him, but refrained. There were only moments until . . .

She looked at him, gentleness in her eyes. "My hackman will get word to you concerning Sutton's condition from time to time."

"But you . . . you . . ."

She could not deny him. "When all is resolved, perhaps we can meet again, under the same conditions."

"Will you promise . . . will you pledge . . . will you give me a token. . . ?"

The horses had stopped. Hudson was at the door. She quickly unbuttoned her white glove and handed it to him. He captured the hand, kissed it fervently, then held it tightly while he stooped and kissed her brow.

"May God preserve you, and God save me!" His grasp tightened even more on her hand until she almost cried out.

Then the door was opened and he was gone. Hudson gave her a glance of sympathy before closing her in. Was the tear in her eye for Justin or the pain in her hand, he wondered.

Sarah Belle wondered about the wisdom of her commitment. There was no doubt in her mind that Justin's sudden attachment was genuine and would be pursued with the intensity that was his nature. On the seat across from her lay the elegant ivory- and gold-headed cane and a pair of dove-gray gloves.

CHAPTER NINE

"HUDSON, HAVE YOU EVER WONDERED why the front wall and entrance, and also the lodges, at Cypress Grove Cemetery were built in pure Egyptian style?" Sarah Belle and her driver were on their way to the post office at the Merchants' Exchange after leaving Justin Lahart at the St. Charles entrance to his sumptuous hotel.

"It is a strange story, madame, most unusual."

"I would think with all the various burying grounds, from ornate and restricted to the most ordinary, and including special resting places for Catholic, Jewish, and Protestant divisions, there would be no inclination toward reminders of ancient Egypt."

"A wealthy relative of mine was influential in both the plan of the cemetery and the design of the structures. As you may know, madame, it was built by the Fireman's Charitable Association and there are many free men of color in this. We purchased and improved the spot at an expense of $35,000, and all the revenue that we derive from interments is devoted entirely to benevolent causes. You have seen the place?"

"Indeed I have. Some of the tombs above ground are most elaborately wrought and the marble facings of elegant finish. Walking up and down the narrow streets and avenues named as though in a city, one feels an awesome removal from this time and place."

"There are no restrictions. The costs are reasonable. The Egyptian style seems to have an appeal that reaches through color and creed. As you may know, free colored children of wealthy parents may receive their early education at the Carmelite Convent, and from there some are sent to institutions in the North for higher learning. This relative of mine became enthralled with Egyptian history, immersed in it, almost to the point of mania. And of what application could one make of such knowledge in New Orleans?"

"He might have built himself or some merchant potentate a pyramid, and practiced the forgotten science of mummification."

"Pyramids our mushy grounds would not permit, but the other——"

"You mean he could——"

"He could and did. And right now in one of those lodges, the ceiling covered with stars representing the Milky Way, lie two beautiful marbelized figures like Egyptian god and goddess."

"I didn't realize you had such a creative mind, Hudson."

Hudson protested, "I'm not creating, I'm relating." He was silent.

"I did not intend to offend, Hudson. Please continue. How did this come to be?"

"I think we could say an Egyptian god and goddess made their first appearance in a Shrove Tuesday parade some years ago. It was my relation and his beautiful wife. They drove a vehicle shaped like those sacred boats of heaven illustrated on Egyptian tombs. It was pulled by two white steeds. It was all white and gold as were their Egyptian costumes. They wore masks, of course, according to Mardi Gras tradition, and carried in their hands large bouquets of little stars on sticks, and in the boat were many more such bundles. There were stars arranged in groups and clusters on the boat structure and on their garments, and on an arch that reached over them representing the sky. The crowd, as always excessively festive at this special season, was enthralled with the display and clambered and fought to catch star-sticks as the sacred barge moved along. The celestial pair chanted their little phrases now in one language, now in another, the god, of course, introducing the Egyptian tongue to excite and mystify. 'We travel through the Milky Way . . . Our star is far beyond the moon . . . We come to visit you today . . . But we must sail away eftsoon . . . Though on this earth you fain must roam . . . The starry heavens are your home.'"

"How beautiful, Hudson. What a happy thing to do. But what about the tomb?"

"The goddess later transpired in a fever epidemic. The god prepared her body and placed it in the lodge with the stars over her head."

"And the god?"

"He visited the tomb on certain starry nights; it was not sealed and it was to be the repository of his own body in time. I and one other relative would accompany him on these visits. He would remain several days."

"A vigil of some kind?"

"Yes. In the tomb."

"*In* it?"

"He would have us remove the opening and then place it back. We would come back for him at the time specified, sometimes twenty-four hours, sometimes forty-eight."

"He would be alive——?"

"Not only alive, but renewed, healthy, content with his lot, a comfort and aid to others—until——"

"One time he was no longer alive——"

"Not only not alive, madame, but—you must not think me just an entertainer in telling you this—but his body was in the same beautiful mummified, or more like marbelized, state. And the face—I would not state this to anyone but someone like yourself—the face divinely happy!"

Sarah Belle remained silent until the coach stopped at the post office. "A marvelous tale, Hudson, and more than strange . . . will you get the mail from my private box, while I check at general delivery——"

"We are at the ladies' general delivery entrance now." He called to a boy to hold the team.

"I never fail to take umbrage at the arrangement here," Sarah Belle complained as Hudson helped her from the coach. "Why-ever should they have the general delivery for English letters in the Exchange Place, and those for letters in the foreign languages *and* for the *ladies* here on Royal Street?"

"The Exchange Place is very crowded with men of commerce, madame, thicker than thieves at the gaming stalls. Excuse me if I say that ladies and their charms would delay and divert these mighty vendors where fortunes are made and traded every moment of the open day. And it is a courtesy to those conversing in troublesome foreign tongues to have special mail clerks who can give time and patience to their inquiries, without intruding on the hurried man of business."

"A pretty speech, Hudson, in defense of your sex, but I still feel put aside every time I go to that window, shuttled into my feminine niche, as it were."

She smiled as she spoke, saying inwardly, "I chide myself every time I come here. Why do I come? I have never received so much as a penny postcard. What is it I expect? I've cut all ties. My regular transactions are taken care of through the private box. I care not to communicate with those I've brought to my House. I don't know where Defender is, nor he I, as I suppose. Has he lost his life in the wilderness or in some foreign battle line? I don't wish him dead. I neither desire nor deserve freedom. The only real freedom I could have would be to know he had found surcease in another's arms, and no longer felt the abasement of surrogate lover."

She sighed and turned a friendly face to the clerk, "Please check for 'Belle' or 'Locke'—'Sarah Belle.'"

He pulled out a large handful of B's, began checking carefully, then paused, removed a brown envelope for further study. "Must have got a little damp somewhere—smeared a bit—it's addressed to 'Lady'—yes, that's it, 'Lady Sarah Belle,' and it has Phillipa Street with a question mark. Return's plain as can be———"

"Let me have it, please!" Her heart seemed to stop and then gave a heavy thump. Who could it possibly be? Not Defender. Not somebody putting out a chance inquiry for her whereabouts. No one had ever called her *Lady Sarah Belle*. It could be teasing, irreverent, or maybe complimentary. She had the envelope in her hand. The return address was from New York, and the name *John*

Monroe Sterling. She blushed as she had in the park and rushed back to the coach to be alone with—yes, with John. She saw Hudson hurrying her way. She didn't wait. She quickly opened the door for herself, mounted the step and almost leaped inside. Hudson and the boy holding the team looked at each other in amazement. The boy shrugged. Hudson scratched his ear, shook his head and mounted the seat, not forgetting to pitch the boy a coin.

Sarah Belle sat back against the coach seat, her eyes closed, the letter from John Monroe Sterling clutched tightly in her lap. The name was like a rhythm in her mind.

The coach rocked along over the uneven dirt streets where frequent muddy areas caused Hudson to drive with extreme care that his equipage not be stained. The three-mile drive to her residence seemed an eternity, but she could not break the seal of the letter—felt closed in, and the necessity to be completely alone and unhampered in her movements when she did read and relate to the contents. The fog was still heavy. Hopefully, Fanaalis would have a blaze in the fireplace. She could sit before it as she did when John was a presence in the house.

"Are you well, madame?" Hudson inquired. "The ride is tiring, I know, but it's best not to crowd and we've met more vehicles than usual."

She had not spoken to him since rushing into the coach at the post office. "I'm simply taking a little respite from a rather demanding day, Hudson."

"Yes, ma'm." He spoke no more until he placed in her hands the bundle of papers and journals he had taken from her box. He noticed her pallor and the unopened letter she was holding, and his eyes questioned.

"I'm quite all right," she assured him, knowing the anxiety he felt for her welfare, and his assumption that the letter contained bad news she wanted to face alone.

His eyes caught hers and held in a depth exchange, conveying a personal message, protective, dedicated. "At your service always, madame." He turned and walked quickly back to his coach, was mounted and vanished in the fog before Sarah Belle, her lashes wet and her hand hot upon the letter, entered the door held open by Shealia.

"Did you notice Hudson's gorgeous livery today, Shealia? He could wear the armor of a Sir Walter Scott knight or the trim regalia of one of those Egyptian gods he was talking about to the same effect, I do believe."

Shealia did not answer. She was often silent before the converse of her mistress, who seemed to be talking as much to herself as her attendant.

Sarah Belle placed her letter carefully on the mantel and her mail on the secretary. The small friendly fire was waiting. She hurried to her room instructing Shealia, "Bring me a comfortable house gown. I would rest before the grate and have a hot brew at my side. How is our charge—is he behaving well?"

Shealia whispered, "While we in garden, he slip into music room and pluck strings on your harp, very soft. I not like without your permit, but I let him."

"You did well. What else?"

"He read. He think about leaving, look out windows. I feed him well. He sleep well. He need not move so much."

"In other words, you helped with the herb tea. Use it sparingly."

"Yes, ma'm." Shealia handed Sarah Belle a letter opener and left the room.

She seated herself comfortably, took a deep breath, made an opening in the tough envelope, and carefully pulled out a long folded strip of paper covered on both sides with a scurrying scrawl, as though thoughts ran ahead out of sight of pen. Just looking at his handwriting caused vibrancy in her fingers so that her hands trembled as she held the letter.

My Dear Lady Sarah Belle,

I awoke this morning with a conviction from my heart that in my thoughts and in my conduct I have "done you wrong," whereas you, through your generous self, have rendered me a service I would seek from no one, and did not realize until recently I had received from you. (I pray that this letter reaches you and if I become abstruse in my explanation, that you dig bravely for my true meaning.)

Since our acquaintance fits no social pattern, derives from no book of manners or theories of proper behavior, let us use a medical model.

You are the physician—you come upon the victim of some near-fatal encounter and note a gaping wound. You say, "Come to my house. I can heal you. I'm a different kind of doctor, I practice in secret—I go out and select my patients because I have a specialty, a mission, outside the regular category of medical practice. I have observed and selected you."

This particular patient is suspicious; besides, he's getting some kind of perverse satisfaction in studying his gaping wound and reviewing the circumstances that brought it about. But he goes with the physician and continues his perverseness in an effort to wound the physician.

He over-succeeds in this and has the physician doing a turnabout and saying, "You can cure yourself. Help **me**. See **my** wound. Examine it, that we may discuss this matter of gaping wounds that are in sore need of skilled attention."

Here is an impasse. The selected patient becomes aware of both the wisdom and the need of the physician, and his own pitiful inability to pose or act as physician to the physician. He makes one try at fairness. In privacy, he sits down and writes out his painful story, which is what he thinks the physician would have prescribed his doing had she been able to handle the case. After this exercise, all the circumstances of his wound seem less consuming, the pain begins to subside. After his full retreat, he finds the raw edges have begun to heal and close, and discovers he is thinking more and more of the physician he abandoned.

Now back to identity, let me tell you this, dear lady, which I do not understand, but seem to be certain of, because the more I think of you the more I see you clearly—your mind as well as your person: Since I did not allow you to tell me of your experiences as a "healer" and instead pontificated on the "Pandora's Box," your likely reaction when you came upon my "Web of Passion" was probably a spirited denial of interest in my past. I seemed to be watching you as you snapped open the lid of your fabled casket for the entry of another bleak account, then slammed it shut with some such inner declaration as, "I refuse to gaze upon the starving bodies of your rejected illusions. Stay there with the rest. I may never let you out."

I recall your remark that I carried my own cure. True. But it was yourself that prompted me to effect it. With the written account purging my mind, and some introspection involving reason rather than emotion, I from myself am set free.

I still am going to Palenque but will await the dry season. My friend and mentor John Lloyd Stephens is glad to brief me on how to make the survey without the inconveniences and discomforts he encountered, though there is still much to contend with in unstable governments, Indian temperaments, and Nature's jungle caprices. Mr. Stephens hopes to return, but he must regain full health and is much involved now in forming the first American Ocean Steam Navigation Company.

Since both you and I (I hope) have made our escape from the "Web of Passion," it would seem fitting that we not dismiss our introduction, so subtly contrived by the Fates on the very doorstep of Destiny. It would be gratifying to me just to know that you have read this and have not turned aside in aversion, as well you might. If you are so gracious as to send me a post office box number, or other manner of mail delivery more direct than the generalities of General Delivery, I will respond in a manner more natural than discreet.

John Monroe Sterling

P.S. About the toned jade—it came from the Pyramid of the Sun ruins on the River Gua. It is a kind of talisman, I believe—an amulet with sound. I know not why I left it with you. When I started to pick it up, I could not. Even at the door, I turned and started back for it, but could not go. It is for you. J.M.S.

CHAPTER TEN

"**H**UDSON, LET'S DRIVE OUT POYDRAS, away from centers of activity. I want to remove myself from my own house for a while, have a quiet drive. I have reason to be thoughtful. I'm not searching for a distressed countenance reflecting the outrage of love betrayed."

"Has Mr. Lahart become troublesome?"

"Quite the contrary." She gave him a brief account of Sutton's change since the gris-gris had been removed and his fear allayed. "And since his composition of 'Serenade to St. Valentine' and my rendition of it on the harp, he has been like one moving in an illusory world. No attention to the injured hand—it has healed rapidly; no mention of his lost love, the piano, or of Ange or of Justin. He is fed by Shealia, attended and companioned by Fanaalis. He spends time in the garden bower, just daydreaming. He sits in the workshop where they work on their Jamaican crafts— he has even assisted in drawing the romantic figures on a decorative screen. Most of all, he fills sheet after sheet with musical compositions—I see that he has a good supply for musical scoring. When I'm not in the house, he works at picking out melodies on the harp. Occasionally, I execute one for him."

She paused, wondering how to explain Sutton's attitude toward her: how whenever she appeared, he would murmur, "Ah! ma Déesse de Musique!" and fix his gaze on her as though she were a celestial mirage that might vanish if he looked away.

"And how does he react to your performance of his works?"

"He kisses my hands in excessive approval and rushes to his room to compose more music."

Hudson laughed. "Marie does sometimes overdo her spells when she removes the effects of a potent gris-gris. Now that he has been weaned from his passion for the pianoforte, how shall you loosen him from the harp and —" he hesitated, "and your role as Euterpe that has plunged him into such idolatry?"

"That is my concern, restoring him to reality and a desire to express his talents and affections in the world according to his birthright."

"In other words, you'll be advising a soul who has stumbled into paradise to return to earth and make up for oversights and indulgences."

Sarah Belle did not answer. After a while she inquired, "Are we not about to cross St. Paul Street?"

"Quite close."

"Then make a right turn. I want to see the Wesleyan Chapel that is devoted to the colored portion of this community. It's close by, is it not?"

"Yes, madame. A bit of it is visible from here. It's a simple frame building, not what you'd call invitatory. The street's in poor condition, and——"

"Nevertheless, I've been curious to view it from the front. Please turn."

"Yes, madame."

Hudson made the turn slowly into the narrower street. His team seemed to share his reluctance. They had progressed only a short distance when screams and cries of distress were heard.

"Madame, I'd turn if I could. It's too late. We'll have to drive on by the disorder."

"That's all right, Hudson. I requested the turn. It's as if I've turned upon myself. Out of many days of driving in search of distress, I had selected this one for retrospection. I suppose if you seek long enough for particular situations, they will advance toward you after a while of their own accord."

The screams and cries were intensified: A man screaming maledictions and a woman screaming protest.

"Don't pull your curtain aside. We'll hurry on by."

"We will not hurry. When you get closer, stop. I've already pulled my curtain aside."

"You are an incautious woman! I have all I can do to handle the team."

"You are an overprotective man! That brute is using a buggy whip on a helpless youth and the girl screaming with every strike as if the blows were on her!"

"Don't get out!"

"You hold the team still. I will get out!"

Sarah Belle, her skirts gathered up, raced to the scene. The three in the caldron of violence were whites. The only witness was a mulatto, the minister at the chapel. He was holding an excited horse hitched to a buggy. A saddled horse was prancing and snorting at a hitching post. The mulatto was in an agony of prayer pleading with all his might for God to have mercy, to rout the devil, to strike down the crazy man with the whip.

"Stop! You mindless fool!" Sarah Belle called out, rushing up back of the man and grabbing his whip arm.

Startled, he turned on her, his whip upraised, his eyes wide and hard with fury. And then total surprise at the woman he beheld, blinded as he had been with vicious intent.

"Oh, Papa! Papa! Don't hurt him anymore. I'll do anything you say."

The infuriated parent was back in the scene, as if the interruption had been imagined.

"Look at th' coward layin' there like a whipped cur—you'd be wife to him—mix my blood with hissen—sneaking off to a colored place, ridin' horseback like a shameless woman—married in this shack makes you no more married than in a whorehouse."

"Oh, God, precious Jesus, get Satan out of that wicked mouth and mind," the distressed preacher cried out, tears pouring down his cheeks.

"I wouldn't 'a taken't, honey, Jeanie honey," the youth moaned, "but he'd've used the whip on you if I hadn't, you know that." The girl just sobbed in reply.

"Look at me!" Sarah Belle commanded the man breathing so heavily, swinging his whip without striking out.

He turned on her, bloodshot eyes full of hate and the desire to injure, saliva white at the corners of his mouth. "Maybe you want some of this?"

Motionless, she stared at him until he averted his eyes.

"Papa! Papa!" It was his daughter holding his whip arm now. "Papa, come with me. I'll get in the buggy. I'll go home with you. I shouldn't have left you. Forgive me, Papa." She wheedled, "I'll fix you a hot toddy. You're upset. You'll be all right. I'll take care of you. I love you, Papa." She paid no attention to anyone else. She acted as if they were alone on the scene. The girl's deception hit Sarah Belle like resonance from a heavy gong.

She hates him beyond the telling. She'll poison him, and she mustn't.

The man with the very white ravaged face framed in an abundance of black tousled hair, looked into his daughter's face and believed. They moved toward the buggy; he, too, seemed oblivious of other presence. The girl clung to his arm, gazing all the time into his face, as though holding him spellbound. Sarah Belle called softly, with clear significance, "Jeanie, wait on the Lord!" The girl appeared not to hear her. She repeated, "Wait, I say, upon the Lord!" There was a slight movement of the head that might have been an acknowledgment. At the buggy, the ravager replaced his whip in its socket, turned and lifted Jeanie bodily to place her on the buggy seat, then got in himself.

"Young man," Sarah spoke with loud command, "you need attending. Get up. Go to the coach. We'll send back for your horse. There's always a way out." Sarah Belle hoped Jeanie was listening.

The whip was raised above the horse. The minister released his hold on the bridle and they were gone.

The young man did not get up. He lay with his face to the ground, his fingers digging into the dirt.

"What's your name? I can help you."

He turned his streaked face outward, showing welts from the lashes. "Help me? Help me kill the father of my wife!" He tried to laugh.

"You were married?"

"He thought he got here in time." He tried to laugh again but coughed instead, and raised himself to a sitting position for relief. Then he looked up at Sarah Belle.

"Lady, go away. I'm a coward. I couldn't protect my wife. I have a sharp knife and could have slit his throat on the spot. 'Here's your bloody murdered father for a wedding present,' I could say. But I let him down me with a buggy whip." He coughed longer this time.

"Lament later. Come along with me. We're killing precious time."

"Killing time, did you say? The only killing I'm going to do——" He was getting to his feet with difficulty. "Come here, Reverend." He motioned to the preacher, who came rapidly to Sarah Belle's side.

"The only killing I am going to do——" he reached into his pocket, took out and opened a sharp blade, "— is myself. You, the man who married me so well, can bury me." The preacher moved toward him. "Don't bother me," he threatened with his knife. "You can keep my horse or sell him as you like, for your services." He sneezed painfully—his eyes watered and there was blood on his mouth.

Hudson had made a quiet approach and stood nearby. "Two mourners for my funeral, that's nice."

Sarah Belle spoke softly. "What if I tell you Jeanie meant not a word she said to her father. She was getting him away before he harmed you further, or anyone else. She'll poison him at the first opportunity."

"I will not believe you."

"Then you're a dunce and know little about a woman who loves a man above all else. What of Jeanie's family?"

"None. She's a slave to that wretch. He works at the docks."

"Will you allow me to assist you and Jeanie? If not, please allow me to get out of sound and sight before you make your messy sacrifice to nothing."

Defiant, astonished, he stared at the strange woman, then yielded. "I'll go with you, ma'm."

"Pocket your knife. What's your name?"

"William Moellhausen."

"William, you may go with my hackman, Hudson Recoire, and sit with him. We'll discuss matters as we ride."

As they turned toward the carriage, she addressed the minister.

"Sir, the human condition is a maze through which we all must wander, but not without direction, unless we choose otherwise—I like to think."

"Ma'm, you were sent from God."

"It's good for you to think so. I know not. Let me remind you that William gave you his horse——"

The preacher started to protest.

"I don't think he'll need it or be back. I'll send you word of the young couple's deliverance, if it's accomplished, that you may give God his due. Good day."

Sarah Belle did not look back, but she felt the man's prayers swift upon her heels. Had she looked, she would have seen him statuesque on the small landing at the entrance, his arms raised high to heaven, eyes closed, lips moving with entreaty and praise too burdened for utterance.

As she took her seat in the carriage, she let her thoughts slip back to the day's intent . . . "Dear Sir John . . . During a drive to the outskirts today, I had thought to work out, in order, the matter I would include in this first letter to you, but . . ."

Sarah Belle sat at her secretary, paper and pen at hand and John Sterling's letter spread out for reference. The long day was behind her now and all quiet on her premises. William had been housed in private quarters attached to the Jamaican craft shop. She had given Sutton a lesson on the technical aspects of harp fingering which he found easy enough in spite of muscular tautness in the palm; and she had laid out a plan of future tactics in his and Justin's behalf.

Equipped with information from William, Hudson would get a message to Jeanie, hopefully in time to forestall any acts of desperation on her part, otherwise a Romeo-Juliet denouement was certain.

She sighed and murmured aloud, "Now for myself," and began to write.

My Dear Sir John,

You write well. I shall refer to the end of your letter for my beginning. Your offer is that if I relay my box number, you will respond "in a manner more natural than discreet." That, of course, you realized would excite my expectations. The number is 701, and I am to assume, am I not, that you expect me to respond by the same credo.

Your account of my handling of "Web of Passion" is relatively accurate. Now that I am aware of your quality of expression, I'm tempted to explore, simply for the reading experience, but you spoke so threateningly of Pandora's plight, I shall refrain—at least until such time as I have your sanction and possibly your presence or Allah's favor.

Since you were here, there have been two other encounters, but not in the nature of the usual. Driving out to locate casualties on the battleground of Eros, I now come upon the actual scene of combat. This somewhat enlarges the scope of my mission. I see you raise an eyebrow and feel a flick of light satire. Nevertheless . . . Can it be that your entrance into my life is a causative factor in this change? Certainly, I myself am not the same. The physician you spoke of is discovering a new range and tempo of being. Do such energies sometimes provoke events in a way beyond our awareness?

Have you ever heard of the Voudou Queen of New Orleans, Marie Laveau? I recently made her acquaintance, but not by seeking her out for direction! She presented herself at my doorstep in the form of a grisgris. In order to allay the fears of my "patient," I invited her to my boudoir as a hair-dresser (her entree into many unsuspecting households). We understand each other. In stature and magnetism of person, she is remarkable. I predict that despite severe judgments on her character, she will be more permanently cast in the history of New Orleans than many figures of this city who rate their mundane civic performances as immortal.

She was much drawn to the jade talisman you left behind and I allowed her to sound it. It pierced me with a stricken kind of loneliness and at the same time summoned me to a height of attention and expectation most awesome. Shall I thank you for this record in sound of ageless mysterious portent, or, shall I rue the day I responded to its insinuations and found myself at your side stripped of my self-molded shining armor?

I must tell you how I feel about Palenque after further study of the Stephens accounts. I would like to slip into a disguise such as Shakespeare invented for several damsels in his comedies—that is, look like an adventurous youth attending a more adventurous master, and astride a faithful "macho," accompany you up a haunting and hazardous trail to the ruins such as Stephens describes.

How is it that since receiving your letter, I have come upon plateaus of beauty in my thoughts about existence—all existence—not heretofore realized? Is the mind (or soul) seeded (as are many natural wonders) awaiting conscious realization for dispersement of some cosmic principle? And what shall we call this principle? A word as ambiguous as **love**? *as illusive as* **beauty**? *What you or I call Love, others might classify as sentiment, illusion, passion. What we call Beauty might make no mark on another's emotions.*

Might it be that the principle is something greater than can be discerned through the limited five senses? And, this further question, my dear John . . . might our seeded minds, like our bodies, when joined together (minds of one accord) be able to create **a body of thought** *not possible through either mind alone?*

Sarah Belle

CHAPTER ELEVEN

WILLIAM MOELLHAUSEN SAT on the arbor bench in Sarah Belle's garden drawing no comfort from the beauty around him. Sarah Belle came and sat beside him.

"William, shame and fear leave no room for remedial action when one is floundering in a bog of adverse events. You must believe that Hudson is no mere hackman—he is a man of means and great charities. He is also cautious and a master of deception when needed in any matter of rescue. He may have Jeanie here before the day is out, and if not, then we will expect them in the morning and hurry you to the docks before the *Arrow* sails for Galveston."

William was astonished out of his despair. "Galveston?!"

"Yes, you'll land there, and then on to Houston."

"Houston?"

"I'm sure you have heard of Houston, Texas."

"Ma'm, what I have heard of Texas——"

"Spare me. Certainly, it is a frontier society of rugged aspect.

But you don't impress me as a hapless youth. The Republic of Texas though recently annexed is still an independent land of opportunity, and Houston in a mighty surge of growth. The fiend you and Jeanie would escape is rabid for revenge. He'll comb the area but he'll not suspect you've the means to travel beyond settlement borders."

"And I do not. But I've secured employment in a brass and harness shop located on the far side of the Third Municipality, and I thought——"

"I think you underestimate the hunting-dog ability of a father-possessor——. Would you like to do the same kind of work in Houston with a shop of your own?"

William looked at Sarah Belle, open-mouthed. What a strange woman! Talking about boat trips and a shop in Houston.

"Could you make saddles?" She paused. "Please answer me, could you make saddles?"

"Why . . . why, yes, ma'm."

"Then listen closely. I'll make it possible for you to settle in Houston and have a shop for custom-made leather goods, especially saddles and harness. I'll supply the gold for your establishment. Once you're in the business gainfully, you'll put aside one quarter of your profits for my need—not a return to me here, you understand, but—for my use there."

Mystery replaced astonishment for William.

"Are you following me closely with a clear mind?"

"Yes, ma'm."

"I assume you're well enough educated to manage figures and write legibly and sensibly in case I should be in touch with you by correspondence."

Pride surfaced in William like a spring released.

"Indeed I am, ma'm! My family teaches its own. I could read and write at five years old. My father used the Bible and Goethe for our reading lessons."

"Goethe! Good Heavens!! Then you read of a great man in a great language. You'll find German immigrants in Houston as in New Orleans, building, map-making, and making music, and you'll soon be at home——. Now, the matter of my business there, for which I'm willing to employ you. I'll write a letter that will be in your safekeeping until the proper time for its delivery, when the person to whom it's addressed is located. Also, I'll give you an advertisement to insert in the *Telegraph and Texas Register* once you've opened your business and become acquainted. The matter is personal and will in no way involve you in unworthy intrigue. I'll prepare the written matter tonight and place it and the currency for your enterprise in your hands tomorrow morning."

"Thanks be to God, it's foggy!" William stood at the window looking out, waiting for the carriage that should—must—bring Jeanie. He and Sarah Belle had had little to say to each other since sharing a sparse breakfast. It was past time for laborers to be at their work on the docks. Would Jeanie's father sense something amiss and wait in hiding rather than follow his habitual trek to the loading sites? Would suspicion or some flash of clairvoyance cause him to turn on his heel and hurry back?

Sarah Belle could not remain aloof from the sharp awareness that there were many dismal alternatives to the success of their formula for Jeanie's escape. William was clutching the satchel she had given him, a scarred leather bag that belied its security and the value of its contents with several strands of rope tied around as if to hold it together.

"Don't clutch the case as if your life depended on it, William—casualness well achieved is a great protection—and do try to control your agitation—your face looks like a death mask." Sarah Belle too showed an unusual pallor and eyes darkly shadowed.

"William, I think you need a hot toddy. Fanaalis——"

"Oh God, no!" William moaned, and too late Sarah Belle could hear again Jeanie's, "I'll make you a hot toddy, Papa."

The silence all around stiffened—lengthened—became brittle. And then at last—the rattle of harness, the clank of wheels, a rapid-paced team, a quick stop.

William made the door first and raced ahead, Sarah Belle close behind. The carriage door opened and Jeanie leaped out and into William's arms.

"Back into the carriage," Hudson ordered, and to Sarah Belle, "I'll report to you, madame, after the boat sails." He was urging the team ahead before the door was closed behind the fleeing pair.

Sarah Belle stood and watched them until the fog shut out sight and sound. She walked slowly back and stood in the doorway looking at the gate.

Suddenly the image of Defender Locke and his departure was as fresh in her mind as if it had come out of hibernation, renewed and vivid. And she was running down the arcade to the impressive entrance of the Locke plantation home, calling out to him:

"Defender . . . Defender . . . ," she felt herself choking as if a cord around her neck was drawing tighter. "Defender, please wait! There's something I must tell you. Come back . . . let me try . . . ," he was on his way to the gate and she had run after, caught his arm.

He shook off her touch.

"Please, please, tell me *where* you're going?"

Then the sudden turn on her with the look that was a lash. "WEST!"

That was the way it had been. Last night she had written out what it was she had wanted to tell him more than three years ago—and what it was she needed to tell him now.

CHAPTER TWELVE

J USTIN LAHART WAS A VERY HAPPY MAN. He was quite certain that never before in his life had he been so elated. No triumph or eminence in the financial world had brought such exhilaration to his sharp mind, so much emotional stimulus to his dormant sensitivities as the message just relayed to him by Hudson: "Yes, Madame Vahnia will come to your suite at the St. Charles as suggested for a discussion concerning your brother Sutton's return to his family position."

Justin's desire to assist in his brother's recovery and at the same time bring himself into a situation of more personal acquaintance with the custodian of Sutton's welfare was a consuming one. He was determined that this acquaintance should not be limited to just another carriage ride, and, moreover, that the second meeting should not be the last. He carried her glove in his pocket, placed it before him when he sat thinking and working out the most minute detail of procedure, imprinting her image upon his mental and emotional structure. Concentration and rational pursuit had brought the consent he sought. Phase one accomplished, and the setting for phase two in readiness.

Of course Madame Vahnia was not her name. He smiled at the artifice. It did not fit. But what did it matter? It was pleasing, she had selected it—and therefore to him it was sweetness and light—and more—an element of mystery that augmented desire, intensified the quest. He murmured, "My Vahnia," and liked the sound. He wrote on a pad "Vahnia Lahart" and laughed aloud.

Justin Lahart, merchant prince of New Orleans, had earned his title while still in his prime because he had learned early a secret which men of his stature seldom share or even analyze: Dame Fortune not only smiles but often she offers a perfect wizardry of assistance when Desire is governed by Design, and Design is ornamented with Patience and Order. Justin was a master of this formula, and so the expected "unexpecteds" were supporting him.

First, there was the matter of his beloved relatives in Natchitoches, on the Red River. Here his mother's brother and family, the Férreos, resided and prospered in that remarkable trade center where high finance abounded. It was the end of the supply line for hearty commerce with trappers, traders, and settlers who loaded out in giant ox-drawn freighters for the Western frontier. And now the Férreos were on their way to New Orleans with a wedding party, for Amelia Férreo was to marry Homère Bienville. Cousin Amelia was the darling of the Lahart brothers, especially of Sutton, for she too was a musician. The relatives and attendants accompanying Amelia and her affianced would reside at the Lahart mansion, the wedding would be performed at the cathedral, the Church of St. Louis. Amelia had written in her letter addressed to both cousins that she was requesting special music, a wedding song, to be composed by Sutton. The Férreos were not aware of Sutton's misadventure. When Justin read the letter, he shouted for joy and kissed the glove of promise!

Another matter related to a harp. Justin had dared to write a letter about this and to ask Hudson to deliver it; the contents had brought him the reply he now reveled in.

My Dear Lady of the Glove,
    You can imagine my happiness over Sutton's condition and his accomplishments on the harp. You cannot imagine my gratitude. It defies

word frames, and were I to allow my true feelings a semblance of expression, you would be offended at my presumption, and rightly. You had suggested that I have a harp of high quality (preferably an Erard with the double action mechanism) with which to greet Sutton on his return. You had also advised that I send any personal mail accumulated during his absence that might awaken some desire in him to return to former surroundings. I call your attention to the letter that I am enclosing from his cousin Amelia Férreo, of whom he is most fond. Since the letter is addressed to myself as well as my brother and is opened, I would like for you to read it ahead of presenting it to Sutton. Could Amelia have elected a better time and place to be wed?

And we have another good fortune: at the New Convent I located a magnificent Erard. It is nearly six feet tall with frame of polished sycamore and sounding board of the finest Swiss pine. The gold-leaf ornamentation is rich, a heavy coat skillfully applied, and the grand column is decorated with Grecian maidens, the base showing winged Grecians holding lyres. I was informed that the mechanism Erard invented now makes the harp more versatile than the piano (thus Sutton should have no regrets in the transfer of his talents!), extending the octave range to twenty-one. The main building of the New Convent houses a seminary for the education of young ladies with instruments available for those talented in music. There were a number of harps for instruction but none so "celestial" as the one I secured for Sutton. I made arrangements for a replacement and for expanding the instruction and equipment related to music in general. Yes, I am bidding for Sutton's favor, and not his alone.

There is much to discuss in our plans for his homecoming. I want you to see the harp and some of my further arrangements—a sort of stage-setting, you might say, for its presentation. You can understand, I know, that I am more uncertain of his acceptance of me as his new-found brother than of the harp as his new-found career. I pray your assistance in this matter.

I also crave your indulgence in the request I am about to make. Would you honor me with your presence in my suite at the Exchange? The Erard now graces my private parlor where I hope to present it to Sutton. All will be circumspect with servants at their posts, and if you would like to bring your woman servant as attendant, she will be most welcome along with you. Here we can discuss the delicate matters concerning Sutton's moods and inclinations, and I would act at once on any

suggestions you might have for enhancing the welcoming scene for him.
I am most gratefully your humble servant . . .
and dare not say more.

Justin Lahart

Justin's good fortune in locating the harp so necessary for win-
ning Sutton to his side again was multiplied when his ship of trade
from Constantinople arrived in advance of Sarah Belle's visit to
his suite. The weakness and corruption of the Ottoman Empire
had left trade doors open to the world, and art treasures of the past
were exposed in Constantinople's public stalls and furtively offered in its thieves' markets. The Lahart collector was learned and
shrewd, and on his return to New Orleans was cargo-watchdog on
a treasure ship loaded with offerings for the opulent.

And so it was that Justin's spacious parlor at the St. Charles Exchange was adorned with the choice pieces of this shipment, not
crowded or set about in vain display, but selected and placed with
a sense of composition as creative as Sutton's musical works. It was
a deliberate enhancement of the setting designed to captivate
both Sutton and the elusive lady who would be the first to gaze
upon his masterpiece of arrangement.

The harp under a canopy of baldachin from Baghdad—that rare
fabric woven of gold and silk, formerly the prerogative of rulers of
church and state—was the centerpiece. Its designs flourished over
a dominance of rich Islamic blue like intricate harmonics in a musical score—subtle greens, capricious blues and lavendars, and
dainty starlike florals. It was supported with a three-sided metal-
work enclosure in elaborate filigree of gold. A sultan might have
held audience under its princely shading. Now a woman would
walk across a matchless rug from Samarkand to be seated at this
music-making instrument.

Justin was standing at the impressive St. Charles Avenue
entrance of the hotel waiting for the arrival of the coach bearing
Sarah Belle. He was quick to open the door ahead of Hudson. His
"Lady of the Glove" stepped out unattended. He found it difficult
to speak.

"Madame Vahnia, I am happy."

"Thank you, monsieur. I also."

"Allow me." He touched her elbow and they moved together up

the outside steps to the projecting portico of stately Corinthian columns, and then up twelve lengthy marble steps to the entrance of the main salon where they paused before a beautiful marble statue of George Washington.

"The designer of these steps must have expected troops to march up twenty abreast to salute their general," Sarah Belle observed.

"There are times and seasons when world citizenry fill this expanse in pursuit of pleasure and profit, and they give the image of greatness scarcely a glance," he commented vaguely. Then under his breath requested, "Will you lift your veil and give me a glance that will bring the mystery of your face into clearer view, and at the same time forgive the familiarity of such a request?"

Sarah Belle was wearing a large leghorn hat with tulle veiling of light hazy blue, held to the brim with a circle of small blue flowers. She raised her veil and they looked at each other with something more than appraisal—a kind of recognition—tinged with sadness for Sarah Belle, and for Justin filled with longing so painfully sweet that he could only murmur, "Thank you."

Sarah Belle lowered her veil, as much for disguise as fashion, he realized, and they proceeded to the center of the salon and started up the grand spiral staircase that reached all the way to the great dome. At the second floor they stepped out on the gallery surrounding the stairs and Justin guided her to the entrance of his suite where a footman waited to open the door. Once inside the parlor she raised her veil and gazed about her, amazed and awed by the surroundings. She made no comment while the maid took her hat and gloves, inquired if there was any other service she could render, and disappeared into an adjoining room. Then Sarah Belle faced Justin. "It is unreal, a dream, a perfect shrine for a harp." She looked at the Oriental rug that lay at her feet and on which the canopied harp rested. "The artistry of heart, hand and—and soul—you have assembled in this room could evoke such imagery that one's senses would . . ."

"Would what, my dear?"

"I cannot express it."

"Could you perhaps express it on the harp?" he suggested gently.

"Is it toned?"

"As perfectly as the master of the opera could achieve."

"I should have known." She stared at the rug a moment longer, knowing it was filled with symbolism that would read like a sacred script could one interpret what the artist had set forth in design.

"What do you discern in the rug?" Justin inquired.

"Only a fraction of what is woven there. The six stylized butterflies around the central medallion, a symbol of soul emergence from body cocoon or possibly soul awareness emerging from the darkness of mind. Had you thought of that?"

"No, I had not."

"And you notice that near the butterflies are four groups of pomegranates."

"And what do they represent?"

"Usually, the sensual pleasures. And the design at each end of the field of blue, with its gold appendages, suggests the tree of life so often found in one style or another among the artist weavers of the East. Do you not envision a kind of celestial tree in those delicate golden extensions from the lively flamelike center that might be trunk or roots? What do you think?"

"I think I have never gazed upon a face with such lively expressions as your own, nor been so moved by the sound of a voice, nor realized the beauty and meaning of certain words until you uttered them."

Startled, Sarah Belle looked up at Justin, who stood slightly to one side, his gaze fixed on her. She, who had made such a study of the masculine countenance in matters of the heart, who had been given youthful adoration by Lando and constant devotion by Defender, had been idealized by some, had watched respect and lust run the gamut of facial delineation on others, was confronted now with the most dominant and revealing "language of the look" in her experience.

It read that this man loved her with all that was best in him, and desired her as he had never desired to possess anything or anybody. He cared not for her station, her name, her condition, or her past. He saw her not only as a woman to meet and match his passions, but a person, a being, that he knew and understood and would cherish as a partner, mind to mind as well as body to body. The magnetism of him, and in this setting, was the most powerful she had ever encountered. If she did not move in another direction quickly, she would move toward him, and once she did that, it would be like crossing a river wide and deep, with no possibility of a return crossing. She stood very still, closed her eyes and trembled. "Justin . . ." She said his name pleadingly, her eyes still closed.

"Yes, my dear . . ."

"Will you bring me a drink of water . . . before I . . . before I play . . . ?"

"Yes, my dear . . ." His voice changed, released her with difficulty—and she knew he had moved away, that he understood. She sighed, and moved to take her place at the harp. She sat gazing at the harp, then up at the wonder, the restrained splendor, of the baldachin. She took a deep breath, sighed again and bowed her head a moment, as if in reverence to the harp, before running her fingers over the strings, seeking and activating a rapport with the instrument.

Justin re-entered with a crystal goblet and offered her not water, but eggnog, mild, soothing, nourishing. He smiled at her as she drank.

"The harp is so big, so many strings, I thought you needed strengthening for the demands it must impose."

She was engulfed with a sense of yearning for Justin's happiness. She could not give him herself, but perhaps she could give him beauty that he could claim and hold on to—something beyond the creative power and symbolic expressions resident in the art objects with which he had surrounded her. She would allow the resonance of these to augment her own creative flow through the harpstrings. She looked at the gold pitcher with its design of peacocks and winged human heads, at the jade cup shaped like a gourd—and made him an offering of music—for him alone—of substance invisible, emotional harmonies beyond articulation.

She handed him the empty glass. She smiled. "So thoughtful of you, Justin. Now will you be seated. You are my audience of one. I am not checking the harp for Sutton; it is replete with heavenly sound. Through it I am weaving a gift for you. It will include threads from my own compositions and Sutton's, and a golden strand or two from the masters, and then improvisation for you and for myself alone which shall be played only this once."

Justin was seated. She looked at him intently as if his features were to be incorporated in her offering, and each was lost in oneness until she reached out and touched a harpstring as though to disengage from an embrace—and the music started, flowed, ascended, descended, sang, shouted in joy, whispered with mystery and promise. It plunged into sadness, yearning, touched the desert areas of the human condition, then soared again to celebrate love and light and to salute the inexplicable Eternal.

When she had finished, they both sat silent, eyes closed. Then Justin whispered as if reluctant to cast words into the mood. "Thank you. Thank you."

Sarah Belle aroused and walked toward him. He jumped to his feet and they stood facing each other.

"Justin, the harp is like a part of myself, I'll play it again many times I know, as I know I'll eat and sleep. But I'll never again play it as I've played it for you. And for this, I say, Thank you."

Justin stood motionless, tried to speak, moistened his lips in effort.

"Let us now talk about Sutton and plans for his return."

"Of course." He made a transition into formal posture, studied, controlled. He escorted her to a chair. "We'll sit in comfort. I'll order refreshments."

With Aladdin-lamp precision, servants appeared, a small table was provided and set out, Justin took a chair opposite Sarah Belle, and they were sharing a light repast. Soon they were sipping Turkish coffee from small china cups as delicate as the hummingbird's wing in the rimmed design, and engaged in converse as calculated as a military maneuver, as positive as a nutcracker.

"Does my brother still harbor fears of encountering Ange again?"

"Certainly not by any mention of her. I can easily allay any uneasiness, if he should express it."

"How?"

"She's no longer in the city. She became infatuated with a Sicilian, an importer of fine oil. He was here to establish a business connection. She accompanied him back to Mobile."

"How do you come by such information?"

"Marie Laveau."

"I see."

"I have delayed showing him the letter from his cousin until I can present the whole matter related to his return."

"I'll send you a list of those who'll greet him here and the time for his appearance. It will be a small party, only relatives and close friends of the bride and groom. I hope you'll agree that your presence is most desirable, in truth a likely necessity."

"I cannot share your viewpoint at the present. It's my intent, Justin, to arrange his departure from my house with Hudson to drive him to his destination."

Justin hesitated before speaking thoughtfully, his voice so soft and low Sarah Belle had to give marked attention.

"I've not been the best of brothers, have ignored much to which I should have given witness and applause. But one quality of his I'm intimately acquainted with; that is his dreamy nature, provoking absent-mindedness, emotional and sometimes damaging attractions, and just as pronounced aversions. And once he's latched his affections on to a person, a pet, a place or an object, the lock is set, and remains that way until event or disillusionment blasts it open." He paused.

"You mean he'll be reluctant to leave my house?"

"And yourself."

Sarah Belle was quick to respond openly, "I've allowed no intimacy between us. He sometimes kisses my hand with the joy of accomplishment at the harp, or in gratitude for—for——"

He waited.

"For some idea I've helped to resolve into a composition or a suitable poem for the song."

"Oh, you sing?"

"Only as I write or read, or walk or da——"

"Or dance?" He regretted that he had asked it. His senses so attuned, he realized at once that it had been a long time since she had danced.

"Or dance." It came out like a faint and dying echo.

Justin's control deserted him. He became agitated. He pulled his chair closer to hers, laid his hand trembling upon hers, where it had curled tightly around the slim rosewood arm of her chair. "I beg of you, I implore of you, let me . . . give you . . . protect you, share . . . joy of life . . . forever . . ."

She tried to pull her hand away.

"Don't . . . Oh God, don't withdraw from me."

Her hand was quiet beneath his.

He made an effort to quiet himself. "I know—I know for some reason I cannot know—that you cannot come to me, that you may have other affections more binding, other intentions more compelling, than the golden circle around the two of us. But do not disappear this day—this perfect day." He was holding her hand now, and she submitted, willing the throb of communion into a controlled rhythm.

"If you come with Sutton I'll introduce you, Madame Vahnia, as Sutton's teacher whom he has been privileged to study with during a short sojourn in this city."

"I'll come, Justin." She quickly disengaged her hand. "I'm sure by this time Hudson has notified your footman that he's waiting."

He was quick to respond in kind. "Follow me, the maid will assist you." He opened the door for her to enter the anteroom where the maid waited.

She appeared shortly, veiled and gloved, and they hurried out and down the spiral stairs as if late for the events at the Metairie racetracks. He held her arm within his, his hand under hers with fingers entwined. The carriage was waiting with Hudson at the open door. Justin was not to be cheated out of a parting gesture for remembrance. He had noted the short blue glove had been drawn on hastily. It had loosened more as they hurried along. When he was assisting her onto the step, his free hand with a deft touch to her fingertips had the empty glove concealed by his side before Hudson could notice or Sarah Belle protest. She looked at him through the window of the closed door, frowning a little. He tipped his hat. She gave him a fleeting smile and drew the curtain.

CHAPTER THIRTEEN

VISITORS TO THE HOUSE OF RECOVERY for the purpose of calling upon Sarah Belle in person were
rare indeed. Only occasionally were the ser-
vants called to the front entrance to deal with tradespeople or
strangers in search of residents in the area. Outside services were
engaged by Fanaalis and negotiated from a gate near the craft-
house, and the Jamaicans presented their wares only at St. Mary's
Market. A higher-than-usual wrought-iron yard fence, topped by
a border of points like the decorative heads on a lightning rod,
indicated an exclusion not easily penetrated. The protective enclosure was reinforced by a wall of shrubbery, pomegranate and the
white-blossoming Christ-thorn, thick foliage of crepe myrtle, and
the vigorous interlacing of honeysuckle and trumpet vine. Inside
were several majestic magnolias, cool fanning willows, the wild
banana, and exotic tropicals. Roses flourished as if seeded in paradise, and more modest florals created orderly pools of color. There
was a small bowerlike shelter, screened and canopied, with a tiled
seating arrangement, suitable for contemplation or private con-

verse. A peep into the front or back yard would give the impression that surely Beauty and Mystery must surreptitiously abide in this place.

Shealia interrupted Sarah Belle busy at her secretary to announce with uneasiness an unexpected arrival.

"Someone—woman—in garden—she there—here—for talking to you."

"Do you know who it is?"

Shealia rolled her eyes upward, then down, and turned her head to admit to the wall with a fast nod that she did know her, possibly too well.

"Is she here to bring harm to you?"

Shealia twisted her apron in a kind of frenzy, "Oh, no, no, no, no, madame."

"Who is it then? Out with it!"

Shealia came a few steps closer and whispered, "Marie Laveau."

"Well, for heaven's sake. Don't be in such a tizzy. Show her in."

Shealia was aghast. "In here?"

"Of course."

"Oh, madame! No, no! You do not . . . it is not . . ."

"And why not? She's been to my boudoir. She's been in my house before. After all, Shealia, this is not a French salon. Tell her to join me here."

Shealia hesitated, opened her mouth in protest but couldn't speak.

Sarah Belle placed her pen in the inkwell and rose impatiently to brush Shealia aside and hurry out to the garden.

Marie was standing on the garden path resplendent in rainbow-hued apparel, the skirt straight and ankle-length, the blouse full and low cut, the blue sash of her order tight around her firm waist, setting off the fullness above and the flatness beneath. The black cross was missing and in its place hung a flashing walnut-size crystal ball. Large blue sapphires gleamed in her ears, and the deep glossy black of her eyes was brilliant with anticipation as Sarah Belle approached. It was as if she perceived what was about to happen and relished it.

"Bonjour, Marie. What a living adornment you are to my garden on this sunny morning."

Marie knew the statement was not flattery. She had dressed for the occasion. She acknowledged the compliment in a musical ripple of French that included a comment on the lovely surroundings in which she found herself.

"I know you are here for a purpose. Come along and we shall discuss what brings you here."

Marie did not move to accompany Sarah Belle into the house. "Would it not be better, madame, if we conversed here in the garden alcove?"

"If you prefer," Sarah Belle turned and smiled knowingly, looking straight into the jet orbs reflecting the voudou queen's hypnotic light that could either menace or enchant.

When they were seated, Marie, having made her impression, relaxed into a natural exchange, as if addressing a longtime friend.

"La Belle, I have come to you with a story."

"Concerning the Laharts?"

"No. For me that is done. Your hands will tie the knot that finishes the seam."

"I hope it doesn't come out that the threads are too short to tie."

"No worry, madame. When you are through, the knot will be tight and thread left to clip."

Sarah Belle gave a short laugh. "I like your certainty. Now the story——"

"You know New Orleans, La Belle, but you are not at the heart, you are not of—of the blood—you were not planted—seeded here, and New Orleans' seeds were of many colors and many kinds of—kinds of free! The no-free, the part-free, and the free. Such as you are free, I am part-free."

Sarah Belle smiled. "I'm a woman, Marie. I'm a part-free too. And the free themselves are not free. They wear the bonds of their order. They move within the locked-in strata of their caste. In the dueling code alone, one of the most elite and cherished young men of a French Creole family, with the purest of credentials within the Colonial aristocracy, must fight a duel on the slightest offense to his honor—whether or not he has a personal honor worth defending. Yet a gentleman of the highest order among your free-people-of-color is not allowed to defend himself against the grossest of insults or physical indignities from a white man— cannot strike him, even much less challenge him to a duel."

Marie stared at Sarah Belle in amazement. "You know such things—then you know about the little houses along the ramparts

—the women, free but slave to protectors, kept pure for one man, kept——"

"Marie, you are young-old, wise, and free within a status all your own, but perhaps you don't know that the world knows all about the idyllic cottages, rose-covered outside, regal nests of beauty inside, an intrinsic, established section of the old city—never houses of ill fame, but certainly houses of infamy for many of the 'pretty quadroons' of song and legend."

"It is about one of these that I have come to you," Marie said quietly. "When I came to dress your hair, and you spoke of the dregs of love for the virgins prepared for these places, I read your thinking."

Sarah Belle made no reply. She felt a heaviness near dread for the story she must hear and doubtless act upon in some way. All brought about by a casual comment—a sentence of sympathy for a condition that had existed in one form or another since the beginning of French colonization in Louisiana and the islands of the West Indies when there were no white women in the settlements, only negro-slave women. The free people of color had their origins here when sometimes the father would free the slave mother so that the children might be free. Down the corridors of time, the quadroons and women of lesser color became so famed for their beauty, so nourished in luxury, that they were forbidden by law in 1788 to walk abroad in New Orleans dressed in their silks and jewels and plumes. The madras handkerchief was designated for their headcovering lest they consume the attentions of young men destined by birth to establish family continuity and bloodlines through wedded bonds.

Then came the quadroon balls to which only white men were admitted. These beauties—not prostitutes but reared in strictest chastity, as educated and preserved in innocence as their convent-bred counterparts—were presented as candidates for the security of a cottage ready-made for love and all the physical pleasures that money could buy (never mind the mind!).

The protector acquired at the ball had responsibilities too: when this gentleman, youth in bloom, left the arms of the luscious quadroon for a wife of appropriate status, he would continue to provide for the offspring and mother though he might never visit again the pseudo-dower-house of his preconnubial delights.

The "quadroons" for whom the balls were originated were often the daughters of cottage mothers whose ambition for their daughters (octoroons) was a wealthy protector and for their sons an education in Paris. But the candidate for this protection, trapped in the wonders and passions of a first encounter at the hands of a partner afire with her alluring virginity and versed in the techniques of erotic subjugation, was unprepared for the message that later would be sent (or learned through publication), that he was laced to another innocent with legal bonds that dissolved all lesser ties. So the deserted one languished in her fragrant prison—a prison of satins and laces, of wines and exotic foods, of trays holding diamonds, rubies, pearls, set among furnishings of rare woods, carpets from the Orient—even servants who would remain to attend her lovely but discarded body. And if she were one of those vulnerable to love's torment, she brought reality to the circumstances and truly discarded the body by poison, in the canal, or in other methods more ingenious.

Sarah Belle's awareness of all this, plus her recent concentration on the Stephens books and preoccupation with John's being drawn to the Palenque ruins, had brought about a dream, a nightmare really, in which she was witness to a ritual among an ancient people—the structures like Catherwood's illustrations of the Palenque sites as viewed by Stephens. It seemed that one of those was a housing for dedicated virgins. And then she saw a beauteous maiden coming out of this place dressed in lavish and bejeweled regalia, walking slowly down a path of paved stones—slowly and slowly, as if entranced. And she knew in the dream where the maiden was going and she wanted to scream, "Stop! You mustn't." But she couldn't. And in the dream Sarah Belle knew somewhere there was an altar and a well of great depth and that the pathway . . . She awakened with an attempted scream of warning.

This mood of apprehension encompassed her anew. And whether it was the dream or the effect of Marie's voice, toneless yet rhythmic, emotionless yet penetrating, she was drawn into a state of seeing all, hearing all, feeling all that came into the story.

They were *Suzanne*, descendant of quadroons; *Stephanie*, the blueblood and bride; and *Emile*, the hapless lover and groom. Suzanne, the protected, the prepared, white enough to pass, was the only child of *Silvie*, queen of the quadroons whose ballroom alliance had continued to visit her after his marriage.

Suzanne had none of the regal bearing of her mother. She was an exotic flower, delicate of manner, pure of thought and motive with none of her mother's aptitude for maneuvering on the battleground of love and rigid custom. It was Silvie's ability to display Suzanne's charms to the best advantage at the quadroon balls that brought her to the notice of Emile Nicée—his family wealth vast, their wall of elitism impregnable, and Emile himself, very handsome, almost delicate in stature, well-sized for her almost-fragile Suzanne.

It was to Silvie's great satisfaction that the two were attracted at first sight. He held Suzanne in the dance as though never to let her go, and she, almost fainting in his arms, gave herself throughout the whole network of her sensitivities never before responsive—gave herself before she was given by her mother or taken by her lover.

From the first night of rapture, Suzanne was so possessed and possessing that there was no other world, no other existence but the two of them—no other desire than to welcome him with all the givingness in her nature, and no sorrow except letting him out the door and waiting for his next entrance.

Silvie was disturbed by the obsessive passion that ravished her daughter and at the same time made her more appealing, more precious in her protector's sight, her large luminous mystical gray eyes more bewitching, ever more exciting, ever renewed to meet the lavish design of his love-making.

Then came the news of Emile's betrothal to the incomparable Stephanie, the date for the wedding at the cathedral, the schedule of prenuptial celebrations, impressive detail of family history and connections in New Orleans business and social hierarchy. Suzanne's mother informed her of the change in Emile's status, pointed out that such wealth would mean no scrimping in Emile's support of her, and if she might bear a child . . . Suzanne, like something cast in white marble until this point, shuddered but made no sound.

Silvie hastened to explain to her that since she and Emile shared such mutual happiness it was likely he would return to her from time to time when the marriage was consummated in the wife's pregnancy. Certainly he could never find in another love-bed the perfection of response with which Suzanne was gifted.

The marble became flesh, shuddered again and shook its head as though movement were almost as impossible as speech.

"You must not be jealous," the older woman advised impatiently. "It is destructive. Emile is generous and kind and will always make your life easy. He will not find with his wife or any other woman what he has found with you, and he will be back when he has performed the functions required of him as a family man. I would not be surprised if he does not risk another night with you before he takes on his convent-bred wife."

Suzanne's eyes shot forth such a violence of hate and jealousy that Silvie was frightened and tried to appease with explanations. "There is no reason to hate this young woman. Her innocence has been as guarded as your own and she has not taken Emile from you. These marriages are carefully arranged by the families. She knows nothing and likely will never know about you and the customs that govern our lives. Such brides when they become aware that some men have two allegiances, two families often, believe their husbands are the exception and so let the matter rest—or, if the arrangement becomes obvious, they pretend no knowledge of it, and no harm comes of it."

"No harm . . . no harm . . . ," Suzanne mumbled, then roused. "You do think he will come again before——"

"As I know men, my daughter, I do believe he will come to you before the wedding," she hastened to reassure. Then stopped by the expression of malevolence that ravaged the girl's usually serene features, she exclaimed, "You will not do such things!"

"What things?"

"Think about taking your own life or that of another."

"I am not thinking of such a thing, Maman. No such thing at all. Now leave me alone, Maman. Let me think how I shall prepare for my last night that it may be better than her first night," and knowing her mother's weakness for fine things and devotion to her, she added, "I will let you help me with every little thing, Maman. You must find for me a new and more enticing fragrance—more nightdresses of the softest silks that will wrap me and enclose me until he is frantic." She laughed shrilly and her mother shuddered in apprehension.

"I mean it, Maman. Do not fail me. And a jeweled belt that he will find difficult to unclasp, and my hair so fresh and silken and clinging that it will nearly strangle him when he loosens it. And wine, Maman, so rich and strong that it will make us wild—wild with joy!" She beat her chest with her small fists and laughed again.

"Suzanne! Stop it! You always say, 'no wine, Maman, love is the strongest wine there——'"

"You stop it, Maman! This is my last night—you will humor me—it will be a great party first, for just the two of us with you and Devi attending us. And you will have violins, two sweet violins playing, and they will play the music that was played when I went to Emile's arms the first time at the ball. You know the music?"

"Yes, but——"

"And we will dance—and dance!—and dance!!—and he will not have all of me that night—and I will play with him—feed him wine——"

"Suzanne!!"

"—and he will be here all day and a second night—away, *far* away from her."

"But Suzanne, you do not know that this will be the last time. I know men. I think he will be back. Like your father——"

"You knew only my father. Emile will not be back—this will be the last time for me, Maman—the last time—then there will be the first time for her——" The malevolence was there again.

"Yes, yes, Suzanne, I will help you. I will help you to make it the most perfect——" She couldn't say more. Suzanne was in control. At least, it would keep her from harm until . . . until . . .

One day Suzanne was left alone. Her mother was out busy with seamstresses and shopping, frantic in her pursuit of everything her demanding daughter could think of to be made or bought. The servants had also been sent on errands. Without compunction, Suzanne invaded the servants' quarters and dressed in the plainest and least conspicuous of the maid Devi's clothes. Then she went out to find a childhood friend, now grown and gifted with knowledge that Suzanne had not, and which she coveted.

The friend was Marie Laveau, whose mother had been Silvie's hair-dresser, and the two children had played together during the pleasant hours of the appointed meetings.

"She seemed such a child," Marie commented softly as she continued her account, "and I felt like her grandmother. I thought she was the most beautiful little octoroon I had ever seen—thought so as a child, thought so when she came to me for help."

"What kind of help?"

"A kind you—or I—never heard of, La Belle. She had a plot in two parts. To the first, I agreed at once—that I would provide a potion that she could add to his wine that would——"

Sarah Belle smiled at the hesitancy—for hesitancy was not natural to Marie.

"Marie, read my mind."

"You are amused that I hesitate when we are kin to the same wisdoms. Suzanne simply wanted me to insure that her man would be useless to any other woman after leaving her."

"And you agreed at once to this preposterous larceny on manhood."

It was Marie's turn for amusement at Sarah Belle's phrasing. "Agreed that she should have full measure and running over of the love feast she desired, yes indeed, and that the bride's cup would be empty. But I am not a butcher, La Belle, either in token or kind. He would recover in time."

"In time for what?"

"You are reproving me—you are now reading *my* mind. Let me bring you the second part of her demand, which I held apart from until I realized I must assist or worse things could come to pass. She was certain in her mind Emile must come to her before the wedding festivities. Then after her night in paradise, she would put her soul on the marketplace."

"You mean she would take up——"

"Oh, no, far from it—very far from it. One can but admire this fair child-woman made clever as a fiend by love's torment. She had a plan for selling herself into the family—the bride's family."

"Impossible!"

"Nothing is impossible, La Belle," Marie said flatly. "It was arranged."

"I do not——"

"Do not tell me you do not believe me. I am here because I know you have a thought of me that I would not weave a web around your thoughts for any reason."

"Continue."

"I know a trader who deals in illicit marketing of slaves. I told him this lovely little creamy had been sold to me by an elderly colored on her deathbed—that she knew the girl was not nimble-minded enough to survive on her own and I must place her in a high family where she could be happy attending some kindly lady. I told the trader where I wanted her placed—to find a fawning relative of the bride who would delight in making her a wedding gift of this fair maid."

"How could you?"

"'How could you?'" Marie mocked. "With diamonds and pearls, dear lady, with diamonds and pearls which little Suzanne provided in plenty."

"Horrors!"

"I have heard worse, but no plan of revenge so well put to the harness."

After a small silence, Sarah Belle knew that out of some kind of protocol of politeness she was to ask a question to keep the story going.

"Did she have her night of love?"

"Probably nothing like it since the Fall of Man," said Marie facetiously. "Her mother and I saw to that. Her mother provided the wine and violins and I the potion."

"Did her mother know you——"

"La Belle!" Marie reproved. "I thought you understood."

Suzanne had made sure, had changed the proportion of wine and the liquid from the small green vial Marie had given her. She kept Emile as she had planned for a night and a day and a night. When he departed he looked like a man from whom all vital essences, mental, emotional, and physical, have been withdrawn—like the husk of a human that had experienced so much beyond himself or his imaginings that he was now held together only by the mechanism of sheer existence. At the yard gate his trembling hands held her face, his eyes so dry and wide open

Suzanne wondered if they would ever close. She didn't care. It was five days until the wedding, three until she would be presented to the bride. She would be prepared. Her hands were steady. Her eyes ready to look upon what was yet to come.

"I was with Suzanne, now called Félicité, attending Stephanie as she prepared for the wedding; there were many servants at her call, but we were the most useful, dressing her hair, preparing every dainty for her wedding night."

Suzanne was the devoted maid, pretending inexperience in matters of love as she replied to the excited murmurings of her mistress, listening to the praise of Emile as the most gentle, the most perfect, the kindest of men, gallant, tender, his caresses reserved but oh, so much meaning, so much promise . . . and when they would be alone after the wedding . . . Stephanie gave a trembling sigh. Dear Emile had not been well of late—soon, as his wife, she could attend him, meet his every whim, see that he had strengthening broths and custards.

"Poor dear darling, so excited about the wedding he is exhausting himself. Why just this morning he almost fainted when he called upon me, did you notice, Félicité?"

"Yes, madame, fainting for love, no doubt—swooning at the thought of the pleasures awaiting him before another day dawns." Stephanie blushed and hid her face.

Somehow Emile got through the wedding, stood smiling in a fixed grimace through the hours of ritual and feasting and dancing through all the elaborateness that the St. Charles Hotel could provide—and then to the bridal suite, and after that would come a wedding trip on the palatial steamboat the *Empress*. But there was no 'after that.' Stephanie said she wanted one maid with her, Félicité, as the groom would have one man-servant, both on summons from the quarters provided.

Suzanne-Félicité, having come up by the servant's entrance, was careful not to make herself visible to Emile though she served Stephanie with her bath and bridal night attire. She listened closely through the night and was satisfied when she heard no lovers' talk, or sounds of delectation. In fact, she was quite certain there was muffled weeping. When she was summoned in the morning, she found Stephanie disheveled, red-eyed, and trembling. "Oh, Félicité, I'm afraid he has gone. Something is wrong —so awfully wrong. See if he's in the parlor. I dare not look, I dare not!" And she was weeping now.

Félicité opened the door to the parlor. The man there stared at her like a wounded, terrorized animal then bolted for the gallery and went rushing and tumbling down the long spiral staircase.

"My story moves into the nunnery where Stephanie and Félicité are religious recluses, Félicité-Suzanne, serving a penance serving Stephanie, who hides in God from the puzzles and terrors of life."

"And Emile?"

"He is hidden away in the Charity Hospital in one of the out-buildings for lunatics. His family placed him and his serving man there. He has a brother that is now the son. Emile does not exist."

"Is he really——?"

"He is empty—head, heart, and man-part, and this is on my conscience."

"On *your* conscience, Marie?"

"Madame," Marie drew herself up in indignation. "Can you tell me why my conscience should not be like your conscience?"

"No, Marie, I cannot, and I beg your pardon. So you are here to get me somehow to help relieve your conscience of Emile. That is the strangest part of your story, after all."

"Not so, madame. You see, Suzanne did not follow my directions on the potion. I do not desire to kill the man in any man. My god is ALL MAN—the big, the everlasting HE."

"I see—I mean, I do not see."

"In time and place, Emile can be a man again."

"Not in my time and place, Marie. Not in my time and my place!"

"You will think about it, and I will come back."

"I cannot help thinking about it. And I hope you will not come back."

"I know you better than you know yourself, La Belle. You will think, and I will be back. Bonjour, madame." She rose quickly and was gone.

Sarah Belle sat thinking. Then she wept.

CHAPTER FOURTEEN

"**H**UDSON, LET'S DRIVE OUT along Shell Road this lovely day and just flow along with the people. There's so much color and movement as they pursue their interests at the racetrack or the resort at the lake. Have you noticed that in the great variety of vehicles one can match up their owners as pompous or plain, and the steeds, according to their masters, showy or modest in trappings and paces?"

"Yes, madame, I had thought it would be just the day for such a drive."

"It is only along this highway that New Orleans society parades without stratification into codes, colors, and creeds."

"You forget Mardi Gras. Our society releases much of its restraints during this season of jubilation."

"Ah, but they are masked, Hudson. They are masked! Quite a difference. And it is riotous, almost rebellious, in its extreme expressions. Along Shell Road it is an open mingling, almost a sense of sharing, almost a breath of freedom."

"A very shallow breath, madame. And there is no clanking of chains to taint the sharing. As for masking—are there not many of us who never remove our masks?"

Sarah Belle had no ready reply. Hudson drove briskly until they became a part of the pleasure-stream bound for Metairie or Pontchartrain, or simply participants in the mood of the day. Then he slowed his team to a pace as leisurely as the barges moving along the canal at the edge of the road.

As they drew near the racetrack, Sarah Belle suggested he stop at a stand offering cold lemonade and sarsaparilla. When he had secured the team and brought drinks, he stood near the open door of the carriage and conversed with Sarah Belle inside.

"You mentioned the masks we wear, Hudson. This gave me a helpful idea. I must deal with Sutton very soon on this matter of returning to his brother and the only milieu for which he is fitted."

"And it is quite apparent, madame, that you must deal with the brother along another line."

They both sipped at their drinks for a while without any reply from Sarah Belle. Then he inquired, "About the mask, madame?"

"Yes, quite apart from the one you usually wear."

It was his turn for the reply given in silence.

She began by telling him in detail Justin's preparations for a reception that hopefully would dazzle Sutton with the glory of the harp and the joy of reunion with the Férreos.

"I agreed reluctantly to accompany Sutton to his brother's suite where I will be presented as Madame Vahnia, Sutton's harp teacher."

Hudson smiled. "Monsieur Lahart is a clever man. He understands that disengaging his brother from your presence would be something like provoking a balky donkey to movement against its will."

Sarah Belle laughed, then sobered. Hudson enjoyed the freedom of making such a statement to her. To either of the Laharts such a comparison repeated to them would have been considered the grossest insult and brought about severe reprisal. She sighed and then proceeded in a detached sort of quietness to relate the dilemma she would face in making her departure from the gathering and the manner in which he would assist her.

"He did not tell me, but I know he plans dancing after the affair in his parlor. There is one of those small ballrooms next to his suite, and I am so certain he will do this—certain in a way I cannot explain."

"I understand. I will join in your certainty. And what is it you would have me do?"

"I hesitate . . . I hesitate . . ."

"Why, madame? Surely you have no doubt of my willingness."

"But I question my right to engage this willingness so often in my behalf."

"Please do not tempt me to assert myself in language more plain. If I did, then I would not have the right to the pleasure it will give me to——" he stopped and smiled a tight kind of smile and looked away from her as he finished, "to wear any kind of mask, be cast in any part for whatever drama you may provoke or contrive around yourself."

As she outlined the part she would have him play in Sutton's return, he was very quiet, gazing out at the parade along Shell Road. When she was done, he faced her again, his eyes bright with excitement: "Madame, it is the most exciting part you have ever devised for me! I will rehearse assiduously and perfect it down to the last detail. An unusual drama, certainly, wherein with God's help we will evade an audience and later applaud ourselves." He took Sarah Belle's glass, chuckling as he closed the carriage door and walked back to the stand.

On the road back, from the driver's seat he spoke into the sound pipe. "I shall practice with the himation until I wrap it around me with the ease of a Grecian, 400 B.C. What color shall I be clothed in?"

"Yellow. The rich deep yellow of knowledge—knowledge to share."

"You. What color will you select?"

"Dark red for concealment."

"I once saw a cane that belonged to a Spanish nobleman. It had a head of richly carved ivory, but . . . but . . . when appearing in court, he removed the concealment and there was a head of rubies, emeralds, and diamonds."

"Sutton, your Valentine serenade will always stand as one of your loveliest, most haunting compositions—and the song that evolved from it as well." Sarah Belle spoke softly.

"The song evolved through you, not me."

"Have you ever written a wedding song—a kind of salute to bride and groom? It could be a good companion piece to the serenade."

"I have never written a wedding song, and I have never written a salute to death, though I have thought of it sometimes," he declared in a flat tone.

The morning was still young and they were in the music room, which they frequented after breakfast was done—sometimes alone, sometimes together.

Sarah Belle sensed that he had begun to rationalize within the fantasy cocoon he had woven around himself, and the peepholes he had made in his mind were offering views flawed and repellent. She made an abrupt intrusion.

"Your cousin Amelia is getting married and she wants a wedding song from you."

He looked at her in consternation, then paled, and his eyes filled with suspicion, fixing on her, then darting around the room as if looking for escape. He tried to speak and could not.

"Hear me out before filling your mind with ugly suppositions."

He found his voice and the tone was rough. "I will not listen. You . . . you and Justin . . . you and Ange . . . you . . ." He arose and stood before her—rigid, his fists clenched, his mouth drawn tight against his teeth. "And the filthy ten thousand—has it paid for my room and board and your bedside attentions?!"

"Marie Laveau received the reward."

"Diablesse voudou! Justin dealing with a black witch—on my behalf. Coming down from Olympus to bargain in a filthy back street. Oh, no! Some shoddy cover-up is being laid before me!"

Sarah Belle spoke quietly, as though she were viewing an inanimate exhibit.

"Ah! My vision is enlarged. I see two men where I thought there was one. One is, oh, so gentle and dreamy, romance in his eyes, poetry on his lips, music at his fingertips, sensitive to beauty, but often insensitive to others. The sullen person right beside him, linked to him, it appears to me, leaps to outrageous, absurd, and harmful conclusions, at the slightest prick to the emotional areas of his selfdom. He does not consider using his talent to add to the happiness of others, but of using others that he may bask undisturbed in the ecstasy of his own creative achievements—

then bring them to the attention of others only that applause may feed the hunger of his self-love."

Sutton was still standing. He looked away from Sarah Belle, his shoulders slumped a little, his clenched fists loosened.

She continued. "Let us satisfy this dark and threatening person who must get some kind of illicit pleasure out of plunging to the precipice of dementia———. You mention Ange. She has gone to Mobile in pleasant company, I understand. I can imagine that the new love she has exchanged for the old has left no bridges unburned. You mentioned the voudou queen in imagery of diabolical black visage stirring poison in a sooty pot. She is bronze and the Greek masters really missed the model of the ages in not having her present to enliven their chisels with the graces of form. She was paid well to do what she did, and what she did was done well. Now we will move on to something else. Your brother Justin loves you———. Ah! that double is still with you and he's sneering— sneering in his way of hiding a desire while nourishing its antithesis. Your brother does not know, even now, where you are. Your privacy has been strictly observed. Justin sends you this letter addressed to you both. He is expecting Amelia and her entourage within a few days, and has arranged for a reunion in the parlor of his suite at the hotel. They know nothing of your injury and absence."

He accepted the letter as though it were contaminated. "I will not go."

"What you do is your choice. You can join Justin and Amelia in a family circle that will receive you joyously or you may seek further seclusion as you desire."

"You are sending me away."

"It is better said that your allotted time in the House of Recovery is well nigh at an end. Your future is with the harp and those you choose to make a part of your life."

"Suppose I choose you?"

"I am not on the list of choices before you. That you must understand."

His lips tightened again. His eyes flashed a rage of insult and injury. He turned his back abruptly and left the room.

Sutton remained in his room the rest of the day. Fanaalis took him food and drink, which he refused. In the twilight of evening with only the faintest candle glow, Sarah Belle sat down at the harp and began a gentle flowing improvisation of her feelings about John, about Sutton and Justin, about William and his bride in Houston—and Defender. There was a passing strain for Lando, only a delicate touch on the higher strings, and a soft melody, experimental with major and minor, mysterious as the concealments of river mist and golden twilight like the one in which she played—for a moment it was almost as if Hudson stood listening somewhere within an oasis of their minds.

The motifs of her musical structure were not all in the masculine gender. There were tones of sympathy and a thread of alien harmony for Stephanie and Suzanne in their strange bondage at the nunnery—and a chord on which she stumbled and could not complete as the ghost of Emile flitted by. Then a hearty lowthroated chording salute to Marie Laveau, in her stalwart maneuverings for evil or good, according to her own differential. At one point there was an intrusion of disharmony as sharp as the string of jealousy that was resolved into a staccato of pleasantry, flirting and laughing—a passing thought of the volatile Ange. It ended in a flight and flurry of dancing tempo, truly Jamaican, for she knew that Shealia and Fanaalis were standing nearby, listening, and she smiled at the sound of their delighted stomping on the garden pathway.

Suddenly she realized the servants were not her only close audience. Sutton was standing, a dim figure, in the doorway.

"Madame seems happy," he spoke in an undertone of irony, and continued: "I have made a choice, according to madame's request. I will attend the reunion my beloved brother is arranging for me and my cousin Amelia with such familial concern, upon three conditions: one, that a harp is provided; two, that I escort you to the affair as my guest; and, three, that you are introduced as my collaborator, and as such, you will sing the Valentine serenade to my accompaniment on the harp, and you will help me write the wedding song before we attend the affair."

Sarah Belle was startled and thought: *Sutton, you are so pleased with yourself. You sound like the fox that has found the chicken-house door left open. But there is only a crack in the door, not wide enough for you to get in.*

After a silence drawn out as she absently fingered a string or two on the harp, she spoke, but barely audibly so he would have to listen intently. "Here in the music room, in the morning, we will have a light breakfast and discuss the matter. And now, if you will excuse me, I have allotted myself another practice hour at the harp."

Sutton could not hide his surprise at the scene which awaited him in the music room. A small table for two was set out in fruit and flowers. The aroma of Jamaican coffee brewed from fresh grind was an invitation to come fully alive for the treat of Shealia's small cheese omelets resting on flat crusty hot-cakes. But the feast for the eyes was Sarah Belle, her hair loose and held back with shell-shaped combs, her morning dress of fine linen-lawn, willow-green, gathered here, flowing there. She sat at the table and was pouring the coffee. She looked up and smiled.

"Bonjour, La Belle," he murmured, taking the chair opposite her as she nodded an invitation.

"The name is Madame Vahnia, monsieur. A harp teacher, you know. She sometimes pens a poem somewhat less than masterly and is known to collaborate with a musician now and then in fitting lyrics to original compositions."

Sutton looked at her in astonishment and hastily sipped his coffee as if to stabilize the reality of what he was seeing and hearing.

"Madame Vahnia has been notified of a public appearance she is expected to make at an exclusive family soirée—a family of some distinction in society and the marketplace, I understand—honoring one of their own soon to be wed. Of course, she will request of the head of the family that a harp worthy of her musicianship and that of her talented protégé——" here she raised an eyebrow and smiled at Sutton, inviting his smile, which came, but with a twitch of uncertainty, "be provided and perfectly tuned by competent craftsmen."

Sutton could not trust himself to comment. He could only try to control the trembling in his hand as he lifted the coffee cup or handled the single dainty omelets deftly in his fingers as Shealia had instructed him. It was trivia in such a moment of high personal drama, he told himself, to be thanking Shealia in a passing thought for seeding the large grapes that were complement to the omelets.

Sarah Belle ate with obvious enjoyment and was silent until she had finished. Then she continued her monologue.

"Madame Vahnia has made a few alterations in the order of the program suggested for this affair and hopes they will be sustained. First, she believes her protégé, as he performs his lovely 'Serenade to St. Valentine,' should himself recite or sing, as the passages suggest to him, the words that have been developed for the music. It would be impressive if he presented the harp solo and then gave the words which are subordinate to the high quality of the composition. What do you think of this?"

Sutton roused to speech, "Yes, yes, possibly so," he agreed vaguely. Then made an effort toward repartee. "The protégé is not a vocalist."

"Ah, but he has a fine voice just the same, and after all, it is primarily a family affair. And, monsieur may recall that the words of the ballads are a man's story. 'She was my love/my Valentine, she gave me joy/she gave me life, an ecstasy I thought divine, with promises to be my wife.'"

"Quite so. Quite so."

"And second, concerning the 'Wedding Song': she would agree to present the vocal on this with her protégé performing on the harp."

"How does madame know that it will be appropriate for the female voice since it has not yet been composed?"

"There was a rather autocratic request that I assist with the writing of this song, and forthwith I did so." Sarah Belle left the table and seated herself at the harp.

Sutton sat very still, staring at her.

"The words are finished. I will play a simple accompaniment and you may bring the composition to full form as you like. You will provide an introduction for me. Then the song——"

"When love comes your way like a star in your night
   Glowing and growing until blinding your sight . . .
   When you no longer feel that you're happy and whole
   And your body is sheltering but half of a soul . . ."

"Why have you stopped?" Sutton was transformed—he rushed to her side.

"I simply wanted to give you the idea—not intrude on the structure you would bring forth."

"Intrude? Intrude! My God! You have possessed me again. Give me the whole of it!"

He looked at her as if he would absorb her—then at the harp and his fingers twitched.

"No. I will lay the words before you." She slipped a piece of paper from her waistband and handed it to him. "And I will leave you with your truly true love."

As she stood, he came close, facing her. A breeze from the garden through the open door wafted the sheer linen of her full green skirt against his knees, and as she reached and touched his shoulder, a gentle brace between them, the drape of her sleeve brushed his hand. He trembled.

"Sutton," she said gently, "the harp is waiting for you." Then she quickly left the room.

The next day John's second letter arrived.

My Dear Adventuress,

I address you thus in the most literal sense of the Latin derivative "adventura," meaning "something about to happen." Your letter filled me with this something about to happen between or because of you and me. I cannot define it or account for it, I can only know that it is there waiting and that it is expanding, generating, enveloping. It cannot be simplified into "we are falling in love" and the concomitant "I love you's." Also, it is more than a "meeting of minds," and, God knows, more than the "mating call." While not altogether negating the potential in these traditional factors, one moves on to something more comprehensive and awesome within the man-woman principle, some purpose encompassing, but beyond, multiplication. Dear God, how I want to understand it! And, dear Sarah, how certain I am that this understanding can come only—only through exploring together this "adventura" we have activated.

One request I make of you, that you read "Web of Passion" before we meet again. Yes, we shall meet again and do not seem so surprised. This much, I can, and with your permission, shall arrange—have no doubt of it! When you do open that fated casket, have no thought for the contents except for slipping out my macabre account. Close it quickly, lock it, and return it to its hiding place. I am serious. Do not ask me to explain such a demand. It is neither the time nor do I have the words to justify my motive. Just be assured that it is more sensitive and reliable than superstition or hex-fear. When you have finished reading, throw it in the fire. Forget it. I am having you read it only that we may have an even start. Even? Who cares about "even"? What I really want you to realize is the precipice which was inviting me when you touched me in the park and drew me away. Like Macbeth I had "supped full with horrors" and was savoring his definition of life as a "tale told by an idiot, full of sound and fury, signifying nothing."

You mentioned, facetiously I think, how you might delight in the disguise of an adventurous youth accompanying a "master" to—I believe it was Palenque! Watch how you deal in fantasy when we must search so seriously for the realities to support the adventura. Let me be specific and personal to say I cannot imagine any disguise sufficient to hide the abundance of your "crown of glory"—and those locks shorn—mon Dieu!! It would be like stripping the petals from a magical brown orchid that I beheld once . . . (Careful, John!)

This specific before I close: I am busy here with the details of an estate being settled in my family—a trust from my grandfather that I did not know existed. It favors me with ample means to continue the investigations that so interested me when I ventured into the Valley of the Orinoco and was carried on into a sea of troubles—which I am more and more inclined to classify as learning experiences.

I will come to New Orleans before I go to Palenque, probably in November or early December—if this is right for you, of course, and then on to Palenque so that I can make my observations there before the rainy season sets in.

It is not easy to conclude this letter. How can I suddenly remove all the barriers that lie between us? I cannot. But I can say that I believe any "adventura" with such a beginning as ours cannot possibly be turned from its course!

John

CHAPTER FIFTEEN

A FTER READING JOHN'S LETTER, Sarah Belle went immediately to the fateful casket as he had directed and took out the account of his venture up the Orinoco Valley into the territory of the Guaharibos, and into the life of the woman Guafana. In her bedroom she continued reading as though it were a part of the letter.

How does it feel to pull out the long, heavy, serrated thorn of betrayal sunk in to its joint and broken off? A quick jerk will fray the flesh, draw mottled blood, leave an ugly scar. A gradual twisting will prolong the anguish. Leaving it to rot out may fatally poison the whole body. Quick! A sharp blade, a deep incision, a pry, and it is out! A red gush—but never mind. Blood-letting is good for the system. But what if the thorn has pierced a vital organ? What if the pain persists and the wound will not close? What if this thorn of betrayal becomes a cherished keepsake, preserved in a bath of emotions?

What would you have of me, Mistress Sarah of the House of Recovery? I would not dare to, if I cared to, spend a single night under your haunted roof. Why should I be hostage to your peculiar ritual of penance?—just by being here feeling committed to some kind of effort at personal renaissance in order to bring the records of your Conscience Book into balance?

Oh, yes, I know. I've heard all about the cures. Tell it. Proclaim it. Act it out. Write it out, if you're literate enough. Publish it abroad, if your story is brutishly tragic enough, and your trauma will be diffused through every throb of pseudo-sorrow, every scalding tear of your eager readers.

Now for my ransom: Let us examine the dream of a boy that turned into a nightmare for the man.

I had a hero—through grammar school, through academic studies at New Jersey College, through a period of intensive research and linguistics at Oxford. My hero died two hundred years before I was born. My hero was a favorite at Queen Elizabeth's court. He was knighted in 1584. No man at the court was so tall and handsome—never a prince so resplendent that he could so please the queen with his manners, his wit, and literary talent.

His earlier life (to the mind of a boy) was even more glamorous, a touch of piracy as he captained the ship *Falcon* in expeditions against the Spaniards, a streak of daredevil in his being arrested twice for dueling. (I studied under a fencing master.) I reveled in his vigorous defense of religious freedom, the light of the crusader shining before him when he enlisted a body of English volunteers to serve in battle with the persecuted French Huguenots. Never mind failures and enemies—such is the price of greatness.

I suffered in identification as he lost favor with the queen—and yet how noble his actions, how romantic his love for the queen's maid-of-honor and their secret marriage. Boyish fancy had enthroned him because he spread his coat before the queen that she might not step in a spot of mud, and scribbled on a pane of glass with a diamond to attract her attention. *Sir Walter Raleigh!* . . . In idealistic youth, the dream took on form and plan.

As I grew older, it became important that I compensate for the villainy of James I, who confined Sir Walter in the Tower for thirteen years, then released the aged explorer because he made a wild promise to find a gold mine in Guiana. On pain of death, however, Sir Walter was not to come in conflict with the Spanish.

This old man had a dream that became the dream I must clothe again with the reality of actual pursuit. His vision was of El Dorado—the *real* El Dorado, the Golden Inca, who once dwelt in the fabulous city of Manoa, on the shores of mythical Parima Lake.

Early geographers located this lake in the low country eastward of the Casiquiare, a branch of the upper Orinoco. Sir Walter was not really after a gold mine in Guiana, he was after an abandoned city of gold, the ultimate romance in exploration.

My pursuit of every detail of this matter, my long visit to the Tower where he was incarcerated, caused my associates at Oxford to refer to me facetiously as "Sir Walter Reincarnate" and to predict any such venture as I planned would have similar fateful results—except that I would probably lose my head to the Indians, whereas my hero lost his to the guillotine when he returned to England a failure.

I had little trouble aligning myself with a Venezuelan government mapping commission. General Paez, in charge of the country, was in border controversy with Colombia. My detailed historical studies and linguistic abilities qualified me as an advisor of sorts.

We were up the Orinoco as far as Los Castillos (more than halfway to Casiquiare country) when the venture began to take on a gloomy aspect. It was as if the defeat of Sir Walter's forces at this site of the old Spanish village had invested the place with a fog of bleak remembrance, and, for me, an ominous sense of approaching danger.

The forts at Los Castillos had not been abandoned by the Spanish until recent times. I felt myself standing on the very spot where Sir Walter's elder son was slain while he himself lay in fevered illness at Trinidad. I felt the tragic dismay of his commander, Kemys, who must return with the news of disaster and who committed suicide under the impact of Sir Walter's reproaches. I almost turned back. But the dream reasserted itself. Surely, Sir Walter knew somehow that the city of gold really existed in some hidden valley of the upper Orinoco—certainly the shiploads of Incan gold taken to Spain in the past had not been fantasy.

After more than a month of hazardous river travel, mishaps, and delays, we arrived at a dismal settlement where the mysterious Casiquiare stream wanders off to get lost from its Mother Orinoco and meanders over into Amazon territory. It was our intent to map its capricious waters which early explorers declared flowed both ways, part clear and part muddy. It was my intent to take off on some private meandering of my own when I could enlist natives suitable for my purpose.

I had not reckoned with the enduring hostility of the Guaharibo tribe to any kind of intrusion into their domain. It was as if they had sighted me and my intent. We were no more than halfway to the reputed mouth of the Casiquiare until our camp was raided during the night. Strategic supplies and one of our boats were taken. A poisoned arrow was shot into the tent of the expedition's leader. The project was immediately abandoned, and hasty packing ordered for a return to the junction of the Orinoco.

My mood was desperate. The region just to the east was the reputed locale of Parima Lake. The dream was now master of reason. I had a well-equipped personal pack. I was overconfident of my ability to relate to the Indians. Humboldt had written of the Guaharibos as "indios blancos," which I had equated with something less than primitive. Only when it was too late to matter did I learn that they were cannibalistic, apparently had no knowledge of fire, and ate their food raw.

The path they had used to reach our camp near a scattered village was plain. I followed it. Several miles along the jungle trail, I sat down to rest and contemplate my foolishness.

I was exhausted and dizzy. I presume I dozed. When I came to I could not believe I was awake. I was swinging and swaying in a large net, and indeed felt like a fish gasping and choking for its element. Through a haze I could tell the net was being carried by Indians who seemed to be trotting along at quite a pace. I began to thrash about. The net was dropped to the ground and I was jolted close to insensibility. The net was opened, a gourdlike hollow pipe was thrust into my mouth, and I must swallow the bitter scalding stuff poured into it. I lost all consciousness at once.

My next awakening was stranger than the first. I thought for sure that I was hallucinating—and now that I am about to describe it, you are apt to conclude that I am still in such a state. A beautiful woman was leaning over me—I was in a softness that was cool and fragrant. My old dream was rampant now, the monarch of my mind that had unseated reality. She could be no other than the high priestess, the goddess, a contemporary princess of the City of Gold. Wasn't her waist-length hair like spun gold? Her skin muted sunlight, her eyes a darker luster, but gold like a gentle lioness—oh, no, my fantasy corrected, not a lioness but a most affable feline glow that almost had a sound to it—a purr. I chuckled in my near delirium of shock. A hand reached out and touched my cheek. It startled me, so soft and yet so magnetic that I could not have moved any part of my body or even blinked until she removed it. Then I shivered and closed my eyes tight. When next I opened them, there was a bearded man by my side who addressed me in perfect French.

"I am Pierre Ottoboni, a French Huguenot missionary, and we

are in a valley of the Sierra Parima in the sacred precincts of the Guaharibo. You are lucky to be alive, but now you are safe. Rest. You are our guest. My daughter, Guafana, will attend you. There are servants but she and I alone speak French, which I can see you understand perfectly."

I muttered my gratitude, closed my eyes, at peace—except for one thing. I yearned for the touch of that hand again—for the aliveness that I knew would race through me. I closed my eyes tighter and willed the touch. It came. This time she took my hand. Mine closed tightly over hers, and this wondrous world of sensation, this addendum to my dream beyond anything I had every dreamed, was in full command.

At this point, Sarah Belle found herself shivering and then short of breath. She felt somehow deprived—and could it be, she asked herself, a stinging rise of jealousy for this "wondrous world of sensation" that John had come into from the hand of another woman? The story was becoming so much present with her that it was hard to relegate it to the past. She dreaded going on into what must surely follow. She laid the account aside, felt chilled, though it was midafternoon, donned her houserobe and made herself comfortable in bed before reading on.

I soon came to learn that I was no mere guest, I was in residence and we were all permanent guests of the Guaharibos. Pierre and his wife had entered the area from British Guiana more than twenty years before. He was a descendant of the Huguenots who fled persecution in France during the late sixteenth century (shades of Sir Walter!). His family had settled in Switzerland. Guafana's mother was from the Swiss line. Their long affiliation with the Protestant movement continued through the generations, and in 1822 when the Société des Missions was formed, the Ottobonis had been attracted to Guiana, and, having been told of the heathen, unapproachable Guaharibos, had found a guide who knew the language and dared to take them into this closed region. It was determined later that the guide had intended to turn them over as prisoners to the Guaharibos, thus preventing their intrusion. Instead the guide had himself been killed and the Ottobonis, drugged as I had been, were taken to Parima Lake.

It was Adela Ottoboni and her knee-length golden tresses, which loosened on the journey, that dazzled her captors and converted them, not to Christianity but to idolatry. The missionaries had to content themselves with their lot, learning the language, hoping to transfer the adoration tended them to the Christ concept. Two years after their abduction, Adela died in childbirth. The babe, obviously as golden as the mother, became the alternate object of worship. A surrogate Guaharibo mother in her milk was brought to Pierre, after a shaman of the tribe had put her through a process of purification. She promptly named the child "Guafana" though Pierre had intended that she be called by her mother's name. As soon as Guafana could speak she named her nurse "Shawse." Pierre was given the respect of paternity and allowed to train the child in his ways, but Shawse had her ways too.

Pierre realized that his and Guafana's lives depended on the Guaharibos' being satisfied with a ritual conforming to their primitive concepts. He constructed a dais in the open where he and Shawse could sit with Guafana (and a protective bowl of fire) when the natives came at certain moon seasons to stare and bring tributes. They brought raw fish, cultivated squash, and a rare jungle lichen that Shawse insisted was a delicacy especially sought for the god-child.

Through the years, ever hoping there would be civilized penetration into the area, Pierre busied himself working with rare woods— the abode for himself and Guafana was sculptured architecture, a place of such beauty and harmony of lines and wood textures that the natives could easily pay it reverence as a dwelling place for the gods. A small chapel, the facade carved out in the shape of a rose with a cross at the center, was his personal tribute to his God, his place of prayer, communion, and a blessing ritual for the few who sometimes fearfully came and knelt with him before an altar garlanded with flowers. If he spoke to them in their language, portraying the Christian ethic as best he could, they always listened, but never heard. Instead their eyes were fixed on the flame that was kept burning in a receptacle at the base of the altar.

On one occasion Pierre said to me, "John, you can be thankful that you let your hair go so long without trimming and it is that peculiar shade of golden brown. The Guaharibos believed you were Guafana's long lost brother."

"Did she have a brother?" I inquired.

"No. It has something to do with a myth of origin. And there is some resemblance between the two of you."

"Impossible!" I protested that I should favor this matchless one in any way. "And my golden strands that misled them were purely a freakish circumstance. Some hair-dressing I brought along reacted with the jungle climate and tropical sun to bleach it out, and I lost my trimmers at the first camp."

"God was protecting you that you might reach us unharmed."

If God were involved, I was ready to praise him excessively for bringing me to Guafana. I wasn't worried. We'd get out someway, sometime. I thrived. I reveled. I was constantly exhilarated at the attentions of Guafana, and Pierre's talents had made the place a paradise of comfort and beauty. He was making the best of an imprisonment. I was dwelling in a most private city of the blest. I was in love with an absorption, a passion, an abandonment I could never have imagined existed in any man. Guafana was not above teasing me. She knew her power. Her presence left me so at a loss for aggressive confidence that I had never taken her into my arms, never tried to kiss her, simply caressed a shoulder, held her hand, touched her cheek, dared to stroke her hair.

Again Sarah's breath came short and she let the pages drop and closed her eyes for composure: What was it John had said about her own hair—"crown of glory"—and something about a "magical brown orchid"? Well, thanks be to God, her hair was *not* golden! Reluctantly, she picked up the pages again, resolved to read objectively, realizing the description of his fateful amour had just begun.

Then the time came—a time of the full moon—a worship session which I despised and resented. Afterwards, Pierre, exhausted with frustration that he must serve such a congregation, left us alone to wander back to the portico, holding hands, silent and yearning. We stopped at the steps and stood gazing at the moon. The fragrance of moonflowers nearby was almost suffocating.

"I wish we were there," she said and sighed.

"Where?" I asked.

"On the moon."

"Why?"

"We would be free."

"We are free now," I said wildly, "free to love." I was no longer restrained. I reached for her hungrily, roughly, held her close, kissed her hair and eyes and face and throat, and at last her lips. She returned my passion. Clasping each other as if never to let go, in weakness we sat down on the steps. Pierre appeared in the doorway. "Go to your quarters," he commanded. "In the morning, I will marry you in the chapel."

And he did. We spent our wedding night in the room that had belonged to Adela, on the bed where she had died and Guafana had been born. It was a stately bed, decorated with Pierre's intricate hand-carving. Shawse had sprinkled some kind of powder that sparkled at the doorway and at the foot of our bed. The goddess was taking a mate.

And some eight months later, a golden son, premature but well-formed . . .

Sarah Belle crushed the page and threw it from her, was out of bed and walking the floor, running her fingers through her hair and talking aloud. "So you had a son, you and Guafana had a son, a 'golden son' you call him! Do you know how this makes me feel? Have you any idea! 'Even!' you said. Reading this would give us an even start! What do you mean 'even'?! You listened to my story of Lando and Defender under duress, and utterly calm, utterly!" And then she remembered how he had cried out "Guafana!" in some agony of recall. This agitated her even more . . . "You were moved only when you thought of her!" . . . She stopped, clinching her hands at her side, and looked in the mirror . . . Amazed at the image of her distress, she spoke to it. "Have you lost your senses?" And it seemed to speak back to her: "Where were you in your recital when he called Guafana's name?" In surprise, she whispered, "I had just described my betrayal of Defender by calling him 'Lando' as he made love to me in our marriage bed." . . . "Considering the account you poured out about yourself, would he expect you to be so tormented by this reading?" . . . "No. He called me a 'physician.' Ha! A physician now gagging on my own prescription." . . . "He wants you to know of the precipice he was drawn back from by your approach in the park." . . . "I haven't even come to that part." . . . "Hadn't you better get on with it?"

And some eight months later, a golden son, premature but well-formed, and to me beautiful enough to make the fatherhood passion that had been stirring me since Guafana's announcement come into full flower. Nothing ever like my feeling for Guafana, nothing so surprisingly wonderful as its yielding a son—my son. For the first time, I began to fret. This was no place for my beautiful wife, my precious son to spend their lives. There must be some way—I must devise something. Had my family given me up for lost?

Would the government of Venezuela——? Fickle thought—why should they care about me after my desertion of the party? But there would be a way—I would make it happen. Guafana had no such concern. She could and did obliterate my restlessness as often as it surfaced. After childbirth, she wove an even tighter web of passion around me so that I never desired nor intended to be separated from it no matter what came to pass.

No matter what came to pass . . .

Pierre told me one day that in all the twenty years he had been in the hidden valley, he had seen only one man other than the natives. He called the man Vasco.

He seemed to hesitate about further comment. "What is he like?" I inquired.

"About your age. I judge his origins to be at one of those too venturesome settlements along the upper Amazon: in that he was taken as a baby for adoption into a raiding tribe, or bartered to another tribe wanting such a prize. By devious channels and streams known only to Indians, there are water travel connections between the Orinoco and the Amazon.

"He came here first with a chieftain's family attending the ceremony. Then he came several times alone, at intervals some months apart. I get the impression that the tribal headquarters are some distance away. He was curious and friendly. I felt saddened that one of his fine stature, and apparently with a very alert mind, should be so limited in development.

"He is the only one who ever loved my chapel. I taught him a little French, delved to see if there were any latent memories, and realized he must have been a mere infant when abducted. I surmise he is Portuguese. His hair is reddish bronze, his eyes a piercing blue."

He chuckled—it was plain this young man had relieved the monotony, the dullness of Pierre's associations with the unresponsive Guaharibo.

"And a funny thing," he added, "that gives him a quaint and I must say an appealing quality. He has gold rings in his ears. I surmise they were taken from his mother or father and were a part of the barter that brought him to the attention of the chieftain; he must have truly prized Vasco as a son to have inserted these treasures in the child's ears."

He chuckled again—"and he does have the funniest ears!"

"Have you seen him lately?" I felt ill at ease.

"Almost a year ago. I hope he comes again. It might encourage him—change him—make him want to partake more of my instruction if he saw another of his kind and age. I know he is teachable—if he were only around more."

I felt no eagerness to be an awakening factor in this Vasco's life. But he did come again.

Guafana was sitting in the garden with the baby at her breast. We had named him Ottoboni Monroe Sterling and we called him Otto. Then suddenly *he*, Vasco, was there with us, coming as silently as an Indian, staring at Guafana with an Indian's absorption.

Guafana was staring back at him as if mesmerized. Finally she looked down at the baby. Vasco looked down at the baby. With protective animosity, I looked only at Vasco.

A smile appeared on his lips, spread to his whole face, brought an unearthly glow to his eyes.

I studied him—hated him—even feared him. He was so strong—in some way so sure of himself—his scanty Indian attire did not detract, simply reinforced the impression of a sleek, perfectly formed man-animal.

He sensed my hostility and turned his attention on me. His eyes focused on me with steely blue calculation. He smiled at me, merely a slit to show his teeth in arrogant threat. And then I noticed his ears! My God! His ears!! I thought I was going to retch. . . . Not a sound from Guafana. She sat still as death, her breast exposed. The baby, filled to surfeiting, simply lay back on her arm, gurgled, and turned a blue-eyed acknowledgment toward me. I turned and ran through a hedge, gasping and vomiting as I ran. Oh God, oh God, how could it be? But it was as plain as the stain on my clothing. Otto's ears were exactly like Vasco's, notched and swirled at the lobes.

Sarah Belle's eyes were wide and dry, her hands cold, fever-red spots on her cheekbones. She kept reading.

I kept running.

I arrived at the lake.

I was wearing sandals and only the lightest of loose clothing. In a gesture of loathing and despair, I tore them off and leaped naked into the water. I swam and swam without direction. I would simply swim until I could swim no longer.

Gasping, I found myself beached, for the lake had a tide and I had not been far from shore. I lay on my back waiting to die. It was near nightfall. An enormous jaguar came and looked at me, so yellow and his rosettes of black marking so clear that I tried to laugh—the rosettes reminded me of Pierre's rose on the chapel front.

We stared at each other, the jaguar and I. In my thoughts I addressed him. "You can make a meal of me if you like, but you will still be hungry, for I have already been consumed."

And then a group of five Guaharibos appeared, scaring away the jaguar. I gave them, too, silent converse. "If you want my head, take it (greetings, Sir Walter Raleigh!). If you want to make a game-board of my body, gather round, and let's play torture (the better to forget *you*, my dear Guafana), or let the devil play host and declare a macabre feast."

Sarah Belle groaned, lay back on her pillows, her empathy so intense that she became lost in his desperation for a while before she could read on to the end.

With that, I passed out. When I came to, my clothing was back on me, and I was being transported in the same manner that I had been brought to hell's campground—in one of those reeking hand-woven Guaharibo fishing nets. I tried to curse the carriers but my tongue was too thick and I had found no profanity in their language. I tried to think of something to do that would cause them to kill me and dump me. I ended by sympathizing with all the water life on earth ever caught in a net, and weak tears rolled down my cheeks. I made up a silly nursery rhyme to myself: "Cry, baby, cry, little he-goldilocks wants to die, die, die—cry, baby, cry." So along the way they fed the baby through the same kind of tube used when he was taken to——

Here Sarah Belle saw that John had made a violent gesture with his pen, blotted, scratched through the paper——

I do not intend to set my pen to that name again or describe that jump-off into hell any further, so help me God!

I would add this prosaic statement. With a Shakespearian flourish of poetic justice, the Indians returned me to the very spot on the jungle trail where I had taken off into gold-fringed madness. Through the good fortune of kindly attentions, I was relayed back down the Orinoco all the way to Ciudad Bolivar where messages and funding from my family awaited me should I ever appear.

And this final observation: In every man there must be a fool crouching, waiting for Reason to languish. Then he leaps to the front of wandering mind and instructs: *"Search for the City of Gold.*

Amass endless wealth and you shall be elevated to high places and never again suffer want." With honeyed tones, he will seduce you further: *"Ah! there is a Place where the Beloved dwells—where the Love Feast is daily spread to satisfy all Desire and Appetite. . . . See the Golden Tower glistening! Behold the inviting eyes and waiting lips of the Only One!"*

I say to you, Fool: *"You are a deceiver! You are simply in search of prey for the Web of Passion!"*

CHAPTER SIXTEEN

T HE APPOINTED EVENING for the Lahart reunion at
Justin's suite in the St. Charles Exchange Hotel
had arrived. It was a day cool and invigorating.
A strong clean breeze from the ocean heralded a seasonal transition. No longer the undercurrent of fever fear that rode in and out
of every summer. For a few months the swamps and the sun would
break off collaboration on human discomfort. The air would provide a heady mix of late summer and early fall florals, foods, and
frolics.

Theatricals were more exciting. An empty ballroom was hard to
find. The levees were livelier with a flow of human carriers, a
mighty rhythm of song, command, threat, code calls in languages
from the shipping lanes of the world—the army of loaders and un-
loaders quickly relieving conveyors bloated with overload and filling the swaying empty boats and barges with a gluttony of cargo.
For the pleasure vessels, enormous palatial steamers decked out
like luscious ladies of easy virtue, departure parties were more
gala, arrivals more rousing.

At the House of Recovery a departure was about to take place in the same tempo. Sutton was animated with a feverish concern for every detail of his appearance. Through Hudson he had sent orders to his man-servant at the Lahart mansion to select from his wardrobe an elegant evening attire. There were high silk hat and white shirt with picturesque ruffle showing above fitted white satin waistcoat and matching cravat. Tight trousers and tail coat were of rich-textured thin broadcloth. Giving a concert-maestro flourish to the whole was a white velvet knee-length cape: wide black velvet collar, black satin lining, all styled to hang about him as an adroit background for the whole ensemble. His cane was thin ebony with ivory head. Short white evening gloves would just touch the wide shirt cuff where garnet links sparkled.

Sarah Belle had arranged for Hudson to assist Sutton in securing appropriate dress for the affair, but she knew nothing about how he would appear. She noticed that he had been carefully grooming his wavy hair, brushing it forward a bit over the ears where it met the side whiskers that continued around in a fringe of beard, making a frame that accented his very pale skin and sensitive features where wide dark eyes articulated his moods far plainer than words could express.

He had entered the parlor where Sarah Belle waited. He removed his tall silk hat and made a small bow, then stood unsmiling waiting for comment.

"Sutton! You look positively poetic! All the ladies there will gasp and hold their breath at your appearance. Be sure that you speak quickly or they will doubt your reality."

"And all fall in a dead faint, no doubt. I would like that."

So you're going to be difficult, she thought. He stood hat in hand staring at her, seeming to itemize every detail of her appearance as designed for the occasion and for the personality of Madame Vahnia. First, her hair, multi-curled but otherwise not in conformity to fashion, front and sides pulled high on to the head and held, crownlike, by a band of filigreed gold. Curls clustered unbound and without ornament along the back of the neck. Opals gleamed in her ears and at her throat. Over her costume she wore an exquisite shawl of blonde Chantilly-lace. Her evening dress reversed the pervasive bouffant skirt style that demanded piles of stiff petticoats. Her basic garment was of creamy satin complementing the shawl. It was made with tight bodice, off-the-shoulder neckline, and full skirt. Over this skirt were four gathered skirts of illusion silk in light pastel tones of green, lavender, pink, blue. Delicate nosegays of the same silks were appliquéd on belt and bodice. Short white gloves, a folding fan of gold gauze, and a small reticule of netted silk completed her outfit.

Having carried his scrutiny down to the pearl-studded buckle on her kid slipper, Sutton looked up to meet the cool tolerance in her eyes. "To escort you under the public gaze, and into an assemblage where gentlemen are present, might well cost a man his life or his honor."

"How so?"

"They could not resist an open challenge for your attentions."

"You asked for the privilege. So surely you are prepared. I suppose you've studied with the poet and fencing master, Michel Saint-Pierre, certainly a congenial associate for a gentleman of your temperament."

Sutton did not reply. She had pricked at the exclusiveness in his nature. Saint-Pierre was rated one of the best fencing masters in New Orleans. He was of the *gens de couleur libres* and his published poems were popular; one had been set to music and was widely sung.

He did not answer. He tapped on the floor with his cane in impatience.

Twilight was settling down. The servants came with tapers and the room opened to candle glow that enhanced the romantic appearance of the couple. Fanaalis and Shealia stole glances of wonderment in their direction but dared not invade the silence that failed to echo their visible loveliness. It had been arranged they would leave after dark and would be the last to arrive at the party. It had also been Sarah Belle's instruction to Hudson that he drive to the hotel in a round-about way and that the curtains on the coach be secured so that Sutton would not be able to check their route.

Other plans had been laid for her departure from the St. Charles so that she could not be hindered or followed without difficulty.

They heard the carriage arrive. Sarah Belle and Sutton knew in thought this was good-bye. Sutton moved close to Sarah Belle, stood facing her. "An escort always returns his lady to her dwelling place when festivities are at an end. So this is not a parting."

"I will return alone, Sutton."

"You will not."

He glared at her. "Then——" He placed his cane and hat on a chair. "Then, just in case you are right," he reached out and startled her by pinning her arms to her sides—she was clutching her shawl in one hand, her reticule and fan in the other. He drew her to him and kissed her full on the mouth with all the longing and loneliness that were wracking him. "Oh God," he whispered, "How wonderful you are and how cold!" He kissed her again, but more gently and let her go. "Did the others who left you from this place perform better than I?" he inquired bitterly.

Hudson knocked.

"Apologies, Madame Vahnia," he said with no hint of regret. "Let us be off. Your handsome footman will not understand."

Sarah Belle said nothing. Straightening her shawl a bit, she opened the door. Hudson walked ahead to the carriage door. "Good evening, Hudson," she greeted. "It is a beautiful New Orleans night, isn't it? Moon rising big and beautiful as if expecting high drama and generating the music of the spheres."

"Indeed, madame," Hudson murmured respectfully.

Sutton offered no greeting. Hudson ignored him.

As Sarah Belle took her seat in the carriage, she was amused at Hudson's dramatic irony in bringing the same fine carriage he had brought for her to use in her first meeting with Justin. Sutton, like Justin, took the seat across from her, but unlike his brother sat withdrawn in moody seclusion.

She felt anxiety, uncertainty, even fear building in him. She wondered if he might not open the door and leap out. His only sense of adequacy seemed to lie in creative expression through music, which he had come close to losing. She realized that Sutton must have been dependent on his parents for a sense of security and personal worth, in contrast to Justin's capacity for self-sufficiency. The shattering experience of losing parents and a younger sister in the fever epidemic must have accentuated the brothers' differences rather than drawing them closer. Could these differences possibly be bridged in one evening? Was Sutton capable of controlled response to the intense excitement that would be generated around him—and the attention that would be focused on her?

"Sutton," she addressed him quietly when she knew they were near the St. Charles entrance. "I am glad to be here with you. I had once thought it better that you appear alone. But I believe now that it will be a wonderful evening for us both, full of surprises and delights—one of those delights being our performance at the harp, the other being the happiness you will bring to others as well as yourself."

He looked at her in surprise, started to reply with his usual asperity, but he no longer felt the urge to spar. What he actually felt was sheer dread. He responded weakly. "You think so?"

The carriage stopped and the door opened. Sutton stepped out and extended his hand to Sarah Belle while Hudson stood formally by. Sutton said a hardly audible "My thanks" to Hudson. Then, still holding Sarah Belle's hand, he stood gazing at the grand hotel as though he had never seen it before. For nearly three months, the confines of house and garden, music room and craft shop, and now this splendor—the grandeur of lofty columns, the spacious spread of marble—how had he ever looked upon it with so little notice? He caught his breath, and moved slowly with Sarah Belle along the same path his brother had followed with such exhilaration in her presence. The climb up the graceful spiral staircase seemed to tire him and at intervals he would pause as though contemplating retreat. It was a lively time of evening. Dining rooms filled, ballrooms were being prepared for the night's gaiety, strains of music seeming to wander up and down the stairs with the animation of groups that passed the leisurely paced couple.

When they turned off at the second landing, Sarah Belle felt Sutton's hand tremble under her elbow. The waiting footman opened the parlor door and they were awash in sounds of laughter and high-pitched conversation. As they stepped through the foyer, Justin with his arms spread as if to embrace them both placed a firm hand on the shoulder of each.

"Madame Vahnia, Sutton. Welcome! Welcome!"

There was a squeal in the background and a rush, a whirlwind of white tulle and gold lace, of gold curls wreathed in forget-me-nots. "Sutton! Sutton! My dar-ling!"

Sutton's transition was like that of a stage magician. He saw her coming. "Amelia!" he called out as he threw his hat and cane to a waiting servant and dashed to meet her. He lifted her off her feet until her face was even with his, kissed her on the nose, and held her dangling like a big doll. "You little witch!"

"You wonderful handsome prince, put me down. I am not a brat to taunt and tease. I am a bride!"

"Oh, yes," he laughed. "A bride! And where is your groom, little maid?"

Homère Bienville had been standing near Justin and Madame Vahnia partaking of some of their shock in witnessing the abandoned delight in the meeting of cousins. He laughed, too sure of himself to be jealous. "Let her act like a child this evening," he said good-humoredly as she rushed toward him with Sutton. "Her days are numbered."

Justin, happy to have Vahnia in his care, moved away from Amelia and the excitement she scattered about her to introduce his lovely lady to relatives and friends: to his Uncle Daniel and Aunt Flore Férreo, and Amelia's sister Florence, maid of honor for the wedding; the groom's brother and sister, Frédéric and Sérénité Bienville; the groom's parents, Loraux and Clarissa Bienville, and a variety of kin and intimates, some of whom had not seen each other for several years.

"There are thirty-six of us gathered here, all with close bonds of interest and affection," he explained, "and informality will prevail."

"And I am the thirty-seventh?"

"My dear, if I had any more interest and affection for you, it would overwhelm me. As it is, I am partially in limbo as long as you remain inaccessible."

He looked at her with such open longing that she turned to smile at someone else, to break from Justin's power to move her beyond herself—to draw her with him into a vortex of spiraling possessive energy. He knew this as well as she, and his cool voice brought her back as he continued.

"It sounds as if eighteen conversations are going at once, doesn't it? In a way, it makes for privacy. I want you to know that all here became acquainted with the harp and Sutton's accident before you arrived. The nature of his accident, of course, is a private matter. To them you are a gifted performer and teacher who guided him into acceptance of the harp as a replacement for the piano."

"I notice he and Amelia are at the harp, inspecting and apparently in earnest discussion."

"I suppose you have noticed also that he is ignoring me. It seemed he was about to greet me someway when Amelia burst upon him."

"I doubt he knows the harp is his."

"Amelia has told him by now. I told her where I secured it and that it was a gift to him."

As if in confirmation, Sutton glanced their way, nodded slightly, stared a moment as though he could not relate them to the scene.

"He is having to take things a piece at a time, Justin."

"I think he was relating to us all right. Probably jealous that I am at your side."

"Have you noticed how the groom's sister, Sérénité, hasn't been aware of anything except Sutton since he became visible to the group?"

"Have you noticed that I have not been aware of anyone except you since you became visible?"

"You are aware of Sutton."

"That's different. I have been aware of him since he was born, in some uneasy fashion I cannot explain. From the first time I looked upon his baby countenance, he seemed to view me with distrust."

Sarah Belle smiled. "Then it's about time for a change, isn't it?"

"We shall see. I would welcome it. Perhaps when the six of us are at a single table, Sérénité will get close enough to impress Sutton. I will be close enough that he will at least tender me verbal recognition."

"I see no table, Justin. What do you mean?"

"I have a surprise for you and did not intend giving it away just yet. I think—I hope—you will be happy with the arrangement—and with me."

He looked at her, not quite sure of himself. She waited.

"After the performance at the harp and a few toasts at the punch bowl, we will repair to a small ballroom on this floor where we will dine lightly and dance lively . . . and dance . . . and dance."

He looked at her appealingly, and she smiled. He was encouraged. She was relieved that she had been so right in her planning with Hudson—her certainty that there would be dining and dancing.

Suddenly the harp sounded, like a presence too long in abeyance—a flash of fingers up and down the strings, faster and faster, a crescendo of chording and into lively improvisation that could have been titled "Moods of Amelia." Sutton had removed his tailcoat and, seated at the harp under the baldachin canopy, with the satin waistcoat, full shirt sleeves, and fitted dark pants complementing form and movement, he was the perfect figure of musical mastery and idyllic romance. He finished with a flourish, stood and bowed as his applauding audience called out their delight. Then he faced in Madame Vahnia's direction and, with all the aplomb of an appointed master of ceremonies, announced:

"Ladies and gentlemen, the central figure of our gathering, my teacher and collaborator, to whom I tender every office of respect and gratitude—Madame Vahnia!" Again there was applause. "She has generously agreed to perform with me here. Since this is a private wedding party for our beloved cousin Amelia Férreo and her fortunate choice of mate Homère Bienville, we will present our arrangement of the wedding song Amelia requested. Madame Vahnia."

Justin moved toward the harp with Sarah Belle, but Sutton was quicker, and halfway across the room he was bowing before her, extending his arm and escorting her to the harp. Justin bowed as he released her. Inwardly, he recoiled at Sutton's rudeness toward him and felt a choler that he knew he must control.

Madame Vahnia stood, quiet, composed, gave the audience a brief smile as Sutton spun forth a rhapsodic introduction, then fingered a melodic strain, rising then falling behind her song.

"When love comes your way like a star in your night
Glowing and growing until blinding your sight . . .
When you no longer feel that you're happy and whole
And your body is sheltering but half of a soul
Unless the beloved is close by your side

And filling your heart with ardor and pride . . .
Then it's time for becoming a groom and a bride.

So I sing for you, bride, in your glowing attire,
And I sing for you, groom, while your heart is on fire!"

Homère glanced at Amelia, then smiled broadly at Madame Vahnia.

"I sing for your future, I sing for your past,
I sing for the present that brings you at last
To the feast at Love's table, to the fountain of life,
To the bliss that awaits you as husband and wife.
To the family you harbor in dream and desire

Oh, I sing for you, bride, in your glowing attire,
And I sing for you, groom, while your heart is on fire.

The light of true love I see in your eyes
And the wonder of union that marriage implies . . .
So live in the light with love—rest in the night with love

And in the garden of love
Let harmony bloom for the bride and the groom!"

Sutton, looking at Sarah Belle as she finished, deliberately continued playing, adding passages she had never heard, expressing desire, tenderness, exaltation; so she in repartee spoke lines above his music:

"And in the shadows, the harp played on
Until a dove in the bower told of the dawn."

Sutton was delighted. He raced the strings to a finale, rose, and bowed deeply to Madame Vahnia. The group cheered, and called out for more. He took the singer's hand and led her to the harp, bowing again, then standing nearby.

Before playing she spoke. "The title of this composition is 'Serenade to St. Valentine,' the composer Sutton Lahart, his first composition for the harp. I predict that it will become a ballroom favorite. He wrote a ballad expressing sentiment suitable for the work. He will recite or sing as it pleases him.

As she spoke, she was aware of Sérénité Bienville sitting close to her brother and as near the performers as she could get. Her eyes fixed trancelike on Sutton—they were a strange color, near jade, and the hair that framed the piquant face had a reddish hue like aged Spanish gold. Sutton, by nature intuitively aware of any feminine attention and ready to play on it, if it pleased him, looked straight at Sérénité as he now recited, now sang his ballad. She did not blush or squirm. She paled and was very still, spellbound.

> "She was my love, my Valentine—
> She gave me joy, she gave me life,
> An ecstasy I thought divine
> With promises to be my wife.
>
> But in this world we must beware,
> For jealous eyes may threaten bliss
> With baleful glance to taint the air
> And blemish every sacred kiss."

Sutton's gestures were all for Sérénité, the foil for his *mélodrame*.

> "She broke the bond of our sweet vow—
> We could not praise St. Valentine.
> She sought another to endow
> With favors I had thought were mine."

Sérénité's expressions began to reflect Sutton's affected emotions.

> "But spring was gone and summer waned
> When she so sadly learned the cost
> Of spurning love which she had gained—
> The love her jealous eyes had lost.
>
> But I believed in Valentine,
> And true love now displaces false;
> I praise the saint, an angel's mine,
> And we embrace in lovers' waltz."

Madame Vahnia was engaging the harp in as mesmeric a waltz as Mozart ever devised.

Romeo never did better at Juliet's balcony than Sutton as he approached Sérénité, bowed in adoration, reached out his hand for hers. In hypnotic compliance, she arose as she would have in ballroom setting and became his partner to perform in the small space near the harp while he finished his declaration:

"An angel's mine in dance divine,
    A rosebud lingers in her hair,"

[he glanced at Sarah Belle]

"She has my heart, we'll never part—
    Oh, arms so soft, oh, face so fair!
    An angel's mine in dance divine. Oh, Dance Divine!"

As the harpist executed a short reprise, Sutton took Sérénité through several more turns, then escorted her to a chair, kissing her hand before turning back to Madame Vahnia and the harp. The audience was delighted. There were murmurs behind fans, sly smiles, and glances. "Love at first sight." "What a match!" "Divine indeed!"

Poor Sérénité, Sarah Belle thought.

A clever ruse, but I know where your attention lies, little brother, Justin thought.

"Now Madame Vahnia will favor us with one of her own compositions. A mood sequence entitled 'In the Garden of My Heart,' most suitable for this occasion so full of sentiment for us all." Sutton was indeed taking over. It was his party. He wasn't prepared for Madame Vahnia's additional pronouncement.

"I would like to dedicate my arrangement to our charming host, who has provided this regal instrument and surrounded it with such appropriate splendor. Mr. Justin Lahart, my compliments." She directed a bright smile to Justin and began to play. He moved nearer the harp.

There was nothing casual or undetermined in her performance . . . gathering a bouquet of emotions . . . florals in bloom, beautiful, provocative, enticing . . . petals falling, withering disappointments. Futility, bud and bloom gone. Then hopelessness reversed in slow but accelerating climb to overcoming and rejoicing! The eloquence of love! The warmth of friendship! The wonder of touch-talk . . . the grandeur of the unknown!

The harp and the harpist were one in resonance, sending out an essence of harmony that held the spirit captive for a moment of high rapture, then left off.

It was as if breathing had stopped in the room, then everyone rose and cheered. Justin came close to her side: "You played on the heartstrings of everyone in this room!" They crowded to praise and touch the woman at the harp.

In the background servants were quickly setting up table for the traditional refreshment: large cut-glass punch bowl, gold-banded with matching cups and small gold-plated forks; canapé platters presenting minced clam and cheese browned on sesame wafers, sherried oysters fresh broiled and pierced with toothpicks, ham and turkey in small brown biscuits lined with spiced butter, jellied shrimp on Turkish crackers; trays piled with luscious grape clusters, cherries with stems, pineapple sticks, mint sprigs, and banana slices fluted and lemon-dipped; and a clear crystal bowl filled with pear, mango and melon balls—altogether an assortment to match the Persian rug in delectable color and variety.

The punch bowl held an ice sculpture of a wedding bell and looped around just under the frozen surface was a thin gold chain holding thirty-six gold rings that would become keepsakes for the occasion. As the group moved toward the table, the attendant in charge poured over the ice several cups of a carefully executed recipe using Malayan tea sugared and flavored with brandy and lemon juice. The sculpture was ornamented with this addition of translucent flowing gold. By now all watched carefully as Justin joined the resplendent serving man who with ceremonial graces uncorked the select champagne from Rheims and handed it to Justin to pour immediately over the ice. Justin picked up the ladle, filled two cups for Amelia and Homère, and addressed them:

> "If you were on Olympus
> And the gods of Greece were there,
> They'd bow before your beauty, Cousin,
> And place a garland in your hair.
>
> They'd look upon this man, your groom,
> Pronounce him pure of heart and true,
> A noble man of princely mien
> Approved by them to cherish you.

"As man and wife for all your life—may you be god and goddess to one another with all the verve of maid and lover! Drink! to each other!" They sipped and laughed and kissed, and then Amelia kissed Justin on the cheek. He ladled two more cups. Then one for himself.

"Madame Vahnia and Sutton Lahart."

They came forward. Sutton was impassive in expression. Sarah Belle felt as though she were a partaker in some kind of special communion, and let it be that way. Justin too was serious. He handed them the cups and picked up his own. Sutton at last looked at Justin and they almost touched in feeling, but not quite.

"Madame Vahnia, will you and the bridal couple join me in a toast to Sutton for his significant and highly romantic composition 'Serenade to St. Valentine'?"

Sutton looked surprised and nodded stiffly. Sarah Belle was pleased. Amelia exclaimed, "Cheers! the family genius!"

"Sutton and cousin kin, shall we toast Music and this gallant lovely lady who has so elevated the spirits of us all with the wonder of her gifts?"

Sutton stepped a little closer to Sarah Belle, and supplemented the toast, intentionally indicating that for him and Madame Vahnia there was a private relationship to commemorate. "Indeed, we shall, and for me there has been a special gift that has brought my life from poverty into a whole kingdom of wealth." He touched Amelia's and Homère's glasses and then, almost as an afterthought, turned to Justin.

Amelia raised her glass high: "And to you, merchant prince of New Orleans, architect of family pride, and a positively lovely man, we four toast you for everybody in the room, Justin Lahart!" There were happy shouts of endorsement.

Justin called the parents of the bride and groom to the table to serve by his hand and then passed the ladle to a gaily attired serving woman. The party had begun, trays were being passed. The level of laughter with happy talk and toasting reached higher and higher.

CHAPTER SEVENTEEN

"**J**ustin, what were you trying to do here? Design a paradise?"

"Simply a setting for an evening in paradise—with you."

The party had moved to an adjoining ballroom. At one end was a garden so realistic with trees, vines, florals, and a border of blossoming shrubbery that it appeared rooted and flourishing. There were narrow walks and six tables scattered about, each with place settings for six.

At the other end of the ballroom were the musicians. Their instruments: four violins, two violas, one cello, a silver flute, a harpsichord, and nearby, Sutton's golden harp, the royal guest. On a table in the background were guitars, tambourines, and castanets—also a collection of hard-heeled short boots. The musicians were prepared to play for and upon the moods of those present, their repertoire ranging from the minuet and waltz in the Mozart, Scarlatti, and Chopin style to popular ballroom tempos. They were even ready on cue to fill the room with French and

Spanish rhythms, traditional and free-ranging, as well as comply with the recent faddish mania for the Bohemian polka, dressed up in Paris and hurrying on to New Orleans.

As the party entered, exquisite chamber music was in progress. Justin with the help of his attendants designated tables: the host's table for the bride and groom, Sutton and Madame Vahnia, and Sérénité, its centerpiece miniature sculptures of bride and groom with harpist and instrument; the second table for parents, maid of honor, and best man, centered with a souvenir grouping of six lively violinists with bows in place. The other four tables, festive with garlands, nosegays, and boutonnieres, were free choice for the rest of the party.

The fare offered at the tables, though rich and varied, was not for banqueting but for intermittent-informal dining and refreshment through most of the night. Delicacies offered at the punch bowl were kept available in fresh supply. The rich mixture of coffee and cocoa, almond-flavored and topped with whipped cream; Mocha and Java coffees, Oriental teas, light wines, iced fresh fruit juices—all were at hand.

Justin had remembered some of Amelia's and Sutton's favorite desserts: French pralines with almonds and cherry flavoring added to the cream, brown sugar and butter; napoleons—custard-filled pastry bars, iced and topped with sliced nuts and sugared cherries; and the midnight treat of Eggnog Colbert in which vanilla ice cream was added to the usual eggyolk-milk-nutmeg mixture, with rum and cinnamon achieving an ultimate that ravished taste buds.

Had it not been for Amelia's ceaseless animation and flow of explanations to Homère on New Orleans gustatory delights, the emotions at Justin's table might have surfaced unpleasantly. "Oh, Justin, I was ravenous for Chicken Supreme like this!" she exclaimed, as she tried to tell Homère how it was prepared (pressed chicken meat around a cone of butter, then batter-dipped and fried), taking a mouthful at the same time.

"You have butter on your chin," he laughed and wiped at her chin with his napkin.

Their continued repartee was unnoticed by Sérénité, who only nibbled at a flaky biscuit and sipped at her wine, her eyes wide with sensations unrelated to sound or taste and dreamy with only one image: Sutton.

Sarah Belle with Sutton on one side and Justin on the other was alternately amused, wary, and concerned. Inner voice offered ironic comment: "This is different. Your approach has always been one at a time. At the moment you are shackled. Just be thankful for Sérénité. Be cautious of the cup and the dance. It's been a long time."

When she spoke to Justin in compliment for the gala arrangements, Sutton turned in chagrin to Sérénité with exaggerated interest. When he asked for wine that was not at the table, but soon provided, he was offended when Madame Vahnia declined to share it with him—he offered it to Sérénité telling her he was sure the very grapes of it were plucked for her alone. She thought so too when he touched her glass with his and whispered, "To the jewel in your eyes."

"The musicians are quite accomplished, Justin. Worthy performers aside from ballroom service," Sarah Belle remarked.

"The one at the harpsichord is butchering Giuseppe Scarlatti!" Sutton snapped.

Sarah Belle saw Justin redden and hold back a retort. She caught his eye and smiled. He responded with unexpected verve. "Madame Vahnia, shall we evaluate Giuseppe and his maligned disciple with minuet, Louisiana-style?"

They came out on the ballroom floor holding hands. The musicians saluted them with a stately passage and provided opening tempos. They exchanged bows and curtseys, then with courtly demeanor they began the dignified, graceful movements of the minuet's golden reign in the court of Louis XV. As they emulated the pauses structurally provided for an exchange of compliments, they spoke to each other of Sutton.

"He insulted you! He deserves to be slapped!" . . . "He hates harpsichords, and it reminds him of his piano playing. He was lashing out in frustration. Be charitable." . . . "God help me, it's not easy, when I know the percentage of jealousy in that frustration." . . . "Out of sight, out of mind. When I'm gone, there'll be Sérénité." . . . "He's cruel. He's playing cat with mouse, hoping to irritate you." There were other couples following and mimicking the precise glides and steps of the leaders. "Don't discount those jade green eyes. Sérénité may be the cat and Sutton the bird. She could be the winner." . . . "Anybody who wins Sutton is a loser." . . . "You told me at our first meeting that you loved him." . . . "My love for him, such as it is, is not blind." . . .

The tempo of the music was changing. It left King Louis' royal strictures far behind, crossed the ocean, and in New Orleans recovered some of the lively rusticity of its origins at Poitou centuries before.

Justin bowed low over Madame Vahnia's hand, kissing it, letting his lips linger in pressure against her hand (hoping Sutton was watching) before swinging his partner into the mood that would accelerate in emotion and pace through the festive hours ahead.

Sutton had dutifully brought Sérénité into the dance shortly before intermission, but when partners broke, hurried her to the table, excused himself, and rushed to Madame Vahnia.

"Forgive me, brother, may I claim an escort's privilege?" He placed a hand on Sarah Belle's arm. "If Madame Vahnia will allow me——" He smiled at Justin with feigned courtesy, then with raised eyebrows turned the same expression on her. She merely nodded.

"Sérénité is alone at the table, brother. It would be kind of you to address your attentions to her."

"I shall, and with a different kind of kindness than you have exhibited in leaving her there."

The musicians issued an invitation to Mozart, and the first waltz of many to come was in progress. It was provocative romance in sound imagery; lovers in a gondola gliding along on a moonlit lagoon, lovers embracing in a sheltered bower while the music played on . . . lovers dancing alone under the stars, toward the inevitable kiss, the lovers enchanted with the simple wonder of touching and moving as one in the rhythms of the dance.

Sarah Belle soon realized that Sutton was the best dance partner she had ever had. Waltzing with Lando had been a dreamy delight of youth, with Defender a happy sharing of attunement, with other partners a mixture of lighthearted physical expression and polite compliance. There was with Sutton the exuberance of articulating in movement the very structural pattern of the music as well as the resultant play upon the emotions. She put aside anxieties and gave herself to the dance. Sutton realized this and was happy. . . . She forgot she was dancing with Sutton. She felt an elevated sense of floating, floating and rocking in a pool of music with the pool in a circular motion of its own. And a thought floated in: What would it be like to waltz with John Monroe Sterling? With the thought came his image and infinitely pleasing it was.

. . . Ah! together they would not only dance, they would *be* music!

With a shock she heard Sutton say, "I wish you were not here! I wish to God you had refused to come." His hand that had been against her shoulder in gentle pressure gripped now the shoulder joint so that she felt a streak of pain. She gasped. The evenness of his step was unbroken. His hand was back in place. "Why?" she whispered hoarsely. "Then, by God, I would never have danced with you and been expected to let you go!"

Sarah Belle's rough protest was to herself: "Oh God, help me; I've done it again. I'm not cured. I substituted John for Sutton."

The dance done, Sutton and Sarah Belle stopped and stood like statues, staring at each other. Amelia and Homère rushed to them.

"Madame, with your permission, it is my turn." Sarah Belle was rescued.

Amelia teased: "Don Sutton Lahart, you are not only permitted to dance with me, you are commanded. And when we are done, we shall join the orchestra for fun—you at the harp, and I at the harpsichord." Sutton was diverted.

"I will watch you perform antics at the harpsichord, if you insist, but I will not play the fool and partner it."

"I am the Queen of the Ball, dear cousin, and could banish you from the court for your impertinence. You would not like that, would you? Being shut out from the presence of Madame Vahnia," she gave him a sly look. He frowned darkly.

"When you frown like that, you look so gloomily romantic!"

Sutton grabbed Amelia and took her into several dizzying whirls as the orchestra took the cue and supplied a regular whirlpool of action—first Spanish in style, then modulated into a dreamy flow that suggested unrequited love and passion's plea denied.

In the pause that followed, Amelia kept her hold on Sutton, and Justin reclaimed Madame Vahnia. The musicians presented a series of French madrigals, the love poems sung and styled with music; now the flute alone, then with harpsichord; violins with gentle improvisation here and there. Sutton relented to Amelia's wishes, and gave harp accompaniment, while she performed at the instrument he disdained, selecting poems that were her favorites. The dancers, an entranced audience in motion, were like instrument and poem combined.

Justin drew Sarah Belle apart and to the table in the "garden"; they were alone. He had the chain of rings from the ice sculpture in his pocket. He took it out and carefully selected three rings from the string of thirty-six. He placed one at Amelia's plate and one at Homère's, then left the chain in the center of the table.

"Souvenirs for all," he explained, "but three are special—a small diamond inside the one for the bride, and a pearl for the groom—and for you——" He handed her the ring. In astonishment she saw that, could the ring have been turned wrong side out, there would have been a complete circle of tiny rubies set flush into the gold.

"Justin——!"

"Let me have it."

Startled, she passed it back to him.

"Now let me have your left hand." Sarah Belle wore no rings. "Don't be so startled my dear. Allow me my moment of pretense. Please, your hand."

As though under a spell, she slowly raised her arm and extended her hand. From the moment he touched it, she regretted her compliance. He slipped it on. It fitted perfectly.

"How——"

"Your precious little glove, my darling."

His voice. She quivered in the sensation it aroused.

"Pretend with me, just this evening, dear one, I plead with you. Just this night of music and dance. My heart tells me I will not see you again. But as long as the music plays for us here, we are engaged, promised to each other. Wear the ring for me, each ruby a drop of my heart's blood, and it will have a hard time beating when you are gone. A very hard time."

She couldn't speak. The ring was there, on the hand he held so tightly, and there was no way to reverse what was taking place.

"It is a pretend night, Vahnia. You are pretending, I know not what. Sutton is pretending with Sérénité, trying to conceal his loneliness and hunger for you . . . and there are others, if all were revealed. I have dwelt in dreams very little in my life, and have pretended even less. Will you indulge me in the one great dream of my life?"

She smiled and went back into the dance with him—into the resonant dreamland of the ballroom where love was enthroned in chanting voices and the harmony of strings. Justin began murmuring to her such a stream of possessive adoration that she found the power of it more appealing than she desired. The same magnetism that she had resisted when visiting with him alone was now augmented with his closeness and the cocoon of tonal beauty that encompassed them. The force of his attraction became a current racing from his touch at her shoulder and waist through her body and eliciting a response that she would have avoided had there been a chance for volition. She was aware that he gave some kind of cue to the lead musician that the performance was to continue longer than might have been expected.

He guided her into the garden space again, speaking softly. "You know, dear heart, that back in the old countries where our dances originated, kissing was an intrinsic part of form and movement. And now I claim a privilege from the past—a ceremonial kiss, my beloved, and a betrothal kiss, I am due."

Suddenly, she was pressed close to him with his lips brought to hers in such immediacy and intensity that she seemed to be flung out of herself and into a oneness that was inescapable and ineffable.

There was another and another. And then he simply held her in his arms. . . . The music stopped.

He released her and seated her at their table. They heard tambourines being shaken vigorously.

"That's Amelia," he said quietly. "It's midnight. She wants her Eggnog Colbert." He rang a small bell and waiters appeared with trays of eggnog for the tables.

She sat very still, withdrawn, her glance remote, her lips pale, her countenance without expression. "Do not leave me," he pleaded. "You cannot shut me out. You cannot, you must not, disappear!" He could not suspect how well-fitted was his remark to her thoughts.

She hardly heard him. She had evoked upon herself a complete and sudden exile from dreamland and pretense. She was thinking of Hudson and their intricate plans for escape.

CHAPTER EIGHTEEN

THE DANCE WENT ON with energies renewed, tempos more varied, and spontaneity on a loose tether. The personality of Madame Vahnia switched to that of a Southern belle in full flower with no one but Justin and Sutton aware of the transition. Whereas her partners had been limited to the immediate family of the Lahart and Férreo menfolk, now protocol for guest and escort or host was abandoned. Madame was given a rush matching that of the bride. Justin was too astonished to invade the circle of admirers and Sutton too proud, knowing his outburst merited alienation.

Her partners forgot she was harpist and teacher—her dancing was the perfect complement to steps they indicated or contrived. Her comments made a man feel important and debonair. She laughed not at all but her smile was infectious.

Musicians brought guitars and tambourines into their repertoire and turned to Spanish rhythms: first there was gliding, yearning, dreaming—then the desire, the fervor, staccato stances, excitement, and whirling. Sarah Belle's thoughts were whirling too as she met all the demands of the exhilarating rigid pauses and spinning climaxes.

I've never danced this way before. Will I ever dance this way again? Will I ever care to? Will I ever get away? Do I want to? This is cultural voudou! How do these musicians cast such a spell? Did Marie Laveau supply each one with a hair from a Frenchman's beard and a drop of blood from a Spaniard's toe?

She executed a final twirl as her partner released her, holding the tips of her fingers high while he stood statuesque. She was breathless. He laughed and lavished compliments. In the brief interlude, Justin appeared and claimed her as Amelia and her father led several couples into the orchestra area where they slipped into short boots and picked up castanets.

"On with the fandango!" Daniel Férreo called out.

"The Férreos in action!" Justin explained. "Their Spanish blood is churning. Shall we watch?"

"Shouldn't you be among them, Justin?"

"What Spanish blood I have does not run that hot." He guided Sarah Belle to a seating area and a small divan where they sat side by side. After a moment of attention to the dancers, she turned to him.

"Justin," she took off the ring with the ruby lining and offered it. "It is time now for me to return this ring."

"Must you?" He did not reach for it.

She slipped it into his coat pocket.

"Then I will place it with the glove. Empty glove. Empty ring. Empty heart. . . May I have the next dance?"

"If the music happens to be more akin to reverie than revelry."

"They'll give us something Chopinish now—melancholy and moonlight—respite in preparation for the polka."

"The polka? What is it like?"

"Rowdy. New and rowdy, but all the craze. I'll happily sit it out with you. Then we'll go back to the enchantment of some lovely waltzes—I shall see to it, and later a hearty repast before departure time. Will Sutton escort you home?"

"I think not."

"To your carriage?"

"We shall see——"

Sarah Belle sat very quietly, as though she were tuning her own instrument of inner awareness, watching for a time to repair to the ladies' parlor where the women gathered in luxurious private quarters, not alone for physical comforts, but for tête-à-têtes, fanning, lounging, sipping frosted drinks. She wanted to leave the ballroom floor under a pretext that she could declare openly so that her disappearance would not at once be suspect.

"I wish I could read your thoughts, dear Vahnia. You have been silent so long.". . . The polka was done . . . and the intermission music . . . then the magic of the waltz like a palpable atmosphere filled the room, offering imagery of lovers taking a stroll together, holding hands, swinging along in time with rippling waters, soft winds, and distant songs. Spellbinders were again singing with the music, adding the force of song to seductive rhythm.

"You are like a memory in my arms . . . and I am holding this lost sweetheart, so real, so precious to my touch, and yet removed. . . . The evening is already like an echo sounding through my being, hollow, haunting, and oh, so, so beautiful. The echo keeps saying, 'I love you, Vahnia, whoever, whatever you are—love you, love you, love you.'. . . You have added no words of love to the echo, but there is forever our time of oneness in the garden. In those moments I learned all about love—all about love." For an instant, he transgressed propriety and drew her very close, and then they danced wordlessly and evenly, he in a haze of longing, she in a state of increased clarity, poised for flight— poised and waiting.

Sutton came at the end of the dance, approaching them directly. "Brother, I owe an apology to Madame Vahnia, and I need a word with her privately. Will you excuse us?"

Sarah Belle looked into Justin's flashing eyes. His lips were a straight hard line. She kept looking, willing an exchange of understanding, of relenting, and more, the purpose for which she had come to him, and the memory . . . the memory . . .

His expression softened, and he nodded to her, leaving them alone together.

"Shall we return to the table for refreshment?"

"Not now, Sutton."

"You are chastising me. I should not have hurt you. You should know my feelings by now. I had never really danced until I danced with you tonight. It was almost like—like you were the harp of me. I want you in my arms again tonight for another, and another! and another!! Then, if you insist, I'll take you to your carriage. If you do not intend for me to step beside you and press my claim, I'll search you out. I'll find you. I swear it! You can't deny me! You *won't* deny me! I'll see to it! You'll be mine, all mine!" He grasped her arm in a tight grip, pulled her closer and whispered hoarsely into her ear, "We'll tour the world together . . . we'll go to Paris . . . Venice . . . Prague. . . . We'll dance the lovers' waltz in Vienna."

He stayed in the cigar and whiskey sanctum too long, Sarah Belle was thinking—he's babbling.

The gentlemen's parlor, like the ladies', provided amenities and provender according to gender.

"We'll give concerts together in all the grand capitals of Europe and be housed in the castles of kings and noblemen. We'll seek out the havens of Eros. I'll woo you in Persian splendor and Polynesian paradise. We'll be wed on some unspoiled Grecian isle, the famed Madame Vahnia and the harp master Sutton Lahart . . . Madame Vahnia always, no Sarah Belle ever." He grasped her arm tighter and gave her a sly conspiratorial glance.

Amazed, Sarah Belle was answering him mentally. I can't believe it. You've crashed the barrier. You suspect I might be color-tainted, but you'd provide the ultimate—the marriage bed—that is, from now until the barleycorn wears off.

The polka music started again.

"Damn that polka!" Sutton stormed. "I'll put a stop to it!"

At that moment, Sérénité put a stop to Sutton.

"There you are! You promised me, remember? You'd teach me the polka. Isn't the beat of it thrilling?"

She had him by the arm—she was standing between him and Madame Vahnia. She looked up at him and pierced the resistance in his glance with the sheer hypnotic force of her green eyes. It had been a long time since a woman's eyes had invited so much and long since he had yielded. He was snared.

Sarah Belle took full advantage of the interruption. She saw Flore Férreo going toward the ladies' parlor. She said to Sérénité more than to the dazed Sutton, "Madame Férreo was inquiring of me concerning her daughter's study of the harp. I must speak with her."

She hurried away.

In the enormous spread of the St. Charles Exchange Hotel with its lengthy porticos, spacious galleries, and miles of stairways, the chances for a hasty, unobserved retreat from its precincts were in the range of absurdity—for a lone woman of any status such a venture would prove ignominious and more. In the predawn shadowed light of a descending full moon and the limited range of gas fixtures and lamp posts, it would be dangerous.

For Sarah Belle to leave without detection was dependent on Hudson's detailed arrangements through a network not available to whites. Though the matter relayed was in oral, rather than written, form, it was generally reliable; service rates were flexible, often free, sometimes gold-dusted—also the service reached greater peaks of efficiency when deceit and intrigue were involved. When Sarah Belle had expressed surprise to Hudson at the ease with which he seemed to complete the intricate chain of assistance, he quoted Plato, "Everything that deceives may be said to enchant."

And now, at the moment of entering the ladies' parlor in the hotel ballroom, Sarah Belle remembered, and thought whimsically that she was exchanging the enchantment of the ballroom for the enchantment of deceit. She had already discovered the maid named Astar, and they had acknowledged each other with knowing glances. Now she sought Astar's services to repair a hemline and they retreated to a place apart. As the girl pretended to work at her hem, Sarah Belle handed her two envelopes. "These are for Monsieur Justin Lahart. Wait until he looks about and grows concerned, and deliver them—just be sure I have had time to make my change and be on my way."

"Yes, madame."

"No one is watching. I'll go now."

Astar brought out Sarah Belle's shawl and reticule and led her to a door that opened into a hall, narrow and dimly lit. "At the end you will find the servants' stairway and someone waiting. I wish you a safe journey through the night, madame."

"And you through life, Astar."

She picked up her skirts and ran down the hallway to the door that opened on the landing of a long stretch of stairs. Another serving girl with a big smile and voice of delighted conspiracy was waiting. "Right down the stairs after me, madame, and watch your step." A small point of light beckoned far below. "There is no one about and a small room at the foot is where we make the changes."

Once in the room, the girl assisted Sarah Belle out of her over-skirts and tucked them into a neat pack along with shawl and re-ticule. "This bundle will be in the carriage that takes you home, ma'm," she explained, "and this—this—you must show me how to help you." Puzzled, she held out multifolds of dark-red soft cotton cloth without cut or seam.

Sarah Belle began by pinning one end of the material securely to the right shoulder of her dress, and then with a series of deft manipulations that were like magic to the astonished maid, wrapped throat, shoulders, head, breast, waist, hips, until she was draped from head to slipper soles with only eyes, nose, and one hand visible. The himation fully achieved, she struck a pose as graceful as a fifth century figurine on a Grecian vase. The transition was awesome. The maid gasped.

There was a knock. It was Hudson, and Sarah Belle's time to gasp. He was attired in the himation and sandals of an Athenian orator, replete with white hair and beard and holding a rolled parchment. He wore no head covering, and the soft tan of his skin carried no ethnic label.

After a moment, they both laughed. Then Hudson was directing. "Come with me. We will enter the main floor near the grand staircase, and go out through the front entrance. There is a scattering of drifters from the ballrooms. We will be taken for entertainers or leftovers from a masked ball. To exit at the back would appear strange to the watchmen. At the front, novelty is the expected."

They moved at a moderate pace along their marble pathway. The masking was provocative of a sense of freedom. Friends, walking in trust together, savored the sharing and daring in a personal drama of their own contrivance. They were not reining their pace against urgency as they passed through interior colonnades—here a shadowed space, there a lighted circle—rather, they were extending an experience they would not repeat, and which, without complete disguise, could not have taken place at all.

Any observance of them was casual. They were obviously a couple whose energies had subsided and their departure, strolling at ease with occasional comment to each other, uneventful. Between themselves, however, their dialogue became a distillation of their relationship, and an island of personal exchange not to be revisited.

"Should we not converse as we move along?"

"Indeed we should, madame."

"In this regalia, I do not feel at ease being addressed as 'madame' or calling you 'Hudson'."

"We might use names appropriate to our period costumes."

"What would you suggest?"

"For yourself 'Zantea' perhaps. For me 'Zeuxis'—the spelling always fascinated me."

"Both names are strange to me." Sarah Belle felt a peculiar delight, a sense of escape into another realm, release into another identity.

"Zantea was a story-singer of ancient Arcadia. The lyre was her instrument. Zeuxis was a painter, his realism so great that birds flocked to partake of a grape cluster that he painted."

"Yesterday you quoted Plato. How did you come by this knowledge of the Greeks?"

"I have a library."

"I should have known. Do you paint?"

"Now and then. Do you write lyrics?"

"Occasionally. I left two poems, of a sort, behind tonight."

"For the Lahart brothers?"

"Yes."

"I don't suppose you would quote them for me, Zantea?"

"For you, Zeuxis. For no one else."

Sarah Belle paused a moment as they were passing the George Washington statue at the entrance, remembering the time she had entered here with Justin; then as they moved on down the steps she quoted: "For Justin——

"*Place no watchman over me . . .*
Send no watchman after me . . .
I must be free to be not-free.
If you would find me, truly find,
Seek through the music of the mind.
There is a place of rendezvous,
For you and me, for me and you . . .
Just venture out of time and space

And I will meet you face to face;
There'll be communion, friend to friend,
For shared transcendence has no end."

They had descended to the portico with its long row of stately Corinthian columns—they were alone in its lengthy expanse moving in and out of the pillared shadows, their appearance so appropriate to the setting, touched by lingering moonlight, they might have been ghosts from the fifth century B.C. misguided into trespassing on a facade of the future.

"He will abide by your desire. His regard for you is a pure flame—a worthy man, almost worthy of you."

"What do you mean, Zeuxis—almost?"

"The unanswerable question, Zantea. And what was your poetic admonition to the transient musician?"

Before descending the long tier of open steps leading to the grounds, they paused by a majestic column and leaned against the marble balustrade, so completely alone in the eerie fading glow of moonlight and the hazy blue flickers of gas lights that they felt world-removed, capsuled in a floating sort of unity, vibrant, fragile.

After a pause in which their breathing had seemed suspended, Sarah Belle gave a small sigh and quoted in answer to his question, her voice so softly distant that he had to lean closer to hear:

"Give Genius Spirit half a chance—
The Self within will sing and dance.
The ones you touch with music's wand
Will dream new dreams—will wake, respond
With Hope for now and Light beyond—
For Music builds a bridge, the span
From common clay to Magna-Man."

"The goddess of music should bestow favors for those words. As for Sutton, I'm sure he would have liked something entirely different from you."

Hudson's use of Sutton's given name, standing alone, came into Sarah Belle's mind like the tinkle of a very small freedom bell, and she felt warm and pleased and continued her confidence.

"When I wrote the lines for the two of them, I thought Justin would be the one most likely to pursue beyond this evening's affair. Now———"

"It is the other one who refuses to let go."

"Yes, but he will hesitate. It will not be soon, perhaps not at all."

"He will seek you out. He will be back."

A very human sound jarred them into the blunt reality of their place and presence. A man was running full speed down the portico toward them.

Sarah Belle froze. Could it possibly be Sutton? He had been so very drunk. Justin would not have given him her letter this soon, if he delivered it at all. But he could have missed her and now be in a frenzy trying to locate the carriage that might be bearing her away. Hudson drew close and placed his arm around her waist, and whispered, "We are lovers caught up in the magic of the night. Ignore him. If he stops, keep your face averted. I will be provoked."

She shivered and leaned against him.

The runner stopped. "Oh, for God's sake excuse me." He was breathing hard. "But have you seen anybody . . . *anybody* . . . a lovely woman alone, most likely . . . along here . . . out there . . . ," he waved over the handrail, "or maybe with her footman . . . I hope . . . she shouldn't be alone . . . shouldn't be . . ." Justin was gasping for breath.

Sarah Belle moved against Hudson. His arm tightened.

"Why, no, sir, no one at all. We have been alone here for some moments, sir, saying farewell to the beauty of the night."

"Yes, yes, I . . . beg pardon . . ." He turned from them, ran back up the portico toward the entrance, stumbling and swaying a little, then stopped to lean over the balusters. They heard a sound from him. Was it a sob or retching?

Sarah Belle gasped in sympathetic response and pushed against Hudson. He took his arm from her waist but remained close and instructed, "We must not hurry away. I see several other couples strolling out. We will converse a while longer."

"He may need help."

"He has recovered and is moving away. Tell me something. Did you quote *all* the poem you wrote for Monsieur Justin?"

Sarah Belle made no haste with her answer, then replied, "All that I prepared for his reading. Why do you think there was more?"

"Zantea would have been more expressive of the heart's alliances."

"I suspect that Zantea sang freely upon the air. All that I sing is not sung in voice or even transcribed."

"I see."

"You often see with the inner eye, Zeuxis." And why, Sarah Belle inquired of herself, did she have the urge to quote those four lines that she had deleted? Probably because she wished now that they had been included. So she spoke them aloud more for the heartsick man who was moving away from her than in response to the man at her side.

> *"The heart's refrain for you and me*
> *A song unsung must ever be*
> *For 'tis not categoried here*
> *On this restricted little sphere."*

Hudson's silence was so weighted, Sarah Belle realized too late her ineptness. He moved so that he was no longer touching her and murmured with an edge to his voice she had never heard. "Too bad for him. He missed the best part. We will go now."

A young coachman was in place on the driver's seat with the team readied. The carriage was not one that Hudson had ever provided for her tours over the city and countryside. It was a one-seater of commonplace design but well cushioned and equipped with lamps up front and a small sidelight in the passenger compartment. Hudson helped Sarah Belle inside and then was seated beside her. The coachman set the team to a moderate pace, as instructed. His two passengers occupied themselves a while seeking comfort and compromise with their disguises. Sarah Belle, twisting and turning about, unwound the himation until it was draped about her like a long shawl. Hudson removed wig and beard. Sarah Belle was combing her hair back with her fingers and shaking her head to get it in place over her shoulders. The coach lamp was just above her head and she was unaware of the romantic frame its mellow light formed over her face and hair. However, she soon sensed that Hudson was unnaturally still beside her and his gaze strong upon her. She turned and smiled, then purposely broke the spell.

"Hudson, even without wig and beard, you still look very much the philosopher."

"If Zantea looked as you look now, the Olympian gods must have vied for her favors."

"The other day I was reading the *Times* and noted under the 'Quote for the Day' a passage that reminded me of you: 'A faithful friend is a strong defense; and he that hath found such a one hath found a treasure.' I forget the source."

"Ecclesiasticus."

"Hmmm—tell me about your library and you will be telling me of yourself."

Hudson sighed audibly. He had no relish for opening the door of himself any further to this woman. Simply by talking about what made him as he was would strengthen the ties between them which for him already were too tight for comfort. But he answered in a voice dulled by longings and denials.

"It has been almost a century in the making, beginning with an ancestor who brought a few treasured volumes when he fled from Jamaica to New Orleans during a rebellion of slaves and freedmen. My forefather, like the history of that island, was a blend of Spanish, African, British, and a few drops of the Asiatic. His mating here was French-mulatto—all have remained nonslave and part-free. Books have been their greater freedom. I have not been to Europe, but friends and relatives going there continue to augment my collection."

He paused. Sarah Belle was silent. Then he continued, as though speaking in the abstract, talking to himself. "Aeschylus said centuries ago, 'Destiny waiteth alike for them that men call free and by others mastered.' And now and then Destiny bestows a gem upon us in this life. Such a gem has been given me tonight. I have walked beside you. I have touched you. I sit beside you now."

There was no further word spoken between them for the rest of the drive to the House of Recovery. But the silence was resonant with understanding and acceptance:

You know and I would not hide it that I am committed to the very
roots of my being and there is entwinement between our lives that
will never be torn apart. *Hudson.*

I love you with an affection that stretches the boundaries of
friendship but does not go beyond. I would leap over them gladly
if the feeling were the same as I have for John—or, I must say
honestly, if my feeling for you matched yours for me all the way.
And I'll tell you something further—if there were no John, if I
hadn't come to realize the oneness in which we are caught up,
and I were to select between you and Justin—at this moment you
call your "gem"—I would select you. *Sarah Belle.*

His hand rested on the cushion between them. She reached
over and covered it with hers. Her hand remained there, like a
covering over his mind and spirit, transmitting the unique dimensions of their relationship. There was no movement of either hand
until the linkage was broken when the carriage stopped.

When they stepped down from the carriage there was the faintest dawn in the east. Shealia had lights burning and was waiting at
the door. The sheen of Sarah Belle's satin underdress partially covered by the dark red shawl of the himation cloth was a blend of
dawn-dark and rising sun. Hudson stood tall, the bright yellow
himation still draped about him and a scroll in his hand; grave of
countenance, he still looked the part of a Greek scholar.

Sarah Belle said simply, "Good night and day, Zeuxis. Did you
hear the applause of the invisibles for our drama?"

"Most certainly, Zantea. The sound of it was deafening, our
success assured. The denouement on the portico held them
breathless . . . I submit this scroll as an epilogue. I pray Zantea
may give the words writ upon it immortality with her lyre."

"It will surely give her a song to sing, Zeuxis, that will keep
fresh the memory of this night. Adieu."

"Bonne nuit."

He stood watching until she reached the doorway. As he turned
away, she called to him, "Hudson, I must see you soon to discuss a
very distressing condition about a man named Emile——"

"I know the story, madame. I know about Emile."

"Oh—oh, I see. That should be very helpful."

"I hope so. At your service, madame."

In the expanding glow of the coming day, they each stood in silence, their thoughts turned from themselves, caught up for a moment in the Emile calamity.

Hudson was the first to move. He turned quickly to the carriage and mounted to the driver's seat, pushing the sleeping youth aside and setting the horses to a fast clip.

CHAPTER NINETEEN

D EAR JOHN,
Your instructions concerning the "Web of Passion"
have been followed. Watching the sheets curl and
burn, sitting in the chair where you had sat, I became an observer at a
funeral pyre in which the flames were feasting on sensitivities other than
yours and mine. What relationships followed in the wake of Vasco's return taunt the imagination with visual tenacity and repulsion. I could
wish your "City of Gold" pilgrimage were simply a fantasy of horror,
but I accept the reality of it as I accept the reality of your having been
here in my house—and the reality behind the image of you plunging into
the inner sanctum of my thoughts while I exercise no desire and little will
to dismiss you.

This is much more than a letter—it is a tablet of information. I have
come as near being shattered over recent events as I think I ever shall be.
I feel compelled to share the matter with you before we meet again for I
cannot predict what condition my household may be in when you arrive.
The House of Recovery is committed to an arrangement from which it

may not easily recover, at least to its accustomed state of insularity. The account I enclose reveals a state of unhinged passion so extreme that a free woman sells herself as a slave in a macabre plot of revenge. You will agree with me, I think, that the New Orleans "jungle" is a fair match for the wilderness of the Orinoco as a stage setting for lovers in ultimate travail. There is something weirdly fascinating in the alliteration of the words "Guaharibos" and "quadroons."

At this point, John, stop and read about the triangular tragedy of Emile, Suzanne, and Stephanie as I have set it down for you separately, and then follow me through an enlargement of the story to include another victim of the self-sale.

I had thought I might step aside from the whole affair in spite of Marie's determination to involve me. Her concern that the deprivation of Emile's manhood might be a permanent affliction was in my opinion misplaced guilt. She gives undue credit to the power of her potion and too little to the power of Suzanne's intent to slay and consume all but the physical shadow of Emile. Regardless, the situation was made more personal for me by Hudson Recoire, my coachman, trusted messenger, and friend—a gifted and charitable man of the gens de couleur libres. I was amazed to discover that Hudson knew more of the bizarre drama than had come to me through Marie Laveau. He and I visited in my garden where Marie had sought my attention. He enlarged on the cast and the scope of the play, not yet into the final act. As a result, I find myself on stage in a major role, untutored and unrehearsed, and no prompter backstage.

The other victim sealed into the cycle of tragedy with Emile was his slave, Maury, who had been attending him on that fatal wedding night.

Maury had grown up with Emile and had been legally consigned to him by Emile's father, binding them into man-servant status for life. Emile was a gentle master. When Maury and a free maid-of-color, who was hired as a seamstress for the Nicée household, were carrying a lovers' cross because wedlock was forbidden between slave and free-born, Emile promised a solution: when he married with a household of his own, he would free Maury so that he could legally wed the little seamstress, and they could together serve his family if they desired. Maury's happiness was soaring on his master's wedding night because freedom and love's consummation were close at hand. Instead he must witness the awful revelation that sent his beloved Emile tumbling and screaming down the grand staircase at the St. Charles Exchange Hotel. Not only was his dream of freedom and plan for mated love shattered, but he was incarcerated in the Charity Hospital to care for Emile. His exile from the Nicée family and his own relatives was complete. The Nicées made an endowment to the hospital for permanent residence of the two inmates and they were to be considered without family connections of any kind.

Hudson, because of his own charities to the hospital and concern for the ones brought there, was allowed to go into the lunatic quarters and visit with the desolate Maury and his deranged master.

I asked him about Emile. Was he dangerous? Did he try to take his own life?

"The hospital lists his condition as 'Lunacy, in extremis,'" Hudson replied. "So far he is harmless—pays little attention to Maury or to the Sisters of Mercy attending their needs. He eats little, but Maury gets bits of food down him when he has exhausted himself talking and walking round and round his cell."

"What does he talk about?" I inquired.

"His 'moon maiden' and the man 'up there' who abducted her from his arms. He is a monumental example of 'moon madness' from which the word 'luna-tic' derives and the connection is rather literal for him— the night on which he made his exit from the St. Charles, Maury carrying him, was full moon and Maury says he kept screaming, 'She's up there—take me up there!' and gesturing to the moon."

I don't know, John, whether it is that Hudson and I are Thespians by nature, or whether it is our limited freedom that makes us so; his restrictions of caste and ethnic derivation, mine simply as a female of the species and a married woman sans husband. Anyway, his description of the Emile-Maury condition as he had observed it brought us together in a plot with a denouement most uncertain.

"That is Emile's obsession," Hudson explained. "All that is left of his mind. He and his true love had soared to the moon in their rapture when they were torn apart, and this man in the moon pushed him off and he went rolling down, down into a dark pit and he must find his way back, back to Suzanne who wants him, calls to him, cries for him. Stephanie is erased from his mind—the only name he seems to know is 'Suzanne.' Maury says when the moon is very bright with its radiance close to full or just after peaking, his lunacy accelerates."

Hudson spared me no details. "Sometimes Emile becomes frantic," he said, "weeps and flings himself about, saying over and over, 'She crooned to me, she crooned to me and said it was our last night, there'd never be another. How did she know? There has to be another! When the moon is bright again, get me to the moon, Maury, for God's sake, get me to the moon!' Then Maury, who is a big man and has shielded Emile like an older brother, weeps too, takes the fragile Emile in his arms, and promises over and over to take him there. I witnessed the spectacle: 'I promises, I promises, baby brother, I get you to the moon, I get you to the moon, by and by, sure nuff.'" Hudson spoke almost in a whisper and stopped as if witnessing the scene again.

I asked him how he contained himself. He said he did not. He wept with them. He said that Maury was ill and that soon his mind, too, would be affected. Hudson did not believe that Emile would die as soon as his caretakers expected, that eventually there would be two mad men and they would go together. Hudson should indeed have been an actor. He can draw a listener up tight into his own emotions.

I spoke to him for building such a scene in my mind and knowing his purpose for doing so: "Can you tell me out of your sane mind what you and I could possibly do to relieve such an impossible entanglement of deranged man and ghastly series of events?"

"Nothing is impossible, madame," he said quietly, "if heart and mind unite in the purpose."

I recalled that Marie had said practically the same thing when I scoffed at the idea of Suzanne being able to place herself on the market as a slave.

Now I felt as if I were having a nightmare in which I had been pirated onto a market platform where Marie and Hudson were the bidders, with Emile, Maury, and the maid Celeste the helpless sacrificials. Should I attempt an escape?

(I will interject right here that I was sold and the nightmare continues.)

But more of the details of the sale . . . There was a weighted silence between Hudson and me after his challenging aphorism. I knew that we could sit for hours before he would suggest to me any move that we might make. The decision and the action to follow would have to be made verbal by me.

First, I explained to him that I knew nothing of Maury's plight— Marie had spoken only of Emile—and that I had been bereft of any ideas for an approach to the solution she seemed to expect of me. My conscience seemed to demand no more of me than that I pass the sorry tale along to him.

My conscience and Marie's are not very well acquainted. Yet mine, in Hudson's presence and with the expanded version roiling in my emotions, plunged me right into the eye of the hurricane. I heard myself asking: "Could Maury's freedom be achieved if he and Emile were out of the hospital, in your custody, and concealed here in the private quarters by the craft shop?"

His response was instant. "I can get them out of the hospital. Those in charge will be glad to be rid of them if I give proper writ of responsibility and assurance of secrecy. Also, Maury is legally registered as Emile's property and I can secure formal writ of release by guiding Emile's signature on the paper. No questions asked if a gold piece of the appropriate size accompanies the request."

"What about Celeste?" I inquired.

"She left the Nicées when Maury was taken away with Emile. I know where she is. She grieves for Maury as if he were dead."

"Then you have my permission to bring the three of them here. I'll arrange quarters," I instructed briskly, at the same time doubting my own sanity. "You can advise me about procedures. I'm . . . at your service," I concluded, mimicking a bit the phrase he so often uses with me.

He found it difficult to speak. "Madame . . . madame . . ." His eyes sought mine for some kind of release from his own inner struggle, "About Emile . . . madame . . ."

"We'll speak of him more when he is here," I said. "Don't worry about Emile—and——" I sensed his concern for my welfare, now that he had me enlisted in the cause. "Don't worry about me. I'm a convert to your credo, so let 'mind and heart unite' to save Maury as well as Emile." There was a slight edge to my statement. He gave me a look that I could not fathom, bowed, and left quickly.

I was totally unprepared for the next episode. The gate had hardly closed behind him before I faced the severity of practicalities. Shealia had heard every word spoken by my two visitors in the arbor—nothing unusual because I have never forbidden this, even found it useful.

She pounced, came close to me, and exploded in rage.

"That voudou devil got you spelled! That madman Hudson put spell on too. He belong lock up with loonies at Charity! My God say, 'flee from evil'! You bring devil-demons here, I flee! Fana flee! Maybe we burn down roofs before go—bring down God-fire on devil-works!"

She moaned and gnashed her teeth in unbelievable convulsions. I realized that she equated lunatics with demons—you know: 'without mind, without God.' I had to get physical control of her—she extended her hands toward me like claws, made hoarse sounds in her throat like an animal, and seemed ready to attack me. My gentle, loyal, trusty Shealia. There had always been affection and mutual need between us. The very premises are willed to her and Fanaalis in case of my demise. I couldn't carry out my impulsive agreement with Hudson without them. I resorted to physical measures. I grabbed her arms, pinned them to her sides, pushed her out along the path, then suddenly shoved her into the lily pond. She is almost childlike in stature and I felt like a bully. I waded in, pulled her out and placed her in a sitting position on the rock ledge of the pool. I pushed her long black hair from her face and sat down beside her. I explained as best I could the essence of demons and the Lord's admonition to "fear not." I had no response from her except shrill sputterings and maledictions with an Oriental tinge—something from her Jamaican origins that I'd never heard before. She rolled her black eyes around in their pools of white gloss that made her look more witchy than Marie could ever have looked, and surely as demonic as her fearsome imaginings. I tried another tack.

"Shhh!" I almost whispered. "I have a secret that I've kept from you." I began gesturing. "These roofs that you would burn are your forever home—should I go to live in far places, even as far as the shores of heaven, all this would belong to you and Fanaalis. More than servants, you're my friends, my family." She was silent. She heard me, but would not speak. She began to shiver. I helped her to her quarters, and, reversing our positions, waited upon her with dry clothes, broth, and brandy.

Fanaalis had been watching and now stood by. I said to him: "Let's wait until the sick guest and the two we would rescue from wretchedness are with us. And then, if you and Shealia must go in fear, I'll not delay you."

She was soon about her duties again but averted her gaze from me, spoke no word, just nodded or shook her head when addressed.

So much for that hurdle. . . . I had only begun. I'll skip now and move on to the most critical, for THEY ARE HERE! When they arrived, Emile was near comatose and carried to his bed in Maury's arms. Shortly after, Celeste arrived with her parents and their minister. Fanaalis uneasily watched over the inert Emile while Shealia hid out. I would not let the ceremony be too commonplace. Celeste came in a pretty white dress. I made a garland of rosebuds for her hair, and Hudson had provided a white suit for Maury. I served an ambrosial wine and angel cake, and then a driver from Hudson's carriage service appeared to take them in a fine coach to a honeymoon abode for a day and night while Hudson stood watch over Emile assisted by a reluctant Fanaalis. For some reason Hudson asked that I not look in upon Emile until Maury and Celeste were in charge. Emile had been placed in a small airy sun-room, its only door opening into the area where his watchful attendants would keep house and sleep when his condition allowed.

The very next day when I went outside to search for Shealia and instruct her about a trip to the market for provisions, who would you suppose I found waiting by the garden gate? Of course—and, most unusual for a person of her demeanor, with an expression of dejection close to fear. I had no word for her until she asked, "How is he?"

"With your divining powers, you should know, Marie."

"I do, madame."

"Then why ask me?"

"I still think you can save him, if——"

"If what?"

"If you attend him yourself."

"You have wooed my services with the best of your mind and tongue to the point of audacity, and by virtue of this, the man has sanctuary and care. Sanity has forsaken him, and the breath of life is nearly drained out, yet you are shameless enough to ask that I——"

"Yes, madame, I am that—shameless. I use my mind and my tongue to get things done . . . and sometimes . . . sometimes just my heart . . . and then my God stands ashamed . . ."

"Marie! If your God——" I couldn't reply to such complexity. She stood before me, head bowed. "Marie! the arts you claim to—the powers—why aren't you busy with your magic for healing Emile? This God that gives you power, doesn't he care about your distress over Emile?"

"He cares not about Emile but he cares about the Eternal **He** in Himself. Oh, madame, it is hard to pass this to a mind such as yours. If Emile dies, my god falls me down and I am done . . . I am done . . ." I knew she wept.

"Marie, I wish you could realize that it is Suzanne who drew the man power from Emile and brought him to this pass, not you! Nothing you could brew up could be as powerful as the words she spoke over and over again to Emile when she had him in condition for eternal imprint. Surely, you know about that age-old residue of power some women can bring forth, not only to destroy manhood but to make of a man a bonded carrier of the thoughts she implants at the right moment."

She raised her head and looked at me through wet lashes with the same inscrutable gaze she had given me on our first meeting, and it touched a strange spark of response in me. It was as if something were settled between us in her favor, and I felt a need to even the score.

"Marie, I make no promises about becoming a bedside attendant to Emile—I have not even seen him yet and do not know when I shall. I shall follow my conscience in directing the care he receives. In return for this task, which you have deliberately placed upon me, I ask of you that never again shall a gris-gris of any kind be placed upon this house or any part of these premises—and this applies whether or not I am in residence here."

"I promise, madame, upon all that is in your heart and mine." And would you believe it, John, she crossed herself in pure Catholic tradition? And then she topped it off by adding, "I go now to pray at the altar where Emile has prayed," turned away quickly and was gone. I sensed that this was no new premise or conversion from voudou, just a simple equation that two Gods are better than one.

Of course, Shealia was listening as I well knew when I so firmly pronounced the request of no more gris-gris. She came forth with her market basket—did not look at me or smile as she usually does, but did speak, "I go now." And that was enough for me to sigh with relief.

Are you weary with all this? There is one more episode, a most strange coincidence I would set down—coincidences are always labeled strange. Are they just strange, or is there something in sequential order but unrevealed within the intricate patterns of our life designs?

I had not yet looked in on Emile, even some days after Maury and Celeste had taken over. Marie had initiated a tugging between us that I felt inclined to resist. But events took the matter out of my hands. Maury had told me that Emile's condition remained almost the same as when he arrived. A few teaspoons of liquid nourishment was all that he would swallow in a day's time. He remained prone most of the time and would not retain a sitting position more than a few moments when propped up.

Then one night Shealia rushed to my bedside with a lantern and told me Celeste had come to her weeping, that Emile lay dying. I grabbed my dressing gown and rushed out. It was a clear night, the moon was in the last phase of the first quarter and intensely bright. The light that bathed Emile's bed, exposed to a wide window, was spectacular, awesome, and the candles in their brackets were like gold moths within a blue-white flame.

Emile lay on his back, his head pillowed, his hands crossed on his chest. His eyes were wide and glazed. I could not see any motion of breathing or blinking of the eyes. Was it the stare of death already in residence? Celeste and Maury stood holding hands and weeping quietly. Shealia had disappeared and Fanaalis was a shadow in the doorway.

I sat on the bedside, took a limp hand in mine and felt for a pulse. Had I imagined a very faint tremor under the cool corded wrist? I reached for the vein along the neck and my fingers again suggested that the blood flow was not altogether stilled. Then I unbuttoned his night shirt and placed my hand over his heart. At first nothing, and then the skin seemed to warm under my hand. I realized that the response was a warmth that could not come from lifeless tissue. Then came a slight trembling that resolved into a feeble throb. I removed my hand, buttoned his shirt and told them, "There is still life." I instructed Fanaalis to bring me a small amount of brandy and honey slightly warmed, Maury to heat stove lids as quickly as possible, and Celeste to demand of Shealia her warmest wool blanket and bring it to me at once. I began briskly to massage Emile's hands and had Maury doing the same with his feet. As soon as the lids were hot, they were wrapped and placed at his feet, between his shoulders and at the small of his back. Though the night was bland I tucked the wool covering tight about him. I rubbed his cheeks, jaws, and forehead trying for animation. As my disheveled hair swept over his face time and again, the eyes began to lose their glaze. With Maury's help, the lips and teeth were parted and the warm honey and brandy spooned in. He swallowed! Leaning over him, my hands tight on his shoulders, my eyes fixed on his, I tried to will his survival. Why did I do this, when by the best reasoning Emile and all concerned would be better off if he were released into spirit? Yes—all but Marie, my senses responded belligerently! Was I trying to save him for Marie's sake? Was she pushing and urging me in some way beyond my control? Perish the thought! I was doing it because saving a life is spiritual intoxicant. Come on, Emile, live! Live! Live! I shook him gently, tried to push him into his weak senses with my strong ones. I made it. His eyes blinked, his lips softened, trembled, and he whispered—whispered clearly so that we all heard it—"Suzanne! My Suzanne! Blue. Blue. You wore blue for me. Blue in the moonlight is . . . is . . ."

An aberration, I thought, as he allowed us to administer the rest of the "potion." I was seated on the edge of the bed. He became drowsy and seemed asleep. I made a move to get up, and quick as a snake strikes (this figure of speech dedicated to dear Marie!) my hand was clinched in his with a grip of steel. "Suzanne!" and the voice was strong. Incredible! But not as much so as the action Maury took. "Massa!" he screamed, "Don't you know you got moon fever! Let go Suzanne or she catch it and she drop dead at your feet, right now!" Emile cringed away from me and started weeping. I left with "moon-fever" nonetheless. My hand was red and aching.

Emile is revived, taking sustenance, talking moon-talk again by the hour, but with a difference. He remembers Suzanne's visit—when the moon comes bright enough he is certain she will find him again—then he will be strong—he will be successful in recovering her, keeping her in his arms. Shealia mixes her strongest sleeping draught to keep him quiet at night.

The **coincidence**: Emile's calling me "Suzanne" was not an aberration—more like a mistake in identity that might have been made by a normal mind. Maury came to me before I had breakfast the next morning, deeply disturbed, anxiety etched on his face, and his posture draped in fatigue.

"Missus, I not sleep a wink all night long. I got to tell you something like a rock on my heart since I lay eyes on you." He swallowed and rubbed his thumbs against his fingers, seeking words and composure.

I waited. His eyes fixed on a spot just above my head somewhere. I knew he prayed. His distress touched me physically. I felt my heart pick up its pace. His gaze seemed locked in space. I must break through.

"Maury, look at me! And speak up!"

He looked at me—rolled his eyes back to the spot on the wall and gasped, "Missus, you th' spittin' image of Suzanne!"

It was my turn to gasp and I almost said "I'd rather be dead than——" but I didn't. And you know why, John? I thought of you. And I thought: this shock is minor to the one John faced. Then I thought: I may see John again. I could take a lot more just for the possibility of seeing John again. I began to pull the details from Maury. I had read accounts of doubles and look-alikes, and I, like many others, have seen strangers who strongly resembled persons I knew, but the enormity of the "double" implication had never entered my mind. I'll confess I probed for the differences!

Maury had often been in Suzanne's presence, for he was the messenger, the only one, between Emile and Suzanne. In my mind, I tried to place us side by side as I built up the comparisons through his agonized search for words and imagery. In features and bodily form we were surely close to duplicate, but I was the taller and "more filled out" he called it, and more active in my "get about." Long brown hair with gold glints and eyes "much gray and little green" appeared identical. He tried for poesy in differentiation: "She more like a delicate flower" (flower with a thorny strength concealed in the stamen, I thought!). And what was I like, I queried. He struggled for equality of compliment but what came out made me feel like a species of sturdy flora, ever-blooming perhaps but not so easily damaged as my counterpart, the delicate one.

Another difference that I combed from him is one that I cherish. His answers to my questions on complexions were hazy and cautious, but I have arrived at definitions. Her skin was "pearly" and she could pass for white. Mine has a natural tint of tan, and I could pass for octoroon or more. This adds color to the coincidence, does it not? The color blue added another touch that enlivened the scene of my meeting with Emile. I recalled Emile's exclamation that Suzanne was wearing blue for him—why was this, I asked Maury. Suzanne often wore blue, a color pleasing to Emile. My dressing gown was blue! Thus expanding the coincidence to absurdity or presenting a finesse of creative intent in human patterning beyond comprehension.

And then I had a revelation—a shock that went through me like a streak of fire. Marie Laveau! She knew about the duality. She had seen us both. She had begged me to care for Emile personally, and thus the sight of Suzanne II would restore his senses and surely his manhood! And she concealed this truth from me until I was in a position of no retreat. . . . And trailing this revelation came Hudson, my trusted friend, confidant, partner in charity. He knew the hazards and had at the other extreme kept me from Emile until Maury and Celeste were in charge. But why did he not tell me, prepare me? I've yet to fathom this. Not knowing of Marie's request to me for personal bedside attentions, he might not have expected Emile to arouse at the resemblance and I would not be burdened with the knowledge. Thus one exonerates one's friends while holding accountable those who conspire with more directness.

You advised me that you would come to New Orleans before Palenque if it were right for me. Indeed it is right for me, if you still consider it right for you after reading about this "sorry tale" unfolding at the House of Recovery. Let me know regarding the time of your journey that I may be supported by expectations. Upon your arrival in the city, you will have no difficulty locating Hudson Recoire's Carriage and Livery Service. Inquire of him in person and he will drive you to my place, as I will have notified.

As I conclude this account, I feel somewhat wicked with spite at the something *that* dared to stamp Suzanne and me from the same mold. Excuse this bit of vulgar verse:

> "I may not be a lily white,
> Or dainty daisy in the dell,
> But I'll put to flight
> This dismal plight
> As sure as Hate is Hell."

Sarah Belle

CHAPTER TWENTY

MAURY'S WIFE CELESTE was as delicate and fast moving in body as the fine stitches she made with her thin flying needle. She had become a key note in the harmony that reigned at the House of Recovery by the third week after Emile had been carried over its threshold. Her skin was light brown velvet—her expressive brown eyes, like her hair, had golden specks and glints. She wore her abundant ringlets piled high and secured with a wide circular band of gold-tinted metal, giving her the appearance of a dignified child playing queen. She dressed in garments toned like cream and garden greens and pomegranate skins. She liked wearing a white rose at her bosom.

After the first few days her acceptance was unanimous in the household. Shealia could not be jealous of such a sweet nature, even though Celeste spent many hours with Sarah Belle alone, taking care of the sewing pertinent to them all. Her work in the sewing room and in the kitchen gave the older woman more time for her beloved crafts and her herb garden. The most unexpected result of her presence was the effect on Emile. Still not able to walk, he now was often placed in a chair by the wide window where the view into the yard offered a diversion of movement, although he might not be responsive to the beauty. Birds, squirrels, bees, and butterflies were constantly expressive of their delight in the abundance of foliage, color, fragrance, that was their provision and shelter here.

Celeste was the only one from whom Emile would take nourishment unprotesting, even manifesting now and then a preference for certain items on the tray. She chatted to him quietly about a bird that fluttered near or a squirrel that looked in at them with curiosity. She placed feeders in close view to attract the feathered and the furry, that she might more naturally call his attention to the outside. There was little response to encourage her. Occasionally his head would turn but there were no words, and his eyes were blank. She would always announce herself when she brought food or came to help Maury attend his needs.

"Here is Celeste, Emile, bringing you good things," or "Here is Celeste, Emile, to give you and Maury a hand." She would sometimes get personal, hoping to bring a spark of attention. "It's so good, Emile, to be Maury's wife and your good friend. Celeste is a lucky woman." And one time when she and Maury were tucking Emile into bed and Celeste had given him Shealia's herbal tea, she dared to say: "We love you, Emile. I am a part of your Maury now. We love you." No response from Emile, but when Maury looked at her, tears were rolling down his cheeks; he reached for Celeste and held her tight.

During this period, there had been no bright moonlight to arouse Emile, and his memory of "Suzanne's" visit became blurry. The fall weather was rainy, foggy, sometimes stormy. Sunshine was elusive, diffused. Weeping willows bent to the ground in simulated grief. Roses dropped their petals. Birds saved their throaty songs for the rare periods when the sun broke through.

Emile's flow of panic talk had ceased. His communication came now and then through sometimes feeble, frantic, and tearful inquiries: "Where is the moon? Has the man in the moon ravished my Suzanne? Is it dark up there? . . . Why can't I find Suzanne? . . . Why can't I see in the dark? . . . Is Suzanne a slave? . . . Did

I buy Suzanne? . . . Did I sell Suzanne? Oh God, who bought Suzanne? Can I buy her back? Is there a mart on the moon?" And then one night piercing screams brought Maury and Celeste in a panic to his side—Shealia and Fanaalis had heard and clutched each other in fear. Even Sarah Belle had been jerked awake with the scream that struck like a pain between her breasts and was thrust out through the top of her head.

Emile was sitting upright in the bed, beating the covers with his fists, his eyes wide and crazed: "You emptied me, Suzanne. I am not here! You took me—you took me hidden inside you to that murky moon! Bring me back! Bring me back!! Bring me back!!!" he shrieked until he was exhausted and fell back on his pillows, breathing in gasps, his eyes closed. Celeste and Maury stroked his hands and his forehead, immersed him in comforting, soothing sounds and words. Maury said, "Hope Miss Sarah didn't hear."

"She did hear," Sarah Belle responded in the doorway. "Feel his pulse."

"He's breathing easier," Maury said. "A nightmare stomping on him, missus. He be all right. You go rest."

Knowing how alarmed Shealia and Fanaalis would be, she stopped by their window. "It was just a bad dream," she said. "You might feel better if you went to the kitchen and made chocolate for yourselves and for me." She had no reply. For a moment, she wondered if they had fled the premises in terror. "You are awake, aren't you?"

Shealia's voice, hoarse with fright and sanctified wrath against evil forces, rasped out, "As devil-man is awake in this place, as demons scream to wake graves open, I am awake and fling myself in front of God."

"Very well. Then I will fling myself into the kitchen in front of the grate and make the chocolate myself while you revel in your own nightmare and Emile sleeps his off."

As she expected, Shealia was in the kitchen before the shavings on the grate were ablaze and Fanaalis was in the living room laying a small midnight fire. Later, as she sat alone sipping her chocolate, she began to ask herself some questions, thinking wryly: there are some advantages in an escape from sanity, yet in both states, there are nightmares, and in both states we lose ourselves.

Where is Defender I wonder? When I think of him there is a

link as fine as a single strand of silk; time and tragedy do not sever it. It was spun from the joy-tone that attracted us to each other. This love is forever silent, but through the link I know that he is still alive. But where? And how does he fare? When I know, if I ever do, will I feel released from my demanding conscience? If the marriage bond were dissolved, would I still feel bonded to the betrayal that catapulted him from my life, making such sudden carnage of his devotion? . . . How long must I carry this on, throwing myself in sacrificial penance upon the stone in his heart where the pulse of an ardent love once throbbed?

Yet, there is a change in my direction. John has effected it. What I did for John I did as much for myself as for him. What I am doing for Emile and Maury has nothing to do with a schedule of penance. I did it for Hudson, and in spite of resistance, for Marie—and yes, for myself, for the satisfaction of rendering aid that I alone could offer. And now where am I? The head of a household of five dependents, none here for recovery alone, all in permanent custody. What will John think of all this? Dear John . . . and why are you so important to me? There are so many dimensions to attraction—to love—to need. Ah! Am I about to become a dependent? That will never do. Yet, this restless churning for his presence, and the wait so long—weeks for an exchange of messages—weeks of travel on his journey here. Will he really come? When? . . .

She went to her desk and picked up Hudson's scroll to read again what he had lettered there. She felt it would reflect something of her own mood.

THE MYSTERIES OF LIFE

The Mysteries of Life move and have their being,
Gaunt shadows in the mist of mind,
Extensions of some giant scheme of things.
When Light breaks through here and there,
Shapes flicker and form, shiny, beckoning, offering wings
For a flight to Freedom's spaces,
For a sight of Freedom's faces;
But in the time of dream-span, they are gone
And the light becomes a burning.
I thirst and press a dew-spread leaf upon my tongue.
I hunger and the mystery yields me nectar drop by drop.

I feel the pang of spirit's deprivation,
The life-thrust stripped of all elation.
I smother in a silence of rejection
Until I dare to breathe the essence of my Source
And reach to touch that which I thought was lost—
To touch and find the mystery soft and vibrant on my skin—
Soft as Hope . . .
Vibrant as Love . . .
Bearing the scent of Freedom, offering Peace within.

She went back to line eleven and repeated aloud: "I hunger and the mystery yields me nectar drop by drop."

She left the room and went to her harp. As she activated the strings, she whispered to them: "For John . . . for dear, dear John Monroe Sterling . . . what a singing name it is for me . . . what a singing name . . ."

The words she first whispered, then softly sang:

"I sing for the part of my life
        that is named John Monroe Sterling.
I sing from the heart of my life
        that I claimed was my own;
But I am half of a whole, I am part of a soul
That was mated and fated
From eons before, on some mystical shore,
In a timeless span before woman and man
        were in flesh and in bone.
The eternal clue for me and for you
        was wrought in a song . . .
I sing it now and it tells me somehow
That all will come round, the key will be found
        though time is so long.
Oh John . . . John Monroe Sterling,
        'I hunger and the mystery yields me nectar drop by drop!'"

Neptune roared and flung his trident about in wrathful display. Over New Orleans lightning flashed in dangerous white and jagged lines of fire. Storm winds roused to shake down flimsy dwellings and fling them about, to twist and fragment trees, and to turn gardens into rags. Boats were flung about like toys in a malicious game that ripped sails and waterlogged cargoes, broke open dikes, played a drum of death and destruction. It was not the worst blast from the sea that the Crescent City had endured but it was left bogged and drooping.

At the House of Recovery the process of restoration was set in motion under a hazy sun with a chilling breeze that deepened despondency at the sight of trees and plants with broken limbs and shattered blossoms. The dripping fern arbors in the yard were like teardrops amplified. Birds and poultry were silent. There were no sounds in the neighborhood of dogs barking or roosters crowing.

Sarah Belle and Shealia made no comment to each other as she brought morning coffee to the bedroom without the usual fruit and pastry, then left. Sarah Belle wrapped a large shawl about her shoulders and sat by the window viewing the wreckage in the yard as she sipped the stronger than usual black potion. Suddenly, her door was flung open and Celeste burst in, garments and hair dripping, feet bare. She rushed to Sarah Belle, fell to her knees, and, in a surge of emotion, grasped Sarah Belle's knees and hid her face. She's panicked, Sarah Belle thought, and then Celeste looked up. The eyes were wide open with an expression that was no less than ecstatic, and the lips were trembling in an effort to find words to fit the expression.

"Celeste, what has come over you? What has happened?"

Celeste seemed to choke and then a whispered blast. "It was a baby squirrel, missus, a baby squirrel!" She grasped Sarah Belle's knees tighter and began to cry.

"What about a squirrel?"

"It was . . . out . . . outside . . . by the window . . . so little . . . so still . . . so still . . . just wet . . . like drowned . . . like drowned . . . and it . . . and he . . . and he . . . ," she sobbed.

"He——? Who are you talking about?"

"He . . . he . . ."

Sarah Belle reached down and loosened Celeste's hands and held them in her own.

"Yes, Celeste?"

"Emile!" The words began to tumble, the eyes pools of joy. "Maury and I sat by him during the storm. He was dead quiet as if nothing happen. Then the dawn came and still we sat and watched, oh so sad. And then he—Emile—he called me, he said 'Celeste!' just like that. Maury and I couldn't move for a minute. Then he called my name again and said, 'Look!' And I looked and saw the baby squirrel. But I didn't say anything. I wanted him to say something else. And he said, 'Look!' again like he was mad at me. And I said, 'Look at what?' He said 'That. Squirrel. Get it.' I didn't answer, and he said, 'Get it!' again, and . . . and . . ." she laughed . . . "and I got it. I rushed out and got it in a towel and brought it back and put it on his lap. It was not dead. Emile didn't look at me, just at the squirrel. He said, 'Feed it.' I got some milk and fed it with my finger. He watched me. He sits there now just holding it and looking at it. Hasn't said another word. Just looks at it." Celeste put her head in Sarah Belle's lap and cried until she was quiet. Shealia was watching from the doorway. She returned with more coffee, strengthened with the froth of egg and brandy. Sarah Belle pulled Celeste to her feet, seated her, and they both drank.

"It must not die," Sarah Belle declared positively.

"Oh, no, missus. Die it cannot! It causes Emile to act alive."

"Yes, it could. But it must be prevented."

"It still shivers, missus," and Celeste herself began to shiver at the image of the dead squirrel in Emile's lap.

"Go right now and talk with Shealia. She knows many of nature's secrets, and she will tell you how to keep it warm but not too warm, how to feed but not too much, how to make a proper nest for it."

"What if Emile will not let go of it?"

"There is no need for him to. The nest can be in a small box he can hold or even have beside him on the bed."

"Oh, yes, yes, missus! I must hurry, hurry, before——" She gulped the rest of her drink, and left the room on such swift silent feet that for a moment Sarah Belle felt reality desert her, then she was filled with an urgency to make haste and join in the work of repair and restoration.

Celeste had filled the room with such an aura of pure elation that to Sarah Belle it was almost palpable; she could even imagine the fragrance of it as she dressed. She found herself hurrying and short of breath, buttons eluding her shaky fingers as if in overanticipation of something akin to rapture, while she quoted to herself the closing lines from Hudson's scroll.

"I dare to breathe the essence of my Source
And reach to touch that which I thought was lost—

To touch and find the mystery soft and vibrant on my skin—
Soft as Hope . . .
Vibrant as Love . . .
Bearing the scent of Freedom, offering Peace within."

CHAPTER TWENTY-ONE

S ARAH BELLE HAD BEEN WAITING impatiently for a
letter from John. More than six weeks had gone
by since she had written, and this was a bit past
the minimal time for postal exchange between New York and New
Orleans—that is, when wind and waves, starlight and storm, and
the stamina of drivers and steeds were in the best correlation.

Another day for hope's renewal brought her to the door watching for Hudson to appear on horseback with the bundle of papers
and mail-order packets he would bring from the post office. The
storm's devastation had made many of the city streets impassable
for vehicles. But now sunshine and an ocean breeze were offering
restitution.

She was waiting on the steps as he came up the walk with his
saddle bags. "Come in, Hudson, come in. There may be matter in
the mail that I will want to share with you."

The relationship between her and Hudson had taken on a more
personal aspect, though he maintained his usual formality in

speech and demeanor. His frequent inquiries and assistance brought to her household an added sense of security and comfort. Though it was never discussed, Sarah Belle understood his feeling of responsibility for those whose freedom he had secured through her provision of sanctuary.

He took special pleasure in supplying attractive raiment for all three and replenishing the stock of foodstuffs with unexpected delicacies and fresh meats. Sarah Belle shared his delight in these things, and Celeste became more and more the object of their attention and love. Her dedication to Emile and her report on every little episode of the squirrel's survival and Emile's attentions to it were related in sparkling descriptions.

"I have named it 'Jasper'!"

"This morning Emile said 'Jasper.' Isn't it wonderful?"

"Jasper turned a somersault! Emile smiled!"

"Jasper leaped to Emile's shoulder! He reached up and touched the frisky little tail, and closed his eyes in pleasure!"

Sarah Belle placed the stack of mail on her secretary and began to go through it. She handed Hudson a *London Journal*. "You may want to look at this." She saw the corner of an envelope, held her breath a moment and pulled it out. . . . It was from Houston, not New York, a letter from William Moellhausen. She said a prayerful "Oh God!", sighed, and reached for the letter opener. Its contents were bulky. Certainly, it contained something about Defender, perhaps some kind of declaration by him in response to her letter.

"Word from William," she said to Hudson, somehow glad that he was there, that she wouldn't be alone as she crossed some kind of threshold in her mind and emotions. William had been gone for several months and this was the first word from him. She had not been disturbed, knowing that William would not consider it proper to write until he had something important to say. She pulled out the folds, remarking more to herself than to Hudson, "We'll see how it is with William, and Houston—and Defender. . . . Here's a clipping of the ad I had him place in the *Texas Register*, rather conspicuous, bold black type and black border, rather funereal." She reviewed it, saying a phrase now and then under her breath, like a ritual in preparation for what she would read in the letter to come.

REWARD IN GRATITUDE AND GOLD FOR INFORMATION LEADING TO
THE WHEREABOUTS OF MR. DEFENDER LOCKE, SOUTHERN GENTLE-
MAN OF IMPECCABLE CHARACTER. TALL, WELL-PROPORTIONED FIG-
URE AND PATRICIAN FEATURES, DARK HAIR AND BEARD, BEST IDEN-
TIFICATION ONE EYE BLUE AND THE OTHER BROWN. PLEASE NOTIFY.

WILLIAM MOELLHAUSEN

BOOT AND HARNESS SHOP

HOUSTON

"William's script is very small and spacing frugal; the other is in an ornate handwriting much larger—certainly not from Defender." She carefully separated the two and read . . .

William's Letter

Dear Madam:

Your advertisement which I have kept in the *Register* since I set up my shop has brought the enclosed response from a most reliable gentleman, Hervey A. Adams, Esq. He refused any compensation for his information. He came here from Ohio in 1837 and I have heard it that he is a descendant of the presidential line. He built the first frame houses in the Houston settlement and was soon a contractor much in demand. I reside in a part of one of his sturdy structures. My business prospers, and I have substantial savings on your division of the profits. I have found here, as you said I might, a German Union, and have become a member. It was formed six years ago by Mr. George Fisher whose name was Faber when, in his youth, he made a daring escape from Hungary to the United States. I have never met a man so learned.

Sarah Belle caught her breath, glanced over at the bookshelf where the travel books of John Lloyd Stephens were kept. "It must be the same one," she said.

Hudson looked up from the journal she had handed him.

"William mentions a person that reminds me of something I have read," she said without answering his look of inquiry and continued her reading.

He knows international law, and he speaks thirteen languages. He early inquired about the ad and assured me that if he ever met up with such a man, or heard of him, living or dead, he would let me know.

Because of Mr. Adams's revelation and because of the good supply of gold I have on hand, through your benevolence, for travel and the hiring of services, I will be able to pursue more diligently the commission you expected of me. Being a newcomer, and having no aptness in matters of search along forest trails and frontiers, I am going directly to my friend Mr. Fisher, who now resides in Austin. Since the recent annexation of the Republic of Texas to the United States, he has been called to an important position in the General Land Office. He has long been a naturalized citizen of both Mexico and the U.S. As soon as I have conferred with him on the matter of locating Defender Locke (who has probably changed his name) and delivering your letter, you will hear from me again.

Jeanie is the same wonderful woman that you brought to my arms. We wish you all Health and Happiness. We look upon you as our Deliverer who snatched us from the Claws of Satan and the Mouth of Hell.

Consider me always your obedient servant,
William Moellhausen

Without comment Sarah Belle passed William's letter to Hudson and began on the Adams document.

The Adams Letter
Dear Madam:

May this account which I am pleased to set down for you be of some assistance or solace in your search for one Defender Locke. I owe him a debt of gratitude that could never be repaid, so extreme were the conditions, so praiseworthy his act of humanity. I will recount the events leading up to our meeting. It happened in the winter of 1842–43, a season so severe that horses sometimes froze to death at their posts. Mexico was a hostile neighbor to the Republic of Texas. Invaders had taken San Antonio. Fifty-five volunteers from my home county rode out to challenge General Woll and and he slaughtered them all. More volunteers rode to San Antonio and I was among them. With General Somervell commanding, we followed Woll back to Mexico. When we turned homeward from Laredo we were in sad condition. We had to divide into small units and shift for ourselves in order to survive. There were five in my group and twelve in another that traveled near us. We starved and struggled through river bogs—we chewed on rawhide—we tried to eat hawk soup. Game was poor and scarce. But one evening at camping time, two men in the other group got a scrawny little deer for supper. The wind blew the odor of cooking meat our way. We knew we would not be invited to share their meager sustenance. It is hard to set down on paper just what it was like. Wet, cold, desperate December, brutal hunger . . . crazed with the scent of the meat flung into a campfire—wild, sweet, juicy meat. Some would be eating it raw and bloody. It became unbearable. My four companions pleaded with me to go over and beg for just a few morsels. I resisted, but since I was much their elder, they thought I could make a better case. One man sobbed. My own hunger and that sound sent me stumbling to the other camp. I was more than unwelcome—they hated the sight of me. I told them our agreement was made in expediency, that humanity overrides expediency. I explained we were too weak even to hunt for ourselves. They railed at me, cursed me, ordered me back to my own fire. I kept begging for just a few mouthfuls to chew on. I told them I was asking for more than meat. I was asking for the gift of life. . . . One became vicious and threatened to attack me. I reminded them that we were men, not animals, and that whether we died in feather beds or starved in the wilderness, we each had a soul, a heart self. My tirade only aroused sarcasm. One who was sucking on the heart of the kill, gurgled, "My heart bleeds for you!" I couldn't stop, the strong odors from the meat seemed to drive me out of my mind. I was preaching to the world about how no people, no country could survive without kindness—*nothing* could *live* without kindness. Then I found myself weeping convulsively, in the same condition as the man at our camp. Suddenly there was a plop at my feet, and there lay the head of the deer. I looked up at the man who had been holding the deer's head, stared into his eyes. *One eye was brown and fierce with hunger and anger—the other was blue and seemed to hold a guarded kindness.* I picked up the head and tried to thank him. "Get out!" he commanded, and I knew if I didn't run, one of the others would grab it from me. I kept thanking him and God as I went thrashing through the brush back to my comrades. I also carried with me a memory to be forever fresh of the man with the brown eye and the blue eye, not knowing his name was *Defender Locke* until I saw your advertisement in the *Register*.

Mr. Moellhausen is pursuing a wise course in contacting George Fisher. No man knows this whole region, its multiracial settlers and unpredictable politics as he does. When he pursues matters, large or small, his intensity and competence leave no margin for failure.

I hope that in outlining this wartime experience in the torturous brush country of South Texas I have somehow done a service to you and the soldier gentleman with the compassionate blue eye.

I am most respectfully yours,
Hervey A. Adams

Not until Hudson was gone did Sarah Belle take down the popular book of John Lloyd Stephens, *Incidents of Travel in Yucatán,* and turn to his description of George Fisher. Stephens had met Fisher at a boarding house in Mérida, Yucatán, that autumn of 1841.

"Just five years ago," Sarah Belle murmured, in wonderment that her life and thoughts were being shaped by the intertwining of such distant events and personages of heroic stature.

"The arrival of the schooner of war 'San Antonio,' from Texas, brought among us a citizen of the world, or at least a great part of it, Mr. George Fisher."

She read on through several pages about this *"citizen of so many republics . . . but his feelings were all Texian . . ."* Although Fisher was first a citizen of the United States and had established family connections in Mississippi, he had spent some years in Mexico, prior to the Texas Revolution.

This was the man who would assist in the search for Defender Locke. So grand was the design of coincidence bringing him into the affairs of her heart that climactic changes in her life seemed inevitable. . . . The Adams and William letters . . . her tightening and demanding attachment to John Monroe Sterling. She continued reading:

"We parted with him in Mérida, and the next that we heard of him was of his being in a situation quite as strange as any he had ever been in before."

Near the conclusion of the lengthy volume she found an account of the situation: *"Island of Cozumel . . . Rancho established by the Pirate Molas . . . Mr. George Fisher."*

"Island of Cozumel" . . . How musical and mysterious the sound. She hastened to read Stephens's account of his visit to this island off the northeast coast of Yucatán and George Fisher's involvement. Natives had called it "The Island of Swallows." Its crumbling temple towers of stone had been the wonder of early Spanish explorers. Sarah Belle studied the Catherwood engravings showing where Stephens's canoa *El Sol* was anchored in the small bay with sails furled . . . and in the background the thatched-roof buildings that had been home to a pirate and family. The solitude, the towering coconut trees and forest wilderness, the intimacy, the invitation to fantasy were all caught in the Catherwood sketch and augmented through Stephens's descriptions. She could see the detail of a hammock and swallows in mystic flight. And what of George Fisher? He had visited the island—had purchased six leagues, or eighteen miles, of it, conducted surveys and set up crosses, envisioning a grand enterprise that would make this lovely isle known to the commercial world.

Sarah Belle felt an affinity for the place and a premonition of connection with her future. Perhaps she and John would go there from Palenque—probably they would——.

Sarah Belle closed her eyes, envisioned herself swinging in the hammock and became lost in a dream of this Island of Swallows. Waves along the shoreline of Miguel Bay lapped gently in metric precision. A late moon shimmering over the waters picked up the remnants of an ancient stone structure almost hidden at the edge of the clearing. . . . And who was standing in statuesque outline at the highest point of the temple ruins as though sighting into the future? Was it George Fisher? In her dream, she reached to a hammock by her side and called, "John, John, wake up and look at the figure there on the temple tower. Who is it? So strange for this place. His sword is flashing and he carries a buckler, like some crusader of old. John! John! Are you there?" The hammock was empty. She shouted, "John!"

Shealia's hand was on her shoulder. "Ma'am, you dream. Wake! I am Shealia. You are here."

"Yes, yes. Shealia. I'm all right. For some reason, I dropped off."

"It is past your meal. You have weary. Stay and the tray will be soon."

She returned to the open book on her lap. Why was her heart beating so fast? She chided herself: Are you thinking George Fisher might sell you a parcel for a House of Recovery on Cozumel? Pirates are passé. Ranchers of dubious intent have fled. Liberated Indians have scattered to mainland jungles. She laughed aloud. But more sober thoughts followed—thoughts about her own liberation. Would she ever leave this house until somehow released from her emotional and legal bondage to Defender Locke? Had she yet put aside her self-imposed "mission"?

She realized more fully than ever that her Southern plantation rearing had been farther from the basic realities of life than an existence on the Island of Cozumel or amidst the ruins of Palenque might be. And were the ruins there because a civilization had built these fabled kingdoms with slave labor, hierarchies of class distinction that invited decadence?

And what of the "fabled kingdom" in which she resided—the Magic Crescent with its bulging slave-based economy and its lofty claim of being "an incubator of the strongest civilization on earth." What payment would be required of it at the toll-gates of Destiny? . . . and more personally, what would be the penalty upon herself for the confinement she had practiced in its precincts for several years? How could she indulge in dreaming of John and Palenque and in fantasizing romantic episodes on the Island of Cozumel!

And the realism of the present: Emile and his attendants and their dependence upon her presence and instruction. Emile was much improved physically, could occasionally walk about slowly, even into the garden now and then with Maury and Celeste in attendance—and Jasper. Every moment the squirrel must be in his sight or at his touch. His vocabulary was meager and his occasional assembly of phrases garbled. His only expressions of clarity related to Jasper and Celeste. Maury was somebody he had named Subrio. Fanaalis and Shealia were no more than objects that moved about in blurred imagery that required no attention. Sarah Belle had looked in on him only when he slept or from her window when he was brought out onto the garden path.

And sometimes she struggled with herself to be sure she achieved an identity entirely separate from that of the woman housed in a nunnery attending another woman destroyed in revenge. At the harp, more than any other time, she felt a creative self emerge that proved a sustaining differential.

One week after her letters from Houston, Sarah Belle was rushing to the door again to greet Hudson. She had heard a carriage coming that she recognized as one of his, and again the surge of hope for word from John, this time more than a hope—a compulsive desire that it must be coming to her hand this day. She would not open the door and rush out to meet Hudson. She would close her eyes, still herself with the thought of deep pleasure to come, opening the letter, reading, reading . . . communing.

She heard him coming up the walk—up the steps. She was shaking—how foolish.

She flung open the door. "Good morning Hu——" Merciful God! She faced a stranger! Cap in hand, portmanteau at his side, hair untrimmed about his ears, long sideburns . . . She closed her eyes, speechless, her heart thumping, "John!"

She opened her eyes. He too was speechless, gazing at her as if she were the stranger sight. And then she realized the image that was before him, the non-Suzanne person, her hair tight and in a knot on her head, large ear loops, a full skirt, saffron in color, and a low-cut loose blouse of a lighter color, thin gold bracelets on her arms; and around her neck, close to her bosom, in a tightly woven cage of golden threads, a large piece of jade peeped through. He looked at her face, skin more tan than olive, then at the peculiar ornament she wore. He whispered, "Can it be you?"

Tears rolled down her cheeks as they had at their first meeting in the park. There was a difference. The blush was not there. Tears made little streaks through the face powder.

"May I come in? I have made so many enemies out of stagecoach drivers and river pilots that I need a refuge."

She stepped back for him to enter. Her lips trembled in a salty smile.

CHAPTER TWENTY-TWO

THEY WERE STANDING before the fireplace . . . he had not laid aside his woolen topcoat, damp with the mist of a chilly November day. He reached into a deep pocket and pulled out a little roll of white cotton rags.

"Dr. Sterling is fresh out of fresh handkerchiefs, but when traveling he always carries an emergency kit for bandages or other unexpected needs." He peeled off one and said, "Look here." She had not faced him since coming into the room, until now. He carefully wiped her cheeks. "Especially useful on colored tears."

She turned from him, then spoke in a low voice. "I have long been disdainful of the soft type of Southern woman who cultivates tears and fainting to escape emotional trauma. But if you touch me again, I think I shall faint."

He chuckled. "How cheering! You boost my spirits. Now move aside while I build up the fire a bit. I presume you do not want to call your servant."

"You are right as well as presumptuous."

He removed his coat and waited for her to be seated, then took a chair beside her. In silence they gazed into the flames that timidly appeared from under the kindling, then began leaping into flashing dance.

"Would you mind releasing your hair from that tight knot so that I can be sure you are you?"

She pulled out several heavy pins and let it fall but made no attempt to arrange it, was relieved that it fell about her cheeks and might veil her expression.

"Thank you." He pushed his hand through his own hair in a self-conscious gesture for it had grown thick and unruly during his long journey.

He is not as much at ease in my presence as he pretends, she thought, herself seeking composure.

"I promise a careful trim before long—that is, if the accommodations once offered are still at hand."

"Never more so, and for any length of time."

After another period of silence, he inquired, "Why the disguise?"

"Emile."

"Emile? Of course, removed through your rescue mission from his web of passion before he could be completely devoured. Your revealing letter, the 'sorry tale,' as you called it, is exactly why I am here in person. Emile mistook you for his quadroon because you look alike."

"You must have read my lengthy account of the whole affair in great haste."

"Yes, indeed, and I have continued in great haste until this very moment, and now I have great concern."

"Suzanne and I are not *look-alikes*, we are *doubles*—'spittin' image,' Maury called it. I related this to you."

"Maury would have been very excitable, hence possibly very inaccurate after the episode with Emile that you described."

"I chose to think not. I have lived through this. And I would remind you that Suzanne was very white, and favored pastels. It is ironical, isn't it, that to look different from her, I must look more like a true quadroon than she did. Emile is now able to be walked about a bit—and sometime there might be another emergency that would bring me to his side."

"And all this time, you have garbed yourself like this against that possibility. Outrageous!"

"You do not like to look at me like this? Is regard measured in color of cloth and make-up and hair fashion?"

"If you intend for me to avoid touching you, do not challenge me."

For the first time since the shock of finding him at her door, Sarah Belle genuinely smiled—inside. And she felt in charge. She stood up and briskly flung her hair over her shoulders.

"I'm sure you would like to freshen up. I'll tell Fanaalis you are here and he will be right with you. Shealia and I will prepare something special for the weary traveler and we will dine together here."

"You are glad I came?" There was an urgency in the question that she relished.

"Very glad, Mr. John Monroe Sterling. Very glad." A long look passed between them and she was the first to hasten away.

Seven hundred miles away in the General Land Office at Austin, Texas, William Moellhausen visited with the Keeper of the Spanish Records and State Translator, George Fisher. The young man marveled anew at the stalwart, picturesque figure of this man-of-the-world old enough to be his father, yet vital enough to quicken the pulse of any woman who might evoke the searchlight penetration of his glance. And the gallant appearance of him: a dash of the cosmopolite from his European heritage, the manners of a Southern gentleman, which he had absorbed at his Mississippi homesite, a streak of Mexican bravado which he found useful, all this animated with an intense patriotic fervor for Texas. One time William heard a Houston official remark that if George Fisher should be offered a halo by a heavenly host, he would accept it only if it were shaped like a map of Texas.

He quizzed William about Sarah Belle Locke with the same acumen that styled his service as an Associate Justice in the courts of Harris County.

"It would take a playwright of incredible genius to contrive a scene such as you have described to me, William, in the rescue of yourself and your heart's choice from the clutches of a depraved father. . . . And this woman, this heroine of such fearless performance, tell me more about her. She took you to her place, you say, and seemed to be the householder, no man about, only two servants. Was her residence lavish, impressive?"

"Oh no, sir, quite modest, but gracious in aspect, beautiful yard and garden, all rather tightly enclosed, you might say."

"You feel quite sure she lived alone?"

"Quite. I could not say exactly why, but I am sure. She was so much in charge, you might say."

"Is her place one of those cottages along the ramparts—you know the ones I mean."

"Oh no, sir. It's located on Phillipa Street."

"I know New Orleans like the palm of my hand. Phillipa Street—not far from—well, I would say a section not so bad, and yet not so good for a woman living alone. Would you say she might be a woman of questionable status?"

"Oh, definitely not, sir, very much the lady—in my eyes."

"You are too young to judge all the subtleties of women, yet we will give some credence to that, and yet——. Hmmm—her name is Sarah Belle Locke, and she wants to locate a Defender Locke. If this man were her brother or father, the ad would have been worded differently and she would likely have signed her name instead of using your name. Would you guess from her appearance and manners that she might have been reared in a Southern plantation style of life?"

"From what I have heard of traditions, yes, sir, that could be."

"The gold she has so liberally placed at your disposal for this search indicates no shortage of that most basic of legal trade. At this point, we will not surmise on how she came by this security, but if it had been family heritage she would likely have been at a different location."

George Fisher wandered to a window and watched a large flock of robins fluttering and wobbling about eating berries from a pyracantha bush. "They are migrating south," he said, "and have stopped by for a drunken spree on the grounds as they do annually, influenced I suppose by the political climate round about——. I have a hunch, William, formed with such sensible order that we shall give it first rank in our procedure. I happen to know of a Locke plantation in southern Mississippi, not far from the Louisiana line. I am going to assume that this Sarah Belle and Defender are related to this plantation family, that they are man and wife, that something came between them—quite possibly a clandestine lover, and Defender was no longer in a mood to 'defend her,'" he quipped. "So he has done what many under similar circumstances have done—gone West, or more particularly, 'gone to Texas,' refuge of the unruly and disenchanted."

William listened in wonderment as Fisher continued with his deductions. "Mr. Locke is not the only man in creation whose eyes are different in coloration. The oddity is such that both legend and literature have given it attention. It has been noted that there is one characteristic in common with those so endowed. They are passionate in attachment and conviction, and have a record of disappearing if they believe their consecration to the idealistic has been violated. And when they surface, they usually have made a 90-degree turn in their way of life. I would venture that we will find this man in circumstances where one would not expect to find the 'Southern gentleman of impeccable character.' He will have changed his name, the 'patrician features' will be well hidden behind as much hair as his countenance will provide, and 'impeccable' will fit no discernible aspect of his appearance or condition."

"He will be hard to find," William remarked, depressed with the prospects of such a manhunt. "He may not even be in Texas."

"If not, he will be in easy reach of our borders."

"How could you know?"

"There is a kind that comes and goes, and there is a kind that remains in this region of retreat."

"What is the difference?" William wanted to inquire, but felt hesitant before such a positive statement.

"Now I come to the part that saddens me, William. I cannot personally engage in the fascinating game of tracking this man to his hideout. And it will be a hideout. We are a State of Texas now, a certain stability reigns. Defender Locke will no longer be in action as a soldier of fortune. He will have——" He was silent for a meditative moment. . . . "He will have found another self——" He chuckled. "Sarah Belle Locke will be in for a surprise, have no doubt of it."

"But if you can't lend your knowledge to this matter personally——"

"My knowledge, yes—my person, no, much as it would delight

me to place that letter you have with you in the hands of Defender Locke and be able to deliver his reply to your patron in person at the house of seclusion on Phillipa Street. But, never before have I been so bound to a job at such a strategic time in history. I'm the one who translated the State Constitution and the Ordinance of Annexation into Spanish. Now I'm the sole keeper of the enormous volume of Spanish records and state translator of papers and letters received during European negotiations with the Republic. I can't tell you how I feel about Texas. She's like some giant-size spiritual mother, demanding my unswerving loyalty and all the services I'm equipped to render her."

"What am I to do?"

"Have no misgivings. I have a proxy. He is due to arrive here from Matamoros any day now. His name is José de Claración, a gifted writer and linguist, responsive to the novelties of these times, and hot for adventure. I became his mentor when editor and publisher in 1834 of my Mexican liberal newspaper, opposing from Matamoros the nefarious power thrust of Santa Anna. This was just prior to the Texas revolt.

"José's mother was an opera singer from Madrid who fell in love with a famous anthropologist while on concert in Mexico City. I think José must have sprung from his mother's womb fully equipped to espouse liberal causes, riding to Adventure's piping, wearing a charm against hindrance and harm to his person. He loves the elations of escape and pursuit, especially when there's gold in the reckoning, either for his pen or his pocket. Yet he believes that the purest gold is in romance, and he is still seeking that virgin goddess worthy of his heights."

Pleased with his poetic delineation of José de Claración, Fisher turned to the spellbound William and inquired, "Would you like for José to carry the letter of your Lady Benefactor on his person as he searches, rather than return to you or me to report on his discovery?"

"Most certainly, sir. Most certainly." William was warmed and happy that such men of action (and romantic quality, suitable for his valorous sponsor) had come to his aid. "I carry gold adequate for his travels and payment for his services, which I will also leave for your transfer to him. You do feel certain he will be free for such a venture?"

"Free is José's perpetual state. Anything he undertakes is of his own will. He's coming to see me, seeking assignments worthy of his marksmanship in human affairs. Rest easy. As for the gold, keep it in custody until the affair is done. José prefers to envision the rewards ahead, the fruit of pursuit, you might call it."

The setting in which Sarah Belle and John dined together was like a shift of scenery and costume in a suspense drama, creating a mood of intimacy softly glowing, delicately fragrant with food essences and a haunting emanation from an exotic piece of firewood hidden within a tantalizing blue flame.

Sarah Belle was dressed, or in appearance was draped, in a dress which she had patterned from the himation style worn in Greek costume when escaping from the ball in the St. Charles Exchange Hotel. The drape around the neck left flesh exposed above the bosom line as frame for a golden topaz pendant. The soft loose-woven grenadine of the garment was ivory shaded, enhancing skintone. Her long brown hair, held back by two pearl-studded clasps, hung about her shoulders without restraint, and ear loops had been replaced with small gold teardrops.

With the assistance of Fanaalis, John, too, had undergone a transformation, with hair trimmed and face shaven. His portmanteau held no attire designed for suaveness, but fresh-pressed linen shirt with gold-nugget cufflinks, trousers and waistcoat in rich tan woolen were unintentional complement to Sarah Belle's attire.

When he entered the room, they stood in awe of each other, almost like strangers, not speaking. Then she moved toward the table through the soft candlelight and he followed, pulling out her chair, standing behind her gazing at her hair, reaching out to touch it, but drawing back and going to his own place. Again they stared at each other. Shealia brought hot breads, poured scented tea, and departed. Sarah Belle served him, inquiring, "Is this to your taste? do you like this?"

"I like everything," he said, still riveting his attention on her.

She began to eat. Under his intense gaze, she found her hand trembling as she lifted the teacup to her lips. She set it down, almost missing the saucer.

"Why aren't you eating?" There was an edge to her voice.

"Do I have to?"

"I would be more comfortable."

"Then I will. But first tell me something. Yesterday you were wearing the jade tonad I left behind. Tonight you wear a lovely topaz pendant. Why?"

"Why are you so inquisitive?" and to herself, she asked with a feeling of desperation, "Why do I give waspish responses when his interest in me is like a lifeline that I must get a firm grip on and never let go?"

"Because, my dear Sarah, sitting here like this looking at you, I realize that everything I see about you, everything I feel about you has significance for me. You may recall in my first letter that I told you if you answered me, and gave me your box number, I would respond in a manner more natural than discreet. You gave me your box number and you responded in the same manner. You who just this day accused me of reading your communication in haste may be surprised that I can quote verbatim from the conclusion of your first letter to me.

"'*How is it that since receiving your letter, I have come upon plateaus of beauty in my thoughts about existence—all existence—not heretofore realized?*' You commented that mind or soul might be seeded as are many natural wonders awaiting conscious realization for the dispersement of some cosmic principle . . . A mighty deep thought, my dear, mighty deep . . . Then you surmised about the ambiguity of the words *love* and *beauty* and concluded with two weighted philosophical inquiries, which I chose to consider entirely rhetorical since my mind was certainly not ready for such a concept.

"Again I quote you verbatim: '*Might it not be that the principle* (that cosmic principle you had just propounded) *is something greater than can be discerned through the limited five senses? And, this further question, my dear John . . . might our seeded minds, like our bodies, when joined together (minds of one accord) be able to create "a body of thought" not possible through either mind alone?*' Signed, '*Sarah Belle.*'"

"When sitting all alone with one's thoughts, it is much easier to come by such ideas and express them than when face to face with the person dwelling in one's mind."

"Assuming our minds are of one accord (as I am inclined to think they might be at this moment)———" He paused, and drew her gaze to meet his in a merging that left him speechless for a long moment, then drew a deep breath and continued in softer tone, "Isn't it more reasonable to consider we might come upon greater ideas and express them more realistically when face to face than in the gross limitations of the written word?"

"Yes, John, yes," she answered in the same altered tone. "About the jade. I wore it that I might feel the nearness of something that had been close to you and that you had left behind in such a manner that it indicated to me you would return—though you had not thought so at the time. With you here that need for reassurance is gone."

"Did you ever sound it?"

"Yes. In spite of the misery it caused me when I did."

"Misery?"

"Loneliness . . . being haunted by your presence that wasn't there. Loneliness beyond any reckoning."

He moved as if to get up and come to her. She shook her head. "About the topaz. My mother gave it to me when I was sixteen. I do not know its origin or its value. It is an heirloom. This is the first time I have worn it since coming to New Orleans."

"Sarah——"

"John, please eat—and do not ask me why I wore it tonight."

"May I ask one more question, in the manner of a request—and I promise it will be the last until . . . until . . . well . . ."

"Dispensation granted."

"When we are done here, will you sing for me? There is a sound that has haunted and tugged at me equally as much as the temple jade affected you. The sound of harpstrings and a voice in song with words I felt I must make my own, or feel somehow diminished."

"Yes, John, I will sing for you, but a line or two will be altered—to make it—more timely."

She sat at the harp. John stood, too restless in anticipation, deeply moved at the sight of her at the grand harp, her flowing hair, her posture in lines as musical as the harp frame.

For a while, she simply made music for him, and then she returned to the theme that had engrossed her the night he had spent in her house.

"O Thou Desert of My Mind,
  O Thou Guarded Hidden Glory,
  Let me somehow somewhere find
  Essence of the human story.

Let me find within my desert
Secret pools so pure and sweet—
Let me find within my desert
Fellow nomads I can greet.

Let me share the fronded shade,
Offer fruits that satisfy,
Gaze in wonder at the dune shapes
Bonded to a blazing sky.

O Thou Desert of My Mind,
Bathing me in searing sun,
Chilling me through bone and marrow
When the burning day is done."

She paused, let the harp speak of loneliness so deep and wide that John found breathing difficult and his heart thumped heavily and loudly. Then came relief.

"What the light that plays so grandly
On the heartstrings of my brain?
Where the Source that rives the darkness,
Brings dissolve to crystal pain?"

As she continued to play, she turned to John, "This is the stanza that I am revising:

"In the Desert of My Mind,
I have stood constrained and stilled.
But now I have a song to sing,
My cup of life has been refilled."

She played on, gently improvising, until she felt John's hands on her shoulders, his cheek against her hair, and suddenly stopped.

"Please play on," he whispered, his cheek no longer caressing her hair, but hands still lightly on her shoulders. "I have something to say too." Her hands were not so sure on the strings, but she obeyed. He spoke tenderly to the same rhythm:

"In the Desert of My Mind
My spirit crumpled in despair,
But now sweet waters are at hand
And love's enchantment fills the air."

Sarah Belle fingered the strings, not knowing what she played. Having his hands on her shoulders was like a discovery of some missing part of herself.

"Rapture! Pure rapture!!" he murmured, kissed the top of her head and moved away.

Her hands came to rest in her lap and her head remained bowed near the strings.

He spoke quietly, "We are too close to glory and too near to danger. I will go now."

She quickly turned toward him and stood in unspoken protest.

He continued speaking rapidly, filling the distance between them with a barrier of words. "I told the coachman to return for me promptly at nine in the morning. I want to be at the St. Charles Exchange before the rush. I have financial matters to care for, commissions from friends and relatives in New York and some transactions of my own. I will engage a suite there."

Sarah Belle shuddered but he rushed on, not noticing, caught up in the explanations that would straitjacket emotions.

"I will return soon, in a matter of three days or so. I must start arrangements for the Palenque enterprise: supplies, attendants, boat passage to Laguna. I have promised Mr. Stephens to engage in observations and note-taking at Palenque that he was unable to make because of the rainy season closing in. The dry season has already begun so there is no time to lose. Also, certain museums are expecting material for their journals and hopefully a few artifacts. I will be——" He stopped, taken aback by Sarah Belle's utter removal from him, though she still stood before him. Neither her body nor features showed any expression whatever.

"You did not expect me to stay closeted here?"

No response.

"Look, Sarah Belle, please. You surely realize what you—what your presence means to me. I will take a suite at the St. Charles Hotel——" Her expression did change then and he misread it. "I did not mean that—God, no. I only meant that I can send a carriage for you anytime, or can come and get you, and we can dine together."

Frantically her caged thoughts agonized: No, John, no. Not the St. Charles, the business domain of Justin Lahart! Lord of Destiny, how could you?

"We can go to a ball, enjoy the dance and music—in each other's arms. More than music, we can *be* music, go to the opera together—New Orleans outshines New York City. Or, we can just stroll about holding hands, looking in at the shops at the Exchange. I would buy you a present and you would thank me with your mystical eyes."

The barrier was breaking down, straitjacket weakening at the seams. He started toward her from across the room.

Her voice, toneless, carefully precise, stopped him, restored the barrier.

"I cannot go out with you, John, not yet."

"You *can* go out with me. You must break the shell enclosing you in this place, holding you prisoner to yourself. I do not care that, on legal records, you are the wife of Defender Locke. You are no more his wife than I am husband to Guafana."

They were startled at his mention of Guafana.

She spoke softly. "You have broken out of your shell, John, but mine is made of sterner stuff."

He spoke in a rush. "You are the cause of my release. Before I met you, just being alive was a nuisance—more than that, a kind of horror. I had been fascinated by the engravings in the Stephens book. I was going to Palenque to escape. I would amuse myself and lose myself in contemplating those majestic ruins, letting my own ruined existence merge with the millions represented there. After I wrote to you and you replied, everything changed. I would go to Palenque with purpose. I would give meaning to my existence———" he hesitated. "I could hope you would accompany me and perhaps together we would discover more meaning to all existence. I would put substance to that endeavor—I am here to do that. And I am here to . . . Sarah, Sarah dearest . . . you are feeling something I cannot fathom, something I do not like . . ."

"We will talk again in the morning, John. Perhaps we have tried to come too close too soon."

"We have not been trying. We are being drawn . . . propelled. . . . Go with me in the morning. We will have a beautiful break-fast together at the Exchange. I will tell you my plans for us. Then you can drive around or come on back as you choose."

"No, John, no. Not tomorrow." Her words were effortful. She felt tired—more tired than she could ever remember. She wanted John to go, before more questions, more concern.

"We'll have a cup of chocolate together before you leave in the morning. Good night, John."

She turned to place a cover over the harp. He hesitated, but sensed her complete withdrawal. "Good night, Sarah."

CHAPTER TWENTY-THREE

SINCE SHE HAD PURCHASED and prepared the House of Recovery as a secluded residence of indefinite duration, Sarah had never spent a night so troubled. John had come to her. John was in her house this night, and for a few hours the joy of his presence had been overwhelming, truly her cup of life refilled. Now it had been emptied again and filled with retrospect, a concoction of her own brewing, which had proved soothing to her conscience, even stimulating when she reviewed the sharing of her refuge and its recuperative effect on others—Sutton Lahart, for instance, the only one who had left her with a threat of reappearance at her door, the only one with whom she had ventured beyond her threshold, and thus been swept into an emotional current almost beyond control. Justin—it was as if he stood giant-size at the grand entrance of the St. Charles Hotel, waiting for her as she appeared with John to fulfill the happy expectations he had outlined—or, on a ballroom floor, he would tap John's shoulder and beg permission to cut in— or, in an adjoining box at the opera (Sutton with him, perhaps)—

she shuddered at the image and pulled the bed covers about her more tightly—Justin again—with all the poise and assurance of a merchant prince, approaching their table in the dining room, taking advantage of some recent acquaintance with John on matters of financial interest. She could not, would not, bring John and Justin into such a confrontation. She pounded her pillow with her fists, and, as she lay back, fatigue dragged her into a troubled phantasia of sound and color interspersed with animation, bringing in the figures of guests she had brought to the house before Sutton and John.

When she tried to pull back to consciousness, only Lando was there, and she inquired, "Lando, why did you open the box?" Immediately she was plunged again into the dissolving images she was trying to escape.

Most highly visible was the ugly one, the pitifully ugly one, who suddenly became handsome and disappeared . . . And there, that one lying face down on the embankment, *young*, his clothes so muddy, and under the mud you could see stripes (prison garb?) . . . she rushed to examine him, and he turned over, his eyes so blue in the smeared face that they dazzled you . . . a blue mist covered him . . . then a shot rang out, and the sound of running brought into focus the bearded face . . . the torso in buckskin shone out of the dream smoke, two wounds, one in the heart, one in the head . . . she struggled to laugh at the symbolic wounds and say, "It wasn't the gun, it wasn't the gun," and her attempt erased the image. . . .

Immediately there was replacement by a man of the cloth. He had jerked the collar from his neck and was tearing it to shreds. He was acting like a madman—he ran up a gloomy corridor tearing at his robe, then stomping it as he disappeared. . . .

Sarah Belle groaned and came near to waking, but instead a final image was thrust into the dream montage—a man of great dignity dressed all in black, his glossy black hair rumpled, his dark eyes haunted, and behind him the dueling tree.

Finally, the dream-master of consciousness must retire from activity in a mind as fatigued as the body it served.

Shealia was frightened the next morning when she must call to her mistress several times and grasp the sleeping Sarah Belle by the shoulder to awaken her.

Suddenly, she was wide awake. John was in the house, or was he? She flung the covers aside and was hurrying around the room, shaking her hair about, casting aside her night clothes, pouring water from the pitcher into the washbowl and dowsing her face, all the time exclaiming to Shealia.

"Is John still here? . . . Thank Goodness! . . . Have you seen him? . . . Then he's all right. . . . Where is he? . . . Out in the yard? . . . What is he doing? . . . Talking to Celeste! . . . Hurry, Shealia! Tighten my bodice and don't be all thumbs about it! Can't you see I've got to get dressed and get out there before he leaves? . . . And why am I wearing the rust-colored one? Don't bother me. Hand me a skirt . . . Oh, God, not . . . not the blue! Not the blue! The purple one! . . . Stop frowning and fumbling. Hurry, I say! Of course it doesn't look right . . . I don't care how it looks. I can't look like Suzanne, you know that. Emile might come out . . ."

"Emile and Jasper with Celeste——"

"Oh, Holy Father and Saints!" She stopped still, gasping a little as she breathed. Her face reddened. "So he's making himself at home . . . he's ingratiating himself with my . . . with my . . . ?" What, she asked herself, were these people sheltered here? Friends? Servants? Wards? Why was she so protective, or possessive, or, was it fearful? Or was she simply reacting to a remnant of stilted Southern protocol? Hadn't she initiated the "more natural than discreet" relationship? But how could she be natural, cast aside her fears, with Justin and Emile so tightly woven into her emotions, so restrictive of her movements, inside or outside of her own house?

As she fixed gold loops into her ears and knotted her hair into a bright yellow kerchief, Shealia gave a small grunt, accenting her disapproval.

"Leave me, Shealia. Prepare some chocolate and pastries and set them out in the front room, also the coffee whip and fruit. I will retrieve the wandering Mr. Sterling."

Alone, she stood very straight and stiff, her hands clinched at her sides, her eyes closed; then she relaxed and briskly made her way into the garden unobserved. She came upon a tableau that moved her close to tears. John was in animated conversation with Maury; Celeste was close to John and looking up into his face as if transfixed. Fanaalis nearby was holding the hedge clippers but removed in thought and action from any use of them. And Emile, just to the side of Celeste, held Jasper in one hand and was stroking him with another, his face expressionless, but his attention held. Maury burst into laughter and Celeste's flutelike voice joined in; Fanaalis's stonelike features broke up. And Emile? Sarah Belle stared, fascinated. Did he smile? Or was it just a grimace?

John became aware of her, turned. There was a hush.

"Good morning," she greeted with as bright a tone as she could summon, and heard the unnatural sound of it echo back to her.

She stood staring at John and he at her, the amazement at her appearance hardly concealed. Celeste took Emile by the arm and the three quickly moved away and out of sight. Fanaalis's shears began snipping with jerky uneasiness. John came toward her and she could not control her trembling. He came very close.

"I hope he doesn't touch me," she thought. But he did. He reached out and took a cold hand in his.

"Come along, sweetheart, come along. It's time for breakfast, and much cozier here in your sanctuary than anything the St. Charles could offer."

Breakfasting together became an impasse from which it was difficult to free themselves. They stood looking at the beautiful array of food and drink Shealia had set out. Their hands remained tightly clasped as if in a lock they could not release; or, as if each were magnet to the other with a force that was irreversible. It was like a transmutation of all the romantic love and passion which each had experienced, into a shocking discovery that there were unknown, unexplored dimensions of attraction—that in many facets of creation, and especially within man and woman, there was in union a wholeness to be achieved that far transcended the sum of their being. At the same time, for John and Sarah Belle, the imminent danger of failing to relate this transcendency to the binding realities of living in the present held each of them in painful restraint—emotion and reason in fragile balance. Touch-talk was a language of love so powerful that they must abandon it or dissolve into a frenzy that each viewed as an abyss of destruction.

They carefully unlocked hands, then sat and partook of food wholly unrelated and without flavor in competition with the hunger they must deny. They heard the carriage arrive but ignored it for a while. They had spoken little.

When John heard the restless movement of horses in harness, he carefully spaced his words as though penetrating a fog of emotions. "I will probably be gone for three days. Plan for Palenque. There will be a way. There is always light at the end of the tunnel, if you dig *up* instead of down. Let us dig diligently—up!"

Sarah Belle smiled faintly. Shealia appeared and filled small cups with strong brandied French coffee. They dutifully took a sip and left the table.

They stood facing each other at the door. John's portmanteau was already on the steps outside. He reached for the doorknob, then turned for a gentle caress of her cheek with his fingers. "I'm glad you didn't use the powder this morning," he said quickly, opening the door and as quickly closing it behind him.

Sarah Belle did not look outside to see if Hudson had brought the carriage or sent one of his coachmen.

Now she must deal with her thoughts, with her household, and the piercing, surging desire for that part of herself that would be isolated from her in a suite at the Exchange surrounded with the excitement of world affairs, business transactions, and the stimulus of luxury living and entertainment. And she could be there close by, waiting, watching, sharing, enjoying, if . . . She had never felt more like a prisoner to herself. In her self-imposed detachment at the House of Recovery, there had always been the refuge of sharing, of atonement, of giving. Now there was self-denial, the possibility of loss. Would John really return? . . . How had he construed her refusal to go to the Exchange? They were already too close in mind for deception of any kind to flourish. He had sensed her complete withdrawal—had he sensed as well the fright, the feeling of weights and chains that made it imperative she not appear in the New Orleans scenes he had envisioned for their mutual delight? Why had he not mentioned the matter at all, not reinforced the invitation? Instead making an obvious pleasantry about dining on the premises? And the handclasp? Reassurance? Understanding? A pledge, that no matter what came to pass, they would dig out? Tears and laughter mixed as she rushed back into the yard, surprised Fanaalis by invading his tool shed, grabbing up a pick ax, and beginning to dig out a clearing under the pear tree.

*　*　*

José de Claración and his powerful roan stallion, worthy of a knight errant, found the road across Texas from Austin east to Nacogdoches a wintertime test of endurance—rivers and creeks capricious and dangerous with new rain, the main roadway sometimes no more than a raw lane hacked out of the wilderness.

He had taken this route in search of Defender Locke after George Fisher had briefed him on the likely nature of the man and the probable switch in identity that he would seek.

"Like Sam Houston," José, a worshiper of heroes in which pantheon the Savior of Texas ranked high, had exclaimed, "Betrayed by his wife, leaving behind the office of governor of Tennessee to lose himself among the Cherokees."

"Something like that," Fisher had agreed. "But Houston's stay was only temporary; we may find that Defender Locke has achieved and may intend to keep inviolate his change in identity. There are others like Houston and this man Locke who escape from insanity or suicide into a sanctuary for bruised spirits to live as a 'citizen' of one of the Five Nations within Indian Territory just across our northern border. He has a choice of five cultures in which he may douse his senses, taste new life flavors, from the erotic to the holy, from agony to bliss—among the Choctaws, Chickasaws, Cherokees, Creeks, or Seminoles. Though under the general haphazard supervision of the United States, these five tribes have governments of their own quite similar to their territorial guardian. A white man who feels at home among them may be 'adopted' and live with greater dignity than he has experienced within his own social order."

"How about languages?" José inquired. "I can communicate freely in English or the romance languages, but if closed in with American Indian tongues, I would be speechless."

"Sign language can be eloquent in distress, but I suggest, if you get no clues along the way, you take the trail northward to Clarksville, a lively settlement not far from the border. There you must seek out the most spectacular character in the field of newspaper editing in all of Texas, Colonel Charles DeMorse, editor of the

Northern Standard. If a man conspicuous for blue and brown eyes has ever been in the town of Clarksville, the colonel will have known about it, and, if possible, would have caught up with our man and talked to him. Also there is an old scout, sometimes in Clarksville and sometimes in Jonesboro just to the north at the Red River ferry point, who is for hire as a translator in Indian Territory. The Indians call him Shumanhaya, or Many Tongues."

Fisher laughed heartily. "I have never had him as a companion on the trail but from a single encounter, I can predict you will find yourself hitched to a one-man circus."

"If I must venture into Indian Territory, I will probably need lively diversion."

"With Shumanhaya beside you, there will be no avoiding it! I can see you now, riding along through the forest together, you shaking the timbers with vocal homage to Paisiello's *Barber of Seville* in order to raise your flagging spirits and Many Tongues sitting backward on his trained horse, beating on a big tin skillet that is part of the paraphernalia tied to his saddle."

"I hope if I make it as far as the Red River, I find him in residence. It would be a shame to forfeit such novel harassment."

As José made his way over treacherous roads all the way to Nacogdoches, he inquired from Bastrop onward, at river crossings and their nearby settlements—the Trinity, the Brazos at Robbins Ferry where traders, settlers, and Indians made frequent crossings, and at Crockett before making his way across the Neches in a rented canoe while the stalwart stallion Cimaroso swam at his side. Not a hint or a whisper from anyone who might have talked to a tall man with the blue and brown eyes, dark hair and beard, and a face to which ladies would give more than a second glance (he simplified the ad's "well proportioned figure and patrician features").

Not until at a large trading post in Nacogdoches did he come upon a hopeful clue. An elderly man in the stockroom came out when he heard José conversing with the manager. Yes, he had seen such a man, in the early spring of '43. With relish, he took his time giving out choice bits of his observation, taking a seat by the big iron furnace centered in the rambling structure and bidding José to do likewise. A chaw of Brown Mule, masticated to a juicy cheekful and artfully emptied in the spittoon some six feet away, and he was ready to address the restless young stranger with the dancing eyes.

"He'd been on that awful expedition with General Somervell in that rabid winter of '42—you know, the one that went after the Mexicans under General Woll, the bastard that did all that killin' in San Antonio."

The clerk gave José a special scrutiny—the mixed garb of heavy Mexican poncho blanket, coonskin cap and high, waterproof, Indian-made deerskin boots. José, his hands on his knees, simply stared back with mocking exchange of scrutiny, and the old man shifted his glance and continued.

"You could see it was still tellin' on him—thet holler-eyed hungry look of a man who can't fergit being a starving skelletin in the brush country about ready to give his bones back to his Maker. And, surenuff, those eyes were real spooky staring at you, one so blue, one so brown. I had a hard time waitin' on him jest feelin' those eyes on me. If I just asked him some question about what took place on thet wilderness fiasco, he'd give me a burnin' look that made me wanna turn and run."

José was thinking: Maybe it wasn't altogether the Somervell Expedition that made him so hollow-eyed. "Did he give you any idea which direction he would be heading from here?"

"Does the Sphinx have loose lips? Does a man dead inside tell you where he intends to bury himself?"

José waited.

"I can give ya the guess of an old man that's been readin' fortunes written on faces and exposed minds fer as long as this tradin' post has had water troughs and hitchin' racks."

"Tell me, and we'll drink to the salvation of the lost. Surely there's a saloon nearby where your customers hitch up to a bar and quench their thirst."

The old clerk grinned. "You're a sly young sleuth, I like your ways and means—Indian Territory, a'course. That's where you'll be a-movin' into on yer hunt. Come along and when the bottle's half empty, I'll tell ya about gettin' on to Clarksville and about the ferry at Jonesboro. And when the bottle's empty and I got 'nother tucked unner my arm I'll outfit ya with costly furs and free advice.

Then ya can face up to blue northers and the inscrutable red man in proper style." He winked and beckoned José to follow him.

Before he could leave his informant, José found himself suited out in a sheepskin cap with earflaps and a flannel lining that could be pulled down to protect the face in blizzard weather, a sheepskin vest to wear under his poncho, a knee-length buttoned down overcoat that he must add to his pack. He left behind his prized landmark headgear, the coonskin cap, also more gold coin than intended; the old clerk was a miner of sorts, sensing when a customer was a good prospect for ripe gold. And noting that Cimaroso was flaunting silver patches on bridle and breast collar persuaded José to add further luster to his grand steed with a bridle festoon that held in place on the horse's forehead a bright piece of metal painted to represent a red rose. José laughed as he set it in place and Cimaroso flung his head about in sportive play. "You'll be a fine match for Shumanhaya's circus animal," he said.

The trader heard him. "That wretch," he stormed. "Avoid him like the plague."

"Did he skin you at the counter, frisk you at the saloon, or draw all aces and kings?" José asked with gentle sarcasm. The old man was silent but his hand trembled as he helped José fit a mask for Cimaroso, as a protection along the northward trail they must pursue from now on.

The editor of the *Northern Standard* was as helpful as José's mentor had indicated he might be—and as much a patron of romance and adventure as the lively young Mexican journalist he greeted with an abrazo when George Fisher was mentioned. Over a lavish spread of food and drink at the frontier hotel dining room, José related all that he knew of the letter he carried, and the lady in New Orleans who had written it and financed the search for one Defender Locke, who was surely a lost lover or mate. He detailed his own mission to deliver the letter and perhaps carry a reply to the woman of mystery who lived alone on Phillipa Street in the most seductive city in America!

At the end of José's account, the colonel sat back, lighted a cigar, and with great relish added a chapter to José's story.

"Of course I know the man you mean. He came through here in '43 when my newspaper was just gettin' a start and no man, woman, or child entered this settlement that I didn't learn all the who-what-why I could pull out of them. That man, Defender Locke, refused to give me his name. He bought supplies, and was looking for a guide and interpreter to take him into Indian Territory. Also he wanted me to tell him as much as I knew about the tribes of the Five Nations.

"I knew a lot, but tried to hold out on him until I knew who he was—but he talked like a Southern gentleman and I didn't get the feeling that he was running from anybody but himself. He'd let his hair and beard grow and that made those two different eyes shine out good and bright. Still, his face showed good breeding, you might say. I couldn't pry him into identifying himself.

"He asked if I could favor him by not publishing anything about him and not telling anyone who might come searching for a man of his description, meaning his eyes, of course. I made no such promises thinking he might need to be found one of these days.

"Finally, I gave him all the information I thought he could use, and told him about that rascal Shumanhaya that knows more Indian languages than God who gave them tongues. You're lucky, or unlucky, whichever way you look at it, for you'll find the old dunce in his shack at Jonesboro. He doesn't trek around much in the winter. Enough gold will pry him loose though, even if snow is neck deep. I hope I can get a promise out of you to come back through when you find your quarry or give up, and give me an account of your journey."

"Give to a smart editor like you a story that I can sell to the *New York Tribune* or the *North American Review?*" José teased.

"On my word, I'll give you full credit and write only to titillate my limited circulation, and I do mean limited!"

José decided that he would first scout among the Choctaws since they were located between the Red and Canadian rivers and he would be in their territory when he crossed the Red at Jonesboro. But first he would contact the fabled Shumanhaya.

José arrived at Shumanhaya's abode in midafternoon of a dark cold day with light snow falling. The place looked like a refuge although it first appeared as an enormous trash pile, a great collection scavenged from riverbank at flood tide and from the toll of accident and barbarity along frontier trails: abandoned vehicles, lumber, posts, barrels, ox yokes, and harness remnants. Scattered over all were stacks of horns from the beasts of plain, forest, and domestic pastures—many of these still attached to the skulls and fixed to the cabin walls.

But the cabin was no shack. It was high-walled with portholes, built of heavy timbers, and included a large shed room on the south for stable and fodder. A high enclosure of spiked posts fenced off the entrance to the housing for man and animal. At the gate a heavy bell was mounted with a chain for sounding. José rode up and gave a strong tug. It rang out so loud and strong that the tired Cimaroso leaped aside in fright and required a heavy hand to remain in position.

The gate opened, and again Cimaroso was ready to make a get-away. The thing at the opening turned out to be not a grizzly but simply a man in the skin of one. José, bone cold, was neither amused nor alarmed. He addressed the furred occupant in a provocative mixture of English, French, and Spanish.

"Mr. Shumanhaya, my mount and I need hospice for the night. We will pay you well. I have heard that you have a keen sense of smell where gold is concerned; at the same time I have heard nothing of dishonesty—so I trust my belongings in your unusual shelter. Further, I would engage you as translator among the Choctaws while I am upon a grave mission in Indian Territory."

Shumanhaya, equally provocative, addressed him in what José assumed was Choctaw, then opened the gate wide for admittance.

There were no more words passed while Cimaroso was stabled with bedding and provision and there had been an indifferent exchange of whinnies between him and the spotted Indian pony whose quarters he shared. The silence continued between the strangers until both were warming themselves before the fireplace where a seasoned meat fragrance was rolling out from an iron kettle.

José was thinking he had never seen a countenance and forehead so encased with deep folds of wrinkles. Small eyes, set far back, shone glistening black, seemed never to blink, and picked up flecks of red and gold from the fireplay.

José found he preferred not to have eye exchange with his host and, as he had seldom done with any man or woman, shifted his gaze when Shumanhaya looked at him directly. Instead he looked around the one-room living quarters at the stacks of furs and hides for bedding and clothing, at the relics and Indian ritual objects on the wall, and benches holding pottery and basketry crafted to depict life and art as he had never seen it before.

As he looked at the array above the fireplace, he noticed a small glass ball with metal capping suspended by a delicate chain from a peg and dangling slightly above his eye level. He shifted his glance to the old man and met a stare that was more revealing than intended. Suddenly, José thought of the clerk at Nacogdoches who trembled at the memory of Shumanhaya . . . and also Colonel DeMorse's hint of aversion at some experience with the "rascal," the "old dunce."

Why, you old snake charmer, José accused silently. He resolved to break through the image Shumanhaya used to distract and deceive.

"Señor Shumanhaya, most enlightened one, let me inquire of you——" he spoke in soft Spanish, beguiling, reverent, obviously toned with good humor. "I would inquire of you under what circumstances you used your little glass ball on the old clerk at the Wholesale Supply and Trading Post at Nacogdoches so that he sputters, rails, and trembles at the mention of your name." José chuckled, and for the first time looked into the black eyes with a mental challenge.

Shumanhaya looked up at the ball and emitted a shallow cackle, and answered in easy English. "The good man was drunk. He thought it was I who cheated at the game instead of himself. He glared at me and threatened with his knife. Before he could get up I said soft words to him, dangled the ball in front of him, continued my instructions until he was fast asleep, then took my winnings and left."

"And Colonel DeMorse?"

"It was a bit more complicated with the editor. He had heard some tales about what he called my 'strange shenanigans' and had written a 'character sketch,' praising my skill with Indian tongues, though he never knew that I spoke more than broken English, and ridiculing my 'playing with the occult,' as he phrased it. He concluded with the hope that I'd come to town sometime and show him something. This I did. Told him to meet me at a certain saloon. When he got there, I lined up the bartender and six customers, asked them to sit down in front of me and I'd show them some magic tricks. I evoked several sleight-of-hand illusions and then told them I would make the glass ball disappear. DeMorse was behind me watching. I began to swing the ball and give them the necessary soothing syrup of words. They began to nod, then finally dropped their heads in sleep. I pulled them out of their chairs, laid them out in a row, told Editor DeMorse 'good-day' and left. Of course, they were awake soon after. I had seen to that."

Serious conversation followed and José felt free to recite the details of his mission. He was startled when after he had finished, Shumanhaya stated, "Now I shall tell my side of the story, in the French, with your permission, a language that glows with the subtleties of romance, mystery, and tragedy.

"The man of the singular eyes is known to me. I have seen his Anglicized and highly productive farm, about a hundred miles from the Red River into the Choctaw Reservation. The Choctaws, agriculturists for centuries, revere him for what he demonstrates in garden, orchard, and fields. The farm lies in the fertile hill country, where valleys and streams offer little prairies and woods that are a pastoral delight. The house he has built of split logs reflects his past more than he knows—the porch supported with posts of a size that suggest columns.

"He came to me before crossing in. I accompanied him and taught him the rudiments of the Choctaw language, and have called upon him several times since he was adopted into the tribe, given the name of Kashtasha, and selected a dream maiden from among the many offered him—such a winsome one of classic profile and such moon-goddess shaping as I have never seen before among the races of mountain and stream."

"Mon Dieu, quelle surprise! And did he take her——"

"As bride? Of course! By all the stars, the moon, the sun, and the sky! That maid must surely think she has moved into paradise."

"Perhaps Defender Locke thinks so too."

"Just perhaps——"

"What a twist! This missive I carry could be a blight or a blessing to all concerned."

"What is a blight for one could be a blessing for another. Let surmise be put aside and our attention given to the bubbling stew in the kettle."

José and Shumanhaya dined sumptuously from the big iron pot and slept like lords amidst the stacks of furs. Next morning the light snow was gone, the sun bright, and they struck out for the Red River crossing and Defender Locke's adopted country. One thing: Shumanhaya did not refrain from the habit that had startled many a traveler. When the trail was easy, he'd loose the saddle, push it forward, and perch behind it facing backwards. This, he insisted, improved the vision of the eyes in the back of his head!

Since leaving Fort Towson, located in Indian Territory just north of Jonesboro, José and Shumanhaya had enjoyed campsites along rivers and streams where lush grasses were abundant and the woods not yet captive to winter. Shumanhaya talked of Choctaw customs and language, and became fascinated with the operatic arias that José joyously scattered along the way. Opera had not, until now, been added to his wisdom library.

"My mother never sang lullabies to me," José confided. "Just her favorite melodies and arias. She could quiet me anytime with *Die Zauberflöte*; to me *The Magic Flute* was a reality."

After that, Shumanhaya requested a "lullaby" before bedding down. They both were amazed at the creatures, winged and earthbound, that joined them on the trail in response to the universal harmony of Mozart *et al*.

They were near the end of their journey and topped a hill where the view into the valley was segmented by growth along the trail.

"The dwelling of the Choctaw Kashtasha is down there, upstream from the flow you can see from here."

José immediately burst into a lively fragment of *Le Nozze di Figaro* in celebration of trail's end.

"Silencio!" Shumanhaya commanded. "He might be hunting, and disappear until we are gone. Also, it is no time to be singing about marriage!"

They made the descent and stopped near a yard gate where hitching posts were placed. It was midday and smoke rose from the tall chimney that served the two floors of the structure. Two Indian hunting dogs staked in the yard gave vociferous warning of the approach of strangers.

The front door opened and closed behind Kashtasha. He stood on the porch, in no hurry to offer a greeting or admission to his precincts.

He was dressed all in buckskin, Indian handcrafted, the jacket fringed and trimmed with ornamental beading. His hair was full length according to Choctaw custom.

"The Chocks are called 'Long Hairs' by some. And, if he'd been born into the tribe, he might have had a flat head under all that hair. Old-timers used to call them 'Flat Heads' but not many Choctaw babies get their tops squared away like that anymore," Shumanhaya muttered to José. "He recognizes me and doesn't like it that I'm here. He's acting like the Indian he's decided to be. He'll come on out, but he'll talk only Choctaw. You'll see. He'll make me translate. He wouldn't speak anything else if he knew all the languages in the world."

The tall man with graying dark hair and a beard-covering that masked his expression did as expected. He moved with solemn stride and a deliberate gaze calculated to transfix the beholder. He quieted the dogs with a single sound and came forward to the gate where he stood, his hand resting on the gate but showing no intent of opening.

He finally gave a three-word greeting in Choctaw. The two visitors answered in kind.

Shumanhaya took his time, in like manner, before speaking. He mentioned that the man at his side bore a letter that he felt sure was meant for Kashtasha.

The reply was harsh and angry. José recognized the tone and enough of the language to realize that the old linguist was being given a verbal beating—accused of betrayal, since he knew more than any other about how and where Kashtasha had settled in the territory. He looked upon José with obvious antipathy. Then he pointed a forefinger at Shumanhaya as though it were a weapon and ordered him to go and never return.

Shumanhaya didn't move. If he had any expression of response, it was hidden in the depth of his wrinkles.

José's Latin blood was churning. He had stood slightly behind the translator. Now he almost brushed him aside as he moved up to the gate, and came so close to the man he knew was Defender Locke that had it not been for the gate, their bodies would have touched. José glared into the two eyes and for a moment wavered—they were so different—as different as the personalities this man had achieved. Then he spoke with responsive choler.

"You are Defender Locke, or, if you please, you once were Defender Locke."

The eyes changed, the brown one filmed over.

"I am here on a mission that I intend to execute. I shall speak to you in good English and not bother with the charade that you are imposing on our presence."

The blue eye widened, as if in astonishment.

"I bear a letter to you, and I feel certain that it merits a reply. That will be for you to decide."

He opened his jacket, reached inside a deep pocket and drew out Sarah Belle's letter, a small packet that meant many pages. He thrust it out, holding the edge against the buckskin of Defender's jacket.

"Take it, or forever live with something more grave than that which brought you here. I mean cowardice! The letter is from a woman. You do not look like a man too timid to read what the hand of a lady in distress might have penned!"

He held the letter in place. Defender moved as if the touch of it were painful. But he did reach up and take it from José in grim silence.

"I shall make camp not far from here on the stream that flows yonder. I will stay there for two days. Then Shumanhaya shall come back to this gate. If you have a reply, give it to him and he will bear it to me and save us the displeasure of further converse. If you have no reply, God, not I or the woman who prepared the letter, shall be your judge!" He spoke a Choctaw farewell phrase that sounded more like a jeer, turned and mounted Cimaroso so quickly that he was on his way before his companion, caught up in the unexpected high drama, could get to his pony and trail along.

CHAPTER TWENTY-FOUR

I T WAS SHORTLY PAST MIDNIGHT, and Sarah Belle was wide awake in anticipation of John's return during the day ahead. She had worked and raced about in house and yard with such energies in anticipation of she knew not what that her four companions joined in with an alacrity far beyond their usual easy living routine—the house and its contents were cleaned and polished until each room glowed in its particular patterns and gave off special fragrance from fresh cut flowers selected to enhance its purpose. The yard had been trimmed and shaped as though it were to be a setting for rendezvous filled with rare pleasantries and romantic implications.

Shealia and Fanaalis, Maury and Celeste were all aware that John was to arrive in the day ahead, and, utterly wearied, had early retired to sound sleep. Emile, stronger, more relaxed in body, and eating with a fully restored appetite, had been easier to care for, calm, seldom speaking, his awareness of things external being wholly limited to Jasper who seemed also to live for one purpose, to eat and to play and prank and preen with the caresses of his keeper. Sarah Belle had relaxed too in unconscious response to this change in her ward. She still avoided Emile but not with the caution and aversion that had possessed her since the Suzanne revelation. She continued to favor bright colors with earth tones and tied her hair in a kerchief when outside the house, but now was too consumed with her own self-wrought "web of passion" to dwell on the Suzanne enigma. Nothing in her experience had prepared her for the attachment that was binding her so irrevocably to this man that—what would she do? what could she do?—that would keep her in his presence (in his possession) for the rest of her life.

She lay in her bed, her eyes closed, and tried to converse with her inner selves, as had been her custom for so long now. They wouldn't speak to her.

> *"So you've closed me out,"* she complained. *"Even you, Soul Self, harbinger of my Conscience. Would you speak to me if I told you that I feel as if I have only half a soul and John Monroe Sterling were the other half—and that I have only half a Conscience and am waiting for him to provide the other half?"*

She lay in silence for a while.

> *"Tell me, what will I do with Emile? What would Maury and Celeste do with Emile if I were gone, and they were at the mercy of Shealia's idea that Emile belongs to the devil? . . . And Hudson . . . how about him? Why couldn't he take care of Emile? Maury and Celeste could help . . . I'm listening . . . I'm listening."*

> *Soul Self, speaking: "My dear Sarah Belle, you've allowed Emotion to banish Reason. Hudson, at great personal risk, delivered three people from a lifetime of torment. He, with Maury and Celeste, and his family would be destroyed if the Nicées ever knew their will had been thwarted in the matter of Emile's banishment. Surely you would not place him and his loved ones in such jeopardy? Your confidant and protector through your years here! No man will understand you as he does. And why is he so understanding? I ask you, Sarah Belle, of the House of Recovery, WHY? This is a matter of Heart and Soul. I have spoken."*

> *"O Hudson, forgive me such a thought!"*

She sat up in bed, restless with the clarity of her mind and feeling a need to walk about. She let the image of John flood in, holding her hand so tight, caressing her cheek in farewell. The desire she had felt to call him back, rush into his embrace, was then as now a painful yearning hard to bear. She made a move to get out of bed, then she heard it, a small sound at the window that she had been ignoring. Now the tap, tap, tapping was more insistent. She had a small oil lamp burning by her bedside. She blew it out that she might not be visible when she went to the window. She had forgotten to draw the blind.

"Who is there?" she demanded in a low firm voice, "and what do you want?"

"It is Marie, madame, Marie Laveau."

"What in the name of God brought you here at this hour?"

"I did not want to disturb those about you. Only you understand. I have something to tell you about your man."

"My man?" Did she mean John? and if so, what did she know or suspect? "I do not like this—not at all! What do you mean—'my man'?"

"Madame knows as well as I the man. She has been awake because she waits for his return today."

Sarah Belle felt a chill roll up her spine and explode at the base of her skull. It was not so easy to deal with Marie at any time. And now, just as she had become immersed in thoughts of John and what it might be like to have touch dissolve into union, this presence at her window had plunged through fantasy with shattering impact of reality. Or was it real? Had she shifted to nightmare as she had been doing in her sleep so much since seeking out John in Lafayette Square that day?

The reality spoke. "Please, madame, could you unlatch the screen and let me in, for it is not safe for us to talk like this."

"Why should I?"

"Because this man, as you have discovered, is your man. And you will make changes because of him. And there is something about Emile———. You do trust me, do you not?"

"What other choice do I have? I'll let you in. Move to your right when you get in. You will find a chair there. Sit in it. I will light my lamp. The servants know my lamp burns late. Sometimes all night when I fall asleep reading. There is no reason for them to arouse unless something without your affinity for the dark should come stumbling around. By the way, I thought my gates were locked."

"They were."

"You evidently abound in talents, including lock picking." Sarah Belle lighted the lamp and got back in bed, laying a book beside her. "Just behind that chair is a commodious closet—as you know since you have been in this room before. If any of my residents should have reason to disturb me at this time of night, you will conceal yourself there."

"Yes, madame."

"Now recite your tale of woe or intrigue."

"It is *not* a tale of woe. I come for your benefit———"

"Of course. What is a benefit for Emile is a benefit for me. You do insist, it would seem, in making the burden of your conscience a burden of mine as well, a friendly sharing as it were. I get the feeling that your God and mine are having an exciting game of poker as they manipulate us on the table of life. And let me tell you in advance if you continue making me the intermediary in the process of restoring Emile to your full equation of male prowess, you are likely to have a gap to fill in the service of your voudou deity."

Sarah Belle was beginning to relish this chance to release some of her frustration over her bondage to Emile, now becoming such a threat to any future she might devise with John. "Plan Palenque," he had said. Couldn't he possibly realize the dilemma she faced? She had written him the self-sale story in detail and explained how she was involved in the disastrous outcome.

"If you've come for a report, Emile is eating as much as Celeste and Maury combined. And the only rapture of life he knows is in caressing a squirrel and having it move around him during all his waking hours in a ballet of love." Her voice carried a sharp edge.

"I know this, madame."

"What have you come to tell me about John? And how did you come to know what you have to tell?"

"Quite easy, madame. It is true, is it not, that my race is everywhere your people are, waiting on them, working for them, listening to them? And equally true that we share all we learn with any of us who have use of the gleanings———

"What I have to tell you comes directly from one such, who is helping load the cargo for the boat."

"What boat?" Sarah Belle's heart thumped with heavy accent.

"Master Newton's barque called the *Valkyrie*. Your man is seeking passage on it."

"Passage? To where?" Sarah Belle held her breath.

"Somewhere across the Gulf of Mexico."

"Thank God."

"You thought he might be leaving you?" Marie chuckled. She too relished the opportunity to spar. "Now you do not mind that I have come?"

"I am resigned. . . . Now let us get on to the part about Emile. I know you didn't come just to accommodate me."

"Your man has a plan. I want you to agree to it."

"What is the plan?"

"That is for him to tell."

Sarah Belle wanted to command, scream out, get the story from Marie somehow. But she knew on this point she would be faced with humiliating defeat. She must reply with restraint or Marie would be aroused to surpass her in dominance and each would lose the satisfaction derived from their peculiar acquaintance—an exchange between such different minds, generating a regard across barriers seldom breached, especially by women.

"As you wish. Why do you want me to conform to something I feel at this point must be exceedingly bizarre, also distasteful, else you would not want to advise me beforehand?"

"It will be good for Emile."

"Indeed! And will it be as good for me?"

"It can be."

"If I submit to something that may be at least humiliating?"

"I have lived with humiliation such as you could never know, madame—it has been my crown and robe. I have made gain of it. Great gain."

Marie's voice was low and throaty, and Sarah Belle felt an energy that seemed to flow across the room and cover her with cool resolve.

"And you think great gain will come to me, if I accede to the plan I am soon to hear?"

"I can foresee it, madame, but the voudou god of the Arada

does not permit me to pull aside the curtain of certainty so soon. I cannot yet command the demons that serve the Storm Serpent when it coils in wrath."

"But you can talk in runic phrases to confound me."

"I have not come just to ask that you agree to the plan for you and Emile——"

"For me and Emile?"

"But also——"

"To warn and threaten——"

"To let you know that if you do agree, and you do find the gain that awaits, I will know. And you will say in your mind, 'Thank you, Marie.' But, before that, you will say that the voudou queen's hell has been shown to you."

"More runes. But I do not consider your portent at all reassuring. You have succeeded in bringing a flock of haunting thoughts right through my bedroom window, and I shall rest no more this night. But anyhow, good night, Marie. Please make the most cautious exit of your life or a bit of Jamaican hell will be breaking loose right here in my yard. At the moment I must thank you for coming, though I may find reason to curse you later."

"Not so, Sarah Belle Locke. You will never curse me. You have never truly cursed a living thing. Some day when you are far, far from New Orleans, your thoughts of me will have wings, and a bird will fly to my hand and say, 'Hello, friend, Marie Laveau.'"

She stepped over to the bed and blew out the lights. She did not look at Sarah Belle as she did so, but Sarah Belle looked at the face by her bedside in the glow of the lamp that lasted only a few seconds before there was darkness. She would never forget that face—she was sure of that. She lay, breathing shallow and utterly still, and then it was morning. Sun shadows played against the wall. She looked about and saw the screen unlatched at the window where Marie had come and gone.

She was watching at a window in the guest room when Hudson's carriage drove up and John, obviously hurried and eager, had a hasty exchange with Hudson, then almost ran to the yard gate and on to the door. Sarah Belle opened the door as his hand was raised to knock. They stared at each other as if banking controls before speaking or coming close together. Hudson, already aware of what lay ahead, held the team at still longer than he intended, then sent them scurrying away with sudden clatter.

John followed Sarah Belle along to the living room, realizing that her mood was carefully detached, and determined to bring her into rapport with his own. Before they could be seated, he had her by the shoulders and was shaking her gently.

"Princess, awake. Prince Charming is here." He touched her lips gently with his own, then drew back. She was blushing but seemingly unmoved. His eagereness became insistent.

"The adventura, Princess. The adventura! Remember how we dallied with the word in our correspondence? It is upon us. Please do sit down that I may do likewise and I will tell you about the magic carpet that will bear us across the Gulf of Mexico to Port Laguna at the northwest corner of the Yucatán peninsula. Her name is *Valkyrie*, as sweet a barque as you have ever seen, newly built, a bright blue face, tight rigging, clean sails, and a hearty kind of spirit reflecting in its owner and master, James Newton. He has six able sailors for crew, likely men, well paid—no scrubs. The *Valkyrie* has been in service enough to be proved worthy. It is chartered to a Don Vicende de Vives, a kind of Spanish nobleman in exile, who owns an extensive and highly prosperous hacienda upriver from the port. It pulls about 260 tons—its cargo made up entirely of supplies for the Vicende plantation, as it goes out, and of products sent from there to New Orleans market on its return.

"Newton tells me there are elaborate iron grillwork and heavy household furnishings—ebony and custom designed by Vicende himself—stored in the hold. The best part of it is that three compartments for passengers have been built in at the request of Don Vicende. This is unusual in such boats. When not used for the plantation owner and his associates, the compartments are available for a special fare, and more revenue accrues to the boat's owner. There is an ample supply of water and foods on board. Newton suggests that for personal preferences I should purchase some extras which I have already placed aboard. Also, I have a medicine chest suitable for our extended travels. The captain stores only a few emergency items along this line."

Sarah Belle just looked at him as he rushed on with details. Once she smiled slightly so that he would be encouraged to continue.

"The private cabins are quite small and not built for female occupancy, but can be arranged with enough comfort to be bearable for the few days of crossing. There is a lifeboat not yet put to use and the best line of life preservers." He studied Sarah Belle's expression and was puzzled.

"The lady who first mentioned with such daring certainty her desire to visit Palenque, even under disguise, seems to be having second thoughts. Shall I continue?"

Sarah Belle's smile this time was a bit more invitatory. "I'm waiting for the disguise part before I get excited."

A shade of uneasiness crept into John's recital. "Don Vicende has a representative on board in charge of his cargo, Señor Alano, and our good fortune will continue from the port onward to Palenque, less than a week's trek from the coast. Alano will assist me in getting carriers at Laguna and then again at Palizada as we move up the rivers to Las Playas and Palenque.

"All arrangements should be easy to negotiate. The revolutionary turmoil that John Stephens encountered is in the past, natives are friendly, padres happy to have their monotony relieved by the appearance of strangers in their isolated curacies, and helpful in securing supplies we will need along the way. . . . Am I boring you, Sarah? Or, perhaps you are troubled about something we should discuss before I carry on." Her stillness bothered him. He had expected sparkle and urgencies for him to get on with the whole story.

"No boredom. Just bothered that you're holding back on the personal aspects of the plan. Your report that the cabins were not designed with female passengers in mind has not included an explanation about such occupancy. Do we harken back to my original fantasy that we go Shakespearian style with the explorer's female attendant in masculine attire?"

"Hardly. Your womanly structure would scarcely fit into such a part." He smiled teasingly, but got no response.

"What then?" Her thoughts were fastened hard and tight on Marie's visit and the "you and Emile" phrasing. Should she let him carry on while she pretended no knowledge of the Emile factor? She decided against a bargain with pretense.

"What of Emile? Is he a part of the plot? It could hardly be otherwise."

"How did you know?"

"Marie Laveau."

It was he now who was stunned into silence. He got up and walked around the room, seeking calmness. Finally, in low controlled voice, he inquired, "Did that witch tell you about it?"

"She is not a witch in the ugly sense you imply. She is a woman doing what she feels she is meant to do in her place and time. She is concerned for Emile, and to a lesser degree, me also. She did not tell me any more than that she wanted me to agree to the plan. She said you would tell me—that it was not her place to do so."

"Damn her anyway. What gain is it to her that you agree to the plan? And how did she learn of my personal affairs in the first place? Of course, the black-ears connection and the white employers' assumption that their own converse is spoken in an unknown tongue."

Sarah Belle was alarmed. She didn't yet know the plan and John was so aroused that a voudou practitioner had come into knowledge of his proposed exploit that he might cancel the whole thing, or at least her part in it.

"Think back, John, over the whole story of Emile and Suzanne, and reckon with Marie's position, burdened with the conviction that she has been a party to Emile's loss of manhood, which concerns her more than loss of mind, especially as she relates to the vengeful nature of the voudou god over such points of masculine dominion."

"Primitive! Disgusting!"

"Then how about reverence for the 'God of Wrath' of the Old Testament so feared in those times?"

"You should have been a man. A lawyer—or a liberal theologian."

"Think what you would have missed!"

"Touché!" They both laughed, and he came back and pulled his chair nearer hers and placed it so that he could study her closely as he talked.

"I will tell all, and I admit, I have had some reservations about your acceptance of the role I have envisioned for you—and Emile. But you do have an alternative. I'm uncertain about your reaction to that also. May I hold your hand?"

"No. I want to think about what you are saying. With my hand in yours, I'd be thinking about——"

"I understand perfectly. I, too, must keep my mind on what I'm saying. I know you've been struggling with your responsibility for Emile, to the extent that you might forfeit our chance for an escape together into another clime and time. So I decided that we should take Emile with us, and of course Maury and Celeste to attend him."

"Emile at Palenque?"

"Why not? Separated from all aspects of his former life and its functions, he might be shocked into a state of mental response."

"He'd probably think he was at last on the moon."

"What's wrong with that? He's been wanting to go there. He'd have a change of scenery to work with."

"He'd probably run off into the jungle searching for Suzanne."

"I could say 'and that would be that,' but I won't be so crass."

"You are still circling the subject."

"All right. The only condition in which the boat's master would consider having two women aboard would be that they be married couples. He and the cargo manager assured me that the only way we could get acceptance of a strange woman in the native villages would be in the company of a husband, or a part of a family unit. Otherwise, supplies wouldn't be available—taboos would blight the prospects for a safe journey and a supportive campsite at the ruins."

"You may stop there. It comes clear. Maury and Celeste are one couple. And in the charade I have a choice of Emile . . . or," she gave him a look that shattered his composure, "you."

He was on his feet, moving about again.

"And," Sarah Belle continued, "If Emile—Maury could take care of my afflicted husband, Celeste and I could share a shelter, and you would be comfortable in single quarters. There would be need to explain, of course, that my husband is in a state of temporary amnesia, due to an accident—that you as a close friend of the family are taking him and his servants on this journey in the hope that strange sights will be restorative. That you assume responsibility for the whole party—especially the wife," she gibed.

"I . . ." But he got no further.

"In a way, you could say that we would be together a family

unit—very proper. On the other hand, if you and I——" she paused again, and he turned to confront her.

"If you and I——" she repeated, and held him with her eyes as though measuring him body, mind, and soul.

"If you and I——" he mimicked her, grasping her arm and pulling her to her feet. "If you and I!—such a storm would break out on that first night aboard the vessel, that the boat and the whole Gulf would be convulsed with the forces set in motion. Don't you agree?" He pulled her to him, one arm around her waist tight and unrelenting as a leather brace, the other around her shoulder, and his lips seeking from her, taking from her, the pent-up desire that had been ravishing her from the first time he had entered this room, which now seemed to resonate with the emanations of their ardor transmuted into an ecstasy that was virginal for them both in its depth and intensity. Yet, there was more . . . more . . . not to be encompassed in this day and hour, and the realization left them with a weakness that terminated the embrace. John lifted Sarah Belle into his arms and carried her to the sofa.

Finally, she said, "It will have to be Emile. I cannot contain it all. I am not ready. It will be enough to be with you every day, looking at you, touching you. . . ."

"A small shelter on a small boat is not right for us . . . ," John agreed in a low voice so endearing that tears rolled down her cheeks. "We will know the time and the place, when your heart is at ease, and I am full grown, in spirit, you might say—when I am in tune with all that is you and can cope with the grandeur that rises in me when I hold you in my arms."

They leaned against each other, holding hands tightly, murmuring love words now and then, reading the silence in between . . . until Fanaalis crept in like an overdue shadow to light the fire and temper the chill, unnoticed by the entranced pair on the settee.

John was gone. It had been only hours since she had been held so close in his arms . . . only hours since she had said, "It will have to be Emile."

First, she went back to the sofa and sat very still in review of the rapture in his arms, the wonder of the plans for departure, leaving the House of Recovery behind—leaving New Orleans behind, and all that was before New Orleans, with a sense of relieved dismissal. She would be close to John . . . close to John, day after day, sailing over the Gulf, through the menace and mystery of up-river travel in the tropics, along the tangled trails and through the Indian villages; and finally in the isolation of their jungle camp and in their exploration together of the majestic ruins at the Palenque site.

The tide of emotion and elation began receding. She felt herself balancing on the firm sand of reason. John had said that the *Valkyrie* would be pulling out of harbor in five days, and so all preparations must be pressed forward in great haste. He would return in the early morning of the departure date for her and Maury, Celeste and Emile, and all their baggage must be properly boxed ready for loading.

And now the reality of her agreement to play the role of Emile's wife began to seep through—a farcical arrangement in order that the adventura of deliverance might take place. In rational thought it became ironic to the point of despair.

There was no way to foresee or deflect the vagaries of a deranged mind. Perhaps Emile would remain unresponsive to surroundings no matter what the changes. Perhaps the Suzanne image was fractured, dissolved. Yet she, Sarah Belle, would be often in his presence, her impersonation requiring an attentive attitude; and though she would be outfitted in plain and sturdy attire, there were likely similarities beyond the visual. Might some level of voice, turn of head, some sense of touch or easy gesture, trigger the Suzanne likeness into false recognition and frantic reaction?

Also, she must display some affection toward him as well as concern for his welfare, in a distorted way standing in for Suzanne. She felt a thrust of revulsion. Was this because she now was so entwined with all that was John, so sensitive to his touch or even the thought of it?

To act the part of a loving wife to another, hoping for a return of normalcy, seemed all at once to be a betrayal of the selfhood just discovered in John's arms. For a moment she rebelled. She wouldn't carry through with the absurdity. She would brook no barriers to being in his presence unrestrained in the exchange of love-look, love-talk, love-touch. She'd get word to John. If there must be pretense for the crew on the *Valkyrie* and for the village natives, then she would pretend to be his wife from the start.

They would take love, test love, in whatever design or disguise fate might demand. Emile? Take him along as a feebleminded brother, hers or John's, no matter.

What about Marie Laveau's request that she agree to go as Emile's wife? Why should she let this voudou mulatto queen dictate a decision so vital, so root-latched into her very existence? If Marie did have any power to peer into the future, as she intimated, her message was that it would be disastrous for both Emile and his guardian if she did not take the course that John proposed. And what was that about a glimpse of voudou hell? So what? She, Sarah Belle Locke, had had many glimpses, even good long looks, at several different kinds of hell.

She must advise Maury and Celeste about the arrangement. They might be shocked, but compliance was assured, even eagerness to expand their own sense and range of freedom. And certainly Shealia and Fanaalis would be awed and incredulous at their new status but would double their efforts to see that all was in readiness when John came again.

And Hudson . . . ? Did he, like Marie, already know about the *Valkyrie* and its prospective passengers? If so, he should be relieved that their mutual bondage to the three who were sheltered at the House of Recovery was soon to be transferred to her and John and the refugees taken far from their hiding place in New Orleans. And what would he be thinking of the passenger arrangement? Most likely the boatmaster's demands concerning women passengers had fallen easily on the ears of workers getting cargo into place and readying the *Valkyrie* for the voyage. And he had been personally driving carriage for John. Of course he knew! She immediately went seeking Fanaalis and instructed him to go to a small riding stable nearby and hurry to Hudson with a message that it was urgent she see him at once.

Hudson came on horseback and arrived sooner than expected. She asked him in and to be seated with her in the living room. He did not hesitate. Without speaking they both recognized that they were together at this decisive time in a manner that ruled out protocol or pretense. In some strange way, they were crossing over a bridge together and for a while they would both be on the same side, then she would cross over another bridge and he would turn back.

Sarah picked up a pitcher on the armchair table at her side and poured out a rich golden stream of eggnog into the tumblers at hand.

"Hudson, I must admit that the turmoil of mind and emotion that has besieged me in these recent days has assaulted both sleep and appetite."

"You've not been alone in this state."

"I've noted in sacred literature that to sup with someone can imply a bond of supportive understanding."

He nodded.

"I made this from my grandmother's recipe. Shealia's Jamaican skills can not achieve it. It soothes and strengthens. In times of stress, it builds one up; in times of over-elation, it tones one down."

Hudson took the tumbler, they sipped, and he smiled. "I think it will build me up. How will it supply your needs?"

"Both ways. I've been elated to a dizzying level. And then have dropped into dismal regions of speculation."

"Where are you now?"

"In between. You are the only close friend I've ever had, man or woman. I have confided in you, exposed my inner thoughts and motives to you. You have acted many parts in my behalf, servant, escort, protector, partner. You have given me understanding completely free of censure."

"You've given me an inner freedom of mind and purpose such as no law of man could take from me. And I have observed in you some qualities of womankind that life and books had withheld from me."

"Hudson, we will soon go our separate ways. It is my destiny to follow John Sterling."

"Yes."

"You know about the planned voyage on the *Valkyrie*?"

"Yes."

"You know about the passenger arrangements?"

"I know what the requirements are concerning women passengers."

"Has John discussed all this?"

"Not all. But the matter of the four of you going from here. He knows of my part in the Emile affair, of course, and speaks with me freely. I think he is an able guardian for all concerned."

"All, Hudson? Including me?"

"I think you, too, deserve freedom—from your self-enslavement."

Sarah Belle waited, but he did not enlarge upon this.

"Hudson, I must ask you one thing further—and it is not easy. Between us, there has never been subterfuge or a curtsey to taboos. You know that I've been restive as to what has become of my husband, and have efforts being made to locate him. I do not wish to see him again or have him send me word of forgiveness, so to speak. I simply would feel more at ease with my conscience to know that he had received the account which I wrote to him. It had never occurred to me until now that I would want to— 'intend to' says it plainer—spend the rest of my life with another man, and that it would be meaningful to me to have our separation be more a fact in law than just a wall of silence extending over the years."

She paused, then sensing that she had from Husdon a detached but concerned attention, she continued.

"I've not heard from William as to the search being made through George Fisher. The wall of silence may not be penetrated for years, maybe never. I must make my decisions now. You and I have done our share of masquerading, but like nothing I am about to do when I step on the deck of the *Valkyrie* and continue until— well, until masks can be removed. To put it bluntly, I must pretend to be either the wife of Emile or of John. With Emile, my double Suzanne is like a threat hovering over me ready to make a docile lunatic into a lustful madman."

"Madame——"

"Don't call me madame!" Could it be that Hudson was about to laugh?

"I can't refrain. For only addressing you thus can I say without offense: If ever I could guarantee you anything concerning your future welfare, it would be that Emile could not, will not, except in fantasy, become a lustful madman!"

"Well, you must know that Marie——"

"Of course I know Marie—have known her since she was a too-wise child. Let us say we know each other, Marie and I. I have pulled her from several burning brush piles, and she has helped me extricate others doomed to be thrown into some boiling caldron of life. Marie has advised you to travel as the wife of Emile, has she not?"

"Indeed she has, bringing me the admonition, as a good voudou should, in the darkness of midnight at my bedroom window."

"Marie, in her fashion, is circumspect, and there was no other way."

He's defending Marie, Sarah Belle realized, and was amazed, close to resentful.

"I gather, Hudson, that you agree with Marie."

"I do."

"Why do you assent with such conviction?"

"Did you not make the choice when John Sterling told you of the plan?"

"Yes."

"And what was your choice when you were in his presence?"

"At that time, I was under the influence of Marie's visit . . . and . . . the impact of John's plans for crossing the Gulf on the *Valkyrie*. I told him . . . it would have to be . . . Emile."

"Did he protest?" He waited for an answer that did not come. "Did you surmise that he, more likely than Emile, could turn into a lustful madman?"

Sarah Belle's lips tightened. This was Hudson, her loyal confidant, speaking. She looked at him, almost expecting him to say "I beg your pardon, madame." But when his sympathetic gaze, with a small spark of humor showing through, held steady, she took a deep breath and looked away.

"Three to one. I have been baited and cornered." She felt cut off from them all. Did Hudson really believe that it would be better for both her and Emile if she accepted this incognito, this farcical mime; or could it be that he wanted to delay her complete bonding to John as long as possible?

He sensed her alienation but continued with surgical dispatch. "You made the decision knowing quite well why you did so. And then your desire to give yourself to this man without delay brought on this search for a way to reverse your choice. I would think the boatmaster has been advised of the arrangement by now, and it would place things in a peculiar light for you to change husbands after coming aboard."

The visit with Hudson which she had expected to be a source of reassurance and support had turned into something quite different—a kind of confrontation with herself, Hudson voicing the opposition.

"The *Valkyrie* is certainly not the only vessel crossing the Gulf from New Orleans to Laguna. I could refuse to go by that boat."

"And John Sterling could go alone without you and without the encumbrances of those you do not wish to leave behind."

"John is not like that."

"Madame, I am amazed. In the years we have worked together, I would think you could read the masculine mind in broader range. Of course you have not until now been so driven to permanent attachment. You spoke of my understanding. Let me assure you I understand all the elements of 'permanent attachment.' Why do you think I speak so boldly in this matter? Understanding you has meant my seeing John Sterling as our final discovery for recovery. Your own. A remarkable kind of poetic justice."

Sarah Belle had no rebuttal. She looked at Hudson. His eyes held hers and she felt as if she were floating on wave after wave of calmness, quietude, certitude.

He said gently, teasingly, "We could reopen the House of Recovery."

She replied in the same tone, "But that is impossible. For John and I with your help are emptying and closing the house. It will be in the loving care of two old Jamaicans who were the first to come here and recover from a lifetime of misery."

CHAPTER TWENTY-FIVE

COMFORTABLE IN A LOOSE GARMENT, her hair held back with a band of yellow ribbon, Sarah Belle was busy in the sewing room with Shealia and Celeste. It was early morning and only two days until departure. Their work was a day and night process, sometimes one, sometimes all three with needles flying and scissors racing. Sarah Belle had secured bolts of plain cotton gingham in dark blue and brown for skirts and bonnets, gray and bottle-green for waists, and cool muslin for undergarments.

"We will emancipate ourselves from corsets, long drawers, and stacks of petticoats," she instructed Celeste. "We will relate to pantaloons as worn under full skirts for riding when I was a girl, but actually we will be wearing our skirts over loose trousers, and beneath waists and trousers, only short drawers and a chemise. Bonnets will have stiff brim and ties, made to protect us from the tropical sun and the vicious swarms of mosquitoes that Mr. Stephens mentions in his books as such a plague over jungle rivers and at their campsite in Palenque. We will carry veils for further protection. No bright trim on anything. We do not want to attract. We want to blend. We must provoke no unnecessary attention from the natives—or the alligators so plentiful in the waters of the interior."

Celeste shuddered, but remained caught up in the spirit of adventure. "We must see that Jasper is securely chained to Emile's belt. If an alligator should swallow either one, the other would try to go along."

"I wonder if John has told the boatmaster about Jasper."

"No matter, madame. He is such a cheerful and loving bit of life, they will surely consider him a sign of fair winds and smooth waters."

The sewing stopped as they heard a galloping horse approach and come to a halt at the front gate.

"Hudson bringing my mail, no doubt." She hurried to the front door. It could be a letter from William about the search for Defender, she was thinking. If only . . .

A repeat surprise was waiting at the door. It was not Hudson. It was John. As she opened the door, he stepped in and reached for her, held her tight, and with her heart pounding against his, kissed her so long and hard that she felt her strength drained from her body as breathing became so difficult and response so intense.

When he released her, she leaned against him, panting in short bursts.

"This is what I came for," he said. "Though I had it mapped out differently."

"What . . . else did . . . you . . . come for? Isn't this . . . enough?"

"Not quite." And he brought her into his arms again, held her more gently, kissing her eyes, cheeks, nose, and finally her lips with repeated intensity.

"No more, John. Please! No more. Let's sit and talk about . . . whatever you came for . . . and Palenque . . . and all."

"What have you been doing?"

"Sewing, sewing, sewing, night and day, and packing the boxes Hudson secured for us; they have strong leather bindings and braces suitable for such travels. He also brought clothing that he thought would be right for Emile and Maury."

"Good. Now, what I want (besides you) is that I get some measurements from the four of you. I must provide oilskins, rubber boots, and other items you do not have access to, since I will have to shop in boys' or men's wear for some of your needs. I have already purchased two lightweight sidesaddles for you and Celeste. Wooden saddles on mules are not the latest in comfort, even for the male position. And if that becomes too wearying for you before we get to Palenque village, Indian bearers will be available for hire. The carrier attaches a kind of chair, a silla, to his lower back and forehead, and carries the passenger comfortably seated."

"Sounds like a substitute for the mule. I had rather walk or crawl."

"You would. Just for that I will see that you have some sturdy pioneer boots. Now about measurements. Shall I begin with you?"

"Certainly. But in the sewing room. Come along."

When they were done, John reviewed the travel arrangements, the equipment and supplies that he had purchased, and the many details that would be pressing him in the short time left.

They were standing at the door of the sewing room with departure imminent; both were hesitant.

"Sarah, dearest—one more thing before I hurry away, but only if the time's right for you——"

"Yes, John." She trembled. How could it be that she could feel like this? No resistance when in his presence—no resistance about anything, anything at all. There didn't seem any response in her except "Yes, John." If only . . .

"Sarah. Sarah, darling. At this moment I don't believe that you could have a thought or an impulse that I wouldn't read as clearly as a billboard at the Exchange . . ." I'm not about to ask what you're thinking. We decided, remember? . . . Now, do you ever play the harp this time of day?"

"Yes, John."

"Can we go there now, and will you play for me? The first time I was in your guest room and heard it faintly, I left with the sound of it haunting me. The other time it was as if the music was a part of us both. Then suddenly you closed me out, dismissed me. You remember?"

"Yes, John."

"It happened when I mentioned wanting to take you out—to the St. Charles, the Exchange Hotel. I was baffled—stricken describes it better."

Sarah Belle looked away.

"I realized later how stupid I was not to understand that you were fearful of meeting someone who's living there—or doing business there—especially fearful of the consequences should he see you in my company."

Her response now was only a whisper. "Yes, John."

"You could have told me. If I could tell you about Guafana, you surely could tell me about anyone affecting your life, as you told me about Lando and Defender."

"Yes, John." She was crying now.

He came close, turned her face to him. "Do you ever play the harp crying?"

She tried to smile. "No, John. I mean, yes John, many times, many times."

It was he that had to look away for a moment, then he placed an arm around her waist. "Come on then, and do it again. You will have company this time."

As she sat down at the harp he took the ribbon band from her head and scattered her hair about over her shoulders. "More suitable this way," he murmured.

"Go sit down, away from me, John."

"Will you come and sit beside me when you have finished?"

"Yes, John."

"I love that refrain 'Yes, John.' I shall expect to hear it countless times more. But I want you to know that I am sane enough to realize that with you there are boundaries that even I must not transgress if I would avoid the 'No, John's'. . . . There are such boundaries, are there not?"

"I hardly know . . . I mean, yes, John."

"Enough. I am moving swiftly out of range. Please play."

She played to love, to the harp, to John, and seemingly to a universe in which they resided at the core. This was a dimension not touched when playing for Justin Lahart—a dimension that she had never reached in her playing to her own emotions and to those of the broken hearts and tormented minds she had sheltered.

When she stopped, she sat with head bowed, her loose hair against the strings.

"Come to me, Sarah. Come to me for a little while."

It was not yet sunrise on the day for boarding the *Valkyrie* when John and Hudson arrived at the House of Recovery bringing a coach for the passengers and a buckboard-style carrier for the luggage.

Hudson greeted Celeste: "In that raiment, you look like a pilgrim ready to board the *Mayflower*."

"Madame says we must dress plain and conceal our charms."

"I agree. There is need aplenty."

Celeste laughed gleefully as she flashed around from place to place, checking trunks and boxes and identifying them for Hudson who with brush and paint was labeling the contents as he checked ropes and leathers to make certain all were securely lashed.

"How is Emile behaving?"

"Like a lamb. It was no bother getting him dressed in the seaworthy outfit you provided. Jasper was so frisky that he kept Emile as occupied as a child with a winsome toy."

"And Maury?"

"Very serious. He worries. I do not know why. It is a man's way, I suppose."

Hudson did not reply.

John and Sarah Belle had greeted each other with careful detachment. When she could speak to him alone, she said, "I never expect to return to this house."

"Good. Does it mean that your home is wherever I am?"

"If you want it that way."

"I do."

"You say that as though it were a vow."

"It is."

Shealia rushed in. "Madame, I must have you at the kitchen, please. The basket for your foods, I must tell you———"

"John, will you tell Hudson that I want to see him in the music room shortly? I must speak to him alone before I leave."

"Yes."

Sarah Belle and Hudson stood before each other, emotions shielded, posture stilted, exchange difficult. The rising sun scattered hesitant rays of light on the stained glass arches of the east windows, throwing patches of color here and there about the room, on the harp, across their faces.

"Hudson, you may dispose of my mail as you see fit. Eventually, there will be something from William; please read and reply as becomes the content.

"Further, it is my desire that my harp be at home in your library, along with my books, which you may move at your convenience. I have told Fanaalis and Shealia this. They know as well about the arrangements made when you and I went together to the Bank of Louisiana yesterday morning. Since they cannot read, they are pleased that you agreed to be custodian of the papers giving them possession of this property and of the monies to be issued to them should their needs exceed the amount they are able to make with sales at the market.

"I did not advise you at the time that I also made funds available for your charities, to be drawn upon at your discretion. The only personal properties that will go with me, I have packed in a single portable trunk."

"Your wishes have had priority in my life since you first hired a carriage from me. The bond was sealed when you sought my assistance in locating here, told me why you had come, and—how you planned to occupy your time. I was confounded then, and remain so now, as to why you selected me to work with you, and now you transfer your most precious possession, your harp, into my keeping."

"It is no deep mystery, Hudson. When one is living within the very matrix of tragedy, moments of certainty or illumination may come with a clarity not attained in everyday existence. One sees into and through people. In an instant, character may be delineated, danger exposed, even thoughts perceived. I experienced such a moment when you stepped down from the driver's seat that first time and assisted me into your carriage."

They gazed at each other in silence, reviewing that coming together, the seeding of the House of Recovery which had made them partners in what was offered there.

"One last assignment, Hudson. You may come to it in your own good time. I will be out of your life, and might even be out of this earthly life. But do not wait too long. If you think it should not be published until a generation beyond our span, then place it, in finished form, to be published when the time is right for acceptance."

"You do perplex me! Especially the word *published*."

"There on the bench by the harp is a box which you'll take with you when you take the harp. There's a smaller box within—the jeweled casket which was a gift from Lando. You know that I kept a written account of every guest that came here and sometimes my account was supplemented by the one being sheltered. I called the contents 'My Conscience Book.' I had thought I would write a book, most particularly for women, but that resolve weakened and died. I realized how much more meaningful it would be written from a man's viewpoint. In fact, I concluded it would be disastrous for me to attempt it—that its publication would be possible only in Europe and that it would fade into obscurity, out of time, out of season——. I am no longer committed to the box, or the book. I pass it along to you."

"I cannot say I thank you. I have a strong impulse to refuse, to say 'Burn it all and be damned.' But again, it's your desire for me to manifest—and as a book it may have a life that I dare not deny. Some books are like that, created out of Destiny's favored mixes and mortars."

"After Zeuxis presented Zantea with the parchment on which was written the 'Mysteries of Life,' I realized that you were the alchemist who could transmute into the gold of literature the baser materials stored in my casket."

"I feel that I have been knighted for services not yet rendered, my lady." He made a slight bow, his smile gainsaying obeisance.

It was their last charade, very small, but crowded with tacit sentiment.

She placed a hand firmly on his shoulder. "Sir Hudson Recoire, thy services are beyond reward. Let the Lord thy God finish what I have only implied." She kissed his cheek and rushed from the room.

"Two days behind us . . . and all really top-notch . . . it's like a pleasure cruise. . . . Are you happy?" John inquired of Sarah Belle.

They stood side by side at the bow, a brisk wind at their backs as if to blow them on ahead of the barque to their destination.

This third morning of the voyage promised to be a matchless December day on the Gulf. Water and sky were a blue ecstasy, and tall white puffy clouds, high above, roamed about like giant sentinels in silent parade.

Sarah Belle could not answer with an unequivocal "yes." She had no regrets for having severed all ties with the House of Recovery, but it was more than an enterprise, it was home. She had grown to love every part of it—the beautiful gardens and bower, the music room at the core of it all. Before she left, she had managed a visit alone with every room and the cherished possessions she had gathered around her. She had stayed longest in the shop where Fanaalis and Shealia worked with their crafts—the beauties of nature and tradition and human values so vividly expressed. They had come upon her there. The three had spoken no word to each other as she touched a basket, a shawl, a bowl, smiling her appreciation, but with a tightness in her throat that would make a shambles of speech. It was when she bade them farewell at the front yard gate on departure that emotions were unleashed. She embraced Shealia only to have her break away and run wailing back into the house. When she placed her arm around the bent shoulders of Fanaalis, he trembled so that she thought he would fall to the ground. He, too, fled from her, bent almost double, unsteady and coughing painfully as he followed Shealia. How could she say "happy" just yet?

John himself was happy—happier than he had ever expected to be again. He was already envisioning the campsite at Palenque. If he could enlist enough help from the village, he would set up fully protected living quarters at the Main Palace. He and Sarah Belle would be free—free to love, free to explore, to delve into the enchantment of past wonders and into the greater enchantment of themselves. For how long? Indefinitely. They would stay the seasons round. Palenque was near enough to seaboard that ample supplies could be laid by. Let the rains and storms isolate them! So much the better. They would study the ways of the jungle life that frequented the ruins—study and perhaps write together——

"John, you are drifting away. Your eyes are nearly closed!"

"Not so far away that I have lost my hearing. You did not answer my question."

"The power play of winds and sails, and those colossal watchdogs of the sky give one a pagan sense of merging with the elements."

"You are being evasive. Be happy with me. And as far as merging is concerned, just wait until——"

He got no further. They heard the quick steps of Señor Alano
approaching. They were seldom in his presence except at mealtime, for he was constantly busy, either checking his cargo below
("Mus' be somethin' live down there," Maury had quipped) or
moving round and round the deck with his telescope in hand ("say
he lookin' for a whale," Maury reported on that). Maury walked
the deck even more than Alano as he strolled with a tranquil
Emile and Jasper.

Master Newton ran a tight ship, as though it were a major
ocean voyage; routines were so well set and the cargo manager so
preoccupied that Sarah Belle and John could visit together in a
pattern of their own. But now they realized that Alano was not
going to pass them by. Emile and Celeste were seated on a deck
bench not far away. Sarah Belle hastily joined them and sat by
Emile, making some comment across him to Celeste as she laid a
caressing hand on Jasper.

"Buenos días, Señor Alano. This is the kind of day that sails
were made for, no es verdad?"

"Sí, señor, verdad . . . verdad . . . pero . . ."

There was always an uneasy manner about Alano that puzzled
John. At mealtime, he was the first to leave the company and pace
around the deck. The boatmaster had remarked on this as the "impatience of a business man eager to make shore and secure his
commission." But John had begun to realize that the fidgety Spaniard was more fearful than restless.

Early evidence of this came on the first evening out when two
sailors were entertaining with harmonica and song. They were offering the sea version of a cowboy ballad: "O Bury Me Not on the
Lone Prairie," with a robust opening,

"O bury me not in the deep blue sea,
Where the hungry sharks would feed on me!"

Señor Alano had stumbled away to get a lantern and disappeared
through a nearby hatch to check his cargo.

John turned to Alano. "You seem worried, señor. Can I be
helpful?"

Alano did not reply but lifted his telescope and gave his atten-

234

tion wholly to scanning the horizon in as wide an arc as his position allowed.

"I notice you use your glass frequently from all possible vantages, also that you have a man sent aloft several times a day to look out for sails that might be in our lane. Why?"

"I would admit to you, señor—and in confidence, por favor—that I carry a childish fear. It is always with me when I travel like this—the fear of pirates. From the cradle I hear gory tales from my grandfather, a merchant seaman who fought them hand to hand, spike and sword, in bloody combat. He carries many scars!"

"I suppose you have told Master Newton this in order to have him set a watch aloft so frequently?"

"Oh, no, no, no, no, señor, that would be—would be——"

"Would be what?"

"He must not think—must not think I am afraid of pirates—it would not make him feel so good. He might suspect——" Alano looked at John wide-eyed, and bit his lip hard while his face flushed.

"Suspect what?"

Alano tried to ignore the sharp query. "The master just humor me—that's all. He carries my cargo—he does what I like—and he ask no questions."

John decided to work more slowly toward the true cause of Alano's fears.

"You should shed your fears of pirates and enjoy this pleasant voyage. We are not on the high seas. We are in peaceful Gulf waters. No wars to spawn privateers—sailing in a lane traversed mostly by small ships in coastal trade, no spoils worth taking, no cargoes easy to unload away from port. Consider your own cumbersome tonnage. It would take a squad of muscle men to unload."

"Stop! Señor Sterling, silencio! I am coming apart with what I know! O Madre de Dios! Spare me!" He was using his telescope again with trembling hands.

"What do you see?"

"Nada! Nada! But I must . . ."

"You must calm yourself. I would remind you that I'm responsible for the passengers. If there's real danger, I should know about it. If not, I'll pull out something from my medicine chest to allay your qualms."

"Please, please, señor, no brandy! I crave it! But it would dim my eyes, and I must——"

"There are other medications besides brandy. One is available right here. A cathartic for your confusion: Speak out, relieve yourself. Tell me, what is there in the hold that causes such agitation?"

Alano looked about him, especially aware of the three on the bench. He moved closer and lowered his voice to a conspiratorial whisper. "You speak Spanish, señor?"

"Yes, if it's easier for you, go ahead."

To let go in Spanish was somehow like keeping a hold on his secret after all. He opened the floodgates to his emotions and a frantic flow came through in his mellow native tongue.

"Gold, señor! Gold! All in the bullion . . . many, many bars. Many . . . silver bars too—and some minted, shiny and in bags, many bags! . . . And jewels! . . . a king's ransom in gems . . . rubies, diamonds . . . a coronet fit for a prince . . . or princess!"

"Señor Alano, enough! I am not amused by Arabian nights stories!"

"I am a desperate man! I would not amuse!" Alano protested.

"Then explain why Don Vicende would be trafficking in treasure troves."

"He is not trafficking, señor. It is his own. It has been vaulted at the New Orleans Exchange since 1840."

"Indeed, sir."

Alano paused before his next statement and moved closer to be certain of privacy.

"Don Vicende is a *Carlist*." He glanced furtively at John to measure the effect of this revelation.

"Ah, now, is he?" John responded lightly, but felt grim reality about to emerge. He must lead Alano into further disclosure.

"Eighteen-forty—that was the year, was it not, when the forces of Ramón Cabrera in Catalonia were defeated in their opposition to Her Majesty Isabella II?"

"Sí, sí, señor. You know Spain——"

Alano was not sure whether this was good or bad for him.

John knew the Latin temperament responded best to circuitous approach. "And now the little queen, at sweet sixteen, is queen in her own right after suffering through tumultuous regencies since the age of three."

"Yes, señor—bad for Spain."

"Do you admire the fair young queen?"

"I have never stood in her presence. I hear that she is beautiful and has a gentle nature."

Alano did not realize that his voice was resonant with false sentiment. He continued, "And the royal wedding this year to her cousin Francisco de Asís, what glorious festivities! Spanish hearts from around the world yearned for the sight of it!"

Enough was enough. John chuckled in derision. "And many of those Spanish hearts have been yearning terribly, violently, for the sight of her uncle Don Carlos on the throne—ever since King Ferdinand declared against his brother Carlos and in favor of his baby daughter for the succession."

"To declare such was against the law!" Alano was indignant.

"What law?"

"The Salic law of succession for Spanish monarchs since 1713!"

"My God, man, that law originated in the fifth century among the Germanic tribes to deprive women of land or power. Barbaric!"

Alano was at a loss.

"I am inclined to applaud Ferdinand. He believed that women had a right to rule—they rule the world anyway, do they not, Señor Alano?"

Alano was bewildered. He could not switch his mood from heavy to light as this American could.

John pursued the subject. "Poor little Isabella. She didn't have a chance and has less now. She'll always be puppet to the party in power. What is it now? Progressive? Moderate? Liberal?"

Alano's anxieties became more tangled. The mixture of endangered treasure and political complexities was so disagreeable that he felt as if he would retch. He didn't try to answer John's inquiry. But the next question, unexpected, like a thrust to the ribs, jarred him to the pointed toes of his boots.

"You spoke of your admiration for the royal couple. Are you a loyalist?"

"No lo quiera Dios! I am a Carlist! Don Carlos is king, by law!"

"Now, by God, I know who and what you are—a part of the

strong arm of the Carlist movement on this side of the Atlantic. So I believe you, treasure story and all. Understand this: I have no reason or intention to betray you. My loyalties are for my own country and the members of my expedition. If we arrive at Laguna without interference, I will erase your story as though it were heard from a sleepwalker. If we are accosted, I will give you every assistance possible without revealing your secret—unless our lives are at stake."

"Gracias, señor. Válgate Dios." Alano's voice was spiritless, drained. "I am at your mercy. Instruct me. You are strong."

"I do not want you at my mercy. We will support each other. And, after all, we may not be intercepted. We must simply be prepared."

"But how, señor? Our boat is unarmed. Don Vicende commanded me that I give no word or sign that would hint at such a need. We must travel in innocence."

"I have traveled in innocence, and I know the penalty. Do you have a stock of weapons?"

"No, señor. I carry a pistolete. And I rely on my sword—but I will have to fall upon it if Don Vicende ever learns that I broke my vow not to tell what is concealed in the ebony storage spaces he himself designed."

"How did you keep secret the removal from the vault?"

"It was handled by Exchange officials in a manner most cautious. Don Vicende maintains a warehouse near the docks. My cargo was stored there and I alone was present when the transfer was made. The bearers entered disguised as merchants bringing supplies purchased for the plantation."

"Then there is not too much cause for your over-concern."

"There are anti-Carlist spies, and some of them know the fabled wealth of Vicende is in the New World. . . . And the jewels, señor, they are a matter of family record."

"How is that?"

"They were presented to his ancestors by the royal family during the golden years of the Conquistadores."

"I am to believe this too?"

"As if the Virgin Mary herself were by my side and nodding my favor."

The two men stood silent for a while, Alano with his eyes closed and lips moving as if in prayer, his telescope neglected.

John was musing on the suddenness with which fate could reverse the conditions under which a man must think and move: "Sir Raleigh, your ghost has come aboard. You captured my boyhood dreams and infested them with the romance of gold. I followed you and met your ghost first at the old forts of Los Castillos on the Orinoco where the Spanish routed you from the New World. But I wasn't warned. I continued under your spell and on up the river to a defeat not unlike your own—never sighting your city of gold, never seeing so much as a cracker box full of doubloons. And now here I am, on sheltered Gulf waters, aboard a small coastal trading vessel, and all that is precious to me—the real treasure of my life—is threatened."

He turned his attention back to the distraught Alano. "You must realize that we could sight a dozen ships at this season of logwood export and exchange, and all friendly. So, there must be no panic, or even excitement evidenced until we are sure of intent; we might even be hailed for assistance of some kind."

Alano protested. "Señor, you should be *more* excited! Yes, I masked every move as though covered by dead of dark. But there are robber bands who pace the docks like hungry tigers—the unknowables. And they have a sense not created in honest men, señor. Like the tiger they smell your tracks and know you have something worth killing for."

"Life is unknowables. . . . You are overtired. Get some rest. I will keep watch and make plans."

"You do have weapons, señor?"

"Yes, I have weapons. I will make plans and we will talk again."

Alano started to hand John his telescope.

"Thanks, I have one of my own with a wider lens."

Alano slumped in relief. "I get some sleep," he muttered and walked away in a haze of fatigue.

John called Sarah Belle to his side. He put his arm around her waist, drew her close for a moment, then released her.

"Sarah, dearest. Have you ever handled a gun?"

She looked at him in amazement, but answered directly. "How did you know? Yes, of course. I had an older brother who used to take me with him to the practice range. He was fond of dueling pistols." Caught in some kind of memory, she paused. "He thought it was fun to have me compete with him in accuracy. My parents would have been horrified. But Jesse enjoyed breaking rules."

"We may have reason to thank Jesse."

"John! What do you mean?"

"Alano has unlisted valuables in the hold. He fears a raid on the *Valkyrie*. I consider it unlikely, but——" Omitting the details of treasure and intrigue, he explained his plans to break out the weapons and loading supplies intended for use at the campsite.

"You and I will make contingency plans, and I will relay to Alano only what seems best for him. No others must know what we are about."

"Not even Master Newton?"

"No. He may harbor suspicions of his own, and is a man who can make ready on short notice."

"About our pleasure cruise, John——"

"Yes, my dear. Pleasure seems to be only difficulty deferred."

"'Difficulty only sharpens desire,' a French poet declared."

John reached for her hand and held it in a crushing grip. "Oh, God, if only I could hold you—hold you right now!"

"The same poet wrote: 'Desire is a flaming sword, but what shall it accomplish without a graceful handle and a tempered blade?'"

"Damn it, Sarah! Just be quiet. Don't look at me."

"Let my hand go if you expect me to handle a gun!"

CHAPTER TWENTY-SIX

MASTER NEWTON WAS AT THE HELM happily tacking down wind as though he and the *Valkyrie* were in a graceful dance, the wind and sails their musical accompaniment.

In an entirely different mood, John was in his quarters laying out his stock of weapons, thankful to Samuel Colt, and thankful that being a resident of New Jersey, his collection of Colt Paterson revolvers, manufactured at the arms company in Paterson, had furnished him with a choice of weapons for this expedition. He had selected three pistols and two carbines, all with loading levers and five chambers in the cylinder.

He carefully assembled and loaded all five pieces, feeling a little foolish as he did so, yet convinced that Alano was sewn tightly into a perilous enterprise: robbers would slaver and kill for such loot, and anti-Carlists would capture and kill with relish, considering all men on board fellow conspirators, and any women unexpected bounty. And the ship—blown up and sunk—could simply be reported lost in a storm.

While Alano slept, John had sighted sail tips of two vessels, one starboard and one on portside, both moving in a direction opposite to *Valkyrie*. Somehow this was reassuring.

When he had his guns in readiness, he went to join the master at the helm, and the news there was not reassuring.

"Take your glass, Mr. Sterling, and look portside to the edge of our world, so to speak, and tell me what you spy."

John scanned until his eyes blurred. "Nothing, nothing at all."

"Aye, and I thought you were something of a seaman. I can see it with my glassy eyeball, and almost smell it too. Look for a line rising a little wider now at the lip of the horizon; it's blue like a bruise ripening. It'll show ripples and scallops before long."

John looked again, no longer trying to catch sight of sails.

"I see what you mean. It's cloudy at the rim."

"Cloudy, you say. It's old Mad-Woman-Storm that's got us in her sights. She hove into the Gulf from the islands, no doubt, and may be out to tear us apart."

"I thought the season——"

"Anything out of its time is a thousand times worsen' what moves on the seasoned track of the calendar. You've heard of sea monsters no sane man has ever seen, but they're there all right, on the bottom of the ocean. Every once in a hunnerd years or so, one'll rise up and swoller a whole ship—out of season, a'course."

"Are you trying to tell me, we had better batten down for a rough time?"

"You're sayin' it mild, Mr. Sterling. We'll issue life preservers, lash the jolly-boat down, set ladder and lifeboat at ready and secure her somewhat to leeward."

John put a feeler out on Señor Alano. "Alano is a man easily excited with emotions so lashed to his cargo that only God knows how he will act in a storm."

Newton gave him a straight, steely stare. "Devil take his filthy cargo. If he gets in our way, we'll tie him down in the hold with it. Won't we?"

"That, and right merrily, Captain," John agreed. "Human skin being the most valuable commodity aboard."

"You know, a'course, I expect to ride 'er out. You get the women and that invalid with man-servant secured in their bunk-havens at the proper time, with lanterns and warnings to stay-put. I can use a man like you with me. The sailors like a fight with the Old Witch of the Waves even if we come awash. . . . She may smack us straight on or just spin us about playfully and be gone."

"How long before we put out the welcome mat?"

"Some hours yet. May get us into dark as black as a cave in hell."

"I like your cheerful approach, Captain. Good day—for now."

John hurried away to rearrange his weapons and gunpowder in case the boat should come awash and water damage be done. "Make us good prey for raiders," he muttered to himself. "But if there are such on our track, may they flounder to a watery finish!"

The cloud was moving in close, black and threatening.

The thunder had become a continuous angry roar, and lightning in vertical streaks connected sky and sea. The sailors, gearing for combat, moved like streaks themselves. The balladeer of the crew busy at reinforcing a spar, sang out lustily,

"O bury me not in the wild blue sea
Where the belly of the whale my grave may be
Shroud my body in canvas lee
And hold on to me
But bury me not in the wild blue sea."

John, Alano, Sarah Belle, and the other three passengers stood clustered together not far from the helm where the master was giving his full attention to studying the storm cloud and getting all steering parts and controls in tight readiness.

John turned to Alano, who was unable to hide his misery and apprehension. The waters were close to calm, the *Valkyrie* scarcely moving. When the sailor, now clambering aloft, boomed out another line, "Where the hungry sharks may feed on me," Alano's eyes rolled in terror.

John addressed him in Spanish: "Señor Alano, the master just suggested that you might like to stay out the storm in the hold with your cargo, and perhaps take a nip or so to steady your nerves. We are in no immediate danger from other sources. 'One mountain at a time' is all we can climb, you know."

"Sí, sí, señor. ¡Que gracia!" As Alano turned away and tried not to run, Mad-Woman-Storm brought a loud clap from out of her rumble that seemed directed at the very vaults of the treasure in the hold. Alano fell to his knees, scrambled up, and raced for the nearest hatch.

Emile stood close to Maury, his eyes half closed, one hand in a side pocket where Jasper peeped out cautiously with an animal's awareness of nature's moods.

Sarah Belle took command of her charges. "The three of you get to Maury's quarters as we arranged according to the master's orders, and stay there until you're called."

Newton called to John. "The wind is picking up now. It won't be long until she gives us a sound slap. Better get into your oils, Mr. Sterling."

"Sarah, I heard you. Surely, you're not going to take shelter alone?" A strong blast of wind hit the ship broadside and another clap, louder than the first, was deafening. Lightning began to flash and play all around, and the storm brought on a near darkness of its own.

John grabbed Sarah by the arm. She called in his ear, "I'll get into my oils and be right back."

"You will not!" But she was gone.

By the time she had struggled back on deck and toward John amidship, the storm was raging with such violence that only their determination to reach each other brought them together. As they clung to each other, a crack of lightning struck a hawser hole and a ball of fire rose up, and seemed to take flight directly toward them. With Sarah held close, John fell to the deck and rolled, thinking, "Oh God, fire on deck . . . catastrophe!"

A volunteer celestial fireman answered his call. The *Valkyrie* listed sharply and sent a wave washing over the deck.

Then came one of those momentary calms when Neptune on a rampage takes a deep breath.

John came to his feet, pulling Sarah Belle with him. With the speed of a stage magician he unwound a length of rope that he was carrying around his waist for emergency tie-downs, tied one end around Sarah Belle and one around himself, taking up the slack with loops around their waists. Simply by turning, they could adjust the distance between them. Then he pulled her close while torrents of rain poured over them.

Clinging and cautious, they made their way through the blustery downpour to the helm, to where the master fought for the life of the *Valkyrie* and of those aboard. With a movement of his head in their direction he signaled awareness of their presence.

Then another blast hit . . . and another . . . and another. The *Valkyrie* plunged and pitched, a boom snapped like a rifle shot through the din, and then the vessel lifted and listed in a side thrust so sudden that John and Sarah Belle were plunged against the wheel, and Newton was thrown to the deck, his head striking a metal brace. As though they were doing a wild spin in the storm, Sarah Belle and John let out the rope between them. John grabbed the wheel and Sarah Belle went to her knees by the unconscious pilot. She struggled with his headgear until she could push it back and get his head in her lap to press firm fingers against an open cut near his ear.

The storm gave the boat a final twist, the thunder lowered to a rumble while lightning continued in wide illuminating flashes more helpful than threatening. The torrent of rain ceased as if a heavy curtain had been drawn back. The dark red glow in the west gave the eerie effect of a burned-out forest fire with black debris its ground line. The moon, not far from full, began to look through the thin afterclouds as if reluctant to lift the veil. Starlight and storm exchanged greeting in the southwest.

A ragged ghost of a man half-naked and battered appeared by John, lantern in hand. "I be the mate. Take this and do somethin' for the captain. All hands still on deck."

John unwound the rope from himself and looked at Sarah Belle—the blood-stained tableau of her holding the wounded master close in her arms becoming clear-cut in the near constant flashes of sheet lightning.

"I'll be back with help." The tableau remained statue-still. He hurried away.

Soon they had James Newton in his bunk, his wounds dressed with a healing salve. John brought liniment and camphor—Sarah Belle rubbed his brow and cheeks, placed the camphor to his nostrils, but he failed to respond.

"His fatigue is too deep," she surmised. The mate and crew were relieved to have a woman in attendance. The Newton cabin was roomier and better appointed than on most ships of trade the size of the *Valkyrie*, and as behooved a merchant seaman who could count on such patronage as the wealthy Vicende had offered in contract.

Celeste was brought in to prepare hot tea and coffee which John laced generously with brandy and passed out to the sailors with biscuits and dried ham. Soon lanterns were bobbing about the deck lighting the way for the crew to bind up the *Valkyrie's* wounds.

As she moved slowly on her way, wavering a little like a beautiful sea creature that has given blood in a fight, the waters she traversed were iridescent with fractured reflections of moon and stars and dots of lantern light.

John found Maury in close attendance upon Emile who, dazed by his shake-up in the storm, would accept neither food nor drink and was seemingly unaware of Jasper's clambering about trying to get his attention. Maury was depressed and taciturn.

"He may come 'round, Mister John, but storm not all we got to bear. More to come. The devil got his bat-wings spread over this ship—for sure."

"Maury, that's nonsense," John declared, at the same time recalling Maury's gloomy consent to the trip when it was first announced. Was it possible that some word of the Vicende cache had filtered through to him on that mysterious circuit maintained in New Orleans by a secret order of slaves and servants?

"Maury, if you had a gun, would you be able to take a shot at the devil if he got too close to the ship?"

Maury altered like a recruit caught napping. "'Deed I would, Mister John. My soul-brother here on this bed taught me guns for huntin' with him, and to carry the gun when he go into danger spots."

"That's good. I have weapons that I brought for protection on our journey, and to secure provisions at our campsite. I will issue one to you, a revolving carbine that will deliver five shots before reloading."

"Never heard of such." Maury's eyes were round with a relief so plain that John knew he had touched the source of dread. Maury was eager. "You mean I get one while on this ship?"

"In the morning, we'll review the mechanism."

"Praise the Almighty. He provide my sword and buckler!"

"When I show you that carbine you'll think the Lord has greatly improved his armory."

John had been too occupied with the condition of the *Valkyrie* and its master to reach ahead into the threat that had originated with Alano's disclosure. Now it closed in on him more forcibly than ever with Maury's foreboding.

If there were raiders tracking the *Valkyrie* and they had been able to ride out the storm, they would hope the ship they sought to plunder might be weakened, and would take advantage on the day now soon to break on the morrow. After that, the voyage would be too near the end for piratical action, with ships from other directions converging on the port of Laguna.

There had been no question about John and Sarah Belle staying in the master cabin. The crew expected it—the mate came for reports to John as if he were in charge. John put up a cot and one would rest while the other sat at close watch over Newton. Celeste came in at intervals.

During the morning watch, when the two of them were alone and wakeful, John inquired, "Shall we set the stage for the next performance?"

"You actually think there might be an attempt to seize the *Valkyrie*—that she is prize enough to draw violence?"

"My dear, Señor Alano is guardian over vaulted wealth in the hold that could build a pirate's palace on Cozumel, finance a revolution on a whim, and endow his family line for generations. . . . My God, I've just remembered, Alano has not shown up on deck since the storm! . . . I hope we don't have another patient. I'll be right back." He grabbed a lantern and hurried to the hatch leading down to center cargo. He left the hatch open and Sarah Belle could hear him calling the Spaniard's name . . . heard it grow faint as he searched at the far ends of the hold. Then silence . . . a long silence . . .

She stood at the door of the cabin waiting . . . uneasy. The dawn was showing a red line in the east with no clouds to ornament the sky. The *Valkyrie* was moving smoothly now, and most of the crew slept. Water and wind and sails talking were the only sounds, as if the ship might be manned and maneuvered by ghosts. . . .

Then John appeared on deck, paused to put out his lantern, and turned toward the dawn as it spread an orange and gold path for the sun. She could tell he drew a deep breath and probably sighed, before moving on toward her.

He stood looking at her a long moment, then inquired, "How is Newton?"

"Still sleeping."

"You mean still unconscious."

"Yes. Did you find Señor Alano?"

"Yes."

"Is he all right?"

"No, Sarah. He's dead."

"Oh, John! Are you sure? How could it be?"

"It appears the cargo shifted and he was caught between two heavy pieces and crushed."

"You say 'appears'—what else could have happened?"

"He could have been murdered."

"John, do you know what you're saying?"

"I'm saying what I have to say."

"But all hands were on deck working to save their lives and ours."

"None of the crew. A stowaway."

"How do you know?"

"I think I just broke his neck."

Sarah Belle stared at him and waited.

"Suddenly he was standing there in front of me. I had my lantern raised. He was small and wizened like an imp of Hades. He threw a knife—I think he was injured for his aim was off. My first glimpse told me what was to come and I dodged. He came at my knees. The lantern fell. I grabbed him and threw him—just hurled him to anywhere. Then I recovered my lantern and looked where he had landed. As I said, I think his neck is broken. He is as dead as Alano.

"But Sarah—look, darling—never mind that. Walk with me to the rail. Celeste will be in the cabin shortly. We must think straight. This means, of course, that we can be sure the *Valkyrie* is targeted for gutting, probably this very day."

"How can we prepare to reverse the gutting?"

John was startled at her even reply. Here was a woman who required no protective coddling at the approach of raw danger.

248

"What will we do with the bodies?" she added.

"Leave them exactly where they are. And at this point, tell no one on board. Hopefully, Newton will come to and be able to take charge. If not, I'll be pushed into lead position. The mate is a good man, but I alone know the details of Señor Alano's mission with all it implies.

"As for preparations: I'll advise the mate that I have had wind of a possible attack because of valuables Señor Alano secreted in the hold and I think we should be at ready. I'll tell him openly of the weapons I have available."

"What of Maury and Emile and Celeste?"

"Maury has been under a cloud all along, full of forebodings, must have had some inkling of the dangers to be encountered. He knows how to handle guns. So I'll equip him adequately for their defense. And ourselves? What shall we say of ourselves, my love?"

"That we live to survive, and that we survive to love."

"Shall we ask permission of the crew before I take you in my arms?"

"Those that are not asleep are too weary to watch, and if they should, let it flavor their day."

She came into his arms and they stood before the rising sun in long embrace—first their lips drinking deep from love's chalice, and, as their arms tightened about each other with heightened intensity, their bodies began pulsing as one, filling them with the wonder of belonging to each other and the assurance of surviving for greater fulfillment of desire and design. Their only witness was Celeste. She had watched and wept for joy.

It was during the afternoon watch, about midway, when they sighted a schooner. It was portside and moving directly toward them rather than parallel in the same lane.

"It's a fast one, sir, the clipper type, carrying a whole cloudful of canvas," the mate reported to John, "but something not quite right about the riggin'—mayhaps the storm chewed things up a bit. Ah, I catch it now, she's listing some. But she must have just been edged by the blasts or else she'd a toppled with all that spread."

John had already briefed the mate, and he, in turn, had alerted the crew that there were rumors of unfriendly craft in some of these waters and so best be sharp-eyed and check blades as well as sails. The mate himself carried a large sword, sharp-pointed and double-edged, as well as his ever-ready service knife. These he considered adequate for self-defense. He accepted the carbine revolver that John placed at his disposal, however, with rapt surprise, stroking the barrel, fingering the cylinder with a gleam in his eye that reflected yearning for a fracas.

John informed Maury and Celeste of the sighting and explained that the schooner could be a friendly one damaged in the storm and needing assistance.

"It's trouble. I knows," was all Maury had to say.

Responding to John's statement Sarah Belle asked, "Is that what you think?"

"No," he replied bluntly. "I think it is the inevitable but the other must not be ruled out, and it could be both—damaged but with intent to pillage just the same. The mate has hoisted the flag. After a while they'll be close enough to respond, and within the hour we'll take out the speaking-trumpet."

The response from the schooner was a matching flag. "That's no comfort," the mate declared. "Rascals and robbers are the same under any flag. You do the speakin', Master Sterling. You got the voice and manners for it. I'll save my kind of words for any thievin' bastard that tries to climb aboard."

John took the trumpet and called out: "The *Valkyrie* here, the master Newton, the business cargo to Laguna."

The reply came quickly: "The *Retort* here, owner Montclair, business supply transport for loggers up the Usumacinta River. We're in grave trouble."

The mate said, "Don't let any soft talk fool you. That schooner's got an evil spirit in its sails. I can tell."

"What's your need, *Retort*?"

"A sick woman aboard—short provisions—storm cracked our water tub and fouled some food boxes."

"A foul trick," the mate muttered. "They need nothing so much as a torpedo through the hull—wish I had that naval vessel I rode a while back under me. By God! I'd blow 'em to hell and no conscience about it!"

"Shut up," John commanded, and called out, "What's wrong with the woman?"

The schooner was closer and communication more distinct.

The mate was scanning the deck of the *Retort* with his scope. "Nothin' but a scarecrow crew, more under the hatches no doubt —a dirty deck—use rats for pets, I'm swearin'."

"The sick one's been knocked about in the storm," the *Retort* caller assured.

"And I'll bet she has, from the likes of what I see! Master Sterling, they's always a smooth talker aboard such schooners. Don't be ironed out by 'im."

"She needs medicine and a woman's hands . . . ," came the plea.

"Probably manhandling has done her in," the mate surmised.

John tried to ignore the mate's asides. He was inclined to play cat and mouse, casting himself as the cat.

"And what makes you think there are women on the *Valkyrie?*"

"We were moored just down the wharf and saw you pull out."

"Imagine that!" the mate sneered.

"Any medications aboard?" John inquired.

"None to speak of. Do you have paregoric? This woman needs paregoric bad to ease the pain, and she has an issue of blood and cries for a woman's care."

"She's a bloody decoy, that's what!" the mate was close to rage.

"Let down your jolly-boat and bring her over," John invited.

The mate yelled to John, "I'll blast five holes in that jolly and carve up every man at the oars."

"What about the woman, mate?"

"Let 'er sink or swim."

"Mister Mate, I, and only I, know what's in that hold, and as long as Master Newton is unconscious, I must make decisions for him, not about running the ship, you understand, but where the lives of us all are at stake because of what's down there. The woman may be—most likely is—a decoy, but we will fare better to play unprepared and ignorant, and learn more of their plot to take us over."

"Where's that cargo manager who's kept racing aloft to look for such as this?"

"Señor Alano suffered injury when some of his cargo shifted. He's not able to be on deck."

"That's the way with watchdogs. They can run themselves to death before anything happens."

The visiting schooner lost no time in getting the woman into the jolly-boat, swung in a carry hammock and accompanied by an attendant and four men at the oars.

The mate called for two sailors to let down a ladder and help the men get the sick woman on board. Then he stood watching the process with his arms akimbo, wearing a scowl that condemned and only deferred the death penalty.

It was a startling piece of cargo being brought aboard. The woman was wrapped in clean canvas—nothing showing but her hair, very long, pomegranate red, flowing around her as she was moved and keeping her face hidden. All five occupants of the boat crowded up the ladder, though only two were handling the body. They were surprised to see a stalwart vigorous woman standing close at hand directing them at once to bring their bundle to the captain's cabin and deposit it on the cot.

Sarah Belle immediately brushed the hair from the woman's face. Eyes were closed, too tightly, the face flushed, and the long dark eyelashes quivering. Near the corner of the full mouth was a small scar, and it was pulsing.

"Oh my, the poor dear. She *is* very sick!"

The woman groaned.

"Hurry, doctor, the paregoric. She is in pain." Sarah Belle unbuttoned the high-collared jacket, thrust her hand under the bodice, felt the woman squirming under her hand. "And the heart rate is simply frightening!"

John opened his medicine chest, conspicuously placed. The first thing visible was his revolver. He picked it up as casually as if it were a surgeon's knife and laid it on the cot not far from the woman's head. He took out a vial, filled a spoon carefully and handed it to Sarah Belle, who coaxed, "Just open your mouth the slightest bit, little one—that's a good girl, now swallow." The patient swallowed and groaned again.

The five watchers tried to show friendly and concerned faces but their aggressive posture belied good will. Their eyes were taking inventory of everything in the cabin—except the pistol, which after a startled glance they heedfully ignored. The leader, more carefully groomed and more inclined to civility, focused on the bunk where the sleeping master lay with face turned to the wall and bandage not in view.

"Shh!" John cautioned. "He's storm-weary. Needs his rest."

Sarah Belle looked up at the four ruffians who had moved very close to her, formidable, threatening, and reeking with surfeit of ale. She frowned, looked at John, made a motion with her head toward the men watching her so intently.

"The lady would like for you to leave, so she will be free to examine the woman and make her comfortable." He spoke in a loud whisper as he replaced spoon and vial, then reached for his pistol as though it were an item almost forgotten. The men moved back, all but the leader, reluctant to be played down.

"Are you a ship's doc?" he queried.

"Surgeon," John snapped with aloof disapproval. "You may address me as 'Dr. Sterling.' My main interest is with my patients. This woman will get all the attention she needs whether she deserves it or not. If she needs the knife, I will be ready. If she needs extended care, we will keep her here until out of danger."

The leader glared, his eyes glittering with rage at the implications.

John's hand lay on the pistol. He continued calmly, "Remain in hailing distance and I will give you a report as soon as I have time to study the case—possibly by tomorrow. Give us your attention at the beginning of the afternoon watch. As for helping out with provisions, the master here must not be disturbed. I have prescribed unbroken rest. I'm sure he will check stores and share with you on the morrow, if supplies warrant."

"Thank you, Dr. Sterling, and I am Monsieur Montclair, the owner of the *Retort*." The spokesman's tone was insultingly obsequious. "We prize our woman dearly. If anything should happen——"

"I am totally responsible. It is a credo of the profession."

The four men turned away as a unit. As they stepped outside the cabin another surprise performance awaited them.

The mate and three sailors were playing an unusual game. Their knives were flying between them like a horizontal juggling display. The mate caught and threw with only one hand and held his carbine aloft like a signal piece while the knives were whizzing about. He didn't stop or look up as the men came out.

"Get to your oars, stretcher-bearers, and step lively. We keep a deck clean and clear, and if ye leave tracks, we'll get a bucket and put you to swabbing and no tellin' when you'll get back home." He knew where the visitors knives were sheathed and was aware of their temptation to reach for them. "Or, if ye want to join the game——" Suddenly all knives were still and the carbine held horizontal.

Silently, the five witnesses left the boat with a stride that spoke clearly their intention to return under different conditions. The mate was convinced they had come to place the decoy and learn the lay of the deck and the force of the crew.

John turned to Sarah Belle. They were both aware that the woman on the cot, though silently sedated with the paregoric, would hear anything they might say.

John spoke softly, "Lying there in repose, she looks quite lovely with her red hair spread all around, doesn't she? I wonder what color her eyes are? There is a look of innocence about her— strange under the circumstances."

"What circumstances?" Sarah asked, picking up the intent.

"Need you ask?"

"You think she might be—just an ornament for the voyage?"

"And what an ornament!"

There was another groan and movement under the covers.

"We must have more private quarters for her. One good look, and the sailors will be at each other until the best man wins. Or if the master should suddenly arouse, he would think he had passed over and this was his reward. Bring Celeste and we will move her at once."

"Place her on my bed," Sarah Belle directed as she left.

John pulled back the canvas to see what he might be carrying when he picked up his charge.

"Shades of Scheherazade!" he exclaimed, and her eyes popped open, two deep brilliant pools of blue that were full of . . . was it misery? mystery? fright? or some unhealthy obsession? She was clad in silk Oriental-style bloomer-trousers, heavily gathered at waist and ankles, dazzling blue in color. Her jacket of patterned brocade was long sleeved and high necked. Where Sarah Belle had unbuttoned the jacket, a tight bodice of gold satin covering only her breasts was exposed. Her body was small, so formed as to suggest the agility of an acrobat with the bosom overlarge—the breasts like a flamboyant afterthought of the creator, attached in a joyous salute to Eros.

Her eyes fastened on John with the intensity of an animal in obeisance to a master. He looked away from what he read there.

The eyes shuttered at once as Sarah Belle and Celeste entered. Her whole body quivered, she groaned and lay quiet as the two women stared at her in wonderment.

"Let's get moving. Bring my chest and the canvas." He picked up the woman with difficulty. Her body was stiff as his arms went under her, and then grew limp as if she had fainted. As he carried her along, her head was thrown back and her hair almost raked the deck. The mate who had been waiting to talk to John saw the procession.

"Oh, Almighty God!" he exclaimed, as near stripped of profanity as he would ever be. "Thou hast delivered up to us a Jezebel!"

CHAPTER TWENTY-SEVEN

JOHN AND SARAH BELLE were walking the deck.
Maury was grimly standing watch over the inert
ornament from the *Retort*.
The mate was at the helm carefully sharpening his knives.

The *Valkyrie* slipped along as smooth as a dolphin, catching a
modest breeze in her sails, as though independent of human
thralldom and evil omen.

A sailor assigned to the cabin to observe the master turned pale
when Newman suddenly sat up erect with wide open eyes, bloodshot and terrified, and commanded hoarsely, "Check the hold! For
God's sake, check the hold!" and then fell back in a coma.

Celeste was with Emile pleading, "Just another spoonful, baby,
for Celeste and Jasper, just one more." And then sat very still, her
tears falling into the bowl of broth.

"The *Retort* quintet have had a setback," said John. "They had
anticipated that the little killer stored below would have laid out

quite a row of us by this time. They will expect him to accomplish more with the assistance of the enticing, gaudy creature they have given to our care."

"Your description is quite explicit."

"So is their intent."

"She must have opened her eyes when you were alone with her."

"She certainly did, and they carry a blast!"

"Really. Did she say anything?"

"Nothing with words."

"Hmmm . . . John, we must search her. There's no telling what she carries in the lining of that jacket and the pockets of her Persian pantaloons."

"We'll try it as a part of the examination. If that doesn't work, I have another scheme that will."

"Have it ready. She had expected no more than a dose of medicine, no undressing required. She would have snarled and bitten me when I reached beneath her bodice, had she dared."

"The caller from the *Retort* must have overstepped a bit when he said she yearned for a woman's touch and was troubled with an issue of blood."

Sarah Belle pushed back an ugly impulse to comment on whose touch might satisfy the patient and whose blood might issue if. . .

"We'll see," she replied.

Maury pocketed his revolver as doctor and assistant dismissed him, and spoke his piece with acid clarity. "I smell venom when I come through that door. A viper lie on that bed, and if it crawl around this deck, the devil prowl this ship till she sink."

"What a wicked statement, Maury. Get out. I will not have you distressing this sick woman."

Maury walked away puzzled and distressed himself. John closed the door behind him.

John pulled a stool beside the bed and sat down, took up a limp hand and checked the pulse. The wrist tightened and the fingers flared. He felt the forehead, the chin lifted and head jerked back.

"Feverish! Pulse very irregular! . . . Madam!"

Sarah Belle resented the necessity for such a tone, "Yes, doctor."

"Get one of your gowns and prepare this woman for further examination. An issue of blood was mentioned and could be fatal unless attended. I think she will be more responsive to a woman's attentions."

Before Sarah could take the stool, her charge had jerked to a sitting position, eyes wide with fury, and hands grabbing both thighs.

John pushed Sarah Belle aside. "I understand your sickness," he said quietly, his own eyes fixed steadily on the flared pupils engaging his until he saw rage replaced by fascination.

"We'll wait. You must have rest and food, and further medication. You are very ill. I will attend you myself—alone. Will you lie down again, please." She obeyed but her eyes followed him, holding on.

Sarah Belle was close to frenzy. "Jezebel has passed her rage on to me," she was thinking.

John reached into the medicine chest. "Bring me a spoon and a cup of water," he said curtly to Sarah Belle, "and then leave us." She obeyed him, her hand trembling, her heart pounding. In the exchange, he managed to expose the vial he was holding. It was labeled IPECAC.

She left quickly, her emotions in a turmoil that mixed assurance with dread.

It was not long until she heard the retching, severe, violent, racking . . . then John's voice, soothing, sustaining, as though guiding someone through a cave of torment that could and would end. More retching and strangling . . . then gasping and sobbing and inarticulate pleading. Then silence.

Sarah Belle knocked gently.

"Not yet," he requested firmly.

She did not knock again. She waited until he opened the door. She was not prepared for what she saw. On her bed was the form that had threatened with such fury, eyes closed, face pale and drained, the red hair scattered all around, a sheet covering the body, arms resting outside showing that she wore Sarah Belle's gown. Neatly spread along a wall bench was the whole array of clothing that had been removed. On the portable cabin table was an orderly display of quite another kind: three stilettos, flat-handled and of different lengths and design; a coil of fine copper wire; several small metal boxes and vials suitable for poisons; a miniature handgun, and a flat case of phosphorous matches.

John came to Sarah Belle, his brow and face still wet with perspiration, his eyes weary, his expression sad. "The venom has been extracted," he said.

"When she revives she'll be very weak and—malleable. Montclair's decoy is now our decoy, and we must shape her to our purpose."

"And what is that?"

"When I told you that the *Valkyrie* was targeted for gutting, you asked me, 'How can we prepare to reverse the gutting?' There is your answer." He nodded toward the bed. "Jinnee."

"Jinnee?"

"She wouldn't tell me her name. I gave her one."

"John! You used that name when—when——"

"I know. On the day you brought me to your house and wanted to open your jeweled box of confessions for me to read."

"Not confessions! Accounts—records——"

"Call them what you like. There could have been no benefit to either of us in such sharing. I told you the jinnee myth to divert you. It was suggested by the Oriental symbols of enchantment worked into the design. And there are certain truths of the human mind concealed in such tales.

"The jinnee, in myth, is a kind of supernatural being that may appear in animal or human form and is subject to magic control for good or evil. If matters work out as I have 'directed'"——he paused for a side glance to Sarah Belle—"Jinnee may wake up a human being."

"Behold the magician that sneered at the likes of Marie Laveau! After the ordeal you put her through, you expect this jinnee to do your bidding?"

"Yes, I do. With your help—and understanding."

He turned away and began collecting the deadly items on the table. "I'll take these for storage in the master's cabin (enough poison here to wipe out an armada), and I hope he comes alive. We need him—urgently."

"How can I help?"

"Stay here until I return. Do you mind?"

"No, John. I don't mind. Honestly, I don't."

He started to leave, turned to look at her, to say something, but words wouldn't come.

His eyes were hollow, his cheeks drawn, his fatigue so deep that his shoulders drooped.

She yearned to run to him, caress him, care for him. But this she knew was not what he needed now. And she knew that he had read into the tone of "Honestly-I-don't-mind" the whole of her thinking: "I do not want to stay here with this vile woman who would have seen us all dead, and gloated—all but you, that is."

He left in silence and she ached with his unspoken response, and felt a sense of separation more frightening than the dilemma they were trying to resolve.

She sat down beside the bed, studying the face in repose, and the still hands, broad with stout fingers curled inward—in response, she clinched her own into fists. A riot of emotions surged through her . . . Hate? . . . Jealousy? . . . Fear? What close kin they were! Certain degrees of fear she had known, hate or jealousy never to the extent of awareness. She opened her hands, let them lie, palms upward in her lap, and willed self-analysis.

Her thoughts spoke to the body lying there, motionless, and yet shrouded in her (Sarah Belle's) gown, which in itself was an affront.

I acknowledge your hate for me is as fierce as your lust for John. That will not change. No matter how staunch he remains in the bracket of our love, I can hate you almost to madness for what's in your mind. At the very sight of him, or the slightest touch, he is ravishing you. Until you can achieve the reality, this is your obsession, giving yourself to him with every glance—measuring every action to please, to entrance him—slavish obedience your constant surrender. All other loyalties wiped out. Must I compete with the wisdom of your kind and a body that would bring Zeus cavorting down from Olympus? How can I stand aside and not hate you? fear you? envy you? Is this rage flaming in me because I myself have not yet experienced in the physical what John and I have to give each other? . . . that I, too, imagine . . . I must rationalize: You are salvation—you are survival for John and me and all aboard this cursed vessel (with dead men in the hold and disaster hovering). Ah! but I must admit to you, Jinnee, animal-woman, there is something of the same in me, an elemental something. At this moment I do

hate! I'd like to tear my gown off you and . . . and . . . Oh, dear
God, how I need my harp!

She unclenched her hands again and concentrated on the harp,
framing the words that she would bring to it.

In the desert of my mind . . .
Monsters three appear . . . I draw them near,
Stand face to face with Monster Hate
Confronted with his awesome power
Too dread to contemplate;
And by his side, his loathsome bride, veiled
        Jealousy——
O! God, I see them mate!!
The ogre Fear stands very near to urge them on:
        "Let Passion roar and blaze, O lustful
                pair, until you've had your fill . . .
        I'll eat your ashes when they chill!"

Sarah Belle was startled, as from a nightmare, by a hand on her
shoulder. John had entered unawares.

"Sarah, you're wrestling with your soul. . . . Isn't love enough?
I've found it so."

She felt a quivering over her whole body, as if every cell had
done a turnaround. She could not move or look up at him.

"The captain is rousing some. I'm hopeful. Celeste is there
ready with stimulant and nourishment if he revives. She has something waiting for you. Go now."

There was a deep breath and a long sigh from the sleeping
Jinnee.

Sarah Belle stood up as if on signal. For an instant their eyes
met, guarded, controlled, the protocol of acceptance established,
the curfew on emotions declared.

John sat waiting for Jinnee's eyes to open, preparing for the first
glance and what would follow. Here lay his weapon of defense for
all who were yet alive on the *Valkyrie*. He, too, was having a new
experience when he had thought to have run the gamut in the
valley of the Orinoco. He had never imagined making deliberate
use of any woman for any kind of advantage, large or small.

It had been with difficulty that he had administered the over-
dose of ipecac after impressing Jinnee that the dosage would

cleanse her system so thoroughly that no examination would be necessary—that she would feel very sick for a short while then better and stronger than before.

She spoke fragmentary English, but while under stress exclaimed and pled in a patois of French he had not heard before and could not localize. No telling where Montclair had discovered such a prize so fitting to his purposes. "And to mine!" he had thought grimly when he was using the French language to plant confidence as he gave her directions, and cared for her needs, bathing her brow, as she went through the convulsive reactions to the medication. "Why?" she had begged, gasping, tears pouring from her eyes. "Perhaps a demon being cast out," he had whispered hoarsely, and despised himself for the ruse he sensed she would accept.

Now she opened her eyes, the long lashes moving back slowly, revealing the blue depths undimmed, as her head turned to focus on John, eyes more powerful than tongue telling him of the pleasure that coursed through her whole body at the sight of him.

He knew that he must not turn his face away. He forced a small smile, reluctant to say what was necessary, and in most gentle French. "The demon has fled."

Her answering smile was radiant. "Yes, all gone."

"Tomorrow, Montclair will come. Will you go back with him or stay with me?"

She raised her arms and reached out to him. "With you, monsieur. Always." And then as an afterthought: "You may kill Montclair, if you like." She smiled broadly to convince him that she was in earnest.

"But he promised you gold, riches suitable for a queen."

"Oh yes," she agreed heartily. "I think now he lied to me—it was too much gold—and jewels. He said I would have diamonds and rubies, and a crown of emeralds and pearls for my hair." She sat erect and ran her fingers through her hair, managing at the same time to loosen the gown so her breasts were near exposure.

John did close his eyes for an instant. "I wish to God she weren't wearing that garment! I'll burn it when this is over!"

"Is gold on this ship?" she asked bluntly. "Montclair say barrels of gold and silver and jewelry. He say we go to Cozumel—he build palace, be the king and I be his queen."

"The Queen of Cozumel! And you'd give up that for——"

"Then there is gold here. You have gold. But that is no matter. You are my gold!" She leaned toward him again, her arms out, her body moving in invitation.

"I did not say there was gold. You could find out from the cargo manager, but he is dead."

She drew back in fright.

"Grudo did it! Who else is dead? He should have killed more by now. Where is he? He would kill me if he knew I belong to you now. Go find him—take the gun. Kill him! Kill him quick!"

"I have."

Suddenly she was elated, delighted as a child, laughed and made a move to jump out of bed.

"Jinnee! Stay where you are a while." He pushed her back, almost roughly. "Lie down. I will bring you food. Take care how you move about—another dose of medicine might be indicated."

She shivered and inquired meekly, "Why you call me 'Jinnee'?"

"You would not give me your name. So I named you Jinnee."

"I like it. I have no name! You hear me!" she demanded, almost shouting. "No name—never! But now," she smiled sweetly, turning her siren eyes full upon him, "I am your Jinnee. You feed me, dress me maybe when I am well?"

Maury appeared at the door. "Miss Sarah Belle say you wanted me, and she now have food ready for you."

"Yes, Maury, stand by and attend the queen." He smiled at Jinnee, and she let out a trickle of laughter.

"I'll be back soon."

She glared at him. "You stay. Feed me. He bring food," she demanded.

"I will select the food and bring it here. We will eat together."

Her eyes glowed with satisfaction, "Oui."

"I want you to be quiet and still until I come back."

"Oui," she replied and threw her arms over her head, stretching her whole body with feline audacity. "I be still."

Maury standing at the door, turned his back, and growled an inarticulate oath.

Sarah Belle and John talked rapidly in the master's cabin.

"Sarah, do you carry any kind of sleeping draught with you, for Emile, perhaps?"

"Yes, Maury keeps it at hand, a herb compound that Shealia brews, effective and no harm done."

"Get it for me quickly so I can take it back with the food, and give me the dosage. I want her to sleep heavily through the night, but be alert tomorrow for the part I'll have her playing. Montclair will be scanning the deck. There must be calculated entertainment. I will instruct all on board while she sleeps."

While Sarah Belle was gone, John anxiously examined Newton, found deep breathing and regular pulse. If only he really were a doctor able to diagnose such a coma! No sign of reviving had been observed, except the exclamation reported by the watching sailor.

In addition to the draught, Sarah Belle carried a bottle of lotion.

"John, I'm placing this bottle here by Master Newton. When Jinnee is well asleep, if you'll come back and apply this briskly to his face, neck, chest, even legs and arms, it will enhance circulation; it's another of Shealia's Jamaican formulas. It might be restorative. I will stay with Jinnee, even catch a bit of rest on the cot, while you do this."

"Sarah, my partner, come here for a moment and put your head on my shoulder." He drew her to him. They did not kiss or cling. It was strength, not passion that built between them; confidence, not desire.

Jinnee's hunger for food tempered her other appetites. John, seated close beside her, plied her with rich thick chocolate, hearty cheese, and dainties from Shealia's basket that Celeste had selected for him. She took the draught without hesitation, and lay back replete. "You say, monsieur, it will keep me young and beautiful," she spoke in her native patois, throaty and purring. "Then you know I am beautiful, but not how much beautiful."

"You need rest, much rest tonight, Jinnee. We will do many things together tomorrow."

"You place your hand on my head, I sleep quicker." Hoping that Shealia's drug worked quicker than the gesture, he complied. He was surprised, alarmed, at the life, the tingle, the magnetic pull of the heavy waves of hair under his hand. It was as though the strands might fasten his hand to her head. Did she know this? She closed her eyes, lay very still, and seemed to be holding her breath. He wanted to remove his hand, but could not will it. He found that he too was holding his breath. Then as if by mental contact, he knew what she was expecting, what she was willing with all her force of mind—that with the other hand he would touch her somewhere, anywhere! Then she caught her breath, let go the image, and began to succumb to the sleeping draught. Lest he startle her, he left his hand upon her hair until she slept, and it was nothing more than smooth silk beneath his fingers.

Sarah Belle and John spelled the night watch over Jinnee. Leaving only Jinnee's clothing behind, Sarah Belle removed all that belonged to her and Celeste, placing her own possessions in John's quarters and Celeste's with Maury and Emile.

At the beginning of the morning watch, 4:00 A.M., John called the mate and Maury and outlined what was to take place on portside during forenoon watch—a performance that could convince Montclair Jinnee's work was going well.

Montclair had the greatest confidence in his voluptuous lure operating with no handicap of scruples. He rewarded her well for her triumphs, and she would be worthy of all he had promised if she raped the *Valkyrie*, making it ready for a funeral pyre, and bestowed upon him the Vicende fortune. It had been obvious to John that Montclair valued "our woman" for the riches she provided from her body of erotic abundance, as well as those she made available over the dead bodies of others.

John recognized also that Montclair was not a man easy to deceive, and that he would approach the *Valkyrie* in readiness for what might be concealed outside the range of his scope. What he would conclude as he watched the play was dependent upon the realism with which the plot was developed by the cast, especially Jinnee. When John had finished his instructions to Maury and the mate, they left to rehearse Celeste and the crew. John alone would carefully prepare Jinnee for her leading role.

One of the sailors relished an early assignment given him to stand watch at the door where the captive enchantress still slumbered.

John and Sarah Belle were free to talk alone in the master's cabin in this predawn period—alone except for the quiet form of Newton who had not aroused through John's treatment.

"I sense he is more comfortable," John reported, "closer to consciousness than since the accident—but no proof whatsoever. I did a foolish thing . . . I hesitate . . ."

"Tell me, John."

"I talked to him as I applied the lotion—as if he were listening. I related the whole ugly situation, couldn't seem to stop talking until I was done."

"That was all right. You needed the release—of informing him, as it were, of the actions you are taking in his place."

"I feel like a stand-in who hasn't even read the part and must ad lib as he goes along."

"Perhaps this is for our good. You may not be as rigid in performance as he might be. In extremity, unknown resources often manifest."

"We could use a lot of those."

They drank strong coffee and chewed on dried fruit and meat.

"John, let me ask you a question: When this escapade is over, in our favor we'll assume, what will become of Jinnee? What will you do with her?"

"That's the biggest ad lib of all. My strategy is to capture, not eliminate, those who cross over to the *Valkyrie*. Maury and the mate are feeling otherwise but may come around. Port authorities want to lay their hands on those who plunder and despoil in these waters, make examples of them, get the word out. To take them alive is evidence. To kill them as they appear is a kind of execution taken into our own hands and requiring burial at sea. We have two on that list waiting down in the hold already. As for Jinnee, she'll live through it somehow. She is a born survivor."

"John, you realize she had the assignment for execution of all on this vessel—with a few exceptions perhaps."

"True. But now she is the instrument of our salvation."

"No, you are, for you made her so. If she hadn't coveted you from the moment she saw you, set her mind to possess you, body and soul—especially body—she would not have betrayed Montclair. When we are saved, if we are, she'll be running free and her obsession will be intensified."

He did not reply.

"As you say, that's for you to ad lib—for the rest of the voyage."

John's smile was small but she read it clearly.

"Yes, I am jealous. And if she should harm you, or possess you—against your will, of course—I could, and probably would, kill her."

"Sarah———" His smile was broader now. "I've never been possessed against my will, do not expect ever to be. When I am ready, you will be the first choice. Does that say it all?"

She reached over and laid her hand on his. "Just let me know, life of my life, just let me know." She gave him an answering smile.

The sailor assigned to Jinnee rushed in. "Hurry, sir. She's awake and getting out of bed. I'm not going back."

"A wise decision, sailor."

John jumped and ran, overturning his coffee cup. Sarah Belle watched the brown liquid spread. On impulse she rushed over to the prostrate captain, and grabbed him by the shoulder, shaking him. "Master Newton, we need you! We need you!" She let go, ashamed. It was like trying to bring the dead back to life.

John found Jinnee sitting on the edge of the bed, wriggling her toes, playing with her hair, knowing full well how ripe she looked in such dishabille.

"Get into your clothes," he commanded. "We have work to do. Montclair will soon be scanning the deck, and if he suspects that you're not doing what you came on board to do, you may not be alive by sundown! This is no time for play."

She was startled and pulled herself into a huddle. "I only look for———"

"Under the bed, and a cannister of water on the shelf. Wash quickly and I'll bring you breakfast and tell what must be done."

He hurried back to the master's cabin, almost in a panic. He grabbed the coffee pot, his hand shaking. Sarah handed him the brandy bottle. He poured a generous stream. She handed him a loaf and candied apricots. He stuffed them in his pocket and left as if on a relay sprint.

He found Jinnee more rational, less intent on seduction. She had left off her jacket, however, her high breasts covered only by the tight narrow bodice, strands of taunting lustrous red hair falling over and around them.

He took on the role of commander.

"Sit down!"

"Eat!"

"Listen!"

The action on the port side of the *Valkyrie* was slow-moving and significant as played for telescopic view from aboard the *Retort*, now closer in range than when first contacted.

The mime enacted could have been titled, "Death Stalks the Deck" or "The Devil Is a Woman."

When the sun was bright on the deck, Jinnee appeared, her siren's hair lifted and swirled about her, loose to the breeze. A sailor, cautious and looking about, joined her, reached for her, held her roughly. Momentarily, she responded to his advances, then slipped an arm around his neck and fed him a dainty from her pocket. He pulled her tight against him again, then gradually released her, moved away, staggered about to slowly disappear aft. Jinnee stretched like a well-fed cat, her face turned toward the *Retort*.

Celeste appeared, huddling close to the rigging as she crept along, obviously hoping to be unobserved by the devil-woman. Jinnee turned abruptly as though sensing a presence, then crouched and moved threateningly toward her, like a hungry wolverine after a rabbit. Celeste ran frantically back in the direction she had come.

The mate appeared at the helm. Jinnee made a stealthy approach. The mate appeared not to see her. When she was close, she pounced, her hand held aloft came down sharply, they struggled back and forth. Finally he fell.

A close-up would have shown Jinnee a furious harridan, her face contorted with raw desire to kill, but no weapon, and the man seemingly so lifeless at her feet cursing her softly, ready to tear her apart, urging her to invite it. She kicked him. He grabbed a leg and flung her to a hard fall, then fell as though stone dead and taunted her to try again.

She got to her feet, raised her arms in fury. The *Retort* sounded its foghorn as if in applause. Her arms fell, she adjusted her bodice and trousers, flung her hair back.

John appeared at her side, made motions of comforting her, stroking her, helping adjust her clothing, smoothing her hair.

This was an unexpected insert into the order of stage business to calm the protagonist. He instructed what she was to do with him.

They moved toward an open hatch, visible enough to appear center stage from the *Retort*. He embraced her—she clung to him—overly long.

"Montclair is watching—he'll kill you if you prolong this. He knows how quick you make your deadly strikes. He has you in full view. A little more of this and he'll know you've betrayed him. I can see him now, skinning you alive!"

She held one arm tight around his neck, and, with the other over his shoulder, could be viewed as though stabbing him in the back. As he tried to fall from her arms, she clung to him, pressed tight again, then let him fall, appeared to gloat over him, dragged him laboriously to the open hatch, and shoved him in.

As he tumbled down the steps, she rushed down after him. He was on his feet instantly but she pounced, grabbed him, with a grip so strong and unexpected that for a moment he was stunned. She had her lips on his mouth with vampire ferocity, her fingers clawing into his shoulders. He responded in the only language she understood, pulled her away, slapped her hard.

"Get back on deck, or I'll throw you to the sharks!"

When she appeared, self-preservation was in her mind. She rushed to the rail, preened as though the time below had been used to finish off her victim, then raised her right arm high in a salute to the *Retort*.

The foghorn sounded again.

When she turned, there was Sarah Belle running to the open hatch. She had seen John thrown down. It was too realistic, and Jinnee following had been too much.

Jinnee's starring role had not included the appearance of Sarah Belle. John had assigned her to keep watch over the captain while Maury kept watch over Emile. Now there was impulsive improvisation all around.

Jinnee ran after Sarah Belle—a sailor appeared out of hiding and pursued Jinnee, grabbed and dragged her, rearing and pitching in a tantrum of rage, across the deck to the railing and was about to fling her overboard when he realized he was on stage and must play his part. He pulled her struggling and clawing against him, until he had almost squeezed the breath from her. He loosened his grip.

"Now, you bloodsucker, pretend to plunge your knife under my ribs. I'll fall, but close by. Do what you've been told to do, or I'll grab you again and the cobra in me won't turn you loose until you're a pulp to squash on the deck!"

He dropped down. Jinnee, weak and making an effort not to drop beside him, gripped the railing, looked across at the *Retort*, screaming and cursing until her wrath was spent.

The foghorn applauded.

During the violent scene on deck, John was holding Sarah Belle in another kind of embrace.

"Sarah, you shouldn't have! You shouldn't have! If that sailor hadn't intercepted her, the whole plot would have fallen apart."

"It was an anguish I couldn't bear. You had fallen from my sight, and she had pursued. I stopped breathing. I was about to suffocate."

"We're breathing now in each other's arms until we make another entrance."

"John?"

"Yes, darling." She was trembling against him.

"I have never before had such a consuming desire to kill."

"It's an instinct dormant in us all, which, given the chance, can surface instantly with jungle tenacity. Let's avoid it where we can."

They waited.

"The mate and Maury will be the hardest to control. They want to kill the lot on sight."

"I find myself wanting to say: 'Would that be so bad?'"

"If the captain were in charge here, I know what he would do: take as many prisoners as possible and turn them over to the port officials. If we send them all to Davy Jones' locker from here, there will be no news to spread along the coastline, no example to those who plunder and despoil. Our story would be dismissed as a tale told for diversion. . . . The crew have ropes and irons ready. . . . It shouldn't be long now."

"I must go back to my station, John. Master Newton has no watch. And you must be free of concern for me. Jinnee had such a time with that sailor, I don't think she'll give me a run. And the observers will relish the sight of a live and frightened woman."

"You are frightened?"

"I shall pretend to be. But for the work at hand, I have a kind of fierce appetite to get into it and get it done." She gave him a quick hug and was gone.

Jinnee whirled about as Sarah Belle appeared on deck scurrying along like fear was at her heels. Jinnee called out to her tauntingly.

"Keep from that man or I slash you to pieces. You scrawny whore in nun's gutter dress! I hate! hate! hate!" She spat viciously, but did not follow.

Sarah Belle forced herself to keep going, keep pretending until she was out of sight. In the cabin, she clenched her fists, closed her eyes, groaned and called on heaven for control.

The captain groaned in answer. She rushed to him, but his eyes were closed and he was still again. She rubbed his forehead, chaffed his hands, and no response. She wanted to weep, but instead rushed around the cabin preparing every possible attention should he awaken.

There was a suspense emanating from all watching and waiting that seemed to convert the air into a mucouslike texture making breathing difficult. Even the *Valkyrie* and *Retort* floating in water close to calm rocked about like animate forms lost of direction and purpose, floundering without power or pilot.

The expected confrontation began to take form as the jolly-boat of the *Retort* pulled out with Montclair and his four fellow pirates. They seemed in no hurry, pulling easily at the oars. The leader sat relaxed at the prow.

The *Valkyrie* ladder was lowered, and then it happened—like an explosion. Shots were being fired from the deck of the *Valkyrie*—and from the jolly-boat. Montclair and his four predators were not taking chances. This time they had handguns, but no match for the Colts. Soon their boat was floundering. One sailor on the *Valkyrie* deck had an arm hanging loose. The mate had blood in his eyes from a graze, but brushed it off and made ready with his knife as two of the *Retort's* crew thrashed about and grabbed for the ladder. Montclair had been hit before he reached the deck and where he went down was a bloody circle to alert the sharks. Maury had emptied his carbine and refilled the cylinder. Curbing his desire to kill, he had aimed for shoulders and arms. Now he stood ready on deck. John was keeper of the ladder.

"Sheath your knife, mate, and help me get these men aboard before they drown. I think Montclair has gone down. Get busy, all of you, with the ropes. Keep them on deck. We'll attend their wounds."

"Like hell we will! Let 'em bleed to death and good riddance," the mate roared.

"You'll need some attention yourself." John wanted to say, "I'm in command here," but restrained himself, for in truth he was not. "Mate, we'll do more good, we'll save other lives and cargoes, if we take these men to Laguna, and let the news out that cargo ships are not easy prey."

The four survivors, fearing a watery grave more than port authorities, and burning from their wounds, did not struggle against their captors.

"Let's take them starboard and secure them. I'll get bindings and do what I can to staunch their wounds. Maury, watch portside for a bit. It's possible Montclair could surface."

At that moment Sarah Belle screamed. John felt he had been shot in the stomach and that his running was a slow crawl. At the master's cabin, he froze in horror. There was Montclair. He was a tall man, and he held Sarah Belle in front of him, one arm like a vise around her waist, the other with a knife poised at the side of her throat. Newton lay like a corpse on his bunk.

Montclair's teeth were bared in a grimace of challenge. "Touch me, and I'll sink this all the way through. Shoot me and I'll kill her before I fall. Get down your boat. Loose my men and get them into it. Tie up my woman and place her aboard. This woman here will go before me and into the boat. You've held my woman a while. Now I'll hold yours. But I'll play fair." He grimaced again. "I'll send your boat back. Fill it with the Vicende cargo, and I don't mean the furniture. Then we'll make a fair exchange. Your woman for the ransom. You don't trust me? That's strange. Do you have a choice?" The knife twisted in his hand.

John was thinking: this is a nightmare. Did I get hit? How did he get on board?

As if mind-reading, Montclair chuckled. "I just popped out of a hawsehole and on over the bow! There's ways, landlubber, when you come prepared with rope and hook and a float around your belly. Smarter ways to get things done at sea than you can handle with a newfangled pistol for cowboys. Get on with it or I'll take a slice out of her face to show you I mean business."

As suddenly as lightning strikes, Montclair was jerked back, his knife sent flying, an arm of steel around his neck, choking until foam flecked his lips. When he was released, he fell limp.

Master Newton stood over him, remarking calmly, as if to himself, "He's not quite gone. He'll come back. I think we'll take him to port."

To break up the stonelike stillness of shock around him, he issued a hearty captain's command to a bug-eyed sailor standing near.

"Harry, you lousy useful gutsy Texas riffraff, tie this critter up, brand him, put his head in a noose and we'll take him to market."

As though he were just emerging from the darkness of the hold, Harry hollered, "Aye! Aye! Sir!" and raced for his lasso.

Sarah Belle was held tight in John's arms. James Newton did not seem to notice.

"Get back to the prisoners," he ordered the others. "Attend the sails! I've risen from the dead!"

How does he know we have prisoners? John was thinking in amazement.

He turned to John with the answer. "I seem to have known all that was going on but couldn't relate to my body—it wouldn't work for me until Madame screamed, and then I had to play dead until Montclair was engrossed in gloating, and I could take him before he could move his knife."

He pushed his hand through his thick rumpled hair. "God, I'm so hungry!"

Sarah Belle responded, still held close in John's embrace. "Not for long, Captain. I'll attend to that. I'm in charge of the galley. The mate signed me on while you were on leave. John, what has become of Jinnee?"

"Madre de Dios! Who knows! I'll try to get things straightened out."

CHAPTER TWENTY-EIGHT

JOHN FOUND JINNEE where he expected to find her—in Sarah Belle's quarters with the door barred. He knocked and called. Finally, there was a harsh whisper. "You . . . you come to me? . . . who with you?"

"No one at all—no one around. Open the door."

"Montclair dead?"

"No. A prisoner."

"You not kill him for me?"

"No."

"When you kill him?"

"We're taking him to the port officials at Laguna."

The whisper became a screech. "Scummy cowards! All on this boat! Vermin! Rat guts!! Give me gun! Give me knife! I slit his throat. I kill him now!"

John was silent.

"You there? You go away?" Then wheedling. "Please . . . Jean . . . amoureux . . . I help you save gold, save ship. . . . For this, Montclair cut me to pieces, watch my blood run, stomp me with nails in his boots! Jean . . . Jean . . . I your woman now . . . you kill Montclair for me . . . I go with you always . . . I do what you say. As long as he live, I am dead woman walking. As long as he breathe on this ship, grave monster wait outside my door."

"Nonsense! He's bound and chained and carries a wound."

"Nonsense to you! You thought he drown! Slippery eel he is! From him I learn! From him I know! . . . So . . . you kill him . . . then you come to me. . . . I wait for you . . ."

She waited. John could hear her breathing, panting in a rhythm of fear and passion for relief from Montclair and acceptance from him.

"You not answer . . . but think 'yes'? . . ." She tried to command, "You think 'yes'?" She became frantic with another offer. "You not know me . . . you not see me . . . you not hold me . . . you kill Montclair and come here and I show you all of me and you kick out woman who take after you. You hold to me . . . hold on to me!"

She waited again, sensed his rejection, knew he was unresponsive to rage. Her voice softened to sweetness but her primitive approach remained intact. "You brave but no like killing. I do it for you. You get me knife, you hold gun, I do it for you. Nobody care when Montclair gone. You save me for I save all on boat. I like to kill mate and woman, also liking to kill me—but when Montclair I kill, I simply your woman, do what you tell, go to any place with you."

John answered her this time, his tone as soft and reasonable as hers. "I tell you what, Jinnee. I have a plan for all of us. I will not desert you. You can count on that. But I cannot do what you want so soon. Keep your door barred and keep quiet. I'll bring you food when I come again. But you must be patient. You have water and some dried fruit left?"

"Oui—some little."

"You understand what I've said? You believe I'll come back—when my plans are laid, and I will tell you what we are to do?"

There was great variance in their understanding. "Oui . . . oui . . . Jean . . . amoureux . . . amoureux . . ." A sensual purr . . . "You come back and hold me soon, Jean, soon . . ."

But John was gone—was running to the master's cabin. He grabbed up his medicine chest. "Newton, set a watch on the women's quarters, an armed one. Montclair's woman has gone behind barred door and is afraid to come out until we kill Montclair —our good fortune. I'm on the way to the prisoners," he turned to the captain with a wry smile, "to bind up Montclair's wounds with the utmost care—you can count on it!"

Over the food that Sarah Belle laid out for Newton, and the coffee she shared with him as he stabilized from the shock of sudden recovery and exertion, they accepted without comment the mutual confidence and admiration of each other. Sarah knew that Newton had observed and would continue to ignore the attachment between her and John. He told her, "Sterling must share my cabin now that I have revived just as he did during my long sleep. We have much to work out before Vicende boards the *Valkyrie*. And I believe we can make port the day after tomorrow, near eventide perhaps, if the weather continues to bring such fair sailing."

"What is Don Vicende like? After all we've gone through for him and his cargo, I feel a certain excitement stirring over facing a man so treasure-laden, so gifted in conspiracy, and who, at the same time, has the artistic nature to design those palacial pieces of furniture in the hold."

"Don Vicende is one of those personages who stirs excitement in the bosom of every woman who looks upon him and then sinks fathoms deep into the luster of his magnetic orbs. He is fine-featured, suggesting more of strength than weakness. His garb is regal, but not gaudy, his manners derived from all the courtesies of Old Spain, and his sense of power dangerous.

"I have been a guest at his hacienda, and never expect to be indulged in such magnificence again anywhere along this coastline or up its rivers. He is one of the kind that has moved personal fortunes from the Old World to underdeveloped regions on this side rather than endanger family wealth in the power play of monarchs. This has brought prosperity to such coastal towns as Laguna, benefitting from the great logging industries and the produce from vast plantations.

"The lords of these haciendas live in total command of their fiefdoms located far enough up the spreading rivers and into the heavy jungles for natural protection against intruders. They drink from silver goblets, sleep in satin-canopied beds, embellish their furnishings in gold leaf, landscape their gardens in romantic mazes. They have innumerable hirelings, mostly Indian, well enough fed to do their every bidding — and fat curates to preside over their gothic chapels, where they kneel before imported sacred figures guarding the gold festooned altar, and take the blessed wine from a jeweled chalice.

"Do not look at me like that, dear lady. You won't doubt it once you lay eyes upon Vicende. . . . When he knows all that has happened on the *Valkyrie*, his gratitude will flow over us in such streams that we'll have to don our life jackets to keep from sinking! . . . He'll house us at the Posada de la Flor, noted for its beautiful gardens and elegant service. He maintains his port residence there. I understand it was he who financed such a lodging place, designed only for patrons of substance and for Don Vicende to conduct the business of his jungle empire."

"I have only one more question. Is there a Lady Vicende?"

"Madame, how can I say when I have never seen or been told of one?" Newton's eyes and the tone of his voice said something that Sarah Belle thought she understood.

The *Valkyrie* seemed to take on a life of her own, moving smooth and flashy toward Laguna Bay—seemed to command the winds rather than having to set her sails in accommodation to whimsical forces. It was the end of the day that had seen the last of the *Retort* left riding aimlessly with two renegade sailors her depleted crew.

The sun was going down, tinting a flurry of thin clouds with gold and pink. The *Valkyrie* was hosting her first burial at sea. Newton, with John and two sailors to assist him, had gone to the task of removing the bodies of Grudo and Señor Alano from the hold as soon as ship, crew, and prisoners had been reviewed.

He had carefully boxed all of Señor Alano's possessions, except the clothing on the body and a gold cross that was worn on a chain holding the emblem near his heart. On Grudo's body was no mark of identification or symbol of kinship in kind or thought. The captain stripped all the dirty clothing from the body before wrapping it in heavy canvas, remarking to John, "Somehow more decent a burial to send him naked back to his Maker. Maybe his withered soul can get out easier and return to Creation for an overhaul."

Of Alano, he commented, "I know little about him, except

that he practiced loyalty to God, Spain, and Vicende, and courtesy to those he dealt with. I'm glad that Vicende has residence at Laguna. He always comes in from his hacienda and stays during the season when his shipments are due and is ready with port authorities to board the boat by the time it is anchored. I'll want you with me when I bring him to my cabin for briefing."

Sarah Belle and Celeste had joined John and the sailors, who accompanied Master Newton to the point on the deck where the bodies would be lowered as the sun dropped below the horizon.

Newton was not the kind of man to read from Scripture or make ceremonial prayer, but he was attuned to the Sovereign of the Seas, the Lord of the Land, and the Creator of the Constellations.

While the sailors held the ropes that held the bodies just above the water, and stood with knives ready to make the cut at his signal, Newton simply stood straight, as if at attention before a higher command, gazing into the sunset, appearing much taller than he was. After a brief silence, he spoke.

"This man known only as Grudo, is returned to water and earth, the seedbed of Life. We judge not, for we know not all the laws of existence that bring us to Birth and Death. So let it be."

The smooth grind of a sharp knife through a rope, and a gentle splash . . .

"This man dies wearing the mantle of duty to country and to a fellow man he served, at the same time wearing the cross of one who lived and died as example to us all. May his soul sail smoothly into a harbor of rest and renewal. So let it be."

Another sound of severing, but no splash was heard for a wayward gust slapped a wave to starboard as if to complete the ceremony and usher its two passengers into another dimension.

John did not return to his self-confined prisoner until the late morning of the next day—not until fear and hunger and fatigue had accomplished his purpose. Then he knocked, and said only, "I am here as I told you I would be."

There was a rasping gasp, relief, or the dregs of rage—he could not tell.

"There is no danger. We have a guard on watch to protect us. I have brought ale and——" The door flew open as if the bar were already down. As he entered, she grabbed the mug from his hand and drank in great gulps—then looked at him, her eyes wide with fear.

"It is *not* poisoned." He handed her a piece of cheese which she snatched, held in both hands at her mouth, and pushed in with ravenous urgency.

John was astonished at her appearance, though it was favorable to his plan.

"Sit down," he commanded, "and eat more slowly. Here are bread and candies."

"More ale!" she pleaded.

"When we have talked." He scrutinized her closely until she became self-conscious.

"This is not the Jinnee I saw on the deck yesterday with hair streaming in the wind, her body like a Viking goddess as she walked the deck and played the part I required of her."

She looked at him sharply, her tangled hair falling about her tear-stained face, eyes underlined with dark shadows. The large piece of bread she had broken from the loaf and was ready to cram in her mouth did not reach its destination. Her hand dropped into her lap. She looked at her fine trousers, soiled and torn where she had skidded when the mate had flung her across the deck. One strap on her bodice was severed, and there were stains and open seams from her tussle with the sailor who had given her the cobra hug. Her face and hands were dirty and so were her bare feet.

"Where are your shoes?"

She pointed, and there they were, proud and pretty, Oriental turn-up at toes looking appropriate for a dancer's pirouette.

"I run more fast barefoot," she said dully, "Montclair like these. He——" she jumped and grabbed John's arm in a grip that sent pain shooting to his shoulder. "Where Montclair now? Dead? Dead?"

"No."

Her grip tightened. She still had strength for fear though none for rage.

"He is bound under guard. I will leave you here to take care of yourself and will not come back unless——"

Her grasp loosened but she was holding on to his arm with lifeline tenacity. He made no move that might disengage her attention.

"Trust me for your safety. There is no other way. You understand? No *other* way."

She nodded.

"First you must become clean and beautiful again."

The eyes, fixed on his face, brightened, began to glow.

"I'll fetch more ale, and bring a comb, more water, and scented soap. You will remove all your clothing and put on the gown you have here. I'll have your clothes washed and mended. Since your jacket and shoes are unspoiled, you'll then be ready for what lies ahead."

She frowned. "What you do with me?"

"I cannot tell you until I see what you look like when you are—when you are all that you can be."

Her eyes narrowed with anticipation. "I see. I show you."

"You understand?"

"Oui . . . I understand . . . amoureux."

"I'll return soon—very soon."

She went ahead of him to the door, forgetting the soil and scent of her harassed body; she was ready to solicit an embrace that would assuage her fears and hungers.

John stood very still and stared at her, beginning at the blackened nails of the bare toes and slowly taking inventory until he reached her eyes. She quailed as if he had struck her, moaned, and ran to the far side of the cabin, her hands over her face.

When he returned, she opened the door wide enough to take what he had brought and hand her clothes out to him, then slammed the bar in place.

John confided to Sarah Belle and Newton what, with their assistance, he hoped to bring about for Jinnee. Sarah Belle in turn had talked to Celeste, enlisting her help with Jinnee's bizarre clothing.

"It is not easy to work with such things, is it, madame? It's like preparing someone for the slave mart who deserves it."

"Shall we call it a labor of gratitude—to a killer who didn't kill us, but would like to anytime henceforth?" Sarah Belle bit off a thread between her teeth with more force than necessary, then jabbed her finger as she started to repair a torn seam.

"Here, madame, your thimble."

"Thanks." She worked the straight seam, then found it gathered, and ripped it out in jerks.

"Let me care for that," Celeste said positively. "I am the seamstress."

"No, I'll do it myself. But I tell you what you can do. Send Maury to Master Newton and get permission to go down into the hold where our baggage is stored. Then you go with him and get out the trunk in which we packed garments that might be more appropriate for us at times and places we have yet to consider. Bring my blue cape and matching skirt, with the dusty rose waist, and whatever else is fitting. Also something suitable for yourself, for you and I, my dear Celeste, are going to be observers of much that takes place on this boat before and after we go ashore."

"May I also bring up some of the green gauzy material we stored for veiling? There are small snags in this bodice and elsewhere that I could conceal with a drape hanging in folds from around the neck."

"Make it as tantalizing as possible."

"What of Emile while Maury and I are below? We will have to remove rope and boxing from the trunk."

"I will stay with Emile while you and Maury get what we need from the trunk."

Celeste looked up from her sewing in astonishment.

"You never expected me to be alone with Emile? Well, this is the time. I will get two difficulties resolved at the same time. I will take this piece of mending with me."

"Let me——"

"Never mind, I will resist all impulses to tear the mess into shreds. Jasper and I together will manage with Emile."

"I will give him a draught before we leave."

"Give him nothing but what nourishment he needs. He gets enough draughts when we are in trouble. I carry the keys to the trunk and the jewelry box on a cord around my waist. I'll give them to you at once."

"Just the key to the trunk, madame."

"I want something from the jewelry box too. The piece of jade in the woven frame, and the two clasps for my hair that I wear with the blouse."

Celeste looked at her mistress with such a comprehension of intent and mood—such a radiance of love and support that Sarah Belle felt her resolve doubled.

Sarah Belle sat watching Emile now and then as she looked up from mending. He was sitting in bed feeding Jasper bits of pecan and almond. Occasionally he would glance at her with a slight smile of sharing Jasper's antics, accepting her presence as though she were no different from Maury or Celeste.

She tried a bit of converse. "How do you like the name *Emile Palais* which we gave you when we started this journey?"

Not even a turn of the head to indicate that she had spoken.

"Jasper, how do you like the sound of *Palais*?"

Jasper looked up, chewing briskly, his bright gaze at her like a smile of approval which brought Emile to focus on her with direct attention.

She resisted the impulse to look away, simply held his gaze and smiled. She held the smile in a frozen stare when he spoke with a voice of clear sanity.

"Who are you? You remind me of someone I know."

As from a great distance she heard herself reply, "I have assumed the name of Sarah Palais for this journey."

"What journey? And why did you assume such a name? Are we on the way to Europe? We are most certainly on a boat. And why are you, a strange woman, in my cabin?"

"Strange woman——" hit her like a splash of cold water bringing relief and a shred of composure. "What is your name?"

"Emile Nicée, of course." He rubbed his forehead. "What kind of wine did they serve at the captain's table? I can't recall a thing . . . even about being on an ocean trip."

Jasper became agitated, as if the person holding him had changed into a different kind of being. He jumped over into Sarah Belle's lap, landing in the midst of Jinnee's finery. Emile jerked to attention.

"Jasper! Jasper!" he shrieked, his hands reaching out frantically toward the squirrel.

Before he could get out of bed, Sarah Belle had dropped her sewing, grabbed Jasper and was placing the trembling pet back in his hands.

Emile soothed and crooned until Jasper was tranquil. Then closing his eyes with a sigh, he lay back, his hand on the squirrel now curled up on his chest. The shutter of his mind had opened to expose reality for only an instant, then with faint imprint had closed tight again.

Sarah Belle willed her shaky hands to pick up the mending that must be done. She knew as certainly as Jasper that the Emile whom neither of them knew had come and gone.

The events of the last day before landing were ordered and filled with preparations for moving into port. The *Valkyrie* continued her smooth movements and steady speed as if eager to end all uncertainties. The sailors thought they could feel her preening under their scrubbing, polishing, and painting.

Newton was busy writing a full report for Don Vicende.

The prisoners no longer greeted their captors with oaths and threats, accepting food and attention to their wounds with surly readiness, hoping some of their kind might come to their rescue in Laguna.

Montclair, however, made a ritual of greeting anyone who came near with maledictions to be delivered to the "Whore of Satan" who had betrayed him.

The greatest stress lay upon John, dealing with Jinnee; on Jinnee, dealing with John and her survival; and upon Sarah Belle, dealing with her emotions concerning John and Jinnee.

John must manage Jinnee on this final evening in a manner that would prepare her for the events of the next day if she were to avoid being taken with the prisoners to share their fate in Laguna. She must have food and rest, and agree to the sleeping draught as she had done before.

He came to her door with plenty of ale and rich heavy foods, "stoking the vampire" he called it in his mind.

"Jinnee, before you open the door, put on your jacket over the gown and put on your shoes—your clothes will not be ready until the morning. I have your ale and a good supper."

A happy "oui," and then a wait.

She opened the door, pulled it back, while he walked to the table and laid out the repast.

He heard the bar fall. He turned and she was leaning against the door. She laughed, showing her teeth bright and clean, her hair fresh-washed, shimmering silk threads standing out in profusion about her like a wide frame. Her cheeks were scrubbed to a pinkish tint that seemed like a faint reflection from her hair. And her lips (what in heaven or hell did she do to achieve that palpable form and color for titillating the senses so wildly?) . . . then her eyes, colored brown gold, widened as if to draw him to her and into her, and he could have sworn there were sparks flicking out from them here and there and being absorbed in the strands of hair at the corners. He looked down, and there were the curved pointed-toe shoes, looking back at him from under the hem of the gown, inviting, like twin temptresses. He tried to look away, say something, but could not. Instead he noticed the jacket, unbuttoned, its whole glittering overlay seemingly designed just to set off the fine lace of the low-cut gown . . . Sarah Belle's gown! He felt sick, weak, trapped. He knew how a woman felt when she fainted to escape. He was man enough not to faint, he believed, but his eyes were riveted to that neckline; Jinnee knew, and held them there, like thin steel threads she would pull toward her when she was ready. His body was locked in a paralysis. He could not turn his head. His legs were stilts. But she was ready. A rhythm of movements began at the neckline. The stilts took a few short labored steps toward her.

She laughed. He spun around, his fists in his pockets, his back to her. . . . He heard the soft movements. I must not let her touch me! I must not! He felt something cool against his fist. He gasped, and energy rushed through him in full release. He clutched the piece of jade Sarah Belle had secretly placed in his pocket—his wonder at her prescience making him feel giant-size and armor-clad. Jinnee was near enough to touch him, but enjoying her power, was waiting. He turned aside, and suddenly was around the table where the food was spread, and she was looking across at him in a shock that delayed reaction.

He was in command.

"Come to this side of the table," he ordered. "I want you to sit here."

She obeyed as though lost on a trail that had appeared clearly marked.

"But before you sit, come closer." She came, hopefully.

He took her by the shoulders. "Stand straight! Be still!" Then he reached, not for the neckline, but for the top button of her jacket, began closing the gaping front and firmly giving her a little jerk each time he fastened a button securely.

"Now, push your hair out of your eyes, and drink your ale." He uncorked the jug he had brought and filled a mug.

She drank and, like a child, held it out for another.

"Now eat." She was not ravenous, but ate on command while he watched.

He sat down across the table from her. "Look at me and listen closely. . . . You want to live?"

A nod, and fright filled the eyes no longer entrancing.

"When the Laguna officials come aboard tomorrow to inspect the boat before giving permission to land, they will take charge of the prisoners from the *Retort*. Montclair is certain to demand that you be taken too."

She cringed and turned her head aside as if to avoid a blow.

"The lesser fate for you would be that the prison guards would make a plaything of you until the time of execution—and a fate even worse would be that Montclair deprive the guards and, by his own hands, take revenge."

She moaned and slipped to the floor in a huddle of agony.

"I think we can prevent this, you and I, if you do exactly as I say, if you look as beautiful in the morning as you looked tonight."

She crawled to him, took hold of his ankles and looked up in slavish subservience. "I do anything you say—you believe me! Anything . . ."

It dawned on John as surely as if she had spoken it: she was Montclair's slave—he had bought her somewhere, somehow. That's why she had insisted she had no name. The compassion he felt, he knew he must not show. There was only one path he could hope to open for her.

No other word would come—she was stricken dumb in her abjection.

He loosened her hands and pulled her to her feet. "Think of tomorrow and what it could be like if you were a princess in disguise."

She was bewildered and tried to hold on to his hands.

"I'll prepare the sleeping beauty draught now. Trust me as you did before. I'll return with your clothes in the morning."

She was silent as he stirred and offered it to her.

"Poison I would down before the hand of Montclair reach out

for me again." She drank and slammed the mug back on the table in a gesture of defiance.

"You really come tomorrow, Jean?"

"Really."

She turned her back and said, "Go."

He heard the bar slam down . . . was satisfied. The signs were right.

A surprise awaited him the next day when he brought her clothing. She reached for the garments, took them and closed the door without speaking. He hesitated, but decided to play the silent waiting game—but not for long, for she must be instructed, prepared, rehearsed. The captain expected to make port by mid-afternoon in fair weather.

At noon, he came again.

"In a few short hours we will be in port. It is time to talk over brandied chocolate and sweet biscuits."

She let him in. "Look at me," she said, "look at all of me."

She stood before him, still as a statue in a museum, the green veiling Celeste had so carefully added to her costume her only covering. Draped like a long scarf, it fell from her shoulders over her breasts and on to her knees.

The final act, he thought, *and I won't need the jade this time.* With an aside of humor for himself: *It's easier without the gown and slippers.*

"Parfait!" he exclaimed. "It's a pity Rubens and Titian are not here."

She was puzzled. "Who Rubens and Titian?"

"Two men born long before their time. Now turn around."

Only her eyes showed that she was startled as she obeyed.

"Now walk slowly toward the table."

He began to feel like an ambitious artist who had found the perfect model.

He followed her and placed the refreshments on the table.

She stood before him uneasy, uncomfortable, with no comprehension of the mood in which he gave her such attention.

"Jinnee, I have no doubt that we will be successful in rescuing you from the talons of the law or any other threat to your safety. Start putting on your clothes slowly—carefully—please, while I watch."

This she found hard to do but began to comply. She was stooping, pulling on her trousers, the glossy red hair hanging over her breasts.

"If only *Don Vicende* could see this!"

She jerked erect, her hands held to her bosom.

"What you mean, Jean? What you mean? You tell me!"

She knew very well who Don Vicende was. She had been around Montclair enough to know much more than he had suspected she knew.

"Get on with your dressing—slowly now. It helps me with my thinking about how I will present you to him when he comes aboard the *Valkyrie*."

She stopped and looked at him pleadingly, the green silk gauze in a kind of tangle around her, making her appear extravagantly bewitching, much more appealing than in her studied pose at his entrance.

"Not Vicende I want, Jean, not Vicende——" Her eyes glazed with tears ready to roll out and put the finishing touch to supplication. "I want . . . I want . . ."

"Put on your jacket!" He spoke sharply. "You want to live. You told me so. I cannot save you. I can only help you save yourself. Don Vicende will be informed that except for you his valuable cargo never would have made port. I will advise him of the dangers ahead for you unless he takes you under his mantle of power and wealth.

"After he has talked with me and Master Newton, I'll take you to the captain's quarters and present you. He will look at you, speak to you, and provide for you according to his impressions and generous nature. You understand?"

"I understand all you say."

"He is not a Montclair. From accounts, he is more like a prince than a pirate."

"How is a prince not like a pirate?"

"A prince has the gold that a pirate wants to take from him."

"Will a prince look at me like you do, or like a pirate do?"

"You are sharper than I realized, princess. You will have your answer when Don Vicende looks at you. Now pull off your jacket."

"Why this put on—pull off?"

"You want to please him, don't you? He'll take you to his grand hacienda no doubt. Do you want to live out your life stirring stew on his kitchen crew? . . . We'll leave the jacket behind. The bodice with that tantalizing veil stuff is much better."

With a start he realized that this item had been added while the clothes were being restored. . . . *If I knew that—if she—but why? —maybe Celeste—but not on her own——*

"My fine jacket I will not lose—it come from Hong Kong."

"I can't help it if it came from Genghis Khan's harem. The question for you is: will it be the kitchen crew or your own lavish den?"

"I leave the jacket."

"Good. When I come for you again, Don Vicende will be on board and there must be no delay."

He moved to take his leave. "One word more: Do not stare at him. Let him wonder why not, but look at him if he asks you to."

He was about to open the door. "Understand? Don't try to take him—let him wonder if you would like for him to take you, understand?"

An empty mug whizzed past his ear and struck the wall. He was relieved that he had not filled it with chocolate. He returned it so that it flew over her shoulder, tangling in her hair, and made his exit with the next move.

He had another surprise waiting. Sarah Belle was standing nearby. He blinked, ran his hand through his hair, looked again, and hurried to her. "Oh my dear, you are real, and such a vision I could not believe it. Do you know I have never seen you in blue before, and there you are, matching the azure of the sky and the *Valkyrie*'s own hue."

"Careful. You are talking to Madame Palais and she is virtually inaccessible."

"Ah, yes."

"Do you carry any scars?"

"No, but a near miss. A case of over-understanding my attempts at coaching."

"An apt pupil?"

"Over-apt, you might say. I hope you are right about the inference by Newton that Don Vicende was not known to have a single attachment."

"We shall know before you bring her in."

"How?"

"Master Newton has asked me to be present with you when Don Vicende comes to his quarters for a briefing on the whole affair."

"Sarah! How unusual!"

"Isn't it? Fits right in with all the unusual things that are still happening on the *Valkyrie*."

"How will you verify this—Newton's inference?"

"Easier to show you than tell you. And it would be helpful to know before you bring Jinnee in, wouldn't it?"

"Sarah, did you—is this why——"

"Come along. He sent me to tell you we will have a light meal together before docking."

"Yes, it will be helpful," he said thoughtfully, as they walked along together, "to know for sure. Then I can decide whether it will be the bodice or the jacket?"

"What are you talking about?"

"I'll explain later."

CHAPTER TWENTY-NINE

THE SAILS OF THE *VALKYRIE* were furled. She sat at anchor like a servant proud of a job well done and waiting for admiration and praise. Don Vicende had been filled with just that as he had watched her sail into port, shiny blue, sturdy lines, and filled with the family treasure that he had plotted and planned for years to harbor in this place, gateway to his private kingdom.

He had been rowed out to the barque with several of his attendants, and had boarded only slightly behind the customs officials and health authorities who must inspect cargo and crew before docking permit was issued. Don Vicende's cargoes and shipments were of great advantage to business and government in this far southwest corner of Yucatán, and official procedures were normally casual.

But "casual" turned into a chaos of questioning with the sighting of the prisoners being held on deck. A messenger was immediately dispatched to return with a larger boat and prison guards.

Don Vicende hurried Newton into privacy. John was beckoned to join them. The mate was left to spin out details, and did not spare the "she-wolf" who had been sent to destroy them all. Montclair screamed that they must search the vessel until she was found.

Jinnee could hear and sense enough of the commotion to huddle in fear and wait for John.

Sarah Belle waited until the prisoners had been removed—with Don Vicende making it clear to the officials that he and his attendants would be responsible for removing the *Retort*'s female decoy—then came out on deck with Celeste to view the bay crowded with brigs and schooners from foreign ports, cargo ships, even a steamer—and in the distance the town of Laguna on the island of Carmen separating the Lake of Términos from the Gulf of Mexico. Her blue cape rippled about her in the breeze, and her hair was loose except for jeweled clasps holding it secured on both sides.

She knew that Newton would summon her when the initial briefing was done and more detailed discussion was forthcoming.

When Newton came, it was obvious that he was astonished to see her out of the neutral garb she had been wearing, and he was pleased as well to be escorting this gracious lady into the presence of his employer.

"Madame Palais! You are quite an ornament to the *Valkyrie* here on the deck and—I must say so—beautiful. I must repeat how fortunate I am to have had your care, your strength and courage, riding with me during my blackout. And now your good mind to support and further detail the events that Mr. Sterling and I have recounted to Don Vicende."

Don Vicende made no effort to conceal his surprise that such a woman had been passenger on his chartered cargo vessel. Although Newton had explained that Sterling, an acquaintance of the famous John Lloyd Stephens, was an antiquarian on the way to the Palenque ruins, still Don Vicende had noted the hazy reasoning given for his being accompanied by a mentally afflicted friend and wife with two servants. He had expected the Palais woman to be boring and lacking in feminine traits, else why would she be out on such a jungle journey?

He let his amazement show. He kissed her hand with the utmost gallantry, and his eyes danced with appreciation as they missed no detail of her appearance.

He is all that Newton described and more, Sarah Belle thought —the Spanish Don to perfection—the shapely figure that high breeding, precision sword play, superb horsemanship, the social graces, and the exercise of power had structured. The ability to display that figure and power to the best advantage in the elegance of garb and the careful use of jewels not overdone—the one glowing ruby on the hand that had held hers for the moment of a kiss that was almost a caress, and a scattering of emeralds imbedded in the hilt of his sword.

When she was seated, he stood as if in deference, questioning her in soft tones, speaking confidentially as if only the two of them were in the cabin. He expressed his gratitude with poetic eloquence, decorated with French and Spanish phrases, that he sensed a lady from New Orleans would understand and appreciate. He took more liberties with his compliments than he would have in the presence of a husband, but here was a lady, mated to a mindless man, who really merited such attention.

John was a restless observer and Newton was genuinely pleased that Don Vicende was saying what was outside his own range of expression but so much deserved.

"I will search, dear brave gifted lady, until I determine some reward suitable for the services you have rendered Master Newton, others on the *Valkyrie*, and through them to myself."

"It is enough, Don Vicende, that we are all safe and your cargo was not plundered. And we will all be relieved if you find a way to reward the woman who came aboard to kill us all but who in the end betrayed her kind and thereby saved our lives and your shipment."

"I have heard the story. I would like a woman's opinion. Would you say that she is no longer dangerous, no longer inclined to plunder, poison, kill?"

"I have no reason to think she has changed. What is your opinion, Mr. Sterling?"

"I have told Don Vicende that she could kill as easily as she can drink ale—that somewhere human values were erased from her conscience. But the Don is wiser than we, more versed in the whole human equation, I would say,"—he gave Sarah Belle a telling look—"and he could have solutions we know not of."

Don Vicende smiled. He was not only versed in the human equation, but in subtle communication. He knew that the mindless husband had already been replaced, and was amused.

"Why not bring this enigma before us, Mr. Sterling, and we will resolve the matter? But let me say now, since I will be a while occupied with taking her in custody, that once you are on shore, you and your party are my guests, and there are services that I can and will make available to you, not only in Laguna but on your journey to Palenque. And," he added, looking directly at John, "as soon as it is feasible, I will arrange a private meeting with you, Mr. Sterling, if that is agreeable."

The eye exchange between them said quite plainly, *I know that you are the one most likely to have had Señor Alano's full confidence and to know the extent of what is concealed in the secret vaults below.*

And John was thinking the obvious. *We, too, are his prisoners, and watchdogs will be set upon us, or worse, unless I convince him that I am a vault more secure even than his collection of ebony furniture.* He answered simply, "Quite agreeable, Don Vicende," and went to fetch the prisoner before the judge.

"Jinnee, Don Vicende is waiting. The prisoners have been taken ashore in chains. There is no danger. Come with me, quickly."

She opened the door, and he was shocked. The hours of fear she had endured since the boat had anchored and since the enraged Montclair's voice had penetrated her hiding place, had changed her appearance from seductive and tempestuous to vulnerable and fragile; however, the witchery of form and face, the dazzling vitality of the long red hair hanging in wavy clusters over veiled shoulders and around her breasts were more magnetic than ever.

She looked at him, her eyes pleading for approval.

"Parfait, mademoiselle!"

She took courage from the only genuine smile he had ever given her. As they entered the master's quarters, there was a stillness of presence like a solid that is penetrable, but once entered closes in on the intruder. John felt it as much as Jinnee. He walked with her into it and stood before the impassive expression on Don Vicende's face as though he too were waiting for judgment, then recovered and stepped aside.

Jinnee was completely unaware of any presence other than the one she confronted. Automatically, she followed John's instruction, gazing at some point above the princely grooming of the Don's shoulder-length wavy dark hair.

"What is your name?" he asked abruptly.

She opened her mouth, but could not speak. The awesome presence before her was too much. She glanced at John.

"Look at *me*!" the Don snapped.

She looked into his eyes and was held mesmerized, snared.

"You do have a name, don't you?"

She moved her head from side to side and whispered, "No name."

"Then I give you one. Dobla. Say it. 'Dobla'!"

She said the word but it came out soundless.

"Speak it! *Dobla*."

She took a deep breath and made it audible: "Dob-la."

"This is your name, and you will never have another. Understand?"

She nodded.

"Do you know what it means?"

"Non."

"It is the name of an ancient Spanish coin. You have, without intent, become as a good luck coin for me."

She was still held without volition of any kind by the gaze he kept sealed on her. She tried to smile but the eyes remained so steely that she could not.

Then his brows raised a little, his lids lifted further to widen and reveal a different attention—the threatening brown softened in response to a different set of sensations—sensations that "Dobla" recognized. At the same time she was aware of John's rigid attention on her, and stilled the inner tremor, the impulse to react in some way to the scrutiny that had begun and intensified to the extent that she felt her clothes slipping from her, and without thinking reached a hand to her bodice, enhancing the appeal she was generating.

Another switch of attention, and the Don was ignoring her, addressing the three "witnesses," with the detachment of a transaction concluded.

"I shall take the woman with me. My attendants are waiting. It will be my pleasure to meet you on shore and escort you to a place of rest and recuperation while your baggage is cared for and arrangements made for your transportation to Palenque."

He turned to Sarah Belle. "Madame, in extremity, I must beg a favor of you. This woman is not adequately clothed for the trip ashore. If I may have your cape to put about her, you can expect more than commensurate reward for your charity."

"Certainly, Don Vicende." She gave him a special smile and unlatched the fastening at her throat.

He was about to step over to Sarah Belle and take the cape, but John was closer and well ahead of him. He lifted the cape from Sarah Belle's shoulders and handed it to the Don. Newton watched, fascinated.

"Gracias, Señor Sterling." He looked at Sarah Belle, not concealing his added appreciation of her as she was revealed without the cape, rose waist held gathered and tightly belted under the blue skirt. Then he continued to John, "My good fortune has been multiplied many times on this day, aboard the charmed *Valkyrie*, and yours, I surmise, in some ways matches my own.

"Good day, Master Newton, your service is inestimable, and irreplaceable. We will sign new and extended contracts before you leave port."

He placed the blue cape carefully around Dobla, and freeing her hair, carefully closed the latch at her neckline, stared into her eyes for a moment that left her in a hypnotic daze, and led her away.

Posada de la Flor . . . "A House of Recovery, and this time I am the guest," Sarah Belle mused.

She sat on a marble bench in a lavishly floral walled garden with no entrance except through the building. Celeste lay dreamily swinging in a wicker hammock nearby while Maury strolled about with Emile and Jasper.

They had been in a suite assigned to them by Don Vicende for four days: two bedrooms with all accommodations, parlor, and small dining room, servants in attendance for every possible need and comfort. Choicest of foods were brought in and served with ceremonial punctuality—three meals, and refreshments at mid-morning, midafternoon, and late evening.

Sarah Belle was confined to the suite and the garden. It would have been as completely unacceptable for her to appear without escort in the dining room, or any other section of the posada open to the public, as it would be for the servants to seat themselves there.

Also, from her assumed status as Emile's wife, she could not appear with John; and, as for Don Vicende, he had his own status and motives that forbade any overt attention to another man's wife.

But she had not gone without attention from either man. Don Vicende had seen to it that John's suite was in another wing of the posada, adjoining his own quarters. Thus, John's visits to Sarah Belle must be brief and seem to be made simply in the interest of his friends' welfare. There was no time for extended confidence, no assurance that a servant might not be eavesdropping in Don Vicende's interest.

He related to her only what he judged she should know and that in low tones, often in French.

"We are being watched and we will continue to be under watch for some time—until Don Vicende removes every doubt from his mind as to my veracity and lack of interest in his fortunes or political persuasions. This will take time.

"I am sure he will send an agent to New Jersey to investigate my family and financial holdings—to check on all I have told him—my friendship with John Lloyd Stephens, my interests in the same kind of exploration. I hope he brings back no account of my Orinoco venture which he would interpret as a lust for gold rather than misguided heroics."

"Why are you the one exclusively given such attention?"

"There are others, but none that he can feel certain knows exactly the nature of his concealed cargo as I do—and that it is vaulted in the ebony furniture."

"No wonder he designed it himself!"

"He trusted Alano to keep the secret which was spilled in the sickness of fear, and, worse for me, in all detail—including a line of intrigue reaching all the way from his Yucatán hacienda to the throne of Spain."

"Incredible!"

"But as true as time. He questioned me in specifics, if Alano had divulged this or that, and I could not risk being evasive with such a discerning man."

"Is he concerned that you might have confided in me, or may be inclined to do so?"

"I assured him that I had kept my knowledge from all on the boat—the others being only generally aware that there were unlisted valuables. I think he believes me, but he must also believe that I will never open up to anyone—under any kind of duress."

"John! That's dangerous!"

"Our little adventura has become a journey into peril. I regret that I led you into it."

"No, John, never that! I invited myself. As I invite myself right now into your arms and into your thoughts so that you can think of us only as one, no matter what jeopardy we face. My only regret is——"

"Speak casually, my own, no tone of love for attentive ears."

"My only regret is——"

"I know." His lips met hers with all the longing of what could have been and what still might be at some uncertain time and place ahead.

There was a knock on the door.

When Sarah Belle opened the door to a waiter bringing the afternoon refreshment, John was by her side.

"Mr. Sterling, the ices and pastries at the Flor are superb. Won't you join me?"

"Thank you, madam. I wanted to be sure that Monsieur Palais was resting and all was well with you. I am due for an appointment with Don Vicende. He is giving me the benefit of his knowledge of the country and assisting with other matters to insure a comfortable and safe journey for us to Palenque. . . . Good day, madam."

Don Vicende's visit to Sarah Belle was prefaced by a verbal message delivered by his personal liveried servant: "Don Vicende would be grateful for the privilege of calling on you at an appointed time, set at your convenience, that he might express his gratitude in person for courtesies extended him aboard the *Valkyrie*."

"Tell him that I go into the garden for a stroll after siesta and he will find me there awaiting the pleasure of his attentions."

She commented on this to Celeste. "He feels that he has impressed me enough with himself and the circumstances I find myself in to make his convenience my own. He actually expected to come on the heels of his servant, but a delay will mystify him just a little, sharpen anticipation. . . . You, of course, will accompany me. It is the custom, but will give him a bit of a surprise, nonetheless. When he appears, you may move off to a discreet distance, out of hearing, we will say, yet not entirely out of sight."

"This is a strange place here, madame—this posada. It is all too comfortable—too closed in—and all the servants, much more than we need. I am too idle. I would like to do something, but I don't dare. They serve you like a person of high station—and which to me you certainly are," she hastily amended, "but I do not like the way they watch you when you are not looking."

"Not looking, Celeste, but knowing. It is peculiar, but so was all we went through on the *Valkyrie*. Never mind, we'll soon be up the riverways and on to Palenque where we can camp among the ruins and the jungle will be our garden."

Sarah Belle looked in the mirror and handed Celeste ornamental pins for the soft folds of hair being pinned at the back of her neck, addressing herself silently as she did so. "Well, how do you like it? Here you are in reverse position, in another's House, the guest being coddled, then questioned. Don Vicende reads women as you read men. His motives may be different, but the procedure comparable. He knows beyond a doubt that you and John are like two flooding streams plunging over waterfalls toward convergence! He is amused, but also concerned for his own interests, and wary of the Palais arrangement, not yet clear to him. He is also a bit intrigued by the woman you are, and what he cannot know about you. But be careful, he will try. Are you amused that his interest in you might benefit John, as Dobla's interest in John had its rewards? No, you are not amused. Leave that to Don Vicende. But you will go into the game with benefits in mind."

When Don Vicende appeared, she arose to greet him. He hurried to her.

"Please, madame, may I sit beside you? You are gracious to grant me this privilege. I have searched my mind for what would be an adequate expression of my gratitude for your care of Master Newton, for your strength and composure in planning and executing the plot that saved the *Valkyrie* and all she carried in lives and cargo."

"It was John Sterling who was in charge. I assisted where I could."

"Mr. Sterling gives you much of the credit."

"He is a generous man of stable character and remarkable intellect."

"This I believe I have established for myself. You will pardon me for personal questions, but all that happened aboard the *Valkyrie* makes for extraordinary circumstances."

"I understand. What would you inquire of me?"

"How long have you known Mr. Sterling?"

"Long enough to be certain that he is in every sense trustworthy."

Don Vicende smiled in a way that acknowledged the evasion and let it rest.

"He has told me of his family connections in New Jersey. And you are from New Orleans?"

"Yes."

"And Monsieur Palais?"

"New Orleans, of course, and a distinguished family of French lineage."

"Any offspring, madame?"

She shook her head, looked him directly in the eye, and he understood "That's all" without her voicing it.

"Madame, I entreat you, do not think me either disrespectful or childlike, but will you close your eyes, trust me, and give me your right hand?"

She gazed at him steadily until his eyes reflected puzzlement, then closed her eyes and extended her hand. He took hold of her fingers, closed them tight, slipped something over onto her wrist, snapped a fine latch, and her eyes flew open.

As his hand left her wrist, it moved with a caressing glide to her fingers and held them close again.

He had placed a bracelet there and a tiny gold chain had allowed the expansion until a latch closed the gold band. Centered on the wrist was a large ruby, set as the heart of a rose, its leaves in the Spanish art of green gold and the petals of the rose in pink gold.

"Do not protest, dear lady, do not protest! It is small payment. Monsieur Palais would agree you deserve it, were he of an observing mind, and your friend Señor Sterling would be the last to think you unworthy."

He still held her hand.

She said gently, "Thank you, Don Vicende," and no more.

He kissed her hand once, and then again fervently.

She did not move her fingers or try to withdraw her hand. In her mind she said: *It is your turn to prove that you are trustworthy.*

He released her hand in answer to her thought, but not without moving his thumb across her fingers as if loath to let go, and causing her fingers to tremble for release.

"One more request, and I will be on my way. It is customary for the Flor to have a small musicale for guests occasionally, breaking the monotony of everyday routines. Tonight is such an evening. Mr. Sterling and I will call for you, so that all may be circumspect, if you will agree to accompany us."

"Don Vicende, it would be a pleasure, but I have not come on this journey prepared for social occasions. I have no more suitable attire than you see me wearing now, the same as I wore when we met. And——"

"Please, madame. It would not be kind to gentlemen present if you wore anything more enchanting than what you are gowned in at this moment. Besides, this is not a formal affair and only a small gathering. There will be good music, a magician perhaps, and a dancer or two. You will come?"

"The prospect is pleasing."

"Bravo! I am happy!" He stood, bowed with a flourish and hurried away.

When John and Don Vicende came to her suite that evening, a servant entered with them and placed a long case on the table. When polite greetings had been exchanged, Don Vicende suggested with becoming guile that she open the case and show them what had been delivered.

She raised the lid and stood looking in wonderment at the lovely folds inside but did not touch them. Don Vicende came quickly to her side, took out a cape very light in weight and roseate in color, and held it up to view, talking with the enthusiasm of a court designer.

"You did not dream perhaps that here in this place so distant from centers of culture, where the influence of pirates and kings has been felt for centuries, that beauty to grace the feminine form was so readily available. Though not in great numbers, there are lovely ladies to be clothed and gallant men to supply them. The finest of materials are imported along with gifted tailors and seamstresses of various races to ply their lucrative trade here.

"This garment is but a small expression of my desire to replace that which you gave with such quick response in a matter of most delicate concern. It is my added pleasure, with your permission, to place it around your lovely shoulders."

Sarah Belle responded in kind: "Your generosity is excessive, the replacement much more splendid than the original, but you have touched the vanity that in a woman is seldom dormant. I feel my grooming for the musicale will be much more acceptable with this ravishing addition."

She laid aside the shawl she had intended to use, and accepted his pleasurable handling of the cape as he draped it around her.

His presentation of the much more costly apparel in exchange for the cape to cover Dobla was a cunning sort of masculine maneuver that could not be countered.

She didn't look at John. She knew exactly what he was feeling. His unnaturally cool, "Madame Palais, the guests will think Don Vicende and I are escorting a newly arrived European célébrité," was not at all what she wanted to hear.

The coastal town of Laguna, Yucatán, depot of the great logwood country, prospered in its location on the Island of Carmen, which lay with its face to the Gulf of Mexico and its back to the great expanse of Lake Términos, receptacle of a family of jungle rivers and streams.

Here in this remote settlement, privilege and populace, primitive and industrial, the caste conscious, the adventurer, and the revolutionary thrived, schemed, and mixed in cautious but necessary contact.

The Posada de la Flor, though exclusive in its patronage, was revered as a symbol of kinship with the great world across the wide waters. The room in the Flor reserved for entertainment could have been, except for its size, a French salon removed intact from Europe. Its gilt, pastel, and crystal decor carried designs conceived for royalty.

The residents who came for the musicale were a cautious mix in themselves—introductions were acknowledged with deference but little warmth of approach: an agent from a shipbuilding firm in Norfolk; merchants out of New York, Boston, New Orleans, Charleston; a padre on vacation from a jungle outpost; a Protestant missionary and wife called to serve in the wilds of Chiapas; also three innovators of productive land clearance along the rich banks of the Río Palizada present with their families just brought in from the States, seated beside a Texas cotton king on the trail of a get-rich-quicker scheme.

The three that entered last, while the musicians waited, took cushioned seats near the dais—the elegant Spaniard, the tall composed American, and the stunning woman wearing a rose-colored cape of feathery velvet and satin, her brown hair piled high with the ends falling in a cascade upon her neck.

Sarah Belle felt a tremble inside when she saw a harp among the instruments. It was an Erard, smaller and not so ornate as the one that had been her delight and emotional outlet, but important enough in the ensemble to be centered and raised above the others. And an unusual ensemble it was. Around the harp were grouped a guitar, two violins, a marimba, and a trumpet.

It was evident from the moment the program started that the musicians were not casual about their instruments nor careless about their mastery. All performers were men. The young man at the trumpet had the dark skin of a Guatemalan Indian and brought out notes as clear as the droplets on the chandelier. The marimba player was alive all over with Latin rhythms. The violinists were suppliants at the feet of romance, and the guitar wooed the harp so ardently that each instrument seemed intrinsic to the other.

Sarah Belle, her eyes on the harp, her fingers hungering for the strings, realized that there was another passion in her life second only to John. She had dismissed it easily on departure from the house in New Orleans, but now she realized that at the harp she had transformed the darkness of her life into light, the lows into highs, loneliness into sustenance, the energies and demands of desire into her own creative harmonics.

Her yearning intensified into a sharp point of craving that streaked through her body from the top of her spinal column to the pelvic basin. Her fingers curled and trembled.

Don Vicende sensed her strong reaction to the music.

"Do you play an instrument, madame?" he inquired.

She did not reply.

John recognized her tension and the cause of it.

"She is a virtuoso at the harp," he informed Vicende, his voice constricted.

The fear and fascination Don Vicende generated—the banked passion of John's love and concern for her—both were surging so rampant through Sarah Belle's senses that containment became a pain racing from her shoulders into her fingers. A high flush mounted on her cheeks and forehead.

There was a pause in the program, and Don Vicende stepped out in front of the musicians.

"I have just become aware that we have present a distinguished harpist from New Orleans, Madame Palais, who is my guest here. I am inviting her to be seated at the harp at this time if it is her pleasure to perform for us."

There was a polite patter of applause.

"John, I can't resist. I am aching to play."

"Go."

Except for the harpist who bowed as he gave her his seat, the musicians sat attentive and still, their instruments at rest.

God, you must have provided this, she though as she flexed her fingers and began.

A few runs as she and the harp became one, and then she was oblivious of her listeners. The energies spent in living and almost dying raced into sound.

Fears and frustrations . . . desire with all its tauntings . . . the ravages of hate and jealousy . . . all came surging up to be washed out with the forces of courage and strength surpassing muscle and mechanics.

One instrument after the other began to pick up, augment, echo what the harp was talking, crying, singing about.

Finally, there was the purest of romance, the dreamer's dream, the lover's love. The trumpet punctuated, the marimba rippled, the violins gave sensual accent, and the guitar injected rhythmic phrasing that increased the flow of wonder between musicians and audience.

At last, Sarah Belle's energies were spent. She folded her hands and bowed her head.

Her audience applauded as one, stood and continued applauding, calling out their approval and delight. The six musicians crowded around her, exclaiming and praising. She was dazed, the emotional height, the rapture experienced through the support of other instruments like nothing she had ever known.

She stared at the rapt faces, wished it were possible to exchange an abrazo with each. "Don Vicende told me there might be a magician here," she said softly, "and I find myself surrounded by six magicians!"

Then John and Vicende were by her side, escorting her through the excited audience, so warm and released by the music that they were now acting like old friends. And Don Vicende was inviting them all, musicians and performers as well, into the dining room.

The accolades lavished upon her as glasses clicked and toasts were declaimed during the impromptu feast Don Vicende hosted in her honor, were vaguely pleasant but unimportant. She had given herself to music and was at peace, moving in a center of calm among the celebrants.

But John was far from calm. When she managed to whisper to him, "Stay close to me, dear." He answered only, "I'll try."

Don Vicende, elevated out of his natural role as a superior to any in his presence, had spoken an impassioned aside, "Surely you are not going to risk this golden talent to the threats of the jungle."

Her only answer was to nod and smile.

The Don, as well as Sarah Belle, had moved into a new range of sensation during the enchantment of the harp. Though he was not a man to roam for long in the realm of imagination, he had found himself led by this woman's musical revelation into an imaginary relationship far different than he could have believed existed.

His reasoning mind, like that of the merchant prince Justin Lahart, told him that she was not of his world. But he was less scrupulous than Justin in seeking alternatives to what was reasonable.

CHAPTER THIRTY

"CLEOPATRA, YOUR BARGE AWAITS YOU at the shores of Lake Términos. The highest quality matting has gone into the structure of awning to shield you from the sun, and into the carpeting. There is also cushioned seating, and a lady's little private house at the stern, known hereabouts as a movable hatch.

"You have the sturdiest of bogadores known for the speed they attain in upstream travel. Moreover, there is a sobrestante who not only oversees your barge and all of its accommodations but is in charge of the whole expedition—has sent couriers ahead all the way to Palenque to make arrangements for lodgings along the way and carriers where needed. All has been made ready for your early departure tomorrow."

"John, I detect a caustic tone in your announcements."

"I myself come merely as a courier of Don Vicende."

Sarah Belle had received no word from John or Don Vicende the day after the musicale. She had felt no uneasiness—was satisfied to be alone with Maury and Celeste, their union radiating a sufficiency always reassuring. She spent time with them in the garden. Even the abstract presence of Emile fostered a contented stillness as he watched Jasper frisking about. She gave poetic attention to the profusion of blossoms where butterflies and hummingbirds were partaking of the essence. The flooding of exaltation she had experienced at the harp was still a gentle flow in which neither John nor Don Vicende intruded.

But by the time John arrived the next morning, she was restless and wanted out, yearning to see him, hear his voice, touch him, get on to the core of the adventura, the mysterious allure of the Palenque ruins.

She had not expected the cool quick kiss of greeting, the strange aloofness in his eyes, the brisk manner and sardonic tone.

What has Don Vicende done to him? she wondered, covering her dismay and seeking for a response that would break through.

"There will be two extra bungos," he continued, "carrying luggage, supplies, and camping equipment that cannot be secured in the interior. Maury and Emile will ride in one of these. Carriers, mounts, and hamacas will be provided for the trail from Las Playas to Palenque village."

"What is a hamaca?"

"It is a cushioned chair with a long pole at each end. The person being carried sits with face to the side, and four bearers, usually Indians, carry it along. Thus, you and Celeste and Emile, can travel in this manner. Hamacas, rather than mules, are the accommodation used most for heavy men and the padres."

"I am neither! You have brought sidesaddles which Celeste and I expect to use. A hamaca in which Emile and Maury could ride would be useful."

"I anticipated providing this, but all has been placed under the direction of Don Vicende's sobrestante, and he considers the hamaca proper for ladies."

"Being proper is not my idea of adventure—or of romance—or, for the solution of difficulties." (Be careful, Sarah Belle, she admonished herself, you'll make matters worse. How well you should know what happens when a man loses his sense of authority.)

She went to the table where the midmorning drinks and fruits were laid out. "Sit down, and let's have coffee together."

He came and sat silent, bemused, while she prepared his cup and handed it to him.

"How can I be Cleopatra and sit here hostage to my subjects, my lovers, and the high priests?"

"Sarah Belle!"

"Ah! you recognize me! Now tell me, what has happened to John Monroe Sterling that has turned him into a disfranchised conqueror?"

He smiled, and relented. "Don Vicende spins a very tight web. Struggling against it at the wrong time could be fatal. I have refused an overly generous reward in gold for my handling of the Alano matter. To me it would be like a bribe for my silence, an admission of being untrustworthy. Yet, I must allow him to express his gratitude in other ways or he will think my independence both a discourtesy and a threat—a matter of design against him for future manipulation. My knowledge of his political ties abroad is of as much concern to him—or maybe more—as the fortune he has finally been able to smuggle into Yucatán."

"So providing passage for us to Palenque in such a manner as he alone could arrange with influence and hirelings, is the first grand gesture."

"And, added to that (I comment on what you already know), is his fascination with the gifted harpist, which gives him added incentive for added favors."

"I should have resisted the Erard."

"One does not resist the inevitable. He was already under the spell. While he waits in the wings to pursue the woman, he can, as a patron of the arts, watch and protect the great talent that the world is waiting for."

"John, you're being caustic again."

"My dear, I am not. I am being blunt."

"He will follow us to Palenque?"

"Of course not. But the sobrestante will see that we arrive safely, have a well protected and supplied camp, and, as provisions are brought to us at Palenque village from time to time, reports will go back down the line as to our welfare and activities."

"Then we will be under watch all the time?"

"Not quite. Access is not easy. We will dispense with any servants from the village and mother nature will help us along. There will be out-of-season rains and storms, isolating us from time to time, as Mr. Stephens and other explorers have reported."

"And after Palenque, what?"

"How about going native? Become children of the jungle? Making our way to one of those primitive Indian villages in the Guatemalan highlands?"

"You're joking. But I'd do that before I'd part from you."

"Are you serious? Tell me right now!"

He shoved his chair back, his hands gripped the edge of the table and he looked across the table with such demanding intensity that she was startled and stood up too.

So he hadn't been too sure of her—the harp, the celebration, Don Vicende——

"There is nothing in my life that I have ever been more serious about. And only yourself or Master Death could change my direction."

She had not caught her breath until he had her in his arms kissing her fervently, repeatedly, his ardor an effort to break through the restraints that held them captive, and his phrases an effort to control desire. "That's all . . . all I need to know now . . . but not all . . . that I forever need . . ."

"Not all . . . not all . . . that I have to give . . ."

"I have heard . . ."

"What . . . what have you heard?"

"I have heard . . ." His lips released hers at last.

"I have heard that there are secret rooms to be discovered in the Main Palace at Palenque. When I find one, will you——"

"I certainly will—you may even find me waiting there."

"I must go. I have stayed too long. Don Vicende will be waiting."

"Oh yes, Don Vicende. Pay my respects."

Don Vicende came in the afternoon to pay and receive his own respects. He accompanied the servants who came at this time of day with the routine refreshments. But this time, his presence meant extra delicacies in food and drink and an array of small packages quite outside of routine. He dismissed the attendants.

"I am begging a special privilege of you, madame, to sit for a few moments and talk in private about your future, which I make a matter of personal concern for reasons I will explain. Please do be seated at the table that I may serve you."

Into the most delicate of crystal he poured a sweet wine so clear that only by its movement could it be detected. He arranged thin silver plates and small matching forks, then placed bite-size pieces of fruit and meats with a variety of crackers on the two dishes he had set out.

Sarah Belle sat and watched without comment. When he sat across from her, he raised his glass. "To a safe excursion that brings you back even sooner than intended—your loveliness and rare gifts unblemished by the wilderness sojourn." He emptied his glass as if to insure the fulfillment of his toast.

"Thank you, Don Vicende. To a man of generosity and rare discernment." She raised her glass and let the wine touch her lips. She nibbled a cracker, forked a tidbit of fruit.

He hesitated, unsure of his approach, a condition so rare that it brought on an irritation making him more direct than he had intended to be.

"It distresses me to see you, so endowed with womanly attributes and a gift of music the gods might envy, tied to a man who is no longer a man in mind or body—and for some reason inclined to follow the tracks of a man who in spite of an honorable nature is an adventurer, a wanderer scratching among the ruins of the past for novelties."

Sarah Belle put down a desire to defend John and surprised him with her own directness.

"What would you have me do?"

"You dare to ask me that, knowing how I feel about you!" His face reddened. "What I could do! How I am tempted!"

"Most men of power have mastered self-control and know the merits of discretion. I think you are such a man. Now again, what would you have me do?"

"Turn back from this senseless expedition to Palenque. I will find a comfortable residence here for your servants—and the husk you call husband. Put aside your attachment to this Sterling, which is no more than a solace for your deprived womanhood. Let me provide the outlet for your marvelous talent and for——"

"My deprived womanhood? Don Vicende, I do not question your intents or abilities to do all you say. In spite of what appears to you as shackles on my life, all are matters of my own choice and the reasons for these choices are not conditions that all your power or desire could alter. I'm grateful for the generous preparations you've made for the expedition. I'm sure we'll have more comfort and protection than we had anticipated. And your attentions to us here at the Flor have made Laguna a luxurious interlude."

"All of it deserved." In the face of her delicate rebuff, Don Vicende changed tone and demeanor as though nothing personal had passed between them. "The little packets stacked there will be easily added to your luggage—some special dainties from the Flor chef stored in tins that will keep well; a lotion you'll find useful for the swarms of mosquitoes that infest jungle riverbanks and the best of lodging sites; and other tokens of esteem that may relieve the monotony of upriver travel."

"You are too kind."

"And you are not kind enough!" his smile was ingratiating, infectious. He arose, ready to take his leave. At the door she extended her hand to clasp his as she said good-bye.

As he took her hand, fixing his eyes on hers with that certain glow she had witnessed when Dobla was brought before him, she wanted to cringe. Then he bowed over her hand and brought it to his lips with a pressure as telling as it would have been had it been on her lips. Her open sleeve dropped back and he saw the bracelet he had given her.

Her heart was pounding. She had slipped it on in a moment of curiosity when packing, and his appearance at her suite had caused her to forget it was there.

"You're wearing my bracelet. Why?"

"You gave it to be worn, did you not? It is beautiful."

He brought her hand to his lips again—and again before he let her go without another word.

Sometimes Maury wondered if his "little brother," Emile, was as unseeing as he appeared to be. Since being brought aboard the bungo, he had sat at ease under the awning, Jasper's chain secured to his belt. The squirrel, fretful at first, soon picked up the mood of his traveling companions, gazing in wonderment at the gigantic trees of the tropical forest so close to the bungos as they entered the Boca Chica that he could have leaped into the branches. The spread of the vivid green forest lining the banks was supported by naked, gnarled roots several feet above ground, intertwined like huge serpents caught and petrified in an agony of knots.

The three bungos were brought out of Lake Términos through this narrow passage into a smaller lake, and from there into the main current of the Río Palizada. This river was called *Mujer de Máscara* (woman of the mask) by the bogadores, because her depths, even to the banks, often made their setting poles useless. The jungle for many miles was a forbidding wall, its branches arching out from both sides, ready to snatch the sails of any boat that was masted and its rowers careless with the oars.

No habitation would be seen until they reached the municipality of Palizada. This distance against the current could take several days and nights, or, if winds were fortuitous and nights clear, two days after emerging from the lake region.

Celeste was uneasy, being separated from Maury, and found the jungle tunnel in which they traveled frightening, concealing monsters that would pounce if they touched shore. Sarah Belle and John sat much in silence, happy in the removal of all things familiar, feeling transported into another realm of existence with no restrictions of time-place, moving toward further awesome encounters with jungle mysteries and jungle power as displayed at the Palenque ruins. Anxieties were abandoned. Expectations raced joyfully ahead.

They felt no need to touch or embrace. Their eyes carried all the messages that required exchange. John busied himself at the oars from time to time, and conversed with the sobrestante about the conditions of travel and weather up ahead, the river's deceits and whims, and the alligators' domain which they would pass through just before reaching the settlement.

The first day and night, rowers had no assist from the wind god, but the moon, showing more than half her face, gave light enough for continued progress. At dawn, the sobrestante assured John that rain would come before the morning had passed and he should see that the women were ready to take cover.

Deluge (announced by one violent blast of thunder that seemed to explode in the wake of the bungos) was more descriptive of what followed. Celeste clung to Sarah Belle and sobbed in the darkness of the hatch which seemed to slide about as the down-pour pounded.

It soon passed and left a blessing in its wake. The sails were set as a strong wind began to drive the bungos ahead with a steady speed. The sun, often a tropical scourge, came out to serve as a drying agent and hasten recovery from the drenching as thorough as a baptism by immersion.

The night to follow was a fantasy of marvel and terror. The wind built up its power, canceling the river's opposing force with furious gusts. The moon offered a veiled light. The bungos whirled ahead like phantoms caught up in a mad dance with the elements.

Dawn broke the spell. The bogadores, who could not be relieved during the wild spree, fell to the deck exhausted, while others took their place.

Sarah Belle and Celeste, looking like windblown outcasts from a wreck at sea, helped John break out nourishment and stimulants, while they marveled that all three bungos had come through without accident.

The sobrestante, after a long draught of straight brandy, announced with bravado that it was "Nada! Nada!" for he had picked trained marineros who had been seasoned in worse storms. They noticed, however, that he was in such a tremor it took both hands to hold the bottle. . . .

Again the sun god was acclaimed, for it was the morning of the third day, and there was Light! And they should find harbor and a resting place at the town of Palizada before the sun set.

The rhythm of the oars was even again. A slight breeze on the sails and the slow-moving current brought on a chant from the rowers addressing the *Mujer de Máscara.*

"Mujer Máscara! Mujer Máscara!
  You took off your mask,
  Your face was ferocious!
  Your spit was a torrent—
  Mujer Máscara! Mujer Máscara!
  You took off your mask.

  Your breath was a tiger,
  It purred with its claws

And made us your toys,
Your miserable toys!
Mujer Máscara! Mujer Máscara!
It purred with its claws!

O Mujer Máscara! Mujer Máscara!
Your mask is in place,
Your wet lips are sweet,
You give us soft kisses,
O Mujer Máscara! Mujer Máscara!
Your mask is in place
And your kiss is so soft!
            Mujer, Mujer, Mujer Máscara!"

A few hours later around a long bend in the river, the Mujer de Máscara took off her mask again and revealed the face of a monster, for the bungos were entering alligator heaven and navigator hell. Stretched out on a large mudbank, basking in the sun, must have been the Alligator King, his full length not less than twenty feet. Surrounding him was his court, either lying on long limbs bending into the river or floating like huge logs against the bank. The river waters were dotted with heads.

The three bungos, moving in a line among them, kept as near the middle of the river as they could steer.

Celeste panicked, leaning far over the boat, screaming to Maury. "You all right, Maury? You all right?"

"Fine, honey, fine! You get your head back way from that edge!"

"Emile? And Jasper baby?"

"Emile look at them like they pet frogs. Jasper tight in his pocket. You sit down!"

Sarah Belle jerked Celeste back.

John commanded, "Stay by Sarah! A tip overboard and you're gone!"

The sobrestante, with the éclat of one who has seen all and knows all, unraveled horror tales as they moved slowly through the threatening heads. He explained that the boatmen in the region considered the alligators "enemigos de los cristianos" and went among them at the end of the dry season to slay them with clubs and machetes until the river turned red; and how when these hideous creatures were swimming along with mouths open they swallowed anything they saw, whether flotsam or living things; how they swam faster than any fish, and how, when slit open, the maw might carry more than a hundred pounds of fish, besides the digested catch; how the hunters once found an Indian woman whole and clothed who had been swallowed the day before, and in another only gold bracelets and pearls as evidence of a similar fate for a careless woman.

Sarah put an abrupt stop to the horrorlogues by suggesting: "Now tell us about men who have been swallowed, and how long it takes an alligator to digest one of the masculine gender, and what indigestible mementoes might remain."

The passengers on the bungos from Laguna, drugged on fatigue, emerged from the wilderness into the settlement of Palizada wondering if the dreamlike scene would turn out to be a delusion. Strings of fog were teasing the river. The sun was wearing a red and gold veil on the way to a tryst beyond jungle walls.

The long main street was laid out on an elevated plain close to the riverbank. Its houses, some large, two-storied, were showing pastel faces through the evening haze. Bungos were swaying at rest on the Palizada like a string of animate carriers in service to the occupants.

Thanks to Don Vicende's sobrestante and the courier he had sent ahead, attendants were waiting to care for the luggage and offer a bright red and blue hack to carry them to comfortable lodgings. A messenger from the alcalde made them welcome, no permissions or inspections required.

In the days ahead, Sarah Belle found that her memories of the overnight stop at Palizada were fragmentary—the high wrought-iron gates at the posada opened by an elderly keeper of the keys with no expression that she could recall; a matronly Spanish woman who murmured a greeting and led her and Celeste to a large room full of large furniture, then left never to be glimpsed again.

But the little maiden who came to fill the water jar and bring food and drink was unforgettable. "She looks and moves as though molded and animated by a perfectionist," Sarah Belle mused, alerted somewhat by the thick coffee slightly diluted with milk being served to her. The diminutive figure and fair skin, hip-length black hair and limpid eyes to match, suggested a mix of Spanish and Mayan.

"Su nombre?" Sarah Belle inquired.

"Paloma. Paloma de la Pureza."

Not fluent but adequate in Spanish, Sarah Belle commented on the beauty of the name, inquired further.

"Paloma de la Pureza—Dove of Purity. How did you come by such a name?"

Paloma said it was given by her mother who hoped she would become a nun.

No, she did not live in this house. She only worked here. Her mother was very poor, and there were other children. Her father had gone to the coast to get work and never returned. The dona of this big house was her protectora.

Sarah Belle felt such a strong empathy for the little Dove, so tender, so pure, yet more than a child, that she would have liked to have been assured that the dona was a genuine and devoted protector.

The effect of the Yucatecan coffee bean left her dizzy and reeling. Celeste helped her to bed and she had no other sensation until Paloma was in the room again, laying out an early breakfast. The sobrestante had instructed they must be on their way in time to reach the next lodging before dark, if possible, and after that Las Playas, the end of the river travel, and only a day from there to Palenque village.

As she hurriedly dressed, Sarah Belle wished, with a kind of frantic necessity, that she had a parting gift for Paloma. The girl stood in silence watching her every move, hoping to be called on for some further service, her eyes big and sad at the parting.

As she thrust a final pin into her hair, she realized that Paloma's attention was fixed on her hand, and with a start she knew why. It was the ring. A thin, inconspicuous narrow band of gold set with seed pearls. It was a tie with her own youth, and though she had never labeled it good luck or protective, in time of decision or change she would put it on for some intangible reassurance it conveyed.

Her eyes met those of Paloma de la Pureza, and she knew she could part with it. It was on her little finger and tight around the knuckle. As she worked with it, Paloma realized what was about to happen.

"O no, no, no! Señora! No es para mí!" She made the sign

of the cross and held her hands tight against her bosom. "No es para mí!"

Sarah Belle loosened a trembling hand and held it in her own for a moment. A flood of tears washed down Paloma's cheeks as the band was placed on her forefinger.

Sarah Belle hastened to her final packing to hide her own tears and to puzzle over the nature of sudden recognitions that provoke spiritual bondage along life's uneven pathway. Certainly it was not limited to love-at-first-sight between man and woman. It had no barriers of age, sex, ethnic, or cultural origins. It did not emerge from whim or fantasy. It was not announced, expected or time-clad. It could become the enrichment of a lifetime, or it could be encompassed in a glance, a handclasp, a hasty greeting at the crossroads, just an instant reading of coded love blended with the tug of parting.

While she was waiting at river's edge to go aboard the lead bungo, she watched Celeste and Maury embrace after getting Emile settled under the awning on the one to follow.

Here were three other bondings to ponder on, the linkage self-imposed. What effect would they have upon her fixed intent to stay at John's side? Would he tire of this entourage? And what would become of the farcical role she was playing with Emile? When he aroused to full and lasting knowledge of his identity, which she believed was destined to happen, how would he relate to her and to his past? The demands aboard the *Valkyrie* and the journey to this point had left no margin for thought or emotion on this enigma.

Now her attention focused on him sitting so tanned and relaxed in the morning sun, Jasper lively in his lap. She came into a strange removed perspective, her environs insubstantial, dream-like: *the lapping of the wide muddy river, held tight in the embrace of the jungle, playful with bungos and with boatmen pushing out upstream to outwit the Mujer de Máscara, or twirling gratefully into her downflow. The bustling activity ashore—native Indians, rooted Mexicans, trans-planted foreigners intent on a world of their own; peddlers of dried young alligator meat, strings of fermented corn, joints of sugarcane; a few women skittering about with ragged children; a padre, a policía, dogs, and pack mules* . . . all an indistinct montage to Sarah Belle, staring at Emile, in search of their future.

A stranger would see him as a man of ease, she mused, handsome with an air of wealth, traveling for novelty, rather than as a disinherited outcast rescued from life imprisonment as a lunatic. He no longer gave an impression of weakness, his appearance thoughtful, reserved. What would a confrontation between her and a restored Emile be like? What would it mean to a sensitive young man of his condition—born to wealth and privilege, reared in the strictures of a caste system, his senses numbed by tragedy too grim to face—to come alive, to recognize himself among the ruins of an ancient civilization? Might it not promote a frenzy of renewed insanity?

She felt a prick of panic which intensified, for Emile was staring back at her!

A touch at her elbow and she whirled around to face the apologetic sobrestante.

"Perdón! Perdón! Madame Palais, it is time we continued the journey."

Celeste and John arranging the luggage had not noticed her absence.

Why had she placed Emile's return to sanity among the Palenque ruins, she wondered? It could happen now—any time!

She was relieved to be riding separately, in the lead, and did not look back.

Between Palizado and Las Playas, Don Vicende's courier had arranged for the Sterling party to have accommodations at the sugar plantation of Fedor Busch. With German order and enterprise Busch had cleared the jungle with Indian and Mexican labor and in four years was operating two sugar mills driven by oxen. He was a prosperous patrón with a roomy plank house, whitewashed and inviting. The long front porch was furnished with hammocks and chairs of native rushes. The thatched houses of the workers were ringed with gardens and orchards. His household was managed by a widowed sister, Hilda, and her restless daughter, Francine.

Two rooms had been made available for the travelers. As the Sterling party arrived and set to by a three-masted cargo bungo sporting a yellow and green *Busch* burgee, carriers were waiting to handle the luggage for the passengers and show the boat crews to separate quarters.

Fedor, on hand to greet John Sterling, barely acknowledged

Celeste and Maury, ignored Emile, and gave Sarah Belle only a brief guarded glance as he muttered the name *Palais* and turned back to John.

The sun was low but still vampire to body moisture, and the pitchers of lemonade offered as the boat-weary passengers stepped upon the porch were refreshment par excellence.

Maury carefully seated Emile at the far end of the row of chairs and waited for Sarah Belle to make the decision whether or not to sit by Emile. She nodded to him to sit by Emile and she took the next chair, placing herself between her two servants. John and Fedor sat side by side. In manner and attention the patrón reserved his courtesies for the antiquarian.

Hilda was frightened of Emile and had her daughter take the pitcher to the far end of the porch while she served the others. Francine, on the other hand, was enchanted with the speechless stranger and his pet. She rushed to bring a cup for Jasper but stopped to stare at Emile until her uncle startled her with a command cough.

Sarah Belle noticed that Emile had accepted the bright green glass from Francine's hand and nodded.

The only conversation was between John and Fedor on matters of news downriver and conditions ahead.

Sarah Belle kept thinking of Emile but not looking at him. This was the first time since leaving the *Valkyrie* that she had been so near him. She had not been able to bring herself to sit beside him, even though she knew Fedor was watching to see if she would and passing some kind of judgment because she had not. She felt sure that Vicende had instructed his courier to explain the relationships of those in the party as he journeyed ahead of them, but what subtle overlay Don Vicende might have placed on the information made her apprehensive.

The bedrooms were scrubbed antiseptic clean and had matting on the floor. Furnishings were sparse and homemade—plain wooden bedframes and slats with thick straw mattresses, table with clay water jars and bowls, coarse cotton coverlets and towels.

The evening meal was served to them by Francine at the family dining room table without the company of Hilda or Fedor. An extraordinary culinary surprise awaited them. In addition to a large mound of pressed black beans covered with butter, a high loaf of burnished corn-nut bread, garden vegetables, and chicken dumplings, was an enormous chocolate pie, its ingredients processed by the ingenious Busch family from their vanilla vine and cacao trees.

At the table, Maury and his fellow watchers were uneasy about Emile. It was the first time they had all shared a meal together, the first time Emile had not been attended by Maury or Celeste while he ate alone, and certainly the first time a stranger had entered the closed circle around him. It was obvious that Francine had not only entered but had established herself. Jasper accepted her, and Emile was content to have the squirrel in her charge while he ate.

Francine had not the Nordic coloring of her mother and uncle. Though fair-skinned, her hair was black with deep waves and her eyes a strange purple-blue set back and shadowed with long lashes. She was shapely, lithe, and yearning for attention, for relief from the dominating personality of her uncle and the rigidly domesticated mother.

Sarah Belle understood Francine but not her attraction to Emile. Perhaps it was the squirrel. . . . *You know better than that, her reasoning self chided. . . .*

She knows he is here as my husband, yet she manages to touch his hand, his arm, his shoulder, while she takes Maury's place waiting on him. . . .

Maybe she is perceptive too. You are sitting by John, you know, and you look and act as though you belonged there. . . .

How could I act any different? . . .

Well, how can she? . . .

She must know he is not in his right mind, or hardly any mind at all. He hasn't spoken a word since she laid eyes on him. . . .

Maybe he's in the right mind for her. . . .

Ghastly idea! She appears quite normal. . . .

What is normal? For her it might be normal to take him in her arms and make love to him. Jasper approves of her. Maybe that's all that's necessary right now. . . .

When the meal was done, Fedor invited them to sit on the porch again. Shaded torches had been lighted and stuck into the ground along a wide semicircle in the front yard.

Sarah Belle decided to puzzle Fedor and Francine and fortify her position by sitting next to Emile. She took the end chair where Emile had sat when they came and indicated to Maury that Emile would be seated between them, and that way, too, Maury and Celeste could sit side by side in a closeness so much denied them.

More aware of what was to come than Sarah Belle, Francine too had seating plans for fortifying her position. She brought her own chair and placed it beside Sarah Belle. Then, before sitting down, she suggested to Sarah Belle that they exchange seats—that way, she could sit by Emile and take care of Jasper.

"There will be music and a lot of noise," she confided.

"Thank you, Francine. That will be helpful." Sitting so close to Emile had already become discomfiting.

Outwitted, she thought, but relieved.

There *was* music and a lot of noise!

A big bell in the back yard began to clang. The workers and their families appeared from around the house on cue.

"We always have a birthday party when we have overnight guests," Fedor explained. "The one whose birthday we are celebrating will come forward—there is usually one in the crowd, and if not, they have determined among themselves which birthday is the closest and we honor that one.

"I pass drink to the men. They are served spirits only on festival days and occasions like this. The women and children get dulces from Hilda's kitchen. They sing and dance for us—nothing like in the old country, but it has a beat and stirs the blood a little."

By this time as many as half a hundred workers with wives and children stood before him. A teen-age Indian boy stepped out and came forward. He wore green pantaloons and a yellow shirt, honoring the Busch colors. Fedor greeted him formally and gave him two jugs to pass around among the men. Then he called two women by name and directed them to the kitchen to carry out the trays of dulces. None were offered to the guests.

The musicians began to ready their instruments: native fifes, their piping like the genesis of bagpipes—handcrafted xylophone, castanets, drums for hand thumping, a scattering of hybrid strings.

When the two jugs had been emptied and the proud waiter had been given custody of two more, the music began: soft, hesitant, gradually phasing in as leadership was established and emotions unified . . . then chanting low, and growing to insistent . . . then dancing barefoot, in singles, twos, and fours.

The beat and the stirring Fedor had mentioned became demanding, possessive. The dancers swayed, and leaned, and stomped —sometimes pausing in solid stillness, as if commanded by the chanting or humming, then breaking out again.

The audience on the porch was not immune, but propriety kept them in their chairs. . . . until . . . Francine leaned over Emile, and with her lips close to his ear began whispering. . . .

Sarah Belle stiffened and reached out to touch Francine in protest—to interfere with what was about to happen—to break the spell in which she too felt entangled.

She did touch Francine but drew back with a sense of shock, a stinging sensation, as if she had been forcibly repelled. She saw Emile hand Jasper to Maury. Saw Francine take his hands and pull him to his feet and lead him out among the dancers.

Musicians and dancers were elated! This was the first time such a thing had ever happened! A guest drawn into their midst!

The rhythms became more seductive, the tempo more compelling, the accent of the drums more pronounced . . . the xylophone lilted . . . the fifes screeched in ecstasy . . . the castanets carefully trembled to the melody the strings invented . . . the humming was like a weaving in and out so that it all coalesced into a performance that could not be explained or repeated.

In the center of it were Francine and Emile—the isolated heart-starved dreamer whose feet had ached for dancing so long, and the New Orleans ballroom stylist, their movements in such harmony that it seemed like a contest between music and dance: would the music absorb the dancers, or would the dancers draw all the music unto themselves?

The only sound from the porch was Hilda's low-voiced moans in eerie accompaniment to the central beat. It was more than Fedor could stand when the moans gathered into subdued sobbing.

He disappeared and the bell began to clang.

The spell was broken. Francine and Emile stood very still holding hands.

Fedor appeared with two more jugs and called gruffly for the carrier. The workers broke into clapping and bravos.

Emile and Francine walked back to the porch. Francine wore a distant expression in her eyes akin to Emile's. When he sat, Jasper hopped back into his lap. He took the leash and sat motionless, looking nowhere.

Francine looked at Sarah Belle, began to cry, and ran away.

Sarah Belle wanted to run after Francine and say, "I am not married to this man. Sometime he may not retreat from himself, and maybe—then——" But there was no way she could read the future—no way she could make things easier for Francine, interfere in such a strict family or reverse such a fateful attraction.

But she would be wondering for a long time *what were the words that Francine had whispered into Emile's ears?*

CHAPTER THIRTY-ONE

T HE USUMACINTA RIVER, called great, noble, a massive water arm of the Central American region, a river goddess, gathered her waters among the mountains of Petén and released them into the Lake of Términos. She created many paradoxes along her way, and perhaps the strangest of these was witnessed by the Sterling expedition after leaving the Busch plantation.

They continued on the Palizada to its junction with the broad expanse of the Usumacinta. The contrast was awesome; in perspective the bungos appeared as small acorn shells on a forest stream. The sobrestante informed them that after a few hours they would turn into the Río Chico, a small river that would take them rapidly *downstream* to Las Playas. How could this be, since the Usumacinta was giving the boatmen such opposition as they moved against her powerful current? "The travelers must not be alarmed," he said, "if the bungos dance about here and there at the juncture."

Looking ahead from the middle of the Usumacinta as they approached the junction, they could see the convergence of the two flows forming an angle of near forty degrees—the mighty Usumacinta rushing toward them, the Río Chico descending in another direction.

Though the cause was apparent, the effect was dizzying, and the wild forces of nature so rampant in their demonstration that human beings might well question their place in it all. Lying to the left of the Usumacinta's main course was a projecting headland reaching out in challenge to the river goddess.

The Usumacinta broke against the barrier like a juggernaut, forcing her way past. But she lost a shoulder in the sharp angle of turn. A part of her waters was turned back with such a powerful thrust that the plain of Playas was flooded, forming many creeks and streams. One of these was the Río Chico.

After a dancing dervish maneuver, the bungos were moving smoothly along down a sluggish current tightly walled in by impenetrable jungle.

The bogadores shifted positions, released tight muscles and reached for dried meat and stimulants. John left a post he had filled forward and came back to Sarah Belle.

"How do you feel now!"

"As if we had been whirled out of one world and flung into another. I could swear I heard an immense door close behind us!"

"Probably a Mayan god admitting you to the sacred precincts of Palenque. By direct course we could not be more than fifteen miles from the ruins. Also, the door has been closed on domestic amenities except those we create for ourselves."

From the Río Chico, the bungos entered a narrow muddy stream that brought the occupants almost face to face with alligators spread along its banks, but they soon emerged into a shallow lakelike expanse of water, and along its shores lay the village of Las Playas. It presented a dismal aspect, primitive huts to form one grassy street, and at the end a rude thatched church with cross and belfry.

When the boatmen poled to a landing, the bungos were met by the justicia, the padre, and the local sexton; lined up behind them were mozos hired as carriers and a scattering of curious natives.

The padre served Palenque village as well and would conduct them there. The courier had designated the padre to make arrangements for the travelers at both locations. At Las Playas he had engaged villagers to prepare a special shelter, and local Indians to transport camp equipment and supplies.

Their housing was a hut constructed of upright sticks and a thatched roof over a dirt floor with strips of matting. A curtain of split reeds formed a partition and on each side was a rude table and a platform made of reeds, suitable for bedrolls. The door was a piece of sailcloth.

John said, "I think it's time to break out the camping equipment. I'll go load some carriers."

Sarah Belle said, "I see what you meant about that door closing on domestic amenities."

She had observed at one side of the hut a small three-sided open structure made of matting fastened to four poles, evidently meant to afford privacy for sheltered women fearful of the eyes of nature. Thoughtful consideration, she granted, but the open side faced the hut!

The influence of the Vicende courier was still evident. Once camping equipment was at hand, the sexton built a campfire near the door to discourage mosquitoes and insisted on heating water for coffee and for boiling eggs he had brought. Also, he placed on their table an olla of fresh milk, bananas, and tortillas packed in corn husks to be kept fresh.

The bedrolls lay spread out on the reed frames. They had eaten well and Emile was immediately asleep. Sarah Belle and John, Maury and Celeste sat around the table on packing cases, a candle burning between them. The sobrestante had brought them a bottle of light wine, presented with the compliments of Don Vicende and the message, "a toast to your well-being in primitive sur-roundings."

John began pouring the special vintage into tin cups. Sarah Belle quipped, "Let us drink a toast to the ghost of Don Vicende. Better the ghost than the reality."

The four of them had never sat together like this before, so isolated and so pervaded with a sense of unity and relief, harmony and happiness. They clinked their cups and laughed. From here, behind the jungle wall, Don Vicende was more of a memory than a threat, his largess a reward for services rendered.

Past imprisonments of body or mind, agonies of spirit, self inquisitions, were of another world from which they had been whisked away to this very time and place. . . . The world of:

Maury, the slave left to die with his master in a lunatic's cell . . . then part-free, part-whole in hiding with the woman he loved.

Celeste, the woman of color he loved, born free but in servitude to the commandment of her kind: "Thou shalt not marry a slave, a man who is black or a man who is white." To share Maury's hiding place was a larger freedom.

Sarah Belle, the Southern woman, long shorn of the proprieties of plantation rearing—long held in bondage to Conscience at her House of Recovery—never having heard the greater heart-song of love until she approached a man in Lafayette Square whose response, bitter and suspicious, was nonetheless like a call from the eternal, a long lost part of herself.

John Monroe Sterling, a man who followed a boyhood dream up the Orinoco wilderness river in search of Sir Walter Raleigh's El Dorado, fabled City of Gold, only to become entangled in a web of passion that held him taut and tormented until he heard the harp of Sarah Belle and her song: "O Thou Desert of My Mind."

John said, "Another toast: To ourselves, *to the Family Four!*"

Three pairs of eyes were fixed on him in wonderment until the full meaning of his toast, the soul-flavor of it, had been absorbed, then they raised their cups and sipped as if in ceremonial communion.

Maury, hardly audible, inquired, "What of little brother?"

John did not hesitate. "Our ward, a child, a different kind of child who at any moment may become a man."

Maury, close to tears, unconsciously used a phrase for so long natural to him, "Thank you, mastah."

"Maury, don't ever call me or any other 'mastah.' For the rest of your life let your mind as well as body enjoy freedom."

"Yes, Mr. John."

"Another family matter," Sarah Belle said, "no more 'madames,' to me at any time."

"What shall we call you, mada——?" Celeste inquired.

"Whatever you like."

Maury interrupted. "Us call her 'Miss Sarah,' since Mr. John calls her 'Sarah.'"

"Now that name-calling has been resolved, what other family concerns before we retire?"

"Mr. John——" Celeste hesitated. "Whatever we see or hear from now on—I think I will be a woman—not a fraidy-cat child."

"Even jaguars or big snakes, or very large hairy monkeys that sometimes scream?" John teased.

Celeste had a prompt answer. "Not as long as you and Maury are around."

"Soldiers of fortune are we. Count on us to slay the dragons. Now it's time to crawl under the mosquito bars, for we make Palenque village tomorrow."

As naturally as if it had happened countless times, Celeste went to Maury and Sarah Belle to John for a goodnight embrace before each got into the allotted resting place.

By early dawn, the sexton was at the door of the shelter renewing the campfire. The padre and sobrestante were at the bungos loading mules with the heavier supplies, and Indian carriers were affixing headbands to secure backpacks.

The size of the procession assembled at the shelter was a surprise to the Sterling party that, with the Vicende outreach, had brought it to pass. There were three horses to carry John, Maury, and the overseer; four hamacas, each with four bearers and relief teams—these for Celeste, Emile, the padre, and Sarah Belle; six loaded mules with caretakers, eight Indians with backpacks, and several boys carrying the small packets of provender that each Indian provided for himself.

The sobrestante took charge of the lineup, John and Maury were at the hamacas—Maury declaring that he didn't need a horse, he would walk beside the hamaca carrying Emile. John persuaded: "You'll be risking exhaustion and be no use to Emile. You've been too long indoors. Six hours or more of muddy roads and tropical sun, and you wouldn't be able even to climb on a horse. Besides, it's important in the eyes of the Indians that you be identified as one of the men in authority."

Then to Sarah Belle: "I know you're unhappy. You look embarrassed and a bit rebellious."

"My compliments on your discernment. I'm just that! Look at them! All so thin and small of stature, and any who are a little taller than the rest having to stoop so that the poles on their shoulders are in balance. I don't like being carried in this manner. It's degrading when I am able to walk and to ride a horse. I would prefer a mule or an ox to this!"

"Much as I would like to see you riding an ox, and they are available, let's look at it this way: All these men, from the padre to the overseer to the Indians and the villagers, expect it to be done this way. Also, they are happy to be earning good wages and are tending you their respect."

"You do a nice mix of logic and ethics, John dear. But what of my *self*-respect?"

"This is no time to alter the course of Mayan civilization in your behalf. The ancestors of these very carriers were the laborers who gave their backs and bodies literally to building the grand structures for their rulers at Palenque. They were provided a deity using a tumpline as an example of what their lives were cut out for. Of course, He paid no wages. The reward came when out of back and breath he was taken to a place where the load was lighter."

"A limited redemption . . . What is a tumpline?"

"Headgear like you see on these carriers, with ropes much stronger for loads much heavier. They had no knowledge of the wheel, no animals for motive power—manpower only and labor in neolithic style. The great ceremonial city of temples, palaces, and royal courts was built of stone with stone tools for cutting and shaping."

"How long ago was that?"

"Quién sabe? Antiquarians and explorers surmise a thousand years at least."

"It appears they're still serving that tumpline god."

"Hardly. You forget the padres have been around for centuries very busy with baptizing."

Sarah Belle was silent, her gaze inscrutable.

"Slow progress? What is time anyway? They've inherited strong backs and serve as carriers when they please. If it's a season to tend their milpas, you can't find one to hire, and when you can, they set their own wages. The palacial cities are in ruins, and the rulers in their forgotten tombs. But the workers live on."

"Surely you plan to lecture when your studies at Palenque are finished?"

"Not unless the prospect is more inviting than your tone suggests."

"I'll try to be more concerned with scenery and avert my face from the sweating bodies."

"That's a sweet lady."

"Watch your language, and get on with your act at the head of the parade as the proud patrón!"

"You have me confused with Don Vicende."

"Not yet. . . . Look! Something peculiar is going on at Emile's chair."

Emile's Indian bearers, and those in the relief ranks, were gathered around him, talking in their native tongue, low-voiced and solemn. One after the other, they stepped up to face him, reached out and touched Jasper, then made the sign of the cross and moved back.

The padre rode up to John and explained. "They recognize that he is not in his mind, so to speak. They have great reverence for such a condition."

"Why?"

"They think that his spirit moves in and out to converse with the gods. To touch him or something belonging to him could bring longer life and more sons."

"A pagan superstition?"

"Quién sabe? But they are all converts and their families before them. We can't erase all that is considered heretical. We don't try. We have learned better. We just superimpose."

It was puzzling to the padre and surprising to the "family four" that Emile was nodding to each applicant as the sign of the cross was made before him and appeared quite at ease in his hamaca.

Sarah Belle's bearers, when struggling through mud or over some obstacle, would pause to fill their lungs and blow with a whistlelike sound that was painful for her to hear. To control her revulsion at having to be carried in such a manner, she purposefully directed her thoughts away from them.

She thought of her first conversation with John, at the House of Recovery—how it had developed from her question "Is there any place where you'd rather be?" and he had replied, in a camp of his own in the Main Palace of the Mayan ruins near the village of Palenque in Chiapas.

. . . how they had discovered their mutual acquaintance with the explorations of John L. Stephens in Central America and Mexico, she having read the published accounts and he having personal acquaintance with the author.

. . . how she had remarked on the importance of learning why "lost civilizations" became lost and applying the knowledge to preserving the present.

. . . how he had replied that we surmise conquests, drouth, floods, as the destroyers, but no attention given to what the people were thinking, or allowed to think—what were their hungers or denials?—was the accumulated wisdom of the times being abused or perverted?

. . . how she had, with whimsical flourish, suggested in their correspondence that she assume a disguise, making it possible to accompany him "up some haunting and hazardous trail to the ruins."

And here she was experiencing the reality, the literal, being carried up the same "haunting and hazardous" trail that Stephens had traversed on his way from Palenque to the coast.

A parrot flew across her path and she watched it to the jungle's edge.

One of the Indians walking beside his mule pointed and called out "Mico! Mico!" but she saw no monkey. With a rush of memory she recalled the explorer's story of an encounter along this same path.

At a rest stop in a clearing, a frightful sound was heard in the woods and an Indian boy came running to him shouting "Un animal." He grabbed his long gun and ran after the boy. They struggled through the brush to a high tree; all was silent. But—far up the long smooth trunk among the limbs, part of a dark animal with fiery eyes was spotted. The boy said it was not a monkey. Stephens thought it was a catamount, aimed between the eyes and fired. The dead animal, its blood trickling down the tree

trunk, did not fall to the ground because its tail was wrapped around a
limb in a tight lock. It was an enormous ape and more related to the
human family than the monkey, Stephens averred, much disturbed that
he had killed it. The Indians thought it a prize, chopped down the tree,
carried the ape back into the clearing and skinned it. Seeing the creature,
lying on its back, the skin off and the eyes staring, a padre among the
travelers exclaimed "Es hombre," and Stephens recorded that he almost
felt liable to an indictment for homicide.

Sarah Belle, in such nearness to the actual scene of the killing, felt the impact of the author's emotion so deeply that, as they came upon a similar clearing and made a midway stop, she came close to tears. There were several thatched huts and Indian families tending the area for the owner, whose house, the larger of the poled structures, was open to passersby. There were outhouses, stables for animals, corn and coffee for sale, and plantains for the taking. The owner's residence was in Palenque, like others who were developing profitable holdings along this jungle passage.

"Are you all right?" John questioned the silent Sarah as they ate and prepared for the rest of the journey.

She merely nodded. There was no way to communicate the nature of her thoughts—the realization that "the haunting and hazardous trail" was leading to an experience that would encompass more than adventure and romance, more than novelty or escape, or even a lovers' rendezvous.

When they arrived in Palenque village, they found it much as Stephens had described it on his arrival six years earlier—as the most dead-alive place he had ever seen—a single grass-grown street, not enough passage on it to make a direct path, a few weathered white houses placed at random on either side, several vacant. At the far end, on an elevation, sat a thatched church, like a tired watchman, supporting a rude cross and belfry. Outlying was a scattering of Indian huts. Pigs, fowl, and mules roamed without hindrance.

The church stood in the center of a grass-covered square, and on each side were houses built with the forest directly to their backs. A few were occupied by whites with land interests in the vicinity, some empty, some in ruins—a testimony to times past when Palenque was on the route of all goods imported to Guatemala.

The Sterling procession brought out the Indians and a few whites to stare and comment. The greatest attraction was the two women. Sarah Belle learned that the Indian women were inquiring of the bearers: "Which is her man?"

An empty house on the plaza had already been assigned to the party.

A great pile of luggage, camp equipment, and supplies was stacked in one room, horses and mules let free to graze and later receive their rations of corn. The Indians vanished, the overseer was a guest of the alcalde, and once again the Sterling party was alone.

John, not pleased that official matters had been taken out of his hands, sent a message to the alcalde and the government official, the prefecto who kept watch that visitors, local or otherwise, not remove any part of the ruins from the area. John would pay his respects before leaving on the morrow and would expect to interview the most knowledgeable guide available for an introductory tour of the exposed area of the ruins.

Five weary people and a tired squirrel made supper of cheese and bread and chocolate and looked longingly at the five reed beds available, equipped with clean corn-husk mattresses. The springs of nerves and muscles pressed tight with facing the threats and perils of the past weeks were released at last. There was left only a two hour trek to the ruins, so anticipation lay sheltered in their thoughts, and excitement was hoarded for the day to come.

It had been years since Sarah had sunk into such deep and dreamless slumber. When she awoke, John and Maury were gone, and Celeste had Emile ready to travel. From the cocinilla adjoining the house two Indian women appeared with coffee and milk, hot tortillas and honey. "Somebody somewhere is rubbing a magic lantern," she told Celeste.

"It must be a big lantern, Miss Sarah. Come and look." In the shed room where the supplies and equipment had been unloaded, the reloading was underway. And grazing out in front were two horses with sidesaddles. And only one hamaca was placed nearby.

"Oh, Celeste, what a perfect beginning to our great day of arrival! Quickly, let's eat and get the luggage ready."

When John and Maury appeared, an elderly man, his features very Indian, was with them. His height (he was nearly as tall as

John) and the bright blue eyes shining out of a mosaic of wrinkles, indicated, however, that he was not a *puro*. He was slightly stooped, but nothing in his bearing reflected humility or uneasiness. When presented to the two women as "Yapah, our guide," he made a slight bow, spoke a compliment in soft Spanish, and then looked at Sarah Belle with such sharp appraisal that she knew within an instant he had passed judgment and given her a seal of approval. How strange, she thought, that she felt such relief.

John explained. "Yapah has his own mule and he has secured two others for Maury and the sobrestante. The padre will remain here to attend his flock. The bearers for the hamacas have been paid their full wages. Yapah says the stars are in harmony for our visit to Palenque. And it is my personal ambition that harmony will now prevail throughout the whole procession." He looked at Sarah Belle: only his eyes smiling.

The bell in the church began to ring. "Ah, the padre's day begins with the same sentiment, Mr. Sterling. With the stars and the padre on your side, how could we of the weaker sex, only two in number, be so imprudent as to occasion discord? In fact, I have slept so well that on this bright morning it seems the whole course of Mayan civilization has been altered in my behalf."

John tried to keep from smiling, and did keep from answering. And Yapah . . . Sarah Belle had another instant revelation. He had read through their voices what they meant to each other. She was more perplexed than uneasy.

As the procession moved out of the village, strung out from church plaza on past Indian huts at the outskirts, it took on a special order, most of the carriers in single file. Yapah, John, and the overseer were in the lead, Celeste and Sarah Belle just behind, then Emile in the hamaca and Maury in attendance. The open road soon led into a dense forest and on to a jungle trail where the narrow passage admitted the intruders only one at a time, with Yapah and his machete in the lead. Although workers had cleared the trail recently from its rainy season tight closure, still-overhanging vines and limbs left beyond the reach of the machete men were slashed expertly by Yapah while his mule continued on the move.

The path was cool and shady with patches of sun filtering

through, bringing to blossom trees that appeared unreal in their floral excesses of yellow and blue. Colossal oaks were draped in vines, holding on their giant branches growths of strange plants and flowers. Startled flocks of parrots made streaks of color through it all.

When they crossed the River Micol, its muddy waters had receded; it flowed clear and shallow over its stony bed and seemed to murmur of mysteries reaching beyond thought. Here Sarah and Celeste let their horses drink, but were too entranced, too lost in the dream quality of the setting, to speak to each other.

Not all was tranquil along the trail. Life within the jungle gave notice of alien presence. Most frightening was the warning scream of a bird that echoed a piercing alarm from time to time, its screeching anxiety affecting the nerves with a strange uneasiness. Yapah sent back word that there was no harm in the creature and it had no name. The natives called it "the bird who saw Christ crucified."

Another announcement of intrusion came from a lofty watch-tower in the insect world, a thin shrill whistle, with a cutting insistence that gave the ear the burden of its high unfinished note. At the same time, the eye could bear witness to animal awareness of the strange life form entering its kingdom: very large, very fresh cat tracks in a middle course along the path.

Again John relayed to Sarah Belle reassurance: "He says it is the tracks of a full-grown jaguar—very auspicious for us, having the Jaguar-god of the Mayas leading the way to the ruins."

"One could be suspicious of such auspiciousness. You might ask Yapah if human sacrifice was required to propitiate the Jaguar-god."

"Are you really uneasy?"

"Just speculative . . . you know . . . the serpent in the garden . . . the jaguar in the jungle . . . both symbols of power that gets lodged in the mind as threatening or evil."

"In other words if you arouse from your slumbers in the remains of the palacio some night and a jaguar is lying at your bedside, you would not be fearful?"

Sarah Belle bent her head, apparently working with the bridle reins and answered so that he alone could hear, "Not if it were purring, and if you were by my side."

Most of the time on the trail was an ascent that gradually became steeper, the animals struggling upward on a slippery, uncertain footing. The first view of the ruins came at a point where the trail, like the mouth of a tunnel, emerged upon a mountainside. Out in the open, the whole procession came to a standstill—the winded animals and the awestruck beholders. Yapah and the Indians, who were not strangers to the sight, stood in attitudes of reverence as before a shrine.

They looked out across the valley to companion mountains beyond, showing in dim outline through the morning mist. Reaching across the heavy quietness, shocking the senses, came a roar of prehistoric dimension. Would a dinosaur raise its grotesque head and peer out from the fogs across the valley? The roar came again, through a distortion of echoes. Was this some supernatural Guardian of the Dead City that was agitated by the presence of fleshly mankind at its gates?

"The roaring monkeys," Yapah announced. "I often feel they are trying to tell us something about ourselves that we ought to know."

Whatever might be their message, they were not heard again, their roars but a prologue to the scene about to unfold.

The advancing sun began to draw back the veils of mist from fantastic piles of ancient magnificence, rising in wounded dignity above the encroaching rain forests. Pyramid-shaped terraces supported stone structures, some crumbling, some with form intact, but all layered with jungle growth trailing from superstructures, pushing into openings and corridors. On some, trees like weighted warriors pushed against walls with their roots snaking through the cracked stonework, invading interiors.

Yapah led the expedition toward the central complex, the main palace. Sarah Belle, her gaze fastened on the remains of the great tower within the royal compound, rising in defiant memorial to a grandeur long dead, felt a sadness deep and poignant, and at the same time an overwhelming sense of freedom for which there was no accounting.

Before the Palenque pilgrims and their train reached the palace, they passed a temple set high and apart bearing a most peculiar roof comb, very narrow and several stories high. Again, Sarah Belle had a surge of feeling akin to recognition—it appeared to her as a beggar long held in hostage to the jungle, beseeching investigation of its reason for being. She yearned to enter, to look, to touch.

They crossed a lively stream that Yapah called the "Río Ocula" and were soon climbing upward toward the east entrance of the palace. The trail had recently been cleared of stones and trees, but as they pursued a more rugged path along one terrace, and then another, the area was so overgrown that the building was obscured from view.

Then suddenly it was there! Through an opening in the trees.

The sun was focused, like a cosmic spotlight, on the east front of the spreading structure, the colossal figures in stucco relief on the pilasters still exhibiting a life of their own, as the artist had envisioned—a Stone Age professional, expecting his creation to last as long as the solid rock on which it was cast, and whose delight in the richest of ornamentation was only limited by the concepts of the wise men and rulers who employed him.

As Yapah led them up a flight of broken stone steps and on through the massive piers at the main entrance into the outer corridor, and then on through a wide doorway to the walled inner corridor, it was evident that he intended for the whole entourage to follow, mounts and all, right on along the interior passage, and why not? The structural vastness, the huge stones blocked and braced against all natural forces, reduced animal and human forms alike to pigmy size.

On approaching the entrance to a spacious courtyard, Yapah's mule with passive familiarity cautiously descended a series of stone steps into the open court. John halted and helped the women to dismount before carefully coaxing the horses down the steps, then admitted the hamaca and assisted Maury with his mule. The Indians in charge of packmules and those with backpacks followed to cluster around Yapah.

Indian laborers had been brought here ahead of the Sterling party, clearing enough of the area for a campsite. Full grown trees still flourished, some of them the wild orange. Mounds of debris contained fragmented stones, some bearing hieroglyphics and sculptured bits of ornate costumes and the figures they adorned.

On the south side of the court, steps led to an apartment of three rooms well enough preserved for occupancy and recently cleared of rubbish. The only openings in the stone walls of the rooms were the wide entrance and in the back an aperture for ventilation in the shape of the Egyptian tau.

Yapah showed his charges these rooms, which he had selected for their quarters, explaining that the center room would be better for supplies and sleeping since it was the largest (near 25 feet long and half as wide) and the smaller rooms on each side suitable for privacy of the sexes. They could have their campfire in the court or in the corridor according to the weather or their pleasure.

The overseer for Don Vicende had not been to the site before. The workers provided by the alcalde at Palenque village (dealing through the courier and the padre) had been placed in Yapah's charge. So it was he who rousted the carriers into their final labors of unloading and placing their packs according to John's directions.

The sobrestante, eager to get his assignment over and done with, took leave of John with flourishes of Spanish courtesy. John in return sent messages of gratitude, wishes for good health and long life to Don Vicende de Vives. John's offer to provide refreshment was declined, since Indians and animals would be taking a rest stop in the valley by the Ocula before returning to the village. Yapah would remain behind.

Soon, the clatter of the mules in the corridor was gone and the little group in the courtyard, six in number, were alone, at the core of a mighty central city, seat-of-power-that-was—life focus for multitudes whose wise men and rulers never knew the wheel or the strength, mysteries, and uses of metals, but who spawned builders supreme, artisans propelled by a kind of creative madness, mathematicians, astronomers, ardent worshipers of god-forces awesome and unrelenting.

Yapah said he would make the first campfire. Celeste and Maury were already busy with Emile, and getting out supplies for the first meal. Sarah Belle and John were left standing together looking at the double-life-size figures carved on stone in bas-relief, set up as a slanted border on the steps they would be using day after day—figures that would lend their presence to all that took place in the courtyard.

They held hands. They shared a sensation of entering into another dimension of existence—a sort of "coming home," but with eerie implications that increased as they continued to stare at these ancients, some crouched, some kneeling in supplication, faces and bodies expressing the plea piteous, a painful mixture of awe and expectation.

"Yapah says the Indians in the village refuse to spend the night here."

"I can understand why."

"He says he doesn't mind. That it is like a home-that-was to him."

"What does he mean?"

"Perhaps we will find out. I think he plans to spend a while with us, and I have endorsed this. He says he has quarters in another building."

"John, I saw not a single smile, not a sign of joy, on any of the enormous elegant figures that ornamented the grand entrance. I wonder if they had music—if they danced. . . . The expressions depicted are more than serious—they are somber in the extreme."

"Perhaps life was like that. We will explore with Yapah this afternoon. We will search for a smile. Speaking of smiles, you look very serious. Are you happy? We have arrived at the threshold of our adventura. What is your first impression?"

Her hand tightened on his. "That it will be much greater than I imagined, and that I will need a larger meaning than 'happy' to express it. Can we sit on the steps, our backs to these troubled images?"

They sat. She leaned against him. His arm reached around her.

Yapah had the campfire well along and water was heating. He went to a nearby tree and gathered two oranges. He came and sat near them while he peeled the oranges with his machete, handed one to each of them, then returned to the fire—no word spoken.

CHAPTER THIRTY-TWO

THE DOMESTIC ROUTINE set up for the six residents within the next few days was a radical departure in daily living for them all. Even Yapah, usually impersonal toward those he served as guide, was an intrinsic part of the pattern that came naturally into place.

He had the campfire going every morning. In the evening he arranged slow-burning foliage, some of exotic fragrance, on the coals to provide smoke against insects and curious animal prowlers. He kept a second fire in the corridor, against sudden rain or tropical storm, at this season infrequent but of hurricane velocity.

John, self-appointed supervisor of waterworks, provided catches for rainwater and cleared a steep rugged path to a stream at the base of the terrace for a second source. He arranged stone slabs and blocks for a table and seats in the courtyard and in their living quarters.

Yapah cared for the horses and mule, kept in the courtyard. On occasion, they rode out on tours. More often they walked, with the packmule following as naturally as a dog. Sarah Belle took inventory of all supplies and equipment and prepared the daily packs for the mule, the food and water, the tools for digging and brushing, the notebooks for herself and John.

With the help of Celeste and Maury, she had arranged the central room for their sleeping with packing boxes for partial partitions—five cots with bedrolls, personal luggage and candles near at hand. No supplies were kept in the two dressing rooms flanking the center. For the outings Sarah Belle removed her skirt and wore the under-trousers tucked in laced boots.

She found the daily partnership with John exhilarating, the near-constant state of euphoria bringing her into an identity of self so stimulating to mind and emotion that she felt stripped of an outside covering she had worn since adolescence. She was no longer Sarah Belle Locke, or Sarah Belle of the House of Recovery. She was the "Sarah" that John intoned with such nuances of meaning. She was the "Miss Sarah" to which Celeste and Maury gave such loving resonance. And to Yapah—it almost embarrassed her to think about it—she was "Damasacra."

"Couldn't that mean 'sacred or holy lady'?" she inquired of John. "Please ask him why he calls me that."

John's report was, "He says you remind him of the lady in a story that he will tell us someday, perhaps, if we ask him the right question about something that may come to our notice as we explore the ruins."

"He is so strange—and rather wonderful, isn't he?"

"The way I feel about him is equally strange—as though he were my teacher, and something more—as though I had been around him all my life."

"Every day I find it more difficult to express myself, to even think, in terms of time."

"I can think of nothing more outside the bounds of time, Sarah, than my feeling for you, than our oneness of being which seems always to have been lying in keep for us outside the conscious realm. Are you trying to put it all in writing? Your notebook is filling faster than mine. Last night I awoke long after all had retired, and your candle was burning. I heard you scribbling."

"There is as much to set down about the inner adventura as about the delights of exploration we share."

"Am I a part of the inner adventura?"

"You are the one who is bringing it about."

"Hmm. Does it contain any surmises of what lies ahead?"

"Yes, it does. It is all quite personal and confidential."

"And to whom are you confiding?"

"To myself. I am writing it to myself."

"Sarah! You begin to take on the role of palace temptress."

"What do you feel tempted to do now?"

"I'll let you write a few surmises to yourself about it. Is the mule packed?"

"Yes, master. If you'll turn around, you'll see Father Yapah and faithful macho waiting at the entrance."

John was startled. "Why did you say Father Macho?"

Sarah Belle laughed. "What kind of spell are you under? I didn't say 'Father Macho,' I said 'Father Yapah.' Yapah's role is versatile: guide and guardian, sage, seer, parent, priest . . ."

"He calls this place we're exploring today a temple. Do you suppose he could perform a marriage ceremony?"

"Now you're tempting *me*. Ask him?"

"I'll do that. Tell yourself in writing what you'll do about it in case he's qualified."

Before leaving, John inquired of Maury, "Does this location distress you in any way? the desolation all around? the gloomy appearance of the ancients who lived here as we see them on the slabs by the steps?"

"Mr. John, nothing distress me since I taken out of lunatic prison, got my freedom papers and my sweetheart woman. I seen faces alive in old New Orleans more pitiful looking and begging than them on that rock. And I tell you what more—that Mississippi-mouth place more scary for me and my Celeste and Emile than any dead city you take us to!"

"Good! Then the family-four remains intact, and you can feel utterly released, your freedom no longer confined to a house and yard."

"If a man get any more free in this place, he get lost! Now, you and Miss Sarah be free too. Go anywhere. Celeste and me stay here and watch over things. This be like a honeymoon spree and we play king and queen of the palace!"

"We'll be careful to observe protocol. If your majesties promenade along the corridors, take your handgun, just as a precaution. Let's try to keep our peace with the animal kingdom. They've had a longer term residence in these parts than even the original occupants."

Sarah Belle's candle again burned long on the night of their return from exploring the temple that held such an attraction for her on the day of entrance into the city.

Dear Sarah!

What a day! How shall I record it? If I say it is the *most* of any sight or feeling, then tomorrow or the day after there may be *more* to heap on the superlative.

Yapah led us to the temple I had longed to enter since I first beheld it. After we crossed the stream, it was an arduous climb up steep slopes of broken stone terraces to the pyramidal structure at the top. It was much in ruins and shrouded by trees and other growth; but once at its entrance, the expansive display of stuccoed ornamentation along its front, and the wide piers covered in hieroglyphics, spread out its history before my eyes, while I stood there breathless and illiterate, isolated in its future, yearning to interpret.

We followed Yapah inside and on across the frontal corridor into an altar room—all the building, walls, ceilings, pavements such heavy stone that one knew the builder intended it to last for all time. John measured the altar room 13 by 7 feet, both sacred numbers. There was a tablet of sculptured stone completely covering the back wall, lighted only by the wide door at the front entrance. We had arrived at the time of day when the light that was emitted seemed only for the scene depicted there. Had Yapah meant it that way?

The two personages facing the cross affected me as though I, too, were a supplicant before forces awesome and undefined. A huge bird, laden with ornaments, was perched on top of the cross, its claws clutching the rim in determined balance. The two figures were, except for ankle trim, unclothed from feet to hip. Elaborate drapes, folds, twists, and plaits of cloth were garment and headdress for the figure on the left; the one on the right was draped only around the waist and wore a plain high turban with elaborate ear caps—he was much the larger and held me in a vise of attention with the authority of his bearing.

His mouth was open in ceremonial beseechment, his arms fully outstretched in gesture of offering. And what was he offering? O God of the Cross! It's lying on a drape that is flowing from his hands, the exposed lines of its body so tender, the head mask a distortion of some kind. If it were simply an image, it surely would not be lying in a position of sleep or death. The skin of my body quivered. It has to be, it could be nothing other than an infant, a newborn. Was it being dedicated, blessings being sought for a life of service or . . . ? All I could witness was the utter solemnity, the surge of controlled feeling flowing from that mouth! And the child, living or dead, what had it felt of life and what its purpose in being born and lifted up to the cross in those arms! I have never had strong feelings before about a baby—have never held one in my arms. Why was this babe such a mixture of loss and desire to me? I hid my face against John and clung to him. He held me tight, and then we walked out.

My imagination still clung to the tiny form and its destiny. Was the mask covering face and head used to reshape and distort the natural form? We had observed the pronounced head deformity in the sculptures everywhere—an elongation of the upper part of the head, sloping the forehead until the whole skull, in some displays, appeared cone-shaped. When I asked John about this, he said it was brought about by a compression device, most likely made of board bindings and applied from birth. What of the injury done to the housing of the brain? I wondered. Did this account for the mournful, the pain-cast features of the suppliants, the awesome gravity woven into the ornate panels on walls and piers? Was the agony of the newborn when forced from the womb prolonged for years in a harsher mold to become a lifetime implant on the spirit?

When we were seated outside in the shade, Yapah said, "You are sorrowful. Sorrow is useful to awaken the spirit, but grieve not overlong for what you do not understand. We will eat and rest, then explore further as we return to the palace."

While we rested, Yapah sitting against a tree trunk and I propped against a building stone while John lay with his head in my lap, John remarked to Yapah that his Spanish smacked more of academy training than the Mayan inflections of the tongue.

Yapah was pleased. "Ah, you notice. I'll tell you the reason. My native tongue is Mayan and I have never been far from Palenque. I have many years and they go back to the time of the supply route through Palenque village from the Gulf to Guatemala. The padres were busy with conversions and teaching the natives simple translations into Spanish. They built a small convent and brought two nuns from Mexico City. They were with us for three years, an older woman and one much younger." He paused, closed his eyes for a while.

"The young one was an angel in robes. Her eyes were so blue that I always felt life was unkind that the church cut her hair and I could never behold its golden hue. I was sure it was gold. . . . Spanish as she spoke it was a song." He paused another while.

"She taught me to sing, not just in my speech, but in my mind, in my heart. I learned things beyond records and places. Things as deep as God. I learned why I was alive—why I was born in Palenque—why I was Yapah . . . and why she was Sister Adela. . . . I never touched her until we said good-bye . . . she let me kiss her hands. I'm sure she made no amends for this to priest or Mother Mary. She was wise and she made me wise. We understood . . . everything."

After a while, John inquired, "Did you ever have a desire to become a priest?"

Yapah waited, then dropped a rock in the waters of stillness, "I *am* a priest."

On the instant, John sat up and looked at him, searching for humor or whimsy in his expression.

I stiffened and stared straight ahead.

Yapah had inherited intact the Indian ability to show no expression at all.

When John is jarred by a statement he tries to set a sharp little trap in response.

"What order?" he snapped with unnecessary severity.

Yapah gave him stern priestlike appraisal before he answered.

"The Order of Yapah. And in this time I am its only member."

John came back rather feebly, I thought. "Apologies, padre. You should have told me."

I didn't dare smile. Yapah was still stone-faced. John retreated by reclining again, his head in my lap. Yapah closed his eyes, and so did we. I couldn't resist some gentle taps on the back of John's neck which I hoped he decoded as "Now what?"

The priest dialogue is still a puzzle, and John has not spoken of it yet. What we speak of lightly now about our approaching union is in reality a deep current of understanding that it is inevitable and not much longer to be put off. Our companionship, our sharing of mood and thought, the sweetness of courtship interludes when senses swirl to a near delirium that implores *now* . . . all combine in the imperative.

There is some kind of essence left in this place that I cannot comprehend, much less define. Did the Presence of Love walk through the gloom and doom and leave footsteps to be retraced? I am even stranger to myself when, as I go to sleep at night, I can think of no place on earth I'd rather be when we merge flesh and spirit in the gift of self to self.

So far, I have not been lonely for my harp. But once I awake from sleeping in John's arms, how shall I express my wonderment in music? Or will our thoughts and feelings be music enough? a composition that can be executed only as a duet and registered in scales beyond the ones we use for converting sensations to sounds.

And now a goodnight to myself. I will blow out the candle and send a thought-question over the partition: What will it be like when there is no partition?

Goodnight, Sarah, Damasacra of Palenque

Another adventure was of such import that Sarah Belle found it the most difficult yet to record and did not open her notebook for several days afterward.

Dear Sarah:

Surely, there can not be another day in my life to match the *Day of the Storm* if we were to live here until the extant ruins have crumbled!

It began as a day of difference for all of us. Even the air, cool with a heady kind of effect, made one feel restless and very energetic. High-flying clouds were playing games with the sun.

Yapah said the grass was good and he was taking the animals out for a morning of grazing.

Celeste was trying out a stone oven Maury had made, and wanted no one to talk to her while she baked a supply of bread.

John was busy making up some torches as Yapah had taught him, for a complete investigation of subterranean rooms in another part of the palace.

Of more interest to me was a temple that we had hurriedly explored, and it was right at our "back door," its base just outside the palace at the southwest corner. Yapah called it the Temple of Records because of the immense tablets of hieroglyphics in the outer corridor and over the inner walls. The natives spoke of it as an *escuela*, a temple of discipline and instruction for their ancestors.

Yapah was gone before I spoke to John about my plan to climb the pyramid top again. He rejected it out of hand, but I told him I would take Maury and Emile—the exercise would do them good and I no longer felt any anxiety about Emile's condition. He reluctantly agreed.

We left the palace through the underground passages along which John was working and began climbing in steep ascent through a tangle of trees that had loosened and overturned the stone blocks originally forming the stepped approach. The trees had erected such a covering, as they towered over the temple and even flourished on its rooftop, that it did not come into view until our climb was half done.

Yapah had cleared a narrow pathway earlier and provided a resting place at this point with stones upended for seats. Emile sat immediately and let Jasper out on his long leash. Maury was winded and put down the lemonade jug.

I told them to stay where they were—I wouldn't be gone long and the climb would be too much for Emile. Maury uneasily protested. I told him I would be in sight until I entered the building and would stay only a short while. If I prolonged my visit, I would come out and wave to reassure him.

I hurried along on the steep incline, feeling strong and excited to be alone for a little while and absorb the feeling of this temple that held so much of history vaulted until the key to Mayan literacy could be found.

As I held on to branches from time to time for support, swinging or leaping as I made my way over tumbled stones, I could imagine the freedom feeling of monkeys making their way through the forest in a more liberated fashion.

I stopped at the entrance to study the human figures ornamenting the four piers that separated the wide doors to the outer corridor. One I would have addressed as a woman. Though heads and parts of arms were missing on the sculptured forms, it was quite clear that each of three was holding a child. Royal lineage? Could the place be a tomb and all the hieroglyphics filling walls and supports, the story of their lives and times?

As I moved on into the front corridor, the large stone pavements seemed to be more of a seal than a floor covering. I recalled that John had measured it 7 feet wide—again the sacred number. I walked back and forth several times. The place was lighted only by the front openings which were heavily shaded. The immensity of the tablets with their crowded symbols, much use of miniature grotesque faces in countless expressions, became oppressive in their mystery. How I longed for a strong light and a Mayan dictionary! It was more than curiosity that aroused me. Here surely was something of concern to me and my time. My frustration increased as the light seemed to be dimming out on me—then became dimmer still, even darkening.

Suddenly there was a clap as if the mountainside had exploded! Then came streaks and snaps of lightning, and a fierce wind that grabbed the forest with tempest force. Trees on the roof broke and crashed. I backed away from the entrance into a deeper darkness. The thunder god struck with his heavy hammer several more times, then roared in deafening crescendo. A torrent of water plunged through the trees, splashed over piles of stones. Lightning illuminated the tablets of hieroglyphics in fantastic display.

What of Maury crouched along the trail sheltering Emile with his big body? I prayed no one would venture a search for me.

I became aware of movements about me and knew that I was not alone. A blaze of lightning showed two big eyes, like small lanterns at the end of the corridor, and a cat form. A jaguar? The god himself, no doubt, as I had seen him represented in ornament and sacrificial ritual. More flashes—more revelations. Refugees from the storm-tossed trees and drenched stones were joining me. So help me God, a pair of monkeys had entered! And then beyond my comprehension that it could be so, serpents large and small were filling the corridor. I dared not move. I was up against a wall so tight I could feel the imprint of its symbols along my shoulders. I was as still as one of the thousand-year-old sculptures, and a paralysis of terror made me almost as solid.

An image of Marie Laveau popped into my mind. I heard her repeating what she had told me when she came to convince me I should agree to a plan for me and Emile: *If you do agree, and you do find the gain that awaits you, I will know. And you will say in your mind, "Thank you, Marie." But before that you will say that the voudou queen's hell has been shown to you.*

I felt a snake gliding across the toes of my boots and at that moment a sheet of lightning gave me a full view of my dilemma: the symbol of the voudou god himself was crawling around over the whole floor of the corridor. I wanted to scream out, "Marie! You witch! I am *in* your voudou hell!" I wanted to sit down and cry.

The monkeys and the jungle cat were as immobile as I. How long could I remain in this paralysis? When the storm abated, would they all leave?

"These are fellow creatures," an inner voice of reason tried to tell me. "They, like you, sought shelter. That is all. They are not harming each other. Why should they harm you?" . . . "Why not?" I countered. "They are in their own kingdom. I am a trespasser and that jaguar's ancestors exacted tribute from a whole race!" . . . So reason forsook me and desperation presided. . . . The storm seemed to abate, and a faint light, gray and tenuous, began to filter through the doorways. But none of the temple tenants were moving out. The monkeys were still there, close together in the corner—the snakes hardly moving—and the jaguar sitting on his haunches, looking at me, the only one I could be sure was sensing me as alive and alien.

I became conscious of a figure in the doorway—a live human figure. Was it a hallucination? A spirit form? Then a departing subdued flash of lightning revealed the most frightening recognition of my life. Emile! No doubt about it. The linen duster he always wore, clinging to him like an outer skin, and a protrusion in one of the big side pockets—the Jasper pocket. . . . Oh, God! Another cloud must have passed over. It was near darkness again.

A voice, now a very real voice, a very soft voice, said, "Don't be afraid, I'm coming after you." I wanted to scream, "Don't move! Don't move!" but I couldn't speak. He seemed to bring light with him from the doorway as he advanced toward me very slowly, very quietly, very carefully. Then there he was, only a step or so from me. He spoke quietly, all in a single tone. "The hurricane has passed. Move out from the wall. Come closer. I am going to pick you up. Make it easy for me. Be very deliberate. Place your arms around my neck and I will carry you out. Do not protest in any way—no sound or movement."

This I did in a stupor of obedience. Emile carrying me out, a twilight-kind of radiance to guide him, stepping, oh, so cautiously over and around the snakes. I sensed every living thing there watching us, recording our presence, but not a single movement of alarm or interference. Then we were out, the rain and wind tempered, the storm pressure out of it.

He sat me on my feet, supporting me with an arm around my waist. "Can you stand now? Can you walk?" I nodded. I was slow to accept the reality of what was happening. Finally I was able to ask, "Where is Maury?"

"A tree fell on him, but I got him out. He's waiting for us. I think he'll be able to walk. Shall we try it now?" He put his hand into his pocket. "Jasper is drenched, but he'll survive."

We had more light now. He took my hand and we slipped and slid, bruised hands and feet, were scratched and slapped by the weighted branches. We made it to Maury. He greeted us with tears pouring down his cheeks. Hugged me. Hugged Emile. I felt warmed and made rational by his emotional relief—but not so rational that I didn't say aloud, quite loud, "Thank you, Marie, friend! Thank you for Emile!"

We were not done with emotional display. On down the trail we met a distracted John who grabbed me while we both cried. He was not aware of the new Emile until we were back in the palace for a third tearful reunion between Celeste and Maury.

And Yapah? He watched in silence. I learned later that he had tried to convince John that we were safe and that there had been a renewal in the temple.

Emile? He sat on his cot watching us and then said to Maury, "Bring me some dry clothes and help me get into them. I'm very tired. I'm going to sleep and when I awake, you'll explain how we got into this place with these people and what Celeste is doing here. Can she see after the squirrel for me?"

Maury said, "Yes, mastah," under his breath and looked to see if we had heard him. We had. He winked and grinned happily.

Somehow that wink was a signal that all was well, "all had come round," closing a circle: for Maury now entirely free, Celeste dwelling in his happiness, Emile sound of mind again with adjustments to make, certainly "manhood" intact after his performance in the Temple of Records (Marie in harmony with her conscience and her god), and John—he knows I am his and no other claim can deny him.

What about Sarah Belle? What about "Miss Sarah"? As I write, I note the flame of my candle cannot illumine that shadowed corner beyond my cot. No more can I light up the shadowed place in my mind where Defender's destiny resides unrevealed. But I do know that I will withhold no part of my threefold self from John Monroe Sterling, our oneness already indivisible. . . . My conscience? It is at rest, or, at least in obeisance. . . . If it should arouse to question, I shall quiet it with a generous serving of Shealia's Jamaican herb tea!

Sarah of Palenque

After the storm the six inhabitants of Palenque were more closely attuned to each other than before. Maury and Emile took long walks together, and Emile, though not withdrawn, spent much time in silence; on occasion he rode out with Yapah, Sarah Belle, and John, and stayed near Yapah as they moved about.

The storm having had its way at cleansing and ravishing anew the site of the old city, left the sun to brighten and bring to quick blossom exotic vines and trees about the premises and on the mountainside—and left the moon to draw aside her mask and glorify with gentle lighting the monuments to ancient and imaginative architects.

Yapah had noticed that on their tours of exploration since the hurricane, Sarah Belle and John were paying less attention to sight-seeing and note-taking and more to themselves—holding hands and gazing about in desultory fashion—selecting choice spots for longer siestas. On one of these, Sarah Belle asked Yapah to explain further about the gloomy expressions on the big spreads of sculptured human faces and within the hieroglyphic tablets.

"Yapah, I have searched, I mean really sought, for a face that smiled or laughed, or simply showed a pleasant or serene countenance."

"And you have not found even one who laughed?"

"In the temple of records, before the storm, I saw one that might be called a laughing face, but nothing of happiness in it—

the mouth wide open, the head thrown back—it could have been a clown or a madman, maybe under torture, wildly grotesque. If you know the face I mean, why do you think he was laughing? Tell me."

"I know the one, and I will tell you—but not today."

It was the question Yapah had been waiting for.

A few mornings later, he surprised them by announcing that they would make a later start and spend the night away from the palace. He would be taking them to a mound at the top of a steep mountain that rose in a line from the front of the palace and had once commanded a view of the city. Now it was much too overgrown for a lookout, but he had cut a trail to the mound and had prepared overnight quarters there. The macho could be loaded with extra supplies.

The three left behind acted as though such an excursion was nothing unusual and assisted in preparing the backpack for the mule.

The climb was steeper than any yet taken to pyramid tops, brush thicker, trees more intertwined. John and Yapah used their machetes to widen the path at intervals for the packmule's passage. The trail Yapah had opened was a green tunnel where parrots, wild turkeys, lizards, snakes, monkeys scurried and fluttered along their way.

At the summit, they came out upon a flat rock surface, clear of growth but around it trees had rooted between great chunks of stone, and nearby was the mound Yapah had mentioned, the trees upon it raised above all the rest.

"Climb a tree on the mound and you can see the village, the gulf, and over into Tabasco," Yapah said, "and in an earlier time could have viewed all that made the great city in the valley below."

Sarah Belle and John were not listening. Their eyes were upon the small lodging place centered on the flat rock. It was constructed of fresh cut poles and thatched with green foliage. It was three-sided, opening to the east. Smaller poles were bound together to form a table and three stools set out at the front of the hut.

"It will not rain again until the moon has filled and begins her retreat," he said quietly, and was silent as he began unpacking supplies and bedrolls and moving them into the shelter.

John and Sarah Belle were equally silent as they assisted Yapah and set out food for the first meal. Then as they sat down, Sarah Belle spoke for the first time.

"This could have been sanctified ground for certain of the ancients in the sacred city below."

Yapah gave her a startled glance and looked away.

"It must have had special significance," John said. "That mound in this particular place would have—would have—I can't explain it. But it still has—well, drawing power." Then with his usual directness, "Why did you bring us here?"

Yapah evaded, "Did you bring your notebook?"

"Why . . . why . . . did you get the notebooks, Sarah?"

"No. I . . . I . . . simply forgot."

Yapah's smiles were never broad, but they could suggest humor, pleasure, sympathy as he chose, or as now, a hint of teasing.

"Perhaps you won't need them. You are right, this is a place of significance and if you choose, discoveries to be made that require no writing down to be remembered."

When they had finished, he said, "I have my own siesta spot, a small grassy space among the rocks where my pet can graze. I will return when the shadows lengthen."

Sarah Belle and John sat for a while not speaking, not touching, not looking at each other.

Finally John stood and spoke, "Come, my dear, take my hand and let's clamber around among the rocks and see what we can discover."

"That fragrant tree over there with all the blossoms just opening to the slanted afternoon light . . . maybe break off a few boughs for . . . for the bower. No, John, don't take my hand. Don't touch me just now. I want to be composed."

"Why?"

"Because I'm trembling, and I'd rather not."

"Why?"

"Don't keep saying 'why'! Why do you think he brought us here?"

"Now you're doing it. I think you know as well as I do."

"You say it."

"All right. He brought us here because . . ."

"Now, see, John, you're not composed either."

"It's this place . . . this place! I can't explain what it is doing to me . . . to us. Yapah knows, and it's . . ." he took a deep breath.

"It's wonderful, John! That's what you're trying to say."

"That's what I'm trying to say, it's wonderful! If he had given us something to drink, I'd think he had drugged us. You don't suppose he did?"

"Of course not! I made the lemonade and poured it myself."

"Can I touch you now?"

"No. Let's get on to the tree. The priest has us under a spell—or maybe it's just the remoteness of this spot, the complete isolation and our being here all alone, camping between earth and heaven."

"We're not alone. Remember. The priest is watching."

"He's not watching. You know that. Plotting maybe, but not watching."

"Tell me one thing, for very sure, Sarah, and maybe I can begin to think straight. Are you glad we're here?"

"Glad is a weak word, John. Do better than that."

"Are you insanely happy?"

"Yes, I am."

"You know what that wise man, priest, conniving friend, or whatever, has arranged for us?"

"Of course."

"And you will lie in my arms tonight in . . . in that place."

"Tonight, and as many more nights as the priest thinks proper to sanctify our nuptials," she looked up at him, humor and love overflowing.

"Oh, God, Sarah. What a gift you are to this man!" He had her tight in his arms.

"John . . . John . . . let me go. The bride must have her bouquet, you know. And Yapah will be back."

Yapah came and brought wild berries, plump and sweet, which he told them grew only at this height. He built a campfire, for the air was cool and damp, and then brought hot water for tea as Sarah Belle set out the cheese, honey, bean patties, and a loaf of Celeste's fresh bread. They ate in silence. Before leaving, he lighted a green stick and set it in a grooved rock, then placed it at the open side of their canopied sleeping place. He said it was from a branch of the "torch-tree" and would burn through the night.

Before leaving, he told them he had placed a coverlet at their bedside to protect from the night vapors since their bedrolls had

354

seemed lightweight for the mountain air.

They thanked him and could say no more.

The place he had prepared for their bedrolls was made of poles lashed together with bark and laid on rock supports, then covered with a stack of tender branches in heavy foliage.

"I keep feeling like I have been here before," Sarah Belle whispered, sitting on the edge of the bed, unlacing her boots.

"If you were, I'm sure I was around."

"Yes, of course you were. . . . Don't you think Yapah brought us here because this place was a sanctuary and he wanted us to partake of its influence—that there was some ageless investment—well—investment in eternal love that never corrodes or falls into ruins?"

"Most likely."

"There is something a bit lonely, like a yearning unfulfilled . . . drifting around . . ."

"If you're talking about yourself, you won't be lonely long."

Sarah Belle was sitting on the bed in her nightgown, her feet curled under her. John was arranging the coverlet that Yapah had left for them.

"John, dear, my feet are cold."

"They won't be long. Climb under."

He held the covers up. She obeyed as he joined her, cuddled close.

"Those feet! And we're in the tropics! What will hapen if we ever go to the northlands? I am doomed!" He pulled her closer, one hand holding her head on his chest, the other in her hair brushing it across his cheek. "I am doomed to be captive in this love eternal you say is resident here . . . my bonds this magic in your hair . . . the pulse in your throat . . . the strength in your arms . . . oh, Sarah, my life, why am I talking?"

"Because love words enhance love. John, I was yours from that day I saw you in the square. You remember I cried, so overcome was I with yearning—and embarrassment. The yearning never left me. The desire I could control. Being near you, being with you was enough for a while . . . but . . . I knew it would be like this. . . . No, I didn't know it would be like this . . . it's greater . . . I could not imagine . . . I could not believe . . ."

"Sarah, please don't cry. I don't want you to cry!"

"I'm crying for . . . I'm crying for joy! . . . I'm crying for belonging to you . . . I'm crying because I can't tell you how much I love you and love you loving me."

"You're telling me, sweetheart, you're telling me in ways beyond words . . . far . . . far beyond!"

The words echoed through her brain. John was taking her "far . . .far beyond" . . . beyond any boundaries of sensation she had ever thought could be experienced . . . and the same words echoed through her body, "far . . . far beyond" rippling and cascading until she felt herself hurled into a realm of unbearable sweetness where shafts of light dazzled until the spirit soared into freedom inexpressible.

When she awakened, John was at the bedside offering her a cup of honeyed tea.

"Wake, Damasacra, and drink the sacrament the priest has brought along with this mountaintop flower he plucked at dawn—when it is most fragrant, he says."

"I wish he wouldn't call me that, and the fragrance is much too sweet, but tell him I love him."

"I could say I think that message is much too sweet also. . . . I am not in a sharing mood . . . but I will tell him."

CHAPTER THIRTY-THREE

SARAH BELLE AND JOHN stayed on their mountain-top of isolation and love for five days. Yapah had made a trip below to explain that the camping excursion had been extended and he had returned for the notebooks and additional supplies. Celeste gave him a puzzled look as she handed him the notebooks. He gave her one of his rare smiles. "I may have to write something down."

The morning of the sixth day, Yapah suggested it might be time to return to the valley. "Bliss prolonged could grow stale." They both laughed at him. "Besides the rain god is restless and may drench you into consciousness and block the trail if we stay longer."

"What a frightful possibility!" John mocked.

"We could live well on wild berries, love, and rainwater," Sarah suggested.

"And use your coverlet to protect us from night vapors."

"You brought our notebooks and we have not yet found time to use them."

For the first time since he had come into their life, Yapah laughed. "I made a mistake. I will bring the macho now and we will pack."

As they made their way back, down the rough incline so steep they must take care not to cause a loose stone to fall after them, they descended gradually into reality—but a different reality in which they would travel the rough and the smooth, the high and the low, hand in hand and heart to heart.

They were at the entrance to the palace when they heard a shocking sound.

"John what is *that*? Is it my mind or am I hearing——"

"You are hearing the impossible. A man's voice raised in an aria from *Le Nozze di Figaro*!"

"The *Marriage of Figaro*? No one in God's world knows of our—our marriage except those here. Could it be Emile?"

"If he had an operatic voice, he would hardly be in a mood for comic operas or be sounding joy over any kind of marriage. Besides there are other sounds, maybe a whole opera company has come to the palace halls."

"John . . ."

"Yes, darling."

"I wish we were back in sanctuary."

"We're back in life. Let's make the most of it. Come on. Whoever that voice belongs to is a happy man. After all, the Palenque ruins are not a private preserve and we haven't rented the palace."

They found the corridor near the courtyard crowded with pack animals and Indian mozos, and near the steps into the court several saddled mules and horses. They passed them all and entered the courtyard. The resounding voice came from the throat of a handsome caballero, surrounded by several attendants and the three awed residents. He stood with his head thrown back in comic posture as if on stage center at the Palenque opera house performing on royal command. He broke off to rush over to John and Sarah Belle.

"Madame! Monsieur! Many courtesies and so much happiness that I come to you at last. I am José de Claración. On my arrival at this spot of lost grandeur, I could not resist an effort to awake the dead and assure them that the world might be a better place than they knew." He addressed John: "I have heard of the exciting Sterling Expedition," and then turned immediately to Sarah Belle. "I come as envoy from William Moellhausen at Houston and through the good offices of George Fisher, key state official in the land office of Texas. It was through his masterly instincts and instructions that I was able to carry out my mission and locate the man," he hesitated, "to whom your letter was addressed."

Sarah Belle, standing very still, very formal, very pale, simply nodded for him to continue.

"I found this—this—Defender Locke. He accepted the letter and I bring you his reply." He unbuttoned his tight-fitting jacket, reached to an inner pocket and brought out a flat packet securely encased in laced leather. He bowed and presented it.

"Thank you, señor." Sarah Belle felt her hands so cold and stiff it was hard to close her fingers around the packet—painful to contact it.

She made the expected inquiries with difficulty, knew John was in thought and concern giving her all support possible.

"Who informed you that I was on this expedition?"

"Your servants at the house on Phillipa Street told me to inquire of the owner at Hudson Recoire Carriage Service."

"I see. Your mission has meant extended travel under difficulties, I am sure. Have you been amply compensated through my representative in Houston?"

"Madame! I can never tell you how amply I have been compensated! Had you not been at this place, had I never made this trip to Palenque with the stop at Palizada . . . Paloma, my dove! Where are you?"

The little maiden of the water jar, her hair flying, darted into the tableau and flung herself into Sarah Belle's arms.

"Never mind the tears," José explained. "She is such a joyful little bird. I learned of you and your goodness from her. She believes that your ring brought me to her. I say it brought her to me. For years I have searched for such a one, and through my mission for you, I found her. . . . Let the lady rest from your passion of gratitude, little one, and come to my side. I miss you."

Paloma came and stood looking up at him, her eyes glistening with adoration. His eyes glancing down were equally worshipful.

He turned back to Sarah Belle and John, speaking softly as if his statement were a sacred utterance, "We were married in the little church at Palizada, thus my arrival here was delayed for some days. There must always be a wedding celebration."

"I am glad you were delayed," Sarah Belle said, and looked at John for the first time since José had stated his mission.

"Congratulations," John said to José. "Yes, there must always be a celebration when true love finds its own."

Sarah Belle spoke to John: "I must leave you for a while, for this matter so long unresolved must be attended."

She left them, walking across the courtyard to another exit and on into a narrow court beyond. Little had been done to clear this area and it suited Sarah Belle's mood. It seemed much further removed from the principal court than it really was.

She pushed through some brush with an unnatural craving to conceal herself, tripped, and fell to her knees. She began slowly with stiff fingers to untie and unlace the leather packet. Finally she pulled the letter out. It was her own letter, the same paper she had written upon! Her face heated and her breath came short. She crushed it in her hands—but as she loosened her hands to let it drop, she glimpsed another handwriting and retrieved the sheets. There was writing on the back. He had answered . . .

Woman of the Past,

I am Kash-tash-ha, a Choctaw, citizen of the Choctaw Nation in Indian Territory. Kash-tash-ha understands all that you have written much better than the man you addressed ever could have understood for Kash-tash-ha has lived in the wilderness and fought in the wilderness and learned from the wilderness the ways of man and beast.

Kash-tash-ha has found peace in a valley among the hills, his friends the creatures of earth and sky and stream, his work in the gardens and fields that the Earth Mother provides. He brings no pain or loss from the past into his dreams. Your letter has cleared a small wilderness path of memory that his thoughts, sometimes escaping direction, had sought to retrace. Now he can release them for the time of this writing.

Between us now let there be no haunting faults to be exorcised . . . no guilts to be expunged. The path we trod together we walked in ignorance of each other and nature's laws. We kept hidden what should have been disclosed. We fled inward and made much of what was little. We were prudish before naked truth, and in a land of slavery, we accepted the mold of conformity to decadence.

Kash-tash-ha is adopted son of the Choctaw tribe. They are his people forever and he a part of their life's blood, for Kash-tash-ha has a wife. Her name is Lu-shapa. Kash-tash-ha and Lu-shapa have a son. His name is Yowani.

Assert your own freedom, Woman of the Past. Find your own valley and whatever awaits you there of life and truth.

Kash-tash-ha, Choctaw

"I have found my valley, Kash-tash-ha!" Sarah Belle said aloud.

"Sarah! Sarah! For God's sake, where are you?" John was stumbling around through the rubbish and tangles of the courtyard.

"Here."

He threshed through the brush and flung himself down beside her. "In heaven's name, why must you hide like this? Haven't you panicked me enough without burrowing so that I have to ferret you out!"

"John, those are the sweetest words I've heard since sanctuary. I have something to tell you——"

"I don't care what's in the damned letter! You're mine, and forever, do you understand? No matter what!" He grabbed her by the shoulders, shaking her, his fingers digging in.

"Before I hear a cursed word about what you've read, you'll tell me . . ." he let go, his lips tight, his face white, his hair tousled over his forehead.

"Tell you what, John? What is it you want me to tell you? I thought I told you everything on the mountaintop—everything that mattered."

"Yes, you did. And to think anything in that letter might change it—I can't explain. From the moment José handed you the packet, I felt like I was on the edge of a precipice and it was crumbling under me—it was a feeling that simply—simply emptied me of reason."

"John, John dear, put your arms around me, hold me close. It's all right—all right for Defender, all right for us. There is no precipice, darling, there is no precipice!"

José explained to John and Sarah Belle that he and Paloma with their retinue of carriers were occupying a house in the village.

Since there was seldom an Indian for hire who would spend a night at the ruins, he and Paloma would not be camping there but would come from the village to tour the site over several days before departing.

He was not returning to the States by way of Laguna, he told them, but would pursue his travels to the east coast of Yucatán by way of the Lake of Petén and the Belize River. He would go on up the coast to the island of Cozumel to appraise the holdings that George Fisher had surveyed there.

"A route we may take later," John remarked as he and Sarah Belle were both thinking this might avoid further encounters with Vicende.

"Ah, I have heard much of Cozumel and from very strange sources," José enthused. "It is a place of enchantment and mystery, they say. Very ancient temples and fortifications, and in times not so long ago a haven for pirates from over the world. My New York editors will relish my accounts. My Paloma and I go well supplied for a honeymoon of glorious dimensions!"

"While at Laguna, did you happen to make the acquaintance of a prominent Spaniard landowner of that region, Don Vicende de Vives?"

"I heard mention of him in the marketplace, but saw nothing of his personage."

"Were the merchants of Laguna aware that you were on your way to the Palenque site?"

"But, of course, señor, why not?"

"Did you ever get the feeling that among the bogadores you hired, any one of them might be spying on you?"

"I got no such feeling, for I travel free and easy so that there can be no cause for spying."

"Is there any among your carriers that have been with you all the way from Laguna?"

"Why, yes, the custodian of my supplies, Horacio. He checks, bargains, guards all my goods. He will accompany me until I leave Yucatán. He is faithful and honest."

"Yes, of course." . . . Probably faithful to Vicende as well, John thought.

"George Fisher has told me of the wonders of Cozumel. He thinks it would attract travelers from all over the world. I expect to be there for some months. If your expedition could join us there, it would be so pleasant!" He looked significantly at Sarah Belle, his eyes wide and knowing.

"Thank you, José. We will think about it."

"About the spying, señor—you seem not at ease."

"A personal matter, José, that involves you not at all, and no immediate threat to me."

Before leaving for the village, José told Sarah Belle that he had good reason to be grateful to her friend Hudson Recoire. "Through him I was able to hire three responsible attendants to accompany me to journey's end. He, in turn, asked a favor of me, and I rejoice to be of service to him. I am delivering to you a packing case that has made the journey without damage."

Sarah Belle was surprised and at the same time relieved that something from Hudson had reached out to her here. She had thought her departure from New Orleans had severed the tie between them except for warm memories. She knew that whatever he had sent he considered important to her. Had he read Defender's letter? She had instructed him "to read and reply as become the contents" of anything that came from William, but neither had expected such an envoy as José!

When José's attendant brought the case in, she had him place it on the table in the courtyard. John stood by, his expression solemn but undisturbed. "It is a happy thing, John—I know it is. We will open it when they are gone."

She found herself alone in the courtyard staring at the box, her thoughts, all things around her, seeming in a state of transcendence, at the very core of her existence. John had gone to see José on his way out of the palace, and like an accompaniment to her mood, José's voice, distant but clear with buoyant happiness, was sending out a challenge to ruin and decay in a triumphant operatic air.

A soft voice beside her said, "It is *Die Zauberflöte*. He is singing the exultant refrain hailing the magic power of the flute."

Emile's presence did not startle her. She was glad he was near.

"I have delayed too long," he said. "I must thank you for my life and my resurrection."

"There are others more significant in your pattern of recovery." She began to say the names and loved the sound of them. "Hudson

Recoire . . . Marie Laveau . . . Maury and Celeste . . . John Sterling who brought us all to this place of beginning again."

"And Jasper," Emile added softly, stroking his furry companion, "my little key to sanity—the only clear memory I have running through all the darkness. There were, however, two bright visions along that shrouded path: In one, I was at sea, and a strange woman in my cabin," he looked at Sarah Belle and smiled, "still a very strange woman now enshrined in my heart."

"And the other?"

"Francine and the dance."

"It was remarkable her recognition of you beneath the disguise your mind had imposed on you. It was difficult for her to let you go without your knowing this."

"I did know but could not bend the bars of my prison. I'll never return to the shadowed world that evicted me, but Francine shines on the outer rim of it, and on fragrant evenings of peace like this, and in the haunting hours of night, she beckons."

In her thoughts, Sarah Belle addressed Marie Laveau: "Ah, Marie, how happy you should be!"

Only John and Yapah were at hand when she opened the case José had delivered. The sun was behind the mountain and a hazy light veiled the courtyard except for the circle where they stood, in reflections from the evening campfire and a torch near the table.

Sarah Belle watched as the two men removed straps, carefully pried off the heavy boards of the outer packing, and broke the seal on the inner wrappings of cardboard and cloth.

Sarah Belle, hardly breathing in anticipation, was thinking: I know he read the Defender letter. I know it! He is somehow celebrating my happiness—it is like a wedding present from an understanding heart. I am almost suffocating with the wonder of him, and of this, this——"

The gift was exposed—the frame of it glowed in the changing light—and it was Yapah who handed it to her.

It was a lyre constructed in the classic proportions of ancient Greece. She held it close as though it were a living thing.

John said, "There is a message here, my dear."

"Read it to me."

Zeuxis became aware that Zantea, the story-singer of ancient Arcadia, had need of her instrument.

"Is that all?"

"Yes."

"It is enough."

She began to finger the strings and the gentle lovely sounds flowed as though coming through an extension of herself.

"Sit here in the torchlight, Damasacra, so we can have the joy of watching your hands on the strings."

She sat and explored the eight strings, each and in combination. The nocturnal sounds in the trees and crevices of the courtyard were stilled and the invisibles waited, as did the three in the apartment, and the two men so near her.

"You will sing for us, Damasacra?"

She spoke two lines above the melody she was weaving:

"This gift of love comes vibrant from the giver's hands,
  An envoy charged with dreams this kindred spirit understands."

And then as though she and the lyre were in dialogue,

"A song of love invades the strings,
  A song of love the lyre brings
  To capture in this ancient place
  The rapture of true love's embrace,
  The glow of love on friendship's face—
  The sound of love when lovers speak
  And tones play games of hide-and-seek——"

(The lyre playfully searched the hearts of its listeners.)

"When we must cross a shadowed plain
  And live encamped with loss and pain,
  To think of love sheds light ahead
  A song invites, a feast is spread.
  . . . Ah, let me feel the reach of love
  To yearn and learn and teach of love,
  And know the very thought of love
  Can breach the walls of time and space
                And deify the human race."

The strings echoed and re-echoed the theme under the last four statements of the singer, until she laid her hand across them for silence.

Yapah spoke into the quietness.

"Are you comfortable, Damasacra?"

"Yes. Yes, of course."

"It is time for the story I promised. I have saved it through long years for the one who would see the laughing face in the Temple of Records and ask the question you asked: "Why among so many did only one face laugh?"

He turned to John. "Come and sit close beside me, son. The story is for both of you, and I am blessed that it is the two of you and not one alone. Listen, oh so carefully . . . and I will tell you how it happened . . ." His voice was like a fine old instrument, seldom played upon, and he brought it into tune with slow and reverent sounding.

"A thousand . . . maybe two thousand years ago it was . . . and the words I speak are not my own . . . they were planted in my soul by the spirit of a wise man who dwelt here in the time of *The Virgin and the One Who Laughed*."

The great city was being built. The rulers believed no other city would ever be greater. The wise men planned it to endure for all time. And the strength of the people flowed into the shaping of giant stones and timbers for temples ornate and palaces magnificent!

Now there were multitudes of people in the valley of the great city, but in them there was no wisdom or understanding, nor any will of their own. The wise men held close all the knowledge, and the rulers were the laws and the gods.

The people were fed that they might be strong for their labors. They were sheltered that they might live longer to carry and place more stones for the building of the temples. And they were mated that their increase might finish the work thus begun and start new labors designed by the wise men instructed by the rulers.

The people were slaves, but they knew it not—for no small bit of learning was ever given unto them. The wise men too were slaves, but they fretted not—for in the comfort of their cloisters they were unaware of the joys of serving mankind, knowing only the reward of serving their rulers.

It is the relation of man to woman, the attraction that can be stronger than law or custom, that so many times marks the course of history, shattering a kingdom or bringing to pass the rise or fall of a whole race. And so it was at this time and place when a wise man forsook his wisdom and loved a slave girl.

It was the custom that wise men beget sons from the women of the virgins' sanctuary, and seldom were sons born to the wise men of other women because such offspring became common slaves as were the multitudes; and so great was the pride and sacred the heritage of the wise men that they desired above all things to rear their sons in the light of their own wisdom.

But one of these who found all tradition and knowledge obscured in the single flaming desire for one woman and no other, put aside the virgin he was to take as wife and brought to cloister instead the slave handmaiden of the virgin. And when she bore him a son, again he cast wisdom aside, and in secret he taught the slave child the things that only the wise men and the rulers should know. Thus much damage was done.

The wise young slave came to be known to the multitudes. Some difference from the rest made him a strange creature to them all. They called him for a while The Different One.

The Different One was stronger than his fellow slaves. His eyes were brighter. They seemed to hold pleasant secrets hard to keep. Strangest of all were the thoughts he held, not about himself alone, but about all others; and the words that sprang from his thoughts mystified the people.

Most frequent among the things he tried to explain was a condition of life called *freedom*. Only a wise man, they felt, should consider such things; but The Different One loved the word and was much concerned that they understand its true meaning. So they tried very hard, for the warmth of his spirit reached out to them. The ones who began to understand took on a brightness of eye that resembled the brightness which the whole countenance of The Different One gave out.

Soon the wise men and the rulers became aware of The Different One and of the things he spoke among the people. And their awareness grew to alarm. They held council together, banishing from their deliberations the father of The Different One. These wise men knew the nature of humanity. Their awareness was condensed by the ages. Their knowledge was tempered in the furnace of time and it was guarded well from generation unto generation. A knowledge of freedom had always been kept from the people, and it must ever be so kept. The members of the great council were entirely equal to the occasion. Their plans were made with care. They held no fear of failure.

The people were called together in great conclave before the Temple of the Sun where they were accustomed to worship their rulers as their gods. There they waited in all humbleness and fear. Finally, the Supreme Counselor of the Law Court, spokesman for the rulers and chief among the wise men, appeared. He stood in white robes and in silence before all. Then in a high voice he called The Different One to come before him, with all the people for witness.

With dignity The Different One mounted the steep irregular steps of the temple until he reached the feet of the Counselor. There he knelt until he felt the scepter touch his head in the sign to raise his countenance for instruction.

"Young fool," the Counselor thought, "there is no fear in him, only the guileless curiosity of youth. He trembles before me, but it is with eagerness to know what I will say. His eyes glow as if he is expecting some unusual gift . . . and indeed it is a very unusual gift he shall have."

He addressed The Different One, and the sounding walls of the temple carried his words in great amplification and clarity to the furthermost row of kneeling slaves before him. These were his words:

"Slave among many who service these temples, you have spoken among the people of freedom as a desirable condition for man to attain. The people have not understood. Some have actually come to believe this state you herald a more rewarding one than that long decreed by the gods. The Different One in trying to think for himself and for the people has fallen into grievous error. The people shall see and understand this. They shall behold in freedom a misery and madness. For your rulers and your gods declare from this temple that you are henceforth a man with freedom! The people will watch how it becomes you. They shall see how a man, neither slave nor wise man, ruler or god, must live.

They will know at last what is the true nature of a free man. Go! Live in freedom! And when the seasons have once more run their course on the calendar, we will call you here again and the people with you. If then the people would be like unto you, freedom shall be the portion of them all! . . . I have finished."

The Different One felt no threat in the accusation of error. He would refute the wise men! He would live a wondrous example of the joys in freedom and thus make free men of them all! He rose from his knees and flung his arms to the sky in great exultation, and from his throat came such a joyous sound, such a rhapsody of laughter, that the fears of the people vanished, and they were lifted up and shouted as they had never shouted before, sharing this joy of the one free man.

As the people dispersed, the slave-made-free moved among them, still laughing and shedding pure pleasure over them all.

"Watch me," he said, "I shall teach you of freedom."

The people thereupon changed his name and began to call him The One Who Laughed, for laughter was a rare thing among them, so few were the delights in living known to the slave-born multitudes.

But there was one who fled when he heard the laughter that echoed down the valley that day from the Temple of the Sun— fled in anguish and despair, taking himself to a chamber of isolation deep under the palace. It was a room so deadened that a man could not hear even the sound of his own voice. There he cursed wisdom, defied the gods, and prayed madly to some power he knew not, beating the walls about him until his hands dripped blood. Finally, he fell in exhaustion and lay against the cool stone floor muttering soundlessly, "My son! My son! The sacrifice is plain! My wisdom is ashes!"

The people had not long to look and listen to The One Who Laughed. It was he who was free, not they. They must work ever harder, ever faster and more devotedly, to please the gods. The rulers must have more temples, more palaces, and more beautiful ornamentation for the great city. The taskmasters became more urgent. The lash fell harder when the load was light. The reward of food was in proportion to the work done. Hunger and the lash were understood. Freedom was strange and afar off.

And stranger still were the things that began to happen to The One Who Laughed.

When the first exuberance had spent itself and the free man became more quiet within himself, he began to explore in living the things he had learned from his wise father but never tested with his own senses. With time for contemplation, he came to know the ecstasy that can fill a man's heart at beholding the ever-changing wonders and beauties in nature. He greatly desired that the people should become aware of this discovery within his freedom, and there came a perfect time for announcing it in nature's grandest setting.

One day at evening time, when the sun hung low over the hills, when flowers were freshly bloomed and birds' song condensed to sweet essence of sound, there reached across the valley from end to end as glorious a rainbow as ever spread color before the eyes of man. The wise men gathered in the tower of the Main Palace to observe, and the rulers walked with stately bearing in the courtyard to witness some part of the astounding display. Only the free man stood and absorbed with all his being the full expanse of beauty spread over and around him. About him on the paths and along the roadways moved the slave people, thousands of them within sight and sound of him—back and forth along the burdenways from quarry to temple. The day was too brief for the allotted loads they must carry, the pain of hunger was too near—ready to twist and gnaw more fiercely in the night—for them to seek more than the reward of food that could be denied if tasks were not finished. The One Who Laughed raised the melody of his voice in calls that matched the beauty around him, telling the slave people of the wonders he beheld, beseeching them to look up with him and perceive the glory of the heavens. But not one burdened back was straightened, not one step lagged in hesitant desire. The choice between beauty and hunger was an instinct implicitly obeyed. The One Who Laughed became very still indeed . . . and in his loneliness the beauty of the scene was dimmed and his freedom somehow diminished.

Such was the innocence of his experience and the brightness of his mind reflecting his father's teachings that The One Who Laughed was unprepared for the power of evil that flourishes in the darkness of ignorance, and the bleak cruelty of prejudice stimulated by that which cannot be understood or accepted. He knew only that he loved the people and desired above all things to have them set free at the appointed time. So he sought more ways to instruct them and prepare them for the day when, by his own example, the true meaning of freedom would be acknowledged before the Temple of the Sun.

To show that freedom is not idleness, he returned to his work at the Temple of Records, applying diligently his talents for ornamentation. And laughter rose up in him again with experiencing the sheer joy of accomplishment, the satisfaction in good work willingly done.

"Look!" he called out to the slave-men working around him, "Look upon the work I now do as a free man. Then look at the other wall where I worked as a slave. There is a great difference, easy to discern. There is also a new something inside me that puts an eagerness into my fingertips and stirs my mind with pleasant intensity. Look! See what I prove to you!" The slaves looked instead at the taskmaster who must appraise their work, for they were more conscious of his presence than any other. He seemed not to know The One Who Laughed was there, so they appeared likewise. But the free man would not be denied their attention: he moved among then plucking gently at a garment, laying his hand upon a shoulder, explaining fervently all the while the relation of freedom to a man's work. But still these whom he desired so much to help appeared to hear him not, and were at the same time openly anxious to be rid of him.

One finally spoke for them all. "Begone!" he said, "Let us work without interruption. We will be thrown back into the quarry and be put to breaking stone again for your interference!"

The free man left the temple laughing, but the sound was thin and hollow.

But he was not yet to be weakened by disappointment or discouraged by aloneness. The people must believe in the goodness of freedom! The face of the calendar was recording the relentless passage of time. He must not let go of laughter or the people would doubt altogether. He must search without ceasing for the experience that would awaken them. It was a small thing that made him for the first time truly afraid that by his example he might not be able to bring about such an awakening . . . a small thing indeed, hardly intended to be an example.

When he first discovered the fine delicacy of fresh fish taken from the stream and broiled at once on a fire by the water's edge, he could not be content until he had prepared a basketful for certain of his friends. At the evening eating time, he carried the basket to the place where they dwelt. Knowing full well their close acquaintance with hunger, he was eager to observe their pleasure in the new food he would offer. But when he uncovered the basket, their terror was an awful thing to behold. Didn't he know that fish was a sacred food, reserved for the wise and the godlike alone? Did he want them thrown to the crocodiles, as they surely would be if they partook of such food in defiance of the gods? Was he bereft of his senses and his concern for their welfare? The laughter he had brought in his heart to accompany their delight in the gift came up to choke him and escaped finally in a harsh and bitter cry as he hurried away from their panic and accusation.

Through that night he walked in blindness, knowing not where his steps took him, caring not . . . then somewhere out of his own darkness and the darkness of the night a restraining hand upon his arm and woman's voice brought reality back to him, made him aware of danger.

"The precipice," she said, "is there at your feet."

He had climbed a mountainside and stood now on a small natural shelf of rock extending over the clean face of a cliff rising a thousand feet above the valley floor. A late moon shed a tired light over the city below, giving its contours of grandeur the softness of clouds at rest in an obscure whiteness. The woman stood very near him, the pressure of her fingers still firm on his arm. Her face was a dim sweet outline in the night's faint glow. He reached out to touch the indefinite cloud of black hair blowing about with the drapes of her white garment, thus assuring himself that here was no apparition.

"A precipice at my feet," he said, "and loveliness at my side."

She moved closer to him. He caught the scent of the garland in her hair. It was the sacred mountaintop flower whose odor is sweetest just before dawn. Its perfume carried to his senses some faint signal of distress—some premonition of a loss to come.

He wanted to reach out for her, bringing her closer still, but he dared not.

"You are the free man?" she asked.

"Yes, I am that," he answered without laughter.

"Then you will not be harmed," she said. "You are outside the sacred law. For any other to touch me would mean death."

He knew then the message in the perfume from the blossoms in her hair. "You are the virgin who serves at the sacred well," he whispered.

"Yes," she answered devoutly, "I am that honored one."

He had a mad impulse to lock his arms about her and plunge over the face of the cliff. The ceremony of the sacred well was known to him in all detail . . . the hypnotic ritual, the barbarous splendor, the utter beauty and sanctity of the virgin who served at the well through the turn of the seasons before the sacrifice. He had never witnessed the sacrifice—that was for the priesthood alone. His father had assured him there was no wisdom in it, no basic goodness or merit; but the fanatic devotion of the people to the shrine of the sacred well could not be violated, and the power of the priesthood rooted in this zeal could not be disregarded . . . so his father had said. But the free man who was his son disregarded it now, rejecting the monstrous vision of the deep dark waters of the well turbid with the body of the lovely one . . . a body made heavy with costume and jewels and gifts for the gods, cast upon the surface, and pulled by eager forces to the oblivion beneath. Such an act was blasphemy to the power of creation itself! A repudiation of all beauty in life which for him was ultimate in this virgin so near him now! He resolved that it should not come to pass!

Suddenly he felt an exultation such as he had not known since he had risen from his knees on the steps of the temple a free man. Now his freedom had brought him the most wondrous discovery of all! His laughter rang out from the mountaintop in the most undiluted joy that young manhood can know, and the dawn seemed to hurry with its light so that he could gaze more clearly into the face of his beloved. As a slave he could never have seen this woman of his life, looked upon her and loved her completely and chosen her for his own.

"Why are you filled with such gladness?" she asked.

"Because I have found you! Because you are mine!" he exulted, placing his hands gently on the beautiful flesh of her bare arms forfended against any man's profane touch. "Do I please you?"

"You please me greatly," she said in bewilderment, "but are you a god?"

His laughter rang out anew. "I am no god," he said, "but simply a free man choosing whom he shall love."

"Then touch me not further lest I become unfit for the gods and cause the people to suffer their wrath."

He felt the painful emptiness of his hands as she moved her arms away and withdrew from him.

"Follow me," she said, and led him to the tabernacle which was her sacred abode until the time of sacrifice.

"I follow you now," he said, "and I will never cease to follow you through whatever spans of time and existence the gods may devise." In the light of the early morning the perfection of her beauty affected him like a delirium and his words of love flowed in a stream of adoration.

She looked far away as if she heard him not and made no reply to feverish question or impassioned plea.

"You must rest," she said finally, and moved to bring a goblet filled with a thick honeyed mixture. "Here is a potion that quiets the striving of the spirit. Drink." And she placed it in his hands.

He drank with difficulty and a deep foreboding. Then sleep descended with black irresistible pressure.

When the free man awoke, day had passed into night again. His mind was foggy with the drug that had brought such deathlike slumber. He was completely alone. The small tabernacle had been removed. It would be easy to say he had dreamed of the virgin of the sacred well. But spread over him was a covering carefully arranged to protect him from the chill of the night vapor. This concern for him, and also the fact that he had awakened at all, caused him to hope in his heart much more than his mind allowed.

The One Who Laughed made no sound anymore. He became as one without the power of speech. Through the days and the nights he searched for the maiden. But the priests had hidden her, and she chose not to reveal herself. Since he was free to go where he pleased, there was no end to his search, for the city was a mighty city and there were ramifications in its structure that no man or a thousand men might know in a lifetime. There was no aid from any man in the city or on the hills or mountaintops surrounding the city, for it was known he searched for the virgin of the sacred well. For this sacrilege of seeking the one who belonged to the gods they would have taken his life had they not been reminded that the Supreme Counselor had decreed his freedom until the appointed time.

It was with deepest despair, in final acceptance of loss and failure, that the exhausted vestige of the man who was The One Who Laughed crawled to the shelf on the mountaintop where the virgin of the sacred well had guided his steps away from the precipice. Now he planned for deliberate self-destruction. The day was near when the people would be called again to the Temple of the Sun to consider freedom. His condition was worse than that of any slave in the kingdom. That would be an awful day. He could not face the agony of it. And then the day after would herald another horror, for that was the time of sacrifice at the sacred well . . . the time when his love would walk in beauty and devotion to the debauched ugliness of senseless destruction. The thought of it threw him into a rage of jealousy and hate for the gods that were not. His long silence was broken by a fury of wild curses that echoed where his laughter had once proclaimed his gladness. Then came quietness and a decision to fill his mind to the brink of his last conscious thought with the beauty of his beloved.

Freely and easily her perfections flowed into the very channels of his soul, and this brought other visions wherein the beauties of nature were matched with those of the virgin . . . the color in rainbow and sunset . . . the soft sweetness of warm night air . . . the stars in their courses . . . the grace of birds in long flight . . . the sacred white dawn flowers that bloomed for the garlands of her hair. And through it all there came to him a light and a truth that had escaped him until now. No wise man, no gods such as those worshiped in the valley, could cause such things to be. There was a Creator! There was a God unseen and without image moving behind all things that were . . . a God of love and mercy! A free man's God! This was the truth that his suffering and his love made plain to him. This the people could understand! This knowledge would awaken them! It was not too late! They could demand their freedom and seek the true God, abolishing forever the sacrificial shrine of the sacred well.

His frail body assembled a frenzied strength. He stumbled down the mountainside to the valley, shouting as the people of the city came within the sound of his voice.

"There is one God! He has created all things beautiful! Forsake your false gods! Pursue freedom! Abandon your hideous shrine fetid with the blood and flesh of your most beautiful daughters. I have found the secret to the good life!"

"Why don't you laugh?" the people jeered.

"This truth is a joy too deep for laughter," he answered them.

"He is utterly mad," the people cried. "The gods will destroy us if we do not silence him."

So they stoned him to silence. And on the appointed day, they took him in a giant cage and left him at the portals of the Temple of the Sun. The Supreme Counselor did not need to query them about freedom. Here was the answer. And lest someone miss the woeful sight, he was left there through the day and the night to follow. It was just before dawn of the day for the sacrifice at the well when the caged one cried out in his anguish, and then began such frightful laughter that it was a torture to all who heard it.

People awakened throughout the city and were terrified, for any sound from the Temple of the Sun was highly amplified and reached from end to end of the valley. Even the priests and the wise men were filled with dread. But there was one wise man who was drawn from his cloister and mounted the steps of the temple until he was face to face with the mad laughing creature that was his son. And he took from his robe a tool with which to split the bars of the cage. Not for one instant did the sound of hideous laughter cease. When the opening was made, The One Who Laughed leaped from his cage as an animal might, ignoring his benefactor. Unmolested he ran with unnatural swiftness to the Temple of Records. His skillful hands grasped the familiar tools, his laughter never abating, and there he worked in a brief period of darkness before dawn.

When the light of day brought men to their tasks again, there were strange inscriptions freshly carved on the tablets at the Temple of Records, and on one of the main pillars a face in caricature, the face of The One Who Laughed.

One inscription read, NO MAN IS WHOLLY FREE SO LONG AS ANY MAN IS SLAVE.

And another, MIND CAGED IN IGNORANCE WILL DESTROY THE RACE.

Yapah paused . . . it was a long pause. John and Sarah Belle, holding hands tightly, waited, not daring to break the spell of the priestlike voice—not daring to ask what their thoughts were insisting: What happened to The One Who Laughed and the Virgin of the Sacred Well? Did the wise man help her to escape also? Did they find each other? Did they . . ."

The voice answered. "The fate of The One Who Laughed was not known to the people nor to any other. But the hearts of the people were heavy and the gods frowned upon them. They blamed the blasphemy of The One Who Laughed. The gods would surely destroy them for allowing him to escape. . . . They blamed the Virgin of the Sacred Well, for she had disappeared from her sanctuary, leaving them bereft of fitting sacrifice with which to placate their wrathful deities."

Yapah's silence extended until they realized the story was done.

Sarah Belle protested, "But Yapah, you hoard the wisdom of the ages, surely you can tell us. They must have found each other. They *must* have!"

"Quién sabe?" Now it was the voice of their guide and companion. . . . "Is it not enough that we have found each other in this place?"